US bestselling author J. ___ Tyler i_ ___t kn___ ___ for her dark, s___ par___ ___ ___ ___ ___s of ___ on Five series under her pseudonym jo Davis. ___ MAL LAW, the first book in her Alpha Pack series, is the winner of the National Reader's Choice A___ ___ ___ ___mal. She's also been a multiple finalist in t___ ___ Award of Excellence, a finalist ___ has captured the HOLT Meda___ been a two-time nominee for t___ Award in romantic suspense. ___

When she isn't writing, J. D.'s idea of a good ___ ___ isn't cleaning house (sniff), bungee jumping (not in this lifetime, or the next), or camping (her idea of 'roughing it' is a slow bellboy). She enjoys reading, being pampered like the diva she is, and spending time with her awesome family. J. D. lives in Texas, USA, with her two children. Visit her website at www.JDTyler.com and follow her on Twitter @JDTylerAuthor

Praise for J. D. Tyler:

'Readers will fall head over heels for the Alpha Pack!' Angela Knight, *New York Times* bestselling author

'Try Tyler's sizzling new supernatural series featuring the Alpha Pack – a specialised team of wolf shifters with PSI powers. Tyler has set up an intriguing premise for her series, which promises plenty of action, treachery and scorchingly hot sex' *Romantic Times*

'A thrilling, passionate paranormal romance that you will not soon forget. Filled with action, hunky shifters, a feisty heroine, witty banter, danger, passion, romance and love, this is a book I hated to see end ... J. D. Tyler is definitely a "must-read" author' *Romance Junkies*

'In a genre where the paranormal is intense, J. D. Tyler may just be a force to be reckoned with. The book kept me riveted from start to finish' *Night Owl Reviews*

By J. D. Tyler

Alpha Pack series
Primal Law
Savage Awakening
Black Moon

PRIMAL LAW

J. D. TYLER

ETERNAL
ROMANCE

Published by arrangement with NAL Signet,
a division of Penguin Group (USA) Inc.

First published in Great Britain in 2013
by ETERNAL ROMANCE
An imprint of HEADLINE PUBLISHING GROUP

1

Cataloguing in Publication Data is available from the British Library

ISBN 978 1 4722 0086 0

Offset in Times by Avon DataSet Ltd, Bidford-on-Avon, Warwickshire

Printed and bound by CPI Group (UK) Ltd, Croydon, CR0 4YY

Headline's policy is to use papers that are natural, renewable and
recyclable products and made from wood grown in sustainable forests.
The logging and manufacturing processes are expected to conform to
the environmental regulations of the country of origin.

HEADLINE PUBLISHING GROUP
An Hachette UK Company
338 Euston Road
London NW1 3BH

www.eternalromancebooks.co.uk
www.headline.co.uk
www.hachette.co.uk

To my mother, Trena Davis.

You are living proof that there is at least one angel walking the earth, who was put here to touch lives, fill them with joy and laughter, and make the world a happier place to be. God knows where I would be without your unconditional love and support, and I thank Him every day for blessing me with a mother as wonderful as you.

I love you.

ACKNOWLEDGMENTS

Special thanks to:

My family, especially my children and my parents, for their unwavering support through an extremely difficult year. We made it, and we're all stronger for it. I love you.

The Foxes—Tracy Garrett, Suzanne Ferrell, Addison Fox, Jane Graves, Julie Benson, Lorraine Heath, Sandy Blair, Alice Burton, and Kay Thomas. I don't know what I'd do without you, and I'm not about to find out! Bring on the wine!

My agent, Roberta Brown—my cheerleader, friend, and rock. I can't ait to see what fun surprises tomorrow brings for us.

My editor, Tracy Bernstein, for supporting and encouraging me when my personal life got really tough. You're a diamond who allows your authors to shine, and I'm grateful for you.

My publicist, Erin Galloway, for your infectious enthusiasm and all the hard work you do.

Prologue

Jaxon Law crouched behind a Dumpster at the rear of the old brick building, wishing he'd worn gloves to protect his hands. And not just because of the stinking garbage overflowing from the top to litter the pavement around him.

Gloves would have shielded him from the stain of the past, in the most literal sense. If he could stand wearing them, but he couldn't. They were too hot, made his hands sweat.

Too bad, because there was a time and place to utilize his RetroCog gift and this wasn't it. None of the Alpha Pack team, including himself, could afford a single distraction tonight. Something wasn't right. A strange heaviness weighted the air, the sky an eerie yellow-green at midnight. A warning of wickedness. Of evil.

"We've got no business being here," he muttered, eyes fixed on the building.

Beside him, Zander Cole gave a quiet huff in the darkness. "Tell that to Terry. He thinks we're indestructible fucking superheroes—or at least he's convinced *he* is."

His best friend paused and Jaxon glanced over to see those strange onyx eyes glittering, body tense. "Got any vibes?"

"I'm just a Healer, man, remember? The only woo-woo shit I'm getting is the common sense *let's get the fuck out of here* kind."

Zan was much more than "just a Healer," but now wasn't the time to argue the point. Every instinct Jax possessed, both human and wolf, was screaming at him to turn and run. Fast and far, no stopping until he'd put this godforsaken place—and the reality of what he'd become—far behind him. He wouldn't, of course. Like his Pack brothers, he simply wasn't made to do anything but stand and fight. Protect the unsuspecting world of humans from horrors they never dreamed could possibly exist.

Even at the cost of his own death, if necessary. But all his life he'd been protecting those who couldn't defend themselves, so the prospect of dying didn't bother him too much and it wasn't what urged him to flee now. It was the inescapable fact that he'd graduated from battling human monsters to real ones, and the team rarely knew what type of slavering beast lurked behind door number three. It was the awful anticipation, and then the sinking in his gut when they encountered yet another deadly creature they had no idea how to defeat.

Sort of like playing Russian roulette with a loaded pistol.

Bullets, knives, and bombs were pretty straightforward—a soldier knows what to expect and who's wielding them. Fangs, claws, and flesh-eating venom? Not so much. Those types of weapons sorta got left out of the manual.

But over the past five years, they'd learned, and fast. Do or die.

Ryon Hunter, the team's Telepath and Channeler, pushed the order into their heads. *Terry says go!*

They converged on the building from all sides—Jax, Zan, Ryon, Terry, Aric, Micah, Jonas, Ari, and Phoenix, or Nix, as they called him. Soon they'd learn whether their source was accurate. If so, a human family was being held captive by a coven of vampires, used as food and slave labor. They were probably terrified out of their wits, running out of hope that help would arrive in time.

Sidling up to the wall, Jax wrapped a towel around his fist to muffle the sound of the window breaking. He cleared the jagged edges; then he and Zan entered through it, letting their eyes adjust to the gloom. They didn't need flashlights—their animal halves saw perfectly well in the dark.

They listened, but there was no sound. The storage room they were standing in was dirty, piled with boxes and other junk. From the stale smell, nobody had used this place in a long while. The bad feeling between his shoulder blades increased.

"This isn't right," he whispered to Zan. "I don't think there's anyone here."

"Let's keep looking."

He wanted to run. But if there was any chance innocent lives could be saved, they had to check every inch.

A few minutes later, the team met in the large, open area of the building. None of them had found a trace of anyone, living or otherwise. And in their business, "otherwise" didn't necessarily mean dead—but perhaps worse than dead.

"There's not a single fucking soul here," Terry snapped. Their boss was pissed. "What a goddamned waste of time."

"We need to leave," Jax said, glancing around. "I've got a bad vibe."

The boss snorted. "Yeah? Right, like there's—"

A crack sounded and Terry made a soft noise, dark wetness blooming on his chest. His eyes widened in surprise, and then he crumpled to the dirty floor.

"Get down!" Jax yelled.

He and his friends dove for cover, but there was precious little to be found. Jax crawled toward a pile of palettes, but a searing pain in his back drove him to his stomach. The burn spread outward, encompassing his torso, his limbs. The heat fried his muscles, and then seemed to numb his entire body.

Silver. Oh, God.

"Silver! They're using . . ." He tried to shout the warning, but as he rolled to his back, the words died in his throat. There was movement in the rafters of the building. Dozens of dark shapes taking flight.

The things swooped down, and he saw huge creatures. Leathery and black, with gaping jaws full of jagged teeth. Not demons or vampires. Not ghouls. Nothing he'd ever seen in the five years since they'd been dropped headfirst into Psycholand.

He tried to scramble backward, to shift into his wolf, but could do nothing but watch in horror as the things converged on his teammates. His best friends and brothers. Teeth ripped into flesh, the screams of the dying tearing out his heart.

A thud shook the floor and one of the beasts galloped to him on all fours, yellow eyes gleaming with malice, saliva dripping from its maw in a sticky stream to the floor. Jax's pulse pounded in his throat, and terror froze him to the bone.

Then the beast grabbed his right leg in its huge mouth and clamped down, crushing bone and muscle. Jax's scream joined his brothers' as the thing shook him like a dog with a bone. He had to do something. Anything. He concentrated on his right hand. Just that. Sweat poured down his face as his fingernails shifted into claws.

Surging forward, he slit the beast's throat. It fell backward, clutching its gullet in a futile attempt to stop the flow. And then fell dead, twitching.

All around him, his comrades were fighting a losing battle. Some of the beasts were dead, but not nearly enough of them. He had to help. Had to get to them.

Across the space, near the opposite wall, Aric sent balls of fire at the remaining beasts, helping to turn the tide, Jax hoped. But the fire was spreading, the boxes and palettes going up like the dry tinder they were.

First the beasts. Kill them, get his team out.

One of them had Zan pinned, ready to tear into his throat. Jax launched himself the few feet to them and barreled into the thing, taking him to the floor. This one met the same end as his first one, and Jax felt a small satisfaction.

"The others," Zan croaked, coughing.

They looked around, and saw the remaining creatures were dead. Some must've flown, frightened off by the fire. Others had been dispatched by their friends.

Somehow, he and Zan dragged their teammates, one by one, from the hungry flames. Some weren't moving. When Zan tried to use his healing powers to work on his mangled leg, Jax stopped him.

"I'll be okay. Get the worst ones."

Zan's mouth tightened into a grim line, but he nodded and moved off. And proceeded to almost kill himself by doing the impossible.

He couldn't save them all.

Jax drifted, wishing he were in Beryl's arms. That all of this was over, or had never happened at all. He imagined being buried between her thighs, giving them what they both wanted. He could almost hear her laughter.

After a few moments, he realized the sound was real, not his imagination. He opened his eyes to see Beryl standing over him, a wicked smile on her lovely face. Except the cruelty transformed her face into something ugly, mocking.

"Beryl? My team, how are they?"

She laughed again. "Dead. How else?"

"What?" He stared at her, uncomprehending.

Crouching next to him, she ran a bloodred nail down his cheek. "Haven't you figured it out? Terry's contact was actually working for me."

She wouldn't have. The Beryl he knew was loving, fun. Insatiable.

He'd thought . . .

"Why? Why did you do this?" Agony lanced his chest. The pain of betrayal and loss.

"Don't you wish you knew? Someone really important has big plans, and that's all you need to know. Thanks for the good times, lover."

Agony became rage. Sitting up, he ignored the pain, pushed to his feet. Grabbed the front of her blouse and shook her. "Who are you working for? Tell me!"

"Fuck you," she spat.

A red haze came down, obliterating all reason. Limping, half-dragging his injured leg, he pulled her toward the burning building. She'd murdered his team. The men he loved like brothers.

"Burn in hell, whore."

With the last of his strength, he threw the traitorous bitch into the fire. Fell to his knees.

Her scream of outrage, promising vengeance, and the moans of his dying teammates chased him into the darkness.

One

Six months later . . .

Kira Locke had thirty seconds to lift the samples and
get the hell out. Every second counted.

And then, technically, she'd be a thief. A criminal. The
police wouldn't know quite what to do with the items
she'd stolen should she be caught, any more than she
knew what to do with them if she wasn't. Her brilliant
plan had included getting them out of here, not where to
go afterward. Or who to give them to. Who did she dare
to trust when she offered little more than some dead tissue and a couple of wild accusations? Who would believe her?

A metallic scraping noise from somewhere down the
hallway caused her to jump, her hands trembling so hard
she nearly dropped the precious containers. *Scratch that
thirty seconds. Shit.* Quickly, she checked the lids once
more to make sure the formaldehyde didn't leak out, and
then slipped the small film-sized canisters into her purse.

*There. Let's see what Dr. Jekyll and the ghouls are up
to.*

The scraping sound came again, louder this time. Closer. The steady, heavy tread of boot heels on concrete, the systematic opening and closing of screeching metal doors announced that one of the night guards was making his rounds. Checking all of the labs and other rooms in this restricted area of her place of employment that she had no clearance to breach.

Make that *former* place of employment, if she got caught.

The footsteps came nearer, another door squealed open, and she silently cursed the bad luck that A.J. had called in sick tonight. The young guard would've covered for her, considering that he harbored the same suspicions Kira did about something being hidden in this place. Something terrible. Then again, it was probably good that her friend hadn't known what she'd planned to do tonight because now he couldn't be accused of helping her.

Heart in her throat, she considered her options—find a spot to hide and hope the guard moved on, or stroll nonchalantly from the room and try to fool him into thinking she had every right to be here. Play it cool, and then get lost.

A sinking feeling in her gut told her the second choice was out of the question, and that the cops were the least of her worries. Glancing around the lab, she zeroed in on the long worktable built on a solid base, the only object large enough to shield her from view. After switching off the light, she skirted the edge, moved to put the table between herself and the door, and crouched. Just in time.

The door swung open, the light flipping on again. The guard paused and she could picture him eyeing the area, trying to decide if anything appeared out of place. His boots scraped the floor as he moved inside a bit farther, and she huddled like a frightened rabbit in a hole, certain that any moment he'd decide to step around the table. Catch her there and call her boss, Dr. Gene Bowman. And if the pompous prick knew she was snooping, what was in her possession, and what she suspected . . .

Go away, please. Please. Her pulse hammered at the hollow of her throat and she was certain he could sense her fear. Smell it, sour and thick in the dank air.

Gradually, his steps retreated after he flipped the lights off again, and closed the door. Only when his tread faded down the corridor did she slump in relief, dragging a hand through her hair. Taking a few deep breaths, she stood, the temporary reprieve at an end. She still had to get out of the damned building unseen, though at almost midnight with nothing but a skeleton crew, the odds were slightly better.

Right. Keep telling yourself that.

Clutching her purse straps in a death grip, she eased toward the door. Turned the knob and slowly inched the weighty metal door open. A bit at a time, just enough to slip out and close it again. Her patience was rewarded with the tiniest squeak of hinges, but even that small noise sounded like a trumpet blast to her ears.

The corridor was clear. Of course it couldn't be dimly lit with lots of inky shadows to hide in, like in the movies. The tunnel-like space was as brightly lit as a football field at halftime, and if the guard came back, she was toast. At least the lack of cover meant no one could sneak up on her, either.

Walking fast, she forced herself not to break into a run. Just a few more yards and—

"Nooooo!"

She froze, heart thundering, eyes wide. "Jesus Christ," she whispered.

Straining her ears, she listened. Nothing. The faint wail of despair might've been her imagination—the product of nerves and too little sleep. For a crazy second, she felt compelled to turn around and search for the source. To find out once and for all whether the spirit that constantly begged for help at all hours of the day and night was real, or if she was out of her mind.

A door opened at the end of the corridor and a burly guard stepped into view. "Hey! What're you doing down here? I need to see some ID."

Kira turned and ran, ignoring the man's angry shout. Fast as her feet could carry her, scrambling to think of another way out, she hit the door at the far end and kept going. A service elevator loomed ahead, which she assumed was for deliveries, being located at the back of the building and away from the general staff.

And if it was for deliveries, it should open near the parking lot.

She punched the button, nearly frantic. The elevator doors slid open, but the guard wasn't far behind. Leaping inside, she hit the button marked L—*oh, God, let it mean "Loading Zone"*—then the one to close the doors, slapping it repeatedly.

The fat guard rounded the corner, belly jiggling, face red, hand on the butt of his gun. "Stop!" He drew the weapon, kept coming, one pudgy hand reaching out to catch the doors.

Too late. He missed, ruddy mug disappearing from view, and the box lurched, started upward. According to the panel the ride was only one level, but it seemed an eternity. Right now, the guard was probably on his radio calling for backup to stop her from getting away with . . . whatever it was she had in her purse.

And if her suspicions were correct, and she was apprehended? Bye-bye Kira, never to be heard from again.

The elevator stopped, and she held her breath as the doors opened. Nothing but dark, empty space greeted her and she hurried out, scanning the large area. It did, in fact, appear to be some sort of loading area, or garage. A couple of vans emblazoned with the NewLife Technology logo sat empty on the far left. Those were pretty much the contents of the cavernous space, save for a few discarded boxes.

Across the way, there were two big bay doors wide enough for just about any kind of truck to pull through, and to the right of those, a regular door with a lit EXIT sign above it. She took off, not caring how much noise she made. She had to get the hell out of there and to her car, *now*.

She pushed outside, into the night, the heat of June in Las Vegas hitting her like a slap. The still-soaring temperature, however, was the least of her worries. As she ran around the corner of the building toward the main employee parking lot, shouts sounded from just ahead and to her right.

"Shit!"

Two guards, including the burly one, burst from a different exit, clearly intending to cut her off. Her old Camry was just a few yards ahead, and she sprinted faster, fumbling with her key chain, pressing the button to unlock it. As she yanked open the driver's door, a series of loud pops rang out, pelting the side of her car.

"Oh, God!" Jumping inside, she slammed the door, tossed her purse onto the other seat, shoved the key in the ignition, and fired it up.

She peeled out, fishtailed, then straightened the vehicle and sped toward the company's entrance. A glance in the rearview mirror revealed that a couple of men in suits had joined the guards, who were waving their arms in agitation. The men broke off from the guards and jogged toward a dark sedan parked close to the building.

Kira turned her attention to the small guardhouse at

the entrance, the orange-and-white-striped arms extending across both the in and out lanes. Normally, she'd stop and swipe her badge to raise the arm, but with two goons chasing her who were probably also armed and ready to shoot first, ask questions later? She'd skip the formalities.

Flooring the accelerator, she gripped the steering wheel tight and rammed through the barrier, cringing at the awful crunch of wood and metal. She risked another look to see the arm go flying, snapped like a toothpick. The dark sedan was now in hot pursuit.

And unshakable. Whatever the sleek model was the assholes were driving, it obviously had more juice than an ancient Camry held together by wire and duct tape. She was lucky it had crashed the gate and come through in one piece, and from the sound of the gears grinding and the engine wheezing, her dubious fortune wasn't going to last much longer.

Correction: Her luck had run out weeks ago when she'd started hallucinating visions of a sexy dead guy—was that an oxymoron?—begging for help, and she'd actually listened.

Where in the hell could she go? The police station wasn't far. She knew a couple of officers, one a detective. And she'd tell them, what? That she was in possession of stolen property and being shot at? That would turn away her pursuers for now, but she'd likely be arrested, the property returned to NewLife, and she'd have nothing to prove her claims. Such as they were.

So the police were out. Which left the airport. If she could just lose these pit bulls, she'd go there, buy a ticket to anywhere. Somewhere random, get a hotel room. Then she'd call a colleague who was a doctor specializing in genetics, arrange to meet him. With someone in the medical field on her side, she might have a chance at getting somewhere with proving what the docs at NewLife were up to.

Which would have been a great plan if the Camry hadn't given up the ghost. The damned thing coughed, sputtered . . . and died.

"No!" Yanking the steering wheel, she guided the car off the side street and into a darkened parking lot. Coasting to a stop, she put the car in park and took in her surroundings.

She was one street off the Strip, behind one of the casinos and off the beaten path. And the bad guys had just screeched to a stop next to her car, on the driver's side.

Both of them emerged from the sedan, the moonlight reflecting off the guns in their hands. They exchanged a look and then approached with slow, confident strides, wearing identical expressions of malicious triumph.

The man who'd been the passenger opened her door, grabbed her by the arm, and jerked her out, slamming her back against the side of her car.

"Seems you've been snooping where you don't belong," he sneered into her face. "The underground level is restricted for a reason. Why don't you tell us what you hoped to discover down there? Or maybe you *did* find something you shouldn't have." He turned his head, called to his partner. "See what Sweet Cheeks has in her purse."

Kira took advantage of his momentary distraction and brought her knee up hard between his spread legs, doing her best to relocate his balls. Letting out a hoarse cry, the man clutched his crotch and fell to his knees.

Kira took a deep breath, and released a scream loud enough to wake the dead.

"Did anyone ask Hammer if he wanted to ride along this trip?"

Jaxon Law studied Zander Cole's profile as the dark-haired man guided the Mercedes SUV through heavy traffic on the Strip. True to his nature as a Healer, his best friend was always thinking of those who were broken—and how to fix them. Not that Hammer was necessarily broken; the big, quiet man was just . . . scary different. "I did. He said he wanted to go to bed early and read."

From the back, Aric snorted. "Jesus. Is he going to do his knitting, too?"

Beside Aric, Ryon piped up. "Quilting."

"What?"

Jaxon craned his neck and eyed the pair, snickering at Aric's puzzled expression. The big redhead was frowning at Ryon as though he'd uttered a foreign word.

"He doesn't knit—he quilts," Ryon said slowly, as though speaking to a three-year-old. "Says it calms him. He's pretty good at it, too. You should see the detail in his designs—"

"Calms him?" Zan interrupted, brows lifting. "God, if he was any more laid-back he'd be dead."

Jaxon put in his two cents. "I think what we see on the outside of that guy is a carefully controlled mask. Wouldn't surprise me if he's the most dangerous dude any of us know."

On that point, he got no argument. Jaxon, Zander, Aric, and Ryon had been together since they were Navy SEALs—a promising career cut short years ago when their unit was attacked by rogue weres, more than half of them slaughtered and the rest, including the four of them, turned into wolf shifters. But Hammer, along with their new boss Nick Westfall, had only been with Alpha Pack for a few months. Those two were born shifters, a fact that had the team and the doctors and scientists at the Institute of Parapsychology completely fascinated.

Nick, a rare white wolf, had replaced the deceased Terry Noble and brought Hammer with him to the team when they both left the FBI, and Jax had to admit the newbies were working out pretty well. Nick was tough-as-nails, but fair, and knew how to laugh at himself when the situation called for it. Unlike Terry, he wasn't above having a beer with the guys, and he sometimes joined them when their wolves needed to run and hunt. He had their backs, always.

Hammer was cut from the same cloth as Nick, though he was more of a mystery. The huge gray wolf preferred to keep to himself and remain ensconced with their leader at their compound deep in the Shoshone National Forest rather than make the trek to Vegas to blow off steam and get laid.

"Quilting," Aric muttered with a short laugh. "Man, I'm gonna give him hell about this."

Zan shook his head. "Probably not a good idea to harass a guy who can kill you with one blow from his fist. Ease up, Savage." Zan made a right, toward the Bellagio, and grinned. "Here we are. Reservations are under my name. We've got four nonsmoking rooms with king-sized beds and the weekend off, boys. Don't do anything I wouldn't do."

This prompted a round of cheers and whistles.

As Zan found a parking space, Jaxon addressed the group. "Keep your cell phones charged and handy. Is anybody besides me going off by themselves?"

Aric laughed. "Are you kidding? I don't know about these two," he said, indicating Ryon and Zan, "but if I don't find a hot woman with loose morals PDQ, I'm going to self-combust and torch half the Strip." Considering his particular Psy gifts, the man was only half-joking.

"No shit," Ryon eagerly agreed.

"I'm going to hit the casino for a while, just relax,

maybe play some blackjack," Zan put in. "There's something to be said for going slow and anticipating the ride."

"I'll go slow the second time. Or maybe the third. Let's go, ladies." Jaxon got out of the SUV carrying his duffel bag, scenting the air. His blood thrummed hot in his veins, his cock already half-hard at the prospect of burying himself between a pair of silky thighs, sliding deep. Fucking all night long, in every position. It had been weeks since they'd been able to make it to Vegas, and like his friends, he was feeling the burn.

Inside the hotel, Jaxon and the others checked into their rooms and dropped off their bags, but didn't linger. Zan had booked them all on the same floor, so they rode down together again and then split up. Zan went looking for the blackjack tables, Aric and Ryon heading for the front doors and disappearing into the night. Jaxon skirted the gaming area and strolled to the nearest bar, ordering a Jack and cola. He sat with his back to the bar, sipping his drink and scanning the crowd, waiting.

She'd be here. Right on the dot, like before.

Jaxon wasn't one to waste valuable time searching for a "date" when he had only two nights off, and Alexa had been not only reliable on their two previous weekends together, but extremely talented in bed. The blond call girl had taught him naughty things he'd *never* considered doing or allowing to be done *to* him, and some of those tasty memories had him squirming on his stool. Damn, the woman loved her job. *Lucky me.*

As if he conjured her, she stepped around an older couple and came toward him wearing a wide smile, a little black halter dress, matching heels, and nothing else. He knew that from experience. Her long blond mane tumbled over her shoulders, full and teased, in a dramatic style that never failed to call to mind an eighties rocker. But the fluff framed a pair of nice full breasts, the nipples even now peeked through the thin material of her dress and awaiting his tongue. Her face was over-done with makeup in his opinion, and she had the hard look of a girl who'd already seen too much of the crap life had to offer. But even so, she was still attractive.

"Hey, hot stuff," she greeted him in a sultry voice. Stepping between his knees, she twined her arms around his neck, pushed her breasts against his chest, and cap-tured his mouth with hers.

Her tongue slipped inside and dueled with his, seek-ing and tasting. Her nipples grazed him though his dark T-shirt, begging to be appreciated. Wrapping an arm around her waist, he broke the kiss. "My room."

"Not yet."

He frowned. "Why not?"

"I have an idea." Her eyes sparkled with mischief. "Let's go for a walk."

"I'm not paying you to take me for a stroll down the Strip, gorgeous."

"There's plenty of time to play in your room, but this is different. Just trust me."

He hesitated. Inside, his wolf growled suspiciously, not trusting her or any situation that was "different." The man, however, was ready and willing to be led by his cock, especially if she came through once again with her love of the daring and kinky.

"All right." Sliding off the stool, he offered her his arm. "Have it your way."

Raking him up and down with her eyes, she ran her tongue over her lips in an exaggerated come-hither ges-ture. "If you insist."

Pushing down another ripple of unease, Jaxon let her pull him away from the bar and through the front doors, outside. He wondered what game she had in mind as they walked in silence, away from the Bellagio and down a side street to the next block, leaving the hordes of people behind.

He didn't have long to speculate. Tugging his hand, she led him across a dark parking lot dotted with only a few cars, toward the back of small abandoned building that used to be a club or something. At the back wall, she pulled him around the corner to where the side of the store was shielded from view of the neighboring business by a tall wooden fence. She backed him against the brick, attacking the fly of his jeans. Which, admittedly, was bulging with excitement.

"Alexa," he began, shaking his head.

"Shush. This is gonna be so good." Expertly, she freed him, stroked his erection. "You ever had public sex? It's quite a thrill."

"Yeah, but who's going to see us? There's nobody around." There was something wrong with her logic in this, but damned if he could think what it was.

Because at that moment she sank to her knees and manipulated his aching balls with clever fingers tipped in bloodred nails. Swiped the head of his leaking cock with that pretty pink tongue. Began to lick his shaft, laving him like he was the last ice-cream cone in the Mojave Desert. He moaned, burying his fingers in her hair, not caring about the gallon of hair spray making the strands stick to his palm like a damned spiderweb. All that mattered was her mouth, sliding down over his rod, the heat, the suction, taking him deep—

A scream ripped through the night, shattering the mood. Jaxon straightened with a gasp, disengaging himself from his date more abruptly than he intended, pushing her back. He listened, ignoring the hooker's muttered protests. Another scream went through him like a bolt of electricity, the sheer terror in the female's voice calling to something primal within him.

Quickly, he tucked his flagging erection into his jeans and zipped up, and then pulled Alexa to her feet. "I have to see about this. Go back to the hotel, where it's safe."

"Oh, come on," she began, pouting. "It ain't your problem. Let someone else deal with it."

Spinning her around, he gave her a push toward the corner. "Go, now, and don't follow me. I'll call you." In that moment, he knew he never would, but the reason eluded him.

Digging his iPhone from his jeans pocket, he took off at a jog, wincing at the stab of pain in his mangled leg. In human form he could walk with barely a limp, but more strenuous activity such as jogging, running, or sparring with his teammates still caused the injured limb a great deal of agony.

Ignoring the pain, he scented the air. *Fear.* The unknown woman's panic clawed at his chest, more than a stranger's should. He had to get to her, make sure she was all right. Following the scent, he slowed long enough to ring Zander. Thankfully, his friend answered right away.

"What's up?"

"My hookup, Alexa. You've met her."

"Right."

"We went for a walk, but something's going down and I had to send her back. She's coming your way." He gave Zan her location and the intersection he'd just passed.

"I'll call the others and send them as backup. After I make sure she's safe, I'll head there myself. What's going on?"

"Not sure, but I heard a woman scream twice."

"Be there soon."

"Thanks, man." Ending the call, he stuffed the phone into his pocket again and picked up the pace. He didn't understand this driving need to hurry, to get between this woman and whatever threat she faced. He ran full out, knowing by the sweet scent that must be hers that he was almost there. She was nearby.

His route took him farther from the Strip, across another parking lot and past more darkened buildings. Not an area where anyone should wander alone. What had brought the woman to such a desolate part of the city? He'd learn soon enough.

As he rounded another building, he spotted her. The woman whose scent would likely drive him mad if he had a few seconds to savor it. The petite blonde was struggling in the hold of a man in a dark suit, fighting like a rabid wildcat, biting, scratching, and kicking. A second man rose to his feet, gun in one hand, cupping his crotch with the other, and Jaxon felt a surge of pride knowing she'd put him on the ground. Then the first man slammed her against the side of a car and delivered a blow to her face that snapped her head back and made her cry out in pain and terror.

Tear out his fucking heart and feast on it while it beats.

Jaxon's beast rose with a vengeance, burst from his skin without conscious thought. His roar shook the earth, brought the tableau before him to a complete standstill. He stripped off his shirt, was barely aware of the rest of his clothes falling away as skin became fur, muscles and bones contorting and reshaping, the usual pain little more than a whisper in his mind. Hands changed to paws, fingernails to claws, man to pure, raging gray wolf.

All zeroed in on the man who'd struck the small, pretty blonde.

The soldier in him knew the smart move would be to go for the man with the gun; the beast demanded blood from the one with his hands on *her*. The one who'd hit her.

The one who now let her go, twisted around to confront the new threat . . . and stared at him in horror. The predator in him felt a surge of satisfaction. His wolf wasn't nearly as hampered by his leg injury as the man.

The wolf sped across the distance, leaped, and the man screamed, the last sound he'd ever make. His forepaws struck the bastard square in the chest, knocking him backward, into the side of the car. Off-balance, the man stumbled and fell, and Jaxon took him to the ground. Lunging, he went for the kill, snapped his jaws around the vulnerable neck, teeth sinking into flesh, through muscle and bone. The man's scream ended in a rough gurgle, his hands grabbing desperately at the wolf's fur, trying to dislodge him. To no avail.

The struggles weakened as blood filled the wolf's mouth, rich and sweet, and he was hardly aware of the man's companion shouting in terror. The beast longed to linger over his prize, to rip into the savory meat and take his fill. To howl his triumph over the man who'd dared to strike his—

A muffled pop and a searing pain in his shoulder brought him around snarling, his kill abandoned as he faced the remaining threat. This asshole had also wanted to harm the woman, and for that he was fucking dead. The wolf launched himself at the second man, who backpedaled with a yell, pointed the gun and fired again. His shot went wide, and Jaxon took him down as easily as he had the first goon, tearing out his throat. The urge to feed was strong, almost unbearable, now that they were no longer a threat to the woman.

The woman.

Again, the scent of her invaded his senses. With the danger past, he let his limp prey drop from his jaws and finally took stock, letting the aroma of citrus and vanilla fill him, the crisp, clean essence of her imprinting on every cell of his being. A strange rush fired his blood, as though the man inside the beast had mainlined a load of coke, a comparison he could honestly make. A much younger, more reckless Jaxon had flirted with the edge of no return before he'd gotten his act together and joined the Marines.

Instinct told him that the effect of this woman's scent had the potential to be twice as intoxicating as any drug, and much more dangerous to the man *and* to the wolf.

Turning, he saw her. Edging around the front of the dilapidated car with her hands on the hood, eyes wide with shock, trying to put the vehicle between them. The predator in him tensed, focused his attention solely on the woman, and he moved forward slowly. Began to stalk her—but not for the reason she might think.

She was slim and small, fine-boned, with a delicate face that was all angles and dominated by big sky blue eyes. Almost an elfin face, especially with the shoulder-length pale blond hair framing those sweet features. He doubted her head would reach his chin, and all things considered, she'd tuck against his chest and mold perfectly against his much bigger body.

Mine.

And why the hell would he go all possessive over a woman he didn't know? His irritation with himself emerged as a growl.

"N-nice puppy," she stammered, stumbling as she kept moving backward, around the car. "Good puppy. Aren't you p-pretty?"

The wolf snorted, which came out like a sneeze. He'd been called a lot of things, very few of them complimentary, and certainly never pretty. But from her? He could live with that.

She grabbed for the passenger door handle and tugged, only to find it locked on that side. Eyes round with fear, she stared at him, and he recognized the moment she realized she was trapped. There was nowhere to go, no escape.

The woman was his.

Kira stared at the . . . dog? Husky? Wolf?

Wolf-man?

No. She had not seen a pissed-off Rambo wannabe burst from the shadows, strip off his shirt, and turn into a big ball of fuzz. That image had to have been a product of her terrified, overwrought mind. But it had seemed so real. She blinked, studying the animal warily as it returned her regard.

The creature was huge, with creamy white fur tipped in black and gray around its face, ears, shoulders, and back. His eyes were a steely blue-gray and seemed to look straight into her soul. Despite the blood marring his coat on his right shoulder, he was beautiful.

And he'd easily ripped apart two grown men, one of them armed. Another glance at the gore confirmed that part was definitely no figment of her imagination.

He continued to advance on her, and she shrank against the passenger's side of her Camry, heart hammering in her throat. She couldn't outrun him if she tried, a fact reflected in those piercing eyes. They were eerily intelligent, almost daring her to try so he could enjoy the thrill of chasing her down.

"Nice puppy," she crooned again, voice wobbling. Holding out a shaking hand, she tried a command. "Stay!" The beast stopped, cocked his head, an almost bemused expression on his canine face. "Good boy. Sit!"

He did.

Some of her fear began to ease and she wondered how well trained the animal was. Maybe he was someone's guard dog that got lost? He'd certainly protected her from those bastards. "Roll over."

At that, the creature's form began to waver. Sort of reshape. She blinked rapidly, thinking there must be something wrong with her vision. But no, she was simply losing her mind after all, because fur retracted, became skin. Paws became hands and feet with very human limbs attached. Tufted black ears went away; the snout disappeared and was suddenly a regal nose.

And now a black-haired man crouched where the wolf had been seconds ago. A big, very naked man who unfolded his tall body and gazed down at her, one corner of his mouth quirking upward.

"I'll do a lot of things on command," he drawled lazily. "But I don't roll over for anyone, sweetheart."

Her brain fritzed. "I—I . . . you . . ." She trailed off helplessly, unable to form a coherent response.

Her eyes raked his body, and she thought he had to be about six-foot-four and more than two hundred pounds. He was pretty well ripped, his chest, long limbs, and torso sculpted with muscle. Thick, strong shoulders led to defined collarbones and a broad chest sprinkled with springy dark hair and graced by two bronzed male nipples. His right shoulder was marred by a bloody gouge, just stopping at the edge of a large tribal tattoo of gorgeous scrollwork that spilled over the deltoid area and ran down his arm. Did it extend down his back as well? There also appeared to be some sort of design worked into the swirls on his shoulder, but she didn't pause to study it.

Her scrutiny drifted lower to his taut, ridged stomach, the dip of his hips. Skimmed down mile-long athletic legs. A network of scars twisted around his right thigh, knee, and calf, and she wondered how the terrible injury had happened, but it did nothing to detract from his physical potency. Inevitably, her attention settled at the apex of his thighs, to the proof that whatever else he might be, one hundred percent pure male stood before her now. A well-endowed man, even in repose, his impressive sex nestled in a neat thatch of curly dark hair.

A hysterical giggle escaped before she could stop it. Her wolf manscaped. How courteous, since he obviously didn't have a problem with public nudity.

"See something amusing?"

The frown in his tone brought her head up and she studied his face for the first time. A single word whispered through her brain, made her shiver—lethal.

If she hadn't already known he was seriously badass, his looks confirmed the impression. He was no model-perfect pretty boy. His spiky black hair seemed to defy gravity, somehow arranging itself into an artfully messy style that reminded her of tangled sheets. Dark brows were arched above a prominent nose and full mouth with lush lips. His ears each bore a piercing of a shiny black stud. His jaw was strong, dusky with a five o'clock shadow, and a soul patch graced his chin. Normally, she preferred men without facial hair, but on this guy? It fit him.

No, not pretty at all.

Raw. Stunning. Untamed.

He spoke, and it took her a second to realize he'd repeated the question. "No, not really. I was just thinking it's so nice that you find time to stay well groomed. When you're not tearing out people's throats." What am I saying? Shut up, idiot! "Are you going to do that to me? 'Cause I gotta tell ya, I'm probably a little gamey. Really, really stringy and—"

"Relax," he said, reaching out to caress her cheek. "I'm not going to hurt you. I heard you scream and I . . ." Suddenly he went rigid, staring deeply into her eyes.

Lowering his hand, he grasped her wrist, his hold gentle but firm. His eyes glazed and he seemed to be looking beyond her somehow. Into her soul.

"What are you doing?" She tugged, trying to pull free, hyperaware of the warmth of his palm, his manly scent. A mix of fresh leaves, the outdoors, and sweat. God, he smelled good.

He shook his head, the weird moment broken. Just as quickly, his expression darkened, his mouth thinning in anger. "What are you hiding? Tell me what you stole from those bastards—the ones I killed to save your ass."

The blood drained from her face. Oh, shit. Did he work for them, too? "I don't know what you're talking about."

His eyes were flinty. "Sure you do. Spill it."

"Fuck, man. What happened here? Can't leave you alone for a goddamned hour."

Startled, Kira twisted and peered over the roof of her car to see two tall men—one redhead and one blond—step into the circle of light and eye the dead suits with grim expressions. The blond pushed a strand of silvery hair from his eyes and whistled.

"Shit. Cleanup on aisle six." His voice held a note of humor, and his expression was kind as he looked up, spotting her. "Ran into a bit of trouble, huh?" So it was the pissed-off guy with the long, dark auburn hair who'd first spoken.

She nodded, windpipe shrinking to the size of a pin-hole.

"Well, don't worry, honey. We'll take care of you," he said gently.

Hours, make that days, of fear and worry caught up with her in a rush, and she was suddenly exhausted. The empathy from this stranger in the middle of all the chaos, not to mention the anger radiating from his two buddies, just about did her in. Tears stung her eyes and she struggled not to let them fall as her captor dragged her around the side of the car to meet his companions.

"Don't look at them," he ordered her, nodding toward the sprawled bodies.

Which, of course, made her look again. And almost get sick.

"For God's sake, Law, put on some damned clothes before my eyes bleed," the redhead growled.

"Yeah, well, it's kinda hard not to lose the threads when we get furry, dickhead."

Get furry. We?

Red cut her a sharp look. "She see you change?"

"Affirmative."

"Oh, fantastic. You do realize Sweet Thing is now our special guest?" At Red's venomous glare, she pressed backward, into the man who'd come to her rescue. "We. Are. Fucked. Nick's going to shred our asses."

"For what?" A fourth man joined the party, jogging from the darkness. The dark-haired newcomer halted, scanning the scene. "Christ."

"Trust me, it gets better," Red informed him, curling his lip. He flicked a hand at Kira and the man—Law?—who now placed his body protectively between her and the others. "The fair damsel got herself into some shit. Our friend here got his hero goin' on, wiped out the vermin, but oh, wait—the chick saw him do his White Fang impression. So now she goes with us, whereupon we can look forward to a reaming from the boss. That about right?" He snarled the question at Law.

"You got it in one," he said coolly, eyes like steel. A muscle in his jaw ticced. "And I'd do it again. So now we deal with the mess, and if you don't like it, tough. After the cleanup, she's my responsibility. I'll field the heat from Nick and take care of her."

"Damned right you will."

"Knock it off, you two." The blond tossed a pile of clothes at Law. "Get dressed so we can ghost out of here. I'll go get the SUV."

The dark-haired guy palmed a set of keys and tossed them to the blond.

Law let her go and pulled on a pair of jeans, followed by his black T-shirt. As he tugged on a pair of heavy lace-up boots, Kira found her voice. "Hang on a second," she said, edging away from them. "Take care of me? Like you took care of them? No, thanks. I'll be fine on my own."

"No longer an option." Law straightened, shot her a feral grin. "Welcome to Alpha Pack, sweetheart."

Two

"Wh-what's Alpha Pack?"

The woman was about two seconds from short-circuiting. She was tired and frightened as hell, and Aric's sorry attitude wasn't helping. Friend or not, if the red wolf snarled at her again, Jaxon would plant his fist in the moron's face.

Even if she was a criminal on the run.

"I'll explain that later." He gestured to the beat-up car. "You got anything important to bring along?"

She nodded. "My purse."

"Is that where you stashed whatever it is you stole?"

Her shoulders slumped. "Yeah. How did you know?"

"Get the purse. That's part of the talk for later."

Avoiding the bodies, she stepped up to the driver's door, opened it, and leaned in. In seconds she emerged, clutching the bag to her stomach. "Ready."

"What's your name?"

"Kira," she said hesitantly. "Kira Locke."

Kira. He liked it. The name fit her. "I'm Jaxon Law."

"What should we do with these guys?" Zander asked, interrupting the introductions.

Jaxon thought a moment. "We'll take their wallets so we can run their names later, do a background check. See who they worked for. Then we'll put them in the car, one behind the wheel, the other in the passenger's seat, and light a bonfire."

Aric grinned, his mood improved by the prospect. "My pleasure."

"Before you do, let me see if I can get a reading or two." Crossing to the nearest man, the one who'd shot him, he squatted and wrapped his fingers around the wrist, making sure to get part of the coat sleeve.

Objects and clothing often carried better signals than people. The impressions he could pick up from a dead person faded quickly, and the living sometimes shielded their thoughts whether they realized it or not.

In the background, the woman, Kira, whispered, "What's he doing?"

"*Shh.*"

As always, he braced himself for the buzz in his brain, like a thousand angry bees. His vision grayed out, the ground beneath him disappeared, and he was falling, falling. And then caught, snared in a web of someone else's making. Sticky threads brushed at his cheek, snagged his hair and tugged at his clothes, but he no longer tried to brush away in panic as he'd done when he was thirteen and his Psy ability had first manifested.

The strings weren't really there in the physical sense. Rather, he'd come to think of them as the tattered moorings of memories to their owners, ripped free and waiting for someone with his ability to grab hold and use them as a guide to the images he sought.

They were anything but consistent, and he likened latching on to one to catching a soap bubble without causing it to pop. The process was tedious, exhausting, and the quicker he grabbed a thread and made the reading, the better.

The first two slipped away, but he took firm hold of the third, following it to the end. Some memories were mere snapshots, but this one was a snippet of film, and Jaxon found himself looking through the eyes of the initial speaker—the dead man in his grasp. The man's residual anger, his trepidation, enveloped Jaxon.

"I'm telling you, this is not my problem. I don't give two shits what Chappell says, I'm not getting paid enough to deal with his freaky God complex!"

The middle-aged, average-looking man in the white lab coat twisted his lips into a condescending smile. "You're being paid plenty, and you'll do your job. Unless you'd rather volunteer to be his next subject." He reached for the phone on the counter. "I can call him right now and make him aware of your issues—"

"Try it, you nasty little fuckwad, and I'll break your neck. I didn't say I wouldn't do it, just that I'm not getting paid enough to take these kinds of risks. I'll talk with him myself, and you mind your own damned business. Got it?"

Without waiting for an answer, he spun and slammed out of the lab.

"Slimy creep, he's gonna call anyway. Shit, what am I gonna do about . . ."

"Jax!"

". . . and sooner or later the cops will notice . . ."

"Jax! Jesus, wake up!"

The thread snapped and he came back to himself gradually. Sounds of the city at night filtered in, along with the oppressive heat. And the fact that he was no longer kneeling, but slumped backward against a big body. Zander's voice was quiet and anxious next to his ear.

"Scares the hell out of me every time you do that."

"Sorry," he slurred.

"You okay?"

"Think so."

"Get anything?"

"Yeah, but I'm not sure what."

He'd have to think about it. Later. God, he was so tired. Always was after he went that deep into a memory. It was much different from the simple flash he'd gotten from the woman a few minutes ago. He wanted nothing more than to sleep until noon tomorrow. Like that would be an option once Nick got wind of their guest.

"Can you get up?"

No. His leg was screaming. "Yes."

"All right. Hang on to me."

Zander stood, hauling him to his feet, steadying him as he blinked away the rest of the fuzziness. Got his bearings. As their surroundings came into focus again, he saw his friends and their new acquaintance staring at him, obviously worried.

Zander patted his cheek. "Hey, you need a turbo boost from the Z-Man?"

Shaking his head, he gave his best friend a lopsided grin. "Naw, I'm good. I'll sleep it off on the way back to the compound."

"How's your leg?"

"Bitching, but I'll be fine."

"If you're sure." He looked doubtful.

"I am."

The act of using his healing ability hit Zan every bit as hard as when Jaxon tapped into his RetroCog mojo. No way would Jaxon let his friend expend his energy over something that would easily pass with some rest.

Ryon pulled up in the SUV just as Aric and Zander got the two dead men situated in the girl's car and shut them inside. Jaxon walked over to their newest addition, a little unsteady on his feet, and took her arm, began to steer her toward their vehicle. Zander followed, but Aric hung back a safe distance from her car, facing it. Preparing to do his thing.

"Don't watch," Jaxon said as she resisted, twisting to look over her shoulder.

"What's he planning to use to start the fire?" she asked, frowning. "There's nothing in his hands. And what the heck happened to you back there?"

"I'll explain—"

"Later." She snorted. "Right. Got it."

"You ask more questions than anyone I've ever met."

"Maybe because so many people you meet end up like *them*?" she tossed out, waving a hand to indicate her unfortunate attackers. "Just an educated guess."

She had a point. He sighed, thinking this was going to be a long night. And not nearly as much fun as he'd originally planned.

Any retort he might've made was waylaid by a loud *whoosh* and a blast of heat. Automatically he turned, glancing over his shoulder at the orange and yellow flames that engulfed the car and its occupants. The conflagration shot into the air and spread out to lick at the pavement, erasing all signs of the blood Jaxon had spilled.

Aric was standing with his feet spread and arms outstretched, palms out. The inferno intensified in response to his unspoken command. After another few moments, he lowered his arms to his sides and strode toward the rest of the group.

"Oh, my God! Did he just . . . No, he didn't. That man did not just start a fire with his bare hands!" Kira was staring at Aric, a mixture of disbelief and astonishment etched on her pretty face.

"Well, that'll attract attention," Aric muttered as he reached them. "Let's hit the road."

"Come on." Jaxon pulled his reluctant new charge along, forcing her to abandon goggling at the fire and get moving.

Ryon remained behind the wheel and Zander got in front with him. Aric climbed in back without a word, taking up position to watch their tail, Jaxon knew, and eliminate any pursuers if necessary. A fact he didn't mention to Kira as they took the middle seats, Jaxon behind the driver.

Ryon floored it, getting them away from the scene as fast as he dared without gaining unwanted attention from the Las Vegas PD. By the time faint sirens could be heard in the distance, they were well on their way.

Beside him, Kira cleared her throat. "Where are we going?"

If not for the subtle tremble in her voice, he might've snapped at her. But for some weird reason, it made him want to soothe her worries. Protect her from harm as he'd done earlier. Fuck. "To our plane. We have a private jet and landing strip in a hangar not far outside the city."

"And from there?"

"Wyoming." Silence. He looked over to see her holding the purse on her lap in a death grip, eyes wide. Hoping to ease her fears, he elaborated a bit. "Shoshone National Forest. We'll land at our compound, and you'll stay there with us for the time being."

"I don't get a say?"

"No." The thought of letting her leave burrowed under his skin like a stinging nettle, though he had no clue why. What the hell was wrong with him?

Her voice rose on a note of hysteria. "So I'm going to

be held captive at an unknown facility by a group of weird, mind-reading, fire-starting, vicious werewolves?"

"Hey, we're not weird," Ryon protested from the front.

Jaxon ignored him. "You're our guest, not a captive. Besides, would you rather be dead right now at the hands of those guys back there for stealing whatever's in that bag? You want us to put you out and leave you at the mercy of whoever sent them?"

She looked away, swallowing hard. "Of course not."

"Then we're your only option at the moment, so sit back and enjoy the trip. You're in safe hands. Nobody in Alpha Pack will hurt you, including me."

This brought her head around, and she scrutinized his face as though she could read the truth of his words there. "You want me to believe you're the good guys?"

He gave a soft, humorless laugh. "I'm not so sure about that. But we're not the guys you have to worry about. Let's put it that way."

She bit her lip for a moment, then sighed. "So are you going to introduce me to your friends?"

She seemed genuinely interested, and he hoped that boded well for how the next few days would shape up. He didn't want her to be afraid. "Sure. The guy driving is Ryon Hunter, and next to him is Zander Cole." The pair said their hellos, and flashed her charming smiles over their shoulders. "The warm and cuddly pup in the back is Aric Savage."

"Fuck you, man," the redhead responded, but with less rancor than before.

Kira smiled nervously at Jaxon. "Nice."

Jaxon stared at her, struck speechless for a few seconds. He could see in the dark just fine, and the shadows did little to hide how her smile lit the inside of the SUV, which tightened his groin into a painful knot. She wasn't just pretty—she was incredible.

"I suppose I can look forward to more intros when we arrive?"

"Um, yeah. You'll meet our boss and another teammate, as well as a bunch of doctors and scientists who live and work there."

Her brow furrowed. "All of you live on-site?"

"Yes. Why?"

"Hmm. Your compound is located in Shoshone National Forest," she said slowly. "That's government property."

"Right again."

"And if your facility is there, and everyone resides there as well . . . You all work for the government, then. Top Secret stuff. Special Ops?"

"Something along those lines." He grinned at her. "You're quick, Miss Locke."

"Kira, please." She caught his gaze, held it.

The air thickened, the moment stretching taut. To his surprise, he was the first to look away. Even his wolf was overwhelmed, in addition to being aroused to the point of madness. He cleared his throat. "Call me Jaxon, or Jax," he said. "And before you ask, yes, the 'Top Secret stuff' you mentioned includes the abilities you've witnessed in us so far."

"Something tells me what I've seen barely scrapes the surface."

"You're batting a thousand."

At that, she went silent and stared pensively out the window at nothing, because there was literally nothing to see other than the blanket of stars crowning the desert sky.

Jaxon had just begun to be lulled to sleep by the darkness and the motion of the vehicle when they arrived at the landing strip. Ryon hit the opener for the wide door, pulled the SUV straight into the hangar, and the overhead lights came on, activated by motion sensors.

Jaxon straightened as a sudden thought hit him. "Our bags are at the hotel."

"No, they're back here," Aric said. "Z-Man must've worked his charm on the concierge to get 'em so fast."

Zan snickered. "She owed me a favor. I collected."

Ryon parked and Aric handed their bags forward. Jaxon took his and shouldered it as he got out of the SUV, and then headed toward the jet. A cheery blip sounded from behind him as Ryon locked the vehicle, and the clomping of boots on concrete filled the cavernous space.

As they walked, Jaxon noted that Kira stayed close to him. Which pleased him to no end, and confounded him as his every reaction to her had so far. It didn't make sense, this need to protect, to place himself not only between her and danger, but between her and the men he loved like brothers. He barely restrained himself from snarling at Zan, who took her hand and politely helped her step into the plane before Jaxon thought to offer.

And her scent is still driving me freaking insane. I'm losing it.

Kira's voice broke into his musings. "Where's the pilot?"

Aric climbed in and grinned at her. "That would be me, sugar britches. Still feel safe?"

She leveled him with a frosty glare. "I have a name. It's Kira. And I never said I felt safe—*he* said I should feel safe." The look was pointed as she glanced at Jaxon.

Aric laughed and headed for the pilot's chair. "Yep, you've got a live one, pal. Have a blast with your new babysitting gig."

"If anyone needs a babysitter it's you," she shot back. "Or a spanking, more like."

Jaxon winced. She'd walked right into that one.

His friend pounced on the opening. "Don't threaten me with a good time unless you plan to follow through. Whenever, wherever you want me to drop trou, say the word, sugar britches—oops, Kira." He winked, completely ignoring the lip she curled at him in disgust, then turned in his seat and fired up the engine.

"Don't mind him," Ryon advised her as he and Zan took seats behind her and Jaxon. "He's so immature he still hikes his leg on the sofa."

That cracked up everyone. Except Aric, who shot the finger to the passengers in general as he taxied the plane from the hangar.

"Is he always so cranky?" Kira asked in a low voice.

Jaxon shrugged. "Nah, Aric's a good guy. Don't know what's up, except maybe he's not too happy about our aborted weekend off."

"Oh." She grimaced. "Sorry about that."

"Not a problem."

As Aric guided the craft into position at the end of the runway and hit the juice, Jaxon was surprised by how sincerely he'd meant what he said. It wasn't a problem—for him, anyway. He should be at least a little annoyed to be on his way back to their isolated outpost rather than enjoying a two-day romp in Sin City. On the contrary, he just didn't care.

And that was what really bothered him.

He was hardly aware of the plane lifting off. Instead, he conjured a memory of the last time he'd spent a weekend with Alexa in his bed. The bottle blonde on her hands and knees as he thrust into her heat. How hard he'd been, unable to get enough. The delicious throb as he held off coming, wanting it to last.

But here and now... The memory shriveled his dick and filled him with a sense of repugnance. As did thoughts of tonight, when she'd rubbed against him like a cat in heat, and he'd responded. Had allowed the call girl to lead him to a dark corner and suck his cock, with the intention of doing so much more.

Suddenly he needed to take a long, hot shower to rid himself of any trace of Alexa's scent. If only he could scour his brain as well.

I must be coming down with something.

But he didn't buy it. *Kira's going to bring me more trouble than I've ever known. I don't need to be a PreCog like Nicky to know that.* These uneasy thoughts chased around in his mind until he finally gave in to the exhaustion that had plagued him since he'd looked through the eyes of the dead man he'd read.

Settling in for the flight, he fell into an uneasy sleep.

Kira would have to stand in line, because trouble came first in the form of their boss.

The flight was uneventful and Jaxon awoke just as Aric brought the jet in for a perfect landing. The small, lighted runway was a strip carved into the forest and could be seen only from the air. The compound hunkered nearby, silent and dark, shielded by the thick cover of trees. Jaxon had always thought of this place as magical, mysterious, and more than a little dangerous. A line from a movie frequently popped into his head whenever he came home: The Alpha Pack headquarters could be found only by those who already knew where it was.

And his team made up the warriors enslaved to serve it for eternity.

Putting aside fanciful ideas about doomed pirates and bespelled ships, he grabbed his bag. The second Aric pulled the plane to a stop inside the hangar, Jaxon jumped out, careful to put his weight on his good leg, and offered Kira a hand before anyone else had the chance. As she placed her smaller hand in his, he caught a knowing smirk from Zander and chose to ignore it.

"Now what?" Kira asked, glancing around the vast space. Unlike their hangar outside Las Vegas, this one housed not only the jet, but a big military-style helicopter and a variety of vehicles—all armed to the teeth.

"Now we get you settled into a room, and we're all going to get some sleep. Everything will be better in the morning after some rest, lots of coffee, and breakfast."

She shot him a dubious look. "Sure. Nothing like a plate of scrambled eggs to make me forget that I'm homeless, jobless, and on Dr. Jekyll's hit list. Not to mention that I'm feeling a lot like Red Riding Hood realizing that grandma's nose is just a bit bigger and hairier than it should be."

"Ouch."

The young woman shrugged and crossed her arms. He couldn't help but notice the nice things the action did to the pert breasts pushing against her blouse. "If the muzzle fits. You can hardly blame me for being . . . hell, I don't even know the right word."

"Scared? Out of sorts?"

"To put it mildly." She sighed. "I doubt I'll sleep much, but I suppose I should try."

Jaxon could think of one foolproof way to make certain both of them slept like babies. His cock twitched in agreement and he shook himself out of his dirty thoughts. The last thing either of them needed was a messy complication. Even if she was willing. Which she wouldn't be, if she knew what was good for her.

"Come on, I'll show you where our quarters are located."

If she noticed his now-pronounced limp, she didn't

mention it as she fell into step beside him. The others had gone ahead and disappeared one by one through the door at the back that connected the hangar to the corridor leading to the main building of the compound. When they reached the entrance, Jaxon held the door open and ushered her inside.

"Wow, this is nicer than I imagined," she said, gesturing to the decor. The hallway was done in dark green carpet, the textured walls painted a warm beige. Tasteful sconces were placed at intervals, the bulbs just bright enough to allow them to see, but not so bright as to glare.

"You were expecting sterile hospital white walls and ugly industrial tile?"

"You called it a compound, not the Hilton."

"True. But we have to live here, so there's no reason for the place to look stark and gloomy. Besides, there are several women on staff who enjoy sprucing up the common areas whenever Nick allots them more money. They wouldn't let us guys get away with plain and ugly even if we wanted to."

"Nick?"

"Our boss," he reminded her.

"Oh, right. When will I get to meet him?"

Raised voices ahead—one in particular a deep rumble above the rest—answered the question sooner than he would've preferred. "Shit."

"Guess that answers my question."

The trepidation on Kira's pale face made him want to growl at whoever came too close, including Nick. As they reached the end of the corridor and entered the recreation room, Jaxon saw that the head Alpha wolf had met their group and was grilling them intently. He did not appear to be thrilled by what he was hearing as Zander tried to explain why they'd returned mere hours after they'd left.

"We had no choice, Nick. These two assholes were attacking the woman, and Jax had to step in."

The older man's mouth pressed into a thin line. "Fine. And you all had to bring her here, why?"

Wasn't this going to be fun? Jaxon stepped up, angling his body so he was mostly between her and the semicircle of men. "The men had guns, and I had to shift in order to take them down. She saw the whole thing."

Nick's stormy blue gaze stabbed him like twin daggers. "Let me get this straight. You let your wolf out in fucking downtown Las Vegas, killed two men, and brought home their intended victim who witnessed the entire fucking episode. That about it?"

"Yes. I wouldn't do anything different, and I don't believe you would have, either. They were going to murder her, and I had about two seconds to decide." He stood unflinching in the face of the man's formidable anger. His actions had been the right course and he wouldn't apologize, nor would Nick respect him for doing so.

They stood regarding each other for several long moments. His three friends moved slightly toward Jaxon in unspoken support of what he'd done, even Aric. It was a gesture not to be taken lightly. Jaxon had broken a hard-and-fast rule by bringing a civilian into their world, a world precious few could comprehend—or could be trusted to keep quiet about once they knew.

Nick's stance relaxed, just a little. "No other witnesses?"

"No. We would've scented them."

Their leader studied each of them at length before his expression finally softened, replaced by weary resignation. "All right. Jax, I want to speak with you and our guest in my office. Now."

After he turned and strode off, Ryon muttered, "Well, at least he's not going to rip your throat out."

Jaxon managed a small smile. "Yet."

"Good luck, bro," Zan said, wincing in sympathy. The others chimed an agreement, and they took turns butting knuckles with Jaxon before wandering to their own quarters.

Beside him, Kira watched them go, unconsciously biting her lower lip. In his opinion, she'd held up pretty well in spite of everything, resorting to humor-tinged sarcasm when she was afraid or feeling unsure instead of going off the deep end like many would have. Even so, she was quickly reaching the end of her rope for tonight.

"Come on," he said, placing a palm on her lower back to gently guide her forward. "It won't take him long to grill us and lay down the law. Then we can hit the sack."

She was silent for a few moments as they walked. When she spoke, her voice was tired. "I don't have anything to wear. All my stuff is at my apartment in Vegas."

"I'll loan you a T-shirt to sleep in tonight. In the morning, I'll borrow some clothes from one of the ladies until we're able to replace your things."

"Thank you." She paused. "I gather that sending someone to pack my belongings is out of the question."

Looking down at her, he nodded. "Too dangerous, at least right now, and the risk of leading more of your pursuers here is too great. You don't have any pets, do you?"

"Unfortunately, no. I like dogs and cats, but I'm not home enough to have one. It wouldn't be fair to leave it alone so much."

Admirable, and advantageous. He would've gone after her beloved pet, but was glad they had one less worry. Another thought occurred to him. "Is there any evidence you might've left behind that could clue in whoever's after you as to how much you know?"

"No. To tell you the truth I don't *know* anything, but I never put my suspicions in writing. My laptop is at

home, but I never dared to use it to research gene splicing. Instead I accessed different ones in the common areas at work, where it would be hard to prove who was
online."

"Whoa, hold up." Halting outside Nick's office, he
frowned at her. "Gene splicing? NewLife does medical
research, right?"

"Yes."

"Then what's so unusual about genetic testing, or
whatever?"

"It wouldn't be remarkable, except—"

Nick interrupted. "Why don't you both come in and
we'll get the answers we need?" He turned, expecting
them to follow.

Jaxon steered her inside, shutting the door behind
them. They seated themselves in a couple of chairs in
front of Nick's desk, while the man himself parked his
rear on the edge of the desk and folded his arms. Gripping the armrests, Kira spoke first, eyeing his boss nervously.

"There aren't many answers I can give you, beyond
how I met your men and was lucky enough to be rescued
by Jaxon."

If Nick was surprised by her use of Jax's first name, he
gave no indication. His manner was as direct as always,
though his tone was kind and patient as he began the
interview. Nick might be one tough son of a bitch, but
Jaxon had never seen him treat a woman with anything
but courtesy. Unless she deserved to be treated otherwise.

"You're Kira Locke," he stated, startling her.

"Y-yes . . . But how did you know my name?"

"Quite simply? I'm a PreCog. I sometimes 'know'
things or 'see' events before they happen. Earlier, I had
a vision that my men would return early and bring you

with them. But I couldn't see the reason, which is what I was asking the others about when you and Jax walked up."

Poor thing was stunned. She stared at Nick, mouth hanging open. Jaxon and everyone at the Institute who was involved with the Alpha Project had years to come to grips with the often terrible reality that not everything that went bump in the night was the wind. Kira's learning curve was going to have to be a lot quicker.

Jaxon laid a hand over hers, rubbing the soft skin on the back with his thumb, trying to comfort the anxiety he could scent coming from her in waves. She glanced at him in surprise but didn't pull away. Heat seared his hand, spread through his fingers, his limbs. Shot to his groin. He had to let go or embarrass himself in front of her and his boss. Withdrawing, he forced himself to concentrate on putting her at ease.

"We all have special abilities, which you know. You've seen some of them, and it's going to take some adjustment for you to fully accept. But right now, what's important is telling Nick what led you to us."

"Okay. This is going to sound nuts." Realizing the irony, she laughed. Then she licked her lips and took a breath, obviously trying to regroup. "Until tonight, I was a lab assistant at NewLife Technology. They're world-renowned in the medical field for making strides in treating cancer, AIDS, and just about any illness or disease you can think of."

"I've heard of NewLife, and they've made some excellent strides," Nick said. "Go on."

"A few months ago, I began to notice some unusual happenings. The doctor I work under, Gene Bowman, started staying late and sending everyone else home, including me. That was remarkable enough because the man's a dictator when it comes to all of us putting in

extra hours. Not necessarily due to his dedication to finding a cure for whatever we're researching, but because
he doesn't believe in doing the grunt work for himself
when he's got the rest of us being paid to do it."

"So you became suspicious of his project?"

"More like curious, at first. Then I found out from
some of the other techs that Dr. Bowman wasn't working alone. Another doc was working with him, behind
securely closed doors, and *his* assistants were being sent
home, too."

"Who's the second doctor?" Nick asked.

"Ivan Rhodes. He's a few years younger than Bowman, but they're both brilliant. They're also very subtle
about reminding the peons just how great they think
they are." Her nose wrinkled as though she'd bitten into
a lemon.

Jaxon began to form a profile. "Passive-aggressive
types?"

"Exactly. The kind who'll say something with a smile,
and you nod, thinking, *Did he just insult me?* They're
pros at twisting their words, or yours, especially if it will
take you down a peg or two." She shrugged. "I could've
found another job in the field a long time ago, but the
odds of finding a doctor to work for who doesn't have an
ego? Good luck with that."

Nick stood and went around his desk, taking a seat in
his chair. "That's interesting, but a couple of stuffed-shirt
doctors working late, especially when searching for a
cure for any number of diseases, isn't exactly alarming.
What changed?"

"You're right, and I probably would've dismissed it
altogether if the two of them hadn't started acting
strange. To me, anyway. I mean, these guys weren't really
buddies, but all of a sudden they were whispering in corners, acting excited about something. A couple of times

they seemed to have a difference of opinion that got kind of heated. I heard Orson Chappell's name once, and Bowman said something about a meeting with him and the board members."

"Chappell," Jaxon said, sitting up straight. "I got a vision from one of the men I eliminated tonight. He told a man in a lab coat he wasn't being paid enough to deal with 'Chappell's freaky God complex,' as he called it. The guy in the lab coat asked whether he'd rather be Chappell's next subject, making it a threat. The man told the lab coat guy to stay out of it. He was nervous, scared his companion was going to squeal to Chappell, and he was worried about cops."

Kira turned to stare at him. "What did the man in the lab coat look like?"

For a second, he was thrown. He'd expected her to question his vision, or laugh it off as ridiculous. That she seemed to take him at face value filled him with something very much like pride. It was one thing to be accepted by his Pack brothers. But from an outsider, this woman . . . For some reason that seemed significant. Special.

"Fortyish. Medium height and build, brown hair. I didn't get the color of his eyes."

"That could be Dr. Rhodes, but it's hard to say. He fits that description, but so do a lot of men. NewLife is a big place."

"Chappell is the CEO of NewLife." Nick cocked his head, a funny look clouding his face. Sitting back in his chair, he fell silent, staring into space.

"That's right." When he didn't respond to Kira, she turned to Jaxon, keeping her voice low. "Is he doing his woo-woo thing?"

He had to smile at her description. "Yeah. Unlike me, he doesn't have to touch an object to receive a vision, though he can and that will sometimes make the vision clearer to him."

"Will he be okay? Your vision really wiped you out," she observed.

"He'll be fine. He's more powerful than any of us, in either form."

Even so, Jaxon couldn't help but worry two minutes later when his boss finally snapped out of his trance. His eyes seemed more shadowed, darker than usual, and for just a second, as his gaze bounced between them, Jaxon could've sworn he saw a flash of something like regret there.

"Nicky? You cool?"

The man shook himself and swiped a hand down his face. "I'm good. Where were we?"

"Orson Chappell."

"Right." He seemed to be having trouble shaking the haze.

"Did you see something important?"

"Just spaced out for a sec. Nothing too clear."

He won't look at me. He's lying. A chill chased down his spine. But there was no time to press Nick on what was wrong, not that he'd tell Jaxon anyway.

The older man stood abruptly. "You know what? It's damned late and we're all tired. We'll finish this tomorrow after we've all had a decent night's sleep and some breakfast. I'll see you both back here at eight."

"Sure," Jaxon said slowly. What the hell? He frowned, not bothering to mask his concern. "Kira, would you wait outside for a minute?"

"No problem." Glancing between them, she rose and slipped out, shutting the door behind her.

"All right, fess up," Jaxon said quietly. "What happened just now?"

"Nothing you need to be concerned about."

"Bullshit. You look ready to pass out."

"I'm fine. It's you who's ready to crash, not me. Now get the hell out and take care of our new addition before she wanders off." He softened his words with a smile.

Stubborn bastard. "Fine. But I'm here to talk if you need me."

"I'll keep that in mind."

No sense in beating his head against the wall. Once his stubborn boss made up his mind to keep his lips firmly shut, not even a crowbar could pry them open.

He found Kira waiting at the end of the hall a respectful distance from Nick's office, and briefly gripped her shoulder before drawing away. Why he felt compelled to keep touching her was beyond him. He had to stop before—no. Not going there.

"Let's get you to a room. I'll give you the grand tour tomorrow."

"Sounds good." A wide yawn punctuated the statement.

His lips twitched, but he refrained from smiling. She was a thief at best, in trouble with some bad fuckers at worst. Figures she'd have to be so damned cute both the man and the wolf wanted to gobble her up. In the best way, that would leave them both drenched in sweat and cum.

Shit! Willing his cock to behave, he took her through the living area, past the dining room, and down another corridor toward the living quarters. He stopped in front of the second door from the end and flicked a hand at it.

"This is one of several empty units in this wing. They're more like small apartments than hotel rooms, which makes living on-site more comfortable. A few of the women live on this end, including Dr. Mackenzie Grant, who's next door to you. My room is just across the hall and a couple of doors down." He pointed. "You need anything, don't hesitate to knock."

"Thanks." She peered at the small panel on the wall near the knob. "Can we get in? Looks like we need a code."

"This one's not set up yet, but we'll take care of that for you tomorrow. It locks from the inside, so you can feel secure."

Opening the door, he ushered her inside and flipped on the light.

"Oh, my! This is much nicer than I expected." A blush tinged her cheeks and she grinned ruefully. "That didn't come out right. Sorry."

He chuckled, liking the way the corners of her eyes turned up when she smiled. "I know what you meant. It'll never make the cover of *Better Homes and Gardens*, but it's not bad."

She ran a palm over the back of the tasteful sofa. "This will do just fine. Thank you. For everything."

A world of meaning weighted those words as her smile died. He understood what she couldn't express— she'd be dead right now if he hadn't intervened. It was hard to say thanks for something like that.

He should know.

"You're more than welcome." He cleared his throat, breaking the intense moment. "Anyway, let me run over and get you one of my T-shirts."

"Oh, you don't have to. Really."

"It's no bother. Hang on a minute."

Jogging across the hall, he let himself in to his apartment and hurried to the bedroom. He spent a few seconds digging through his dresser, searching for a clean shirt that wasn't too worn. Finding one, he jogged back to Kira's door and knocked.

"It's Jax."

The door opened and she met his eyes. "I appreciate this, but you didn't have to," she said, taking the shirt. Their fingers brushed and he felt that current again. Electric, shooting south like lightning.

He shrugged. "You had to have something for bed."

"No, I don't." Standing on her tiptoes, she planted a kiss on his cheek, and murmured, "I sleep naked, but I appreciate the gesture. Good night, Jax."

With that, she closed the door and left him standing there panting like the wolf he was, sporting a hard-on that was attempting to drill through his zipper.

If he didn't get relief, fast, he was going to explode in his jeans.

I sleep naked.

Time to take care of business. And then he was going for a long, long run. With any luck, he'd be too exhausted to dream about a pretty little blonde with sky blue eyes.

Pacing his office, Nick stared out the window at the night. The moon called him, beckoned him to raise his voice in song, pour out his sorrows. Wouldn't be the first time, nor the last.

Sometimes he fucking hated his "gift" as a seer. Tonight was one of those times.

Two hearts were destined to be bound forever, find a love stronger than any they'd ever known, or would ever know again. Their road wouldn't be easy, but their joy when they gave in would be boundless.

And oh, God, so brief.

Two souls would be torn apart. One heart left drowning in grief.

But Nick couldn't interfere with the future, with free will. He'd made that mistake once, with tragic results.

There wasn't anything he could do to change the horrible outcome.

Not one goddamned thing.

Outside, he stripped his clothes and shifted, hit the ground on four white paws, and ran. If he ran far enough, fast enough, maybe he could forget that real monsters existed. Just for a little while.

And just maybe, he could forget he was one of them.

<u>*Three*</u>

Instead of heading to his room, Jaxon kept walking. All the way to the end of the corridor to the double doors, where he pushed outside, breathing in the lush scents of the forest with profound relief.

Despite his earlier exhaustion and the ache in his bad leg, he'd gotten a second wind and had no hope of sleeping until he expended this strange energy. His body was a powder keg set to go off. He felt too big for his skin, ready to burst. His nerves hummed like live wires, crackling to his toes.

Because of Kira Locke.

No. He wouldn't accept that. Because accepting she was responsible for the weird reactions he'd been experiencing ever since he'd first laid eyes on her, inhaled that alluring citrus and vanilla scent, meant acknowledging an implication he just wasn't ready to face. Not now.

Maybe never.

Haven't you learned your lesson? No woman can love a man who's half beast. Not without Disney manufacturing the ending.

Making his way across the training course and shooting range, he picked up the pace. His wolf wanted out and he was ready to oblige. At the edge of the trees he shed his clothing, leaving it in a pile to retrieve later.

Tilting his face up, he closed his eyes, released his hold over the beast, and let the change overtake him. Muscle and bone reshaped, and he dropped to all fours as his thick coat emerged. The process wasn't without some pain in his joints and in his injured leg, but was nothing like the agony they'd endured five years ago, when the animal within was new and they'd fought it with all their power. Resisting had made it worse and was a mistake each of them had quickly learned not to make.

Embracing their feral nature had brought heartache in spades, closed the door on their old lives forever. But it also included a few benefits, and this was one of the best—to run with the night, hunt and kill. To feast and then howl to the heavens, though whether in triumph or loneliness he wasn't always sure. To simply *be* and leave human worries behind, if only for a while.

He ran, relishing the earth under his paws, the wind in his face. Thankfully, his injury was lessened, as usual, in wolf form, and he was able to enjoy his run. After a while he scented a rabbit and chased it from a cozy burrow near a fallen log, knowing it didn't stand a chance. The need to taste fresh meat, savor the sweet juices, ruled his canine heart and mind.

Until he held the writhing creature down with massive paws and it shrieked in terror, long and loud. Many nights in the past he'd hunted and not been affected by the cries of his prey. The weak fed the strong, and that was the way of the entire world. One slice of his claws, one snap of jaws, and the struggle would be over, the larger beast sustained. Why should the rabbit's valiant will to survive affect his human half tonight?

Slowly, he eased off the rabbit and it wriggled free,

gave a leap, and shot into the underbrush. His wolf whined at his inexplicable actions, giving up a hard-won snack. Maybe he'd had enough killing for one night.

Spinning, he ran again, heading for a stream about a mile from the compound that he liked to visit. The spot was secluded, on Institute property, and relatively safe even at this distance from the main building. Even if the most die-hard camper or hunter ventured this far into the wilderness, they'd be brought up short by a high-security fence topped with razor wire. Should anyone be stupid enough to try to breach it, silent alarms would notify the team as to the location of the would-be intruder and he would be dealt with.

Reaching his destination, he padded to the bank's edge, stuck his nose in the frigid water, and drank. When he'd had his fill, he raised his head, scented the air to make certain none of his team was nearby. Satisfied, he shifted and stood.

Damn, he'd hoped the run would not only clear his head, but rid him of the rampant arousal jutting from between his thighs. If anything, the freedom of his run had only made it worse. Scowling down at his current problem, he wondered at its stubborn insistence. He normally had complete control over his body, but ever since he'd scented *her* it was as though his libido had gone bonkers.

I sleep naked.

Right this minute, Kira was probably sprawled in crisp sheets, sleeping like a fair angel, long dusky lashes curled against porcelain cheeks. Toned limbs tangled with white cotton, sleek back dipping to the curve of a small, tight rear.

"Shit."

Groaning in frustration, he found a soft, spongy spot a few feet from the stream's edge and lowered himself to the ground. On his back, he cupped his balls, already high and tight. This wasn't going to take long.

Grasping his cock, he swiped a thumb over the head, smearing the oozing precum around. Conjuring a delicious fantasy, he imagined Kira half on her stomach, peaceful in sleep. He'd move the sheet aside, exposing her gorgeous little ass—and he had no doubt she'd be beautiful all over—and spread her legs. He'd nuzzle her sex, lick and probe, waking her slowly. Half-awake, she'd moan and beg for more.

He'd give her what she asked for, making her writhe as his tongue explored the dewy folds, teased and sampled the tiny clit. Nearly driven out of her mind, she'd get on her hands and knees, begging to be taken. And he'd gladly oblige, putting the head of his cock to her entrance and pushing home. He'd slide deep, show her the pleasures of being mounted and taken by something more than human. Something primal.

"God, yes."

Fisting his rod, he stroked, gripping hard for that extra bit of rough. He'd do her just like that, sliding deep, faster and faster until he was pounding hard. Her cries would blister his ears, bring his beast forth with wild joy. When he could hold back no more, he would drape himself over her, thrust one final time, pump his seed into her womb . . .

And sink his canines deep into her throat. Claim her. *Mine! My mate.*

"Ahh, fuuuck!"

He shot hard, cum painting his belly and chest in creamy ropes. Again and again he spurted until his hand and torso were slick and he lay spent, out of breath. God, that was so good, fantasy or not. The real deal would likely kill him.

Gradually his scattered brain began to collect itself

and a chill settled over him that had nothing to do with his nakedness and the cool night air. What had he called her?

My mate.

No. Uh-uh. No goddamned way was that ever going to happen. He liked his life the way it had been for the last several years—footloose and able to scratch his itch with a willing female whenever the need became too great to ignore. Alexa might not appeal anymore, and Vegas was a long commute anyway, but there was always Jacee, the sexy bartender at the Cross-eyed Grizzly. The cozy hangout was only a thirty-minute drive into Cody, the town nearest the Institute. Jacee didn't mind being his occasional booty call.

Only because she's as lonely as you are, his conscience nagged. *She deserves better.*

Didn't matter. Guys like him had to settle for what they could get out of life, and for Jaxon, that meant being content with his brothers. Losing himself in a pair of arms once in a while. Fighting the supernatural predators he'd never dreamed existed before they'd been turned.

Surviving one more day.

His life could never include a Bondmate. He wouldn't open himself to that awful rejection and hurt again, not to mention endangering his brothers' lives a second time. Never.

Shaking off those grim thoughts, he rose and washed himself off in the chilly stream. Then shifted and ran.

From here to the equator wouldn't be far enough.

Kira rolled over, stretched, and opened her eyes, squinting against the bright sunlight filtering through the blinds. The dull throb at her temples attested to how little sleep she'd gotten. A strange place, surrounded by strange people who were like beings from the Syfy channel, wasn't conducive to peaceful slumber.

Added to that was the mournful howling that gave her goose bumps and had her pulling the covers over her head. Didn't these guys ever sleep? Or were those *real* wolves doing the serenade? All night, she half-expected Jason Hawes and Grant Wilson to burst into her room carrying thermal cameras and EVP recorders, completing her little side trip to Paranormals-R-Us.

And then there were the renegade thoughts of Jaxon, ones that made her shivery in a good way. Sure, she'd been scared as hell and more than a little freaked out to see a man morph into a wolf and race from the darkness. Tear apart the two guys trying to kill her, and with little effort. But the jerks with the guns had frightened her more, and truth be told, she'd sensed, deep down, that the wolf meant her no harm.

What had he said? That he and his friends weren't the ones she had to worry about.

So far that appeared to be the truth. He'd rushed to her defense like her personal avenger, and had continued to protect her even from his friends. She wondered if he realized he'd constantly put his body between them and her, his glare promising trouble for anyone who dared to touch her.

Okay, am I being a bit too romantic here, reading more into his actions than was really there? Maybe. But he *had* protected her.

Looked damned fine doing it, too. All those rippling muscles, that soul patch, spiky black hair, and the wicked ear piercings lending the man that slight air of irreverence. Confidence. Here was a guy who knew how to handle his business.

She'd love to know whether he could handle himself as well in bed as he could out of it.

"Right. He's probably got a string of women who can answer that question." And why should that make her cranky? Sitting up with an irritable sigh, she got her bearings and then made her way into the bathroom, wincing as she glanced in the mirror. "Talk about ghouls," she muttered, making a face at herself. The mug staring back at her would no doubt make the wolf run for the hills, tail between his legs. Time for a shower, and coffee. In that order.

Before she could turn on the water, a firm rap caught her ear. Heading out, she passed through the bedroom and snagged the T-shirt Jaxon had brought, hauling it over her head. As she went into the living area the knock came again.

Hurrying to the door, she peered through the peephole to see a woman standing in the hallway. Sliding the bolt, she opened up and gave the gorgeous brunette on the threshold a tentative smile.

"Hello. I'm Kira Locke."

"And I'm the welcoming committee," the woman said warmly, holding up a stack of clothes. "I'm guessing you'd like something to wear."

"Yes, thank you! Come in." Stepping aside, she let in her visitor. Though technically, *she* was the visitor here, she reminded herself.

The brunette laid the clothes on the sofa and turned to Kira. "I hope these fit well enough to get you through a day or two. I'm taller and not nearly as slender as you, so you might have to roll up the jeans and wear a belt. Oh, I'm Mackenzie Grant," she said, holding out her hand.

Kira shook, liking her already. "Jaxon told me about you. You're one of the doctors, correct?"

"That's right. I'm a psychologist, though I'm not called on much to use that training anymore. At least not like I was in the beginning, when the men had so much trouble adjusting. Now I'm a scientist and parapsychologist here at the Institute. I study paranormal phenomena, particularly how the changes have affected our Alpha Pack men or will affect them in the future." She blushed. "I'm sorry. I get carried away by my subject, especially since I rarely have anyone new to discuss it with."

Kira grinned. "No biggie. I can see why you'd be excited, Dr. Grant. I can't imagine what it must be like to be on the leading edge of such a fantastic field of study and have to keep it a secret from the outside world."

"It's hell," she agreed. "And please, call me Mac. Everyone else does."

"Okay . . . Mac." Kira paused, curious. "Please, if this is none of my business just say so, but . . . are you a shifter, too?"

The doc shook her head. "No, I'm fully human. I was brought in by my father to help launch the Alpha Project more than five years ago, after the SEAL team was attacked in Afghanistan and turned. He was the team's CO and recommended me to come in and counsel them, and that led to what I'm doing now. When the compound was completed, I just stayed on and never left."

"Sounds like a dream job, studying real-life paranormal stuff and getting paid."

"It is, but it can be frightening, too. There's so much out there that we believed to be fairy tales, and— Well, enough of that for the moment," she said, a bit too brightly. "You must be starved."

So much out there. Like what, besides wolf shifters? Her skin prickled. "I could eat. I need a shower first, though."

"Take your time. Breakfast is served at seven, but there will be plenty of food if you're later than that. You don't have to worry about a schedule, at least not until we figure out what you'll be doing, so it's all good."

All good. Right. Kira almost laughed at the absurdity. "I— Thanks."

"See you soon. And try not to worry, okay? You're safe here."

"That's what Jaxon said."

Mac cocked her head. "Well, he's right. None of our guys will let anything happen to you. You can trust any of them with your life."

"I got the demonstration on that one in living color. Maybe I can return the favor someday."

The other woman winked and headed for the door. "Good luck with that. They're as übermacho as men come."

After Mac left, Kira availed herself of the shower, relishing the hot water on sore muscles that were making themselves known. Her back was especially tender, she supposed from the goon slamming her against the car last night.

Well, he'd paid for it. Both had. Remembering the huge wolf ripping out their throats, she shivered despite the steamy spray.

Out of the shower, she found a fluffy towel in the cabinet and dried off. Frowning, she realized she had no way to comb or dry her hair and cursed herself for not thinking of it when Mac was here. The friendly woman probably would've loaned her a brush, dryer, and even a little makeup if she'd thought to ask. Not that she normally wore much, but she wasn't thrilled about going to sit and eat among a roomful of hotties, sporting wet hair and looking like an extra from *Dawn of the Dead*.

"Fantastic."

After using the towel to dry her hair the best she could, she finger-combed to remove most of the tangles and then gave up. Next came the jeans, which were too big in the waist and about four inches too long. To keep from stepping on them, she rolled them up, making cuffs. Then came the red T-shirt, which was also too big, but at least helped hide the fact that she was about to lose the jeans.

Looking at herself in the dresser mirror, she slumped in dejection. For today, it would have to do. Mac wasn't a big woman at all; Kira was just small. Always had been, which was why she'd never been able to swap clothes with her girlfriends in high school.

"I look like a refugee." Which was pretty accurate.

After slipping on a clean pair of socks and her own tennis shoes, she grabbed her purse and made certain the containers were still inside. Reassured, she slung the straps over her shoulder and headed out. Once in the corridor, she also realized she hadn't asked for directions to the dining room. Hadn't Jax taken her through it last night? She'd been so wiped, she'd hardly noticed, and had no clue where it was located.

She did remember that Mac's place was next to hers. She knocked and waited. No answer. Biting her lip, she stared across the hall to the door Jax had said belonged to him. Might as well give it a try.

But he wasn't there, either. Resigned to finding her way alone, she started down the hallway. At the T-shaped intersection, she hesitated. Had they come from the right or left last night? Taking a chance, she went right.

It was the wrong direction, of course. She made that discovery when she ended up taking a couple of turns and going through a set of double doors to find herself in what appeared to be a waiting room. There were cushioned vinyl chairs and a desk with no receptionist. Probably at breakfast with everyone else, since it wasn't like this was a public facility where they'd be expecting someone. Backtracking, she made the opposite turns that would lead back to the hallway where her room was located. Or so she thought.

"Crap, where the heck am I?"

A minute later, she found herself in another corridor, this one not as brightly lit as the others. Doors lined each side of the hall, each one made of dark, heavy metal with a single window held in place by heavy rivets. Moving close, she inspected the first one, noting the Plexiglas was two or three layers thick.

Beyond the window was a cell. There was nothing else the space could be, furnished with little but a bed, a sink, and a toilet.

"What is this place?" she wondered aloud. In answer, a low, menacing growl echoed down the tunnel, causing her to jump. Hand on her galloping chest, she inched forward, drawn to the source despite common sense shouting at her to run.

As she padded down the right-hand side, she discovered the culprit in the second cell. She drew in a breath to see a black wolf, one almost as big as Jax, pacing the width of the space—as much as the heavy chain on the end of the metal collar would allow. Back and forth, like an animal at the zoo, and she had the impression he was slowly going out of his mind.

Suddenly he stopped, whirled, and raised his head, staring straight at her through the little window. His eyes glittered, though what color they were she couldn't tell. She saw only impotent rage a second before he launched himself at the door, lips pulled back in a feral snarl, fangs white as snow against his dark fur.

She jumped back in reflex but the chain held, and the wolf was jerked off his feet by his own speed and force. He fell, rolled to his stomach, and coughed. Then he leaped up and ran again, to the same result. Tears pricked her eyes and she moved on, out of sight. Poor thing. If he couldn't see her, he'd eventually stop. She hoped.

The next cell, not surprisingly, was empty. Feral creatures probably shouldn't be kept side by side, even though they were surrounded by some sort of thick metal for the walls, floor, and ceiling.

In the fourth cell, she saw something really massive curled on the bed, so heavy the mattress sagged under its weight. Squinting, she saw that it was coiled, its sleek head resting on a pillow, seemingly sound asleep. Now, why on earth would they have jailed a snake? Even if it was as big as a frigging Volkswagen. Perplexed, she moved on, thankful the growling from inmate number one had ceased.

Cell number six, however, provided the second-biggest shock since her life had gone headfirst down the rabbit hole. She blinked to be sure of what she was seeing. A humanoid creature sat on his bed. *Humanoid* because . . .

Jesus, he had wings. Beautiful, deep blue wings matching waist-length hair that was no doubt glorious when the tresses were clean. Though the wings were drawn up against his back, the longest feathers trailed like silk across the bare mattress behind him. He was naked and *very* male, with skin that gleamed like snow. He was no doubt a fine specimen when in full health, but his prominent ribs and collarbones testified to the lack of proper nourishment.

The winged man was rocking, arms wrapped around his middle, staring at the opposite wall at nothing. Almond-shaped eyes fringed with dark lashes were drowning in despair and tears coursed down lean cheeks. Like the wolf, he wore a metal collar but there was no chain. Curiously, only his wrists were bound in irons, and his hands were encased in some sort of silvery mesh gloves.

He was stunning.

And absolutely despondent. He'd not been fed, had no clothes, and no bedding to keep him warm. Outrage left her breathless. Who was supposed to be caring for these poor creatures? Why were they even here, locked away like death-row inmates?

"Oh, God," she breathed. Were they scheduled to die?

Across the way, the opposite cells held an array of different creatures, both lovely and, well, homely. Some were snarling and pissed at the world, some as sad as the winged man. One looked like a small gremlin covered in brown fur, wide mouth showing a double set of razor-sharp teeth as it maniacally chewed on the chain around its ankle. It was easy to see why some prisoners like the feral wolf and the little gremlin would be detained, but what of the others?

Shaking in anger, she backed away. Hit the exit and spun—

And ran straight into a solid male chest.

"What the hell are you doing in a restricted area, sugar britches?" the man rumbled, grabbing her arm.

Tilting her head back, she found herself staring into Aric's light green eyes. Annoyance was stamped on his handsome face, and she wondered if he was capable of expressing happiness. Dark auburn hair trailed over one shoulder and tickled her nose. So did his scent, potent and male. Almost as good as Jaxon's.

She attempted to wrench her arm free. "I didn't know it was off-limits, seeing as how there's no sign."

"There is a sign, down there." He pointed to the end of the corridor. "You must've missed it."

"Sorry. Now let go."

"Not until you answer my question—what were you doing?"

"Looking for the dining room. Obviously I got lost."

His gorgeous eyes narrowed and he jerked his head in the direction from which she'd come. "See anything interesting in there?"

"Plenty," she hissed, seething. Damn, he was impossible to budge. "Why are those poor creatures locked away like criminals? What are you planning to do with them?"

His laugh was not a nice one. "Darlin', any one of those *poor creatures* will gladly rip off your face if given the chance. And *I'm* not planning to do anything with them. We just bring in the rogue paranormals that are causing havoc in whatever part of the world we're sent. We subdue and rehabilitate them if we can. If not, we terminate them."

"What?" she cried, gaping at him. "That's not fair! What kind of monsters are you all to play judge and jury over creatures that aren't even human? They can't possibly understand what's happening to them! They're probably confused and frightened! I'd try to rip off your face too if I was running around lost in a strange world and you came at me with a weapon—hell, I want to now!"

He stared at her for about two seconds before he burst out laughing. Infuriating man! Egotistical SOB.

"Ease up, wildcat. If you were in charge, what would you do differently, hmm?" His thumb brushed over her lower lip in an intimate caress.

Far too intimate for her liking. She jerked her head back, breaking contact and glaring up at him. "The opposite of whatever's being done now, I can tell you that. I think they need someone to show them some compassion, to see that someone cares. If any of them can be sent home—wherever that might be—we should make it happen. If we can't, they need a purpose. Jobs, anything to make them feel useful. Important."

"Wow, a real Pollyanna." From his lips, it didn't sound like a compliment, the words tinged with bitterness. "Spread a little love and the whole universe will hold hands and be healed. How about you start practicing right here?"

Before she processed the challenge, he cupped her face, dipped his head, and took her mouth in a searing kiss. Caught by surprise—and insanely curious—she went with it. His lips were full and firm, his tongue talented. He tasted good, like mint. Yep, the man was a world-class kisser.

But the earth didn't move. His touch didn't carry a fraction of the spark she'd experienced with Jaxon, and he hadn't even kissed her. Gently at first, she tried to disengage. Then with more insistence, pushing at his chest.

"Aric, let me go."

"Sugar, I—"

"I am not your sugar, sweet cheeks, or darlin', and as talented as your lips are? Sorry. They don't make my universe hold hands and sing, or whatever. So for the last time. Let. Me. Go!"

The redhead opened his mouth to say something else, but never got the chance. Suddenly he was yanked from her and bodily thrown against the wall, a seriously pissed-off Jaxon in his face.

"How many times does a lady have to ask you to let go before you get it through your thick skull?" he shouted, gripping Aric's shoulders and shoving hard for emphasis.

"Get the fuck off me, asshole." He shoved back, bared his lengthening canines, and the fight was on.

Kira squeaked in alarm as the two combatants slammed off the walls, throwing punches, shaking the building. After about the fourth bounce they went down, Aric on top of Jax, and shifted right in their clothes. Pants and shoes were kicked aside as one red and one gray wolf rolled, snarling and tearing into each other. In short order, their T-shirts were bloody and hanging in tatters off their broad shoulders, deadly claws and fangs slicing.

Terrified they'd kill each other, she bolted. She had no idea which way to go, but she had to find help. Just before she reached the end of the corridor, Ryon, Zander, and a big bald man she'd never seen before rounded the corner.

"Whoa, dogfight!" Ryon called. He slapped the big man's beefy shoulder with the back of his hand. "Dude, go get Nick."

"Shit," the guy spat. But he did as Ryon said, disappearing the way he'd come.

Ryon took her arm and gently moved her a few feet farther from the fray while Zander got as close as he dared, yelling at his friends.

"Hey, you idiots! Cut it out before Nick gets here!"

Anxious, she wrung her hands. "Can't he do something?" she asked, referring to Zander.

"They're too far gone to listen to anyone but the head Alpha," Ryon said, wincing as the gray wolf sliced the red's shoulder. "Anyone else who tries will be toast."

It seemed like forever but was likely no more than a minute before a white wall of fur barreled into the fight, separating the two warring wolves and knocking each one on his ass. Fangs bared, he let out a low, menacing growl, gazing from one of his errant soldiers to the other.

Kira stared in awe. The white wolf was slightly bigger than the other two, which was saying a lot. He was beautiful, and it was tough not to be impressed with the way he made his subordinates back down. The red wolf caved first, flattening his ears back and lowering his head in submission. Then the gray. Though clearly neither wanted to give in, since they kept shooting side glares and rumbling at each other.

Without warning Nick shifted and pushed to his feet, standing gloriously naked in the middle of the hallway. "Clean up and come to my office. Right fucking now. You'll be lucky if I don't suspend you both." With that, he turned and walked toward where Kira stood with Ryon.

She couldn't help but notice the man, who must be in his early forties, was damned fine. He nodded, then strode past as though he couldn't care less what she saw. As she turned her attention to Jax and Aric, she saw they'd shifted also. She'd have to be dead and buried not to goggle at the taut, tattooed male flesh on proud display. Any second, her brain would overload.

What a way to go.

As though reading her mind, Ryon spoke up with a chuckle. "You'll get used to it. Mac and Doc Mallory did. We're part wolf, and what need do wolves have for clothing? It's in our nature not to worry overmuch about nakedness when we shift back to human form. Saves time if everyone just gets over it and gets on with business."

"Makes sense," she murmured. It did. But . . . wow.

"Not that we ride into town and parade around naked," Zander put in with a wink. "That only flies when we're here, among our own."

"Sure." Seriously hot, naked wolf shifters. Oh, the agony one must endure.

But wait. The other women had gotten used to it? The idea that Mac or any other female had seen Jaxon in the raw didn't sit well. At all. In fact, it downright sucked, though she couldn't fathom why she should care.

Jax and Aric had pulled on their pants and were still glaring. Jax stepped close, invading the redhead's space. "Don't ever touch her again, unless she asks."

Aric's jaw ticced, but he kept his cool. "I didn't intend to. What you interrupted was me about to apologize to her. But you didn't give me the chance."

Kira heard the truth in his words.

Jax's cheeks colored and he backed off. "Then I owe you an apology. I thought . . ."

"Yeah, I know what you thought," he said quietly. "I'm pushy, but I'd never force myself on a woman. And I'd hoped you knew me better than that by now."

"I do, man. I'm sorry." He sighed. "I lost my head and I don't have a clue why."

He gave Jax a long look. "Hope you figure it out."

"What's that supposed to mean?"

"Nothin'. Let's go get our asses chewed out so we can get on with this wonderful day." Aric strode toward her and stopped a safe few feet away. "I'm very sorry, Miss Locke. I didn't mean to offend you. Hell, who am I kidding? I did mean to push your buttons because that's the kind of bastard I am. But I meant no real harm. Please believe that."

"I do, apology accepted. And it's Kira." She tried a smile, which he returned. His real smile, absent of his smartass mask, was breathtaking. Not as much as Jaxon's, but still.

"Thank you." With that, he took his leave.

Jax stopped in front of her, ignoring Ryon and Zan, who looked on with interest. "My apology is next. I'm sorry for scaring you. My wolf went nuts when I saw him manhandling you, not that it totally excuses my behavior. I could've controlled it better, but I didn't."

"It's okay. Apology accepted," she said, drinking in the sight of him. His shirt was a goner. He was smeared with blood, had bites and slices all over his chest, shoulders, and arms. "Don't you two need to get those tended?"

"I'm fine. They'll be healed soon. After we see Nick, I'll go grab another shower and then it should be time for him to meet with you and me." His expression grew concerned. "You didn't show at breakfast. Did you ever eat?"

"No, I got lost and ended up in this restricted area. I swear I didn't see the sign. Aric found me here. Then you found us, and things went from bad to worse."

Glancing around, he raised his brows. "I just realized where we are. Got an eyeful, did you?"

"You could say that." Remembering why she'd been so upset when Aric found her, she felt her mood darken all over again. "Someone is going to tell me what's being done for those pitiful creatures I saw locked away like ax murderers. Especially the guy with the wings."

"Sounds like we have a lot to discuss. Later, though."

"I'm holding you to it."

Using his torn shirt, he wiped a trickle of blood from his temple. "Come on, I'll walk you back. Go get something to eat while I get called on the carpet."

"Yes, sir." She gave him a mock salute.

"That's more like it, soldier."

"Don't get used to it."

His lips curved upward. "Want to bet? I'm awfully good at getting my way."

For some reason, she very much wanted him to try.

Four

Jaxon watched Aric leave Nick's office without bother-ing to rise from his own chair. As expected, their leader had coolly reprimanded them for their behavior, accepting no excuses before dismissing Aric. Jaxon knew without being told that Nick wasn't finished. He'd have more to say before sending him to fetch Kira.

But for the longest time, Nick simply stared at him, expression unreadable. As always, Jaxon had to work not to give away how much it bothered him, wondering what the man saw. Finally he broke the tense silence. "We told you Kira got lost on her way to breakfast, which is how she ran into Aric. But you need to know she stumbled onto Block R."

That unhappy news got a swift reaction. Nick swore. "I should've realized she might have, considering where the fight happened. Why didn't you mention this sooner?"

He shrugged, refraining from cracking, *You're the PreCog. Why didn't you know?* Nicky hated when peo-ple said shit like that. "I'm mentioning it now."

"How'd she react?"

"I could tell she was upset and is sympathizing with their situation. She's particularly concerned about Blue." The team's nickname for the winged creature, since nobody had been able to learn his real name—if he even had one.

"Aren't we all." A grim statement, not a question.

"Yeah. None of them is in terrific shape, but he and Raven are the worst."

At the mention of the feral black wolf, the atmosphere in the office darkened. Raven was a painful subject for all of them, an incomprehensible tragedy. Nick leaned back in his chair and studied Jaxon thoughtfully.

"In addition to being a lab assistant with medical training, Kira seems like the nurturing sort. She's genuine and has empathy. More important, she's going to be here for a while and needs a job. If she's inclined to work with the creatures on Block R, I think we should let her try."

Jaxon found the prospect interesting. "Did you see this in a vision?"

"Not per se. It's more of a strong, positive feeling."

"Then it's as good as a vision." He paused. "Are you asking my opinion on this?" Nick didn't discuss staffing decisions unless they affected the whole team—which they usually did.

"I am. What do you think?"

"I don't know her very well, but from what I've seen, I'm not sure. After all, she did get into hot water, presumably for stealing, someone at NewLife is after her, and she hasn't yet finished her explanation. I say we hear the rest first before you decide to grant her access to sensitive information and place vulnerable lives in her hands."

Nick nodded. "I agree. Why don't you go get her and let's finish this interview? Afterward, I need to meet with the whole team."

"What's up?"

"Couple of items came across my desk this morning from Grant. We've got a potential problem to deal with and four unusual murders to investigate."

"What sort of problem?"

"Reports are coming in of a man hanging around the cemetery outside Cody, possibly a paranormal being. He's starting to spook the locals."

"Think he's connected with the murders?"

"Not sure. I'll bring you up to speed with everyone else."

"Knew it's been too quiet around here." He stood with a grunt. "Be right back."

He found Kira in the dining room, clearing her spot at one of the big oak tables. As it had since last night, the sight of her hit him in the gut. Other places, too. She should look ridiculous, drowning as she was in the red shirt and jeans, but instead she was cute as hell. Looking up, she spotted him heading her way and greeted him, her gaze wary.

"Hey. I was just about to take this to the kitchen."

Had he put that hesitation there? Idiot. Of course he had. In less than twenty-four hours she'd seen him tear apart two men and go after a good friend. As a wolf. Naturally, she wasn't going to be overjoyed to see him.

"Leave it. The cook's two helpers get paid well to keep the place clean."

"Oh. Okay, then I guess I'm ready to face the firing squad." She grimaced, grabbed her purse from the floor beside a chair, and fell into step beside him.

"It won't be so bad. You were lost and that wasn't your fault. I, or someone else, should have made sure you had an escort to breakfast. Don't worry. Nick won't rake you over the coals until after you're officially employed and no longer have an excuse not to break the rules."

She looked up at him in surprise. "Is he planning to offer me a position?"

"Maybe. Let's finish our talk with him and we'll see."

Once they'd settled in, Jaxon relaxed as Nick brought last night's aborted interview up to speed. Kira fidgeted, outwardly nervous.

"Miss Locke—"

"Kira," she blurted. "I'm sorry. But it's Kira."

He smiled, no doubt hoping to put her at ease. But it only made him appear more dangerous, which Jaxon knew wasn't intentional at the moment. "Right. Kira. Let's revisit what you told us before." He shuffled some papers on his desk, notes he must've taken after they'd left last night. "You said you'd become suspicious of Dr. Bowman and Dr. Rhodes. They'd been sending their assistants home, working late, and you overheard them speaking about meeting with Orson Chappell and some of the board members. That correct?"

"Yes."

"I did some checking on NewLife. Chappell is not only the CEO, he's the owner and founder of the company. It seems he has a stranglehold on the board and the buck stops with him."

"That's what I've heard. He's a charismatic public figure, but he's rumored to be very tough to deal with and work for one-on-one."

"But you have no firsthand knowledge?"

She shook her head. "I've never met him in person."

"How long have you worked at NewLife?"

"Four years."

"And you've never met the head honcho?"

"The federal government employs almost two million people, about eighty-five percent of whom live in or around Washington, D.C. How many of those have actually met the president?"

"Good point," he conceded with a half smile. "So that brings us to the meat and potatoes of the discussion. What was the tip-over factor for you? When did curiosity become suspicion that something possibly . . . *unethical* was occurring? If that's the right word."

"Unethical describes what I *thought* I might find. What I started putting together called not only ethics into question, but legality and morality." She looked away from Nick, staring pensively at the wall, as though remembering.

"Quite by accident, I heard Dr. Bowman whisper something in hushed tones to Dr. Rhodes about the restricted area in the basement of NewLife. A security guard found a sanitation worker down there without clearance and the worker was fired, but that wasn't the interesting thing. I'm paraphrasing, but Dr. Bowman was upset, and he said something like, 'Remember the media explosion in the nineties when the first successful cloning of an adult mammal was done with Dolly the sheep? If anyone finds out, this will make that scientific breakthrough look like child's play and that can't happen— not before we're ready.'"

Both Jaxon and Nick sat up straighter, eyes widening. Jax interrupted. "And you believe they were referring to whatever research they're doing in the restricted area that the worker almost discovered?"

"I'm sure that's what they were talking about. But I didn't catch any more at that time because they moved out of my hearing. A few days later, Dr. Bowman was called away from work to a family emergency and I sort of took the opportunity to, um . . ."

"Snoop?" Jaxon suggested helpfully.

Her cheeks flushed. "Well, I had to get a report he'd forgotten to hand to me in his hurry to leave, and when I retrieved it from his desk, I bumped his computer mouse. Naturally, he'd forgotten to log out and shut down for the day and the screen saver went away."

"Naturally." Nick's lips twitched.

"The computer hadn't gone to sleep yet, so the screen and all the icons were right there. He had a document running, minimized at the bottom of the screen and I clicked on it. I know, I know," she said, the blush deepening. "It was wrong of me and I could've been fired."

Nick steepled his fingers and watched her thoughtfully. "You should've been and if it were me, unless you had a reason that was a matter of life and death, you would've been. But considering what came later, getting fired was the least of your concerns."

"I did a stupid thing," she admitted. "But the section I was able to read on the document was alarming. It wasn't text, like written narrative, but was several pages of formulas. Lines and lines of letters and numbers, arranged and rearranged, like notes on any number of experiments on test subjects."

Nick frowned. "Like the doctor was recording what worked and what didn't? Trial and error, and what he or they tried next?"

"Exactly. It took me a minute to realize the patterns that kept repeating on the page were genetic codes and DNA strands. And this is the part that's going to sound off the wall . . . Some of the codes, or more accurately the strands, weren't human."

Jaxon exchanged a telling glance with Nick before he spoke up. "Not so off the wall, from where we're sitting. Our DNA isn't exactly human anymore, either."

She blinked at him. "I hadn't thought of it that way, but you're right. Anyway, as I scanned the document, I had trouble believing what I was seeing. If I was interpreting correctly, it seemed that the lines represented genes being spliced and DNA being forced to mutate."

Leaning forward, she warmed excitedly to her topic. "From the very top of the page, each line appeared to represent a strand of traits, the code and DNA mutated in some small way from the strand before it."

"Hang on." Nick's brows drew together as he tried to follow. "You're saying these lines represented progressive change . . ."

Like Nick, Jaxon struggled to assimilate what she was getting at. Hell, he was a soldier, not a scientist.

"Yes—recorded progression of a single individual from human to something else. That's what was on the page in black and white. From the data, I inferred that a series of tests must've been performed on the individual to get those results."

Nick's voice was low and troubled. "To what end? What are they attempting to force the human DNA to mutate into? And why?"

"That's what I was hoping to find out when I took tissue samples from the lab last night." Opening the purse on her lap, she reached in, dug around, and brought out several small containers. She sat them on Nick's desk and they eyed the contents.

Nick and Jaxon each picked up one and carefully turned it this way and that. A piece of tissue—it appeared to be flesh and a bit of muscle—floated in clear fluid in the one Jax held. A label stuck to the side declared the vial as belonging to "Subject 0013." It also had a string of letters and numbers underneath and was dated almost two weeks ago.

"Freaky," Jax commented in distaste, setting the thing on his boss's desk. Nick put them in a row and studied the labels.

"Three of these are from Subject zero-zero-one-three. The other five are from different subjects." He looked at Kira. "Was there any rhyme or reason to what you took?"

"Zero-zero-one-three was the label at the top of the document I saw on Dr. Bowman's computer. I grabbed what I could see of those, then some others. I was in a hurry. I had a loose plan to take them to a geneticist friend of mine in Los Angeles and see what he could learn." Her shoulders hunched. "Evidently I didn't plan ahead very well."

"I think you might've ended up in the right place all the same," Nick said, raising a brow. "Were you able to print a copy of the document from Bowman's computer?"

"No. I heard someone in the outer office and had to get out of there. I minimized the document the way I found it, and was never able to go back."

"Pity. Would've been interesting to have our scientists interpret it. These should help, though." The older man gestured to the containers. "I'll get these to our lab. Would you be agreeable to assisting down there, if they meet you and decide they'd like to take you on? After I conduct a thorough background check and you pass, of course."

"Hmm. I don't know, but . . . Where else do I have to go and what are my other options?"

"Nowhere and zip," Jaxon put in, not giving Nick time to come up with anything. He pointedly ignored the man, who was trying to hide a knowing smile. "We can't let you leave for the time being, and at least here you'd get to do the lab work you're familiar with, only better. How many people can say they study shifters and other beings?"

"True." Kira brightened, looking excited. "You know, I think I'd like that very much. I'm willing to give it a try, and I know I'll pass your check. I have a clean record with plenty of commendations, up until I ran across something I shouldn't have. And for what it's worth, I have a gut feeling something very wrong is going on at NewLife. I just can't prove it—yet."

A mixture of relief and worry swamped Jaxon. He was glad she'd agreed to stay, but he didn't want her anywhere near whatever Chappell and his scientists were doing. Nick's next words echoed his thoughts.

"Good. But you'll keep the sleuthing to our labs and if any action needs to be taken against NewLife, including more investigating, the Alpha Pack team will handle it. Understood?"

"Yes, sir." She shuddered. "Believe me. I don't want to go anywhere near there again if I don't have to."

Something flashed in Nick's eyes, there and gone so fast Jaxon might've imagined it. "That's the smart route, until we know what's going on. Now we need to discuss what you saw in Block R."

Her good mood fled, and she worked to keep her tone respectful though the anger. "Is that what you call the horrible place where you're keeping those pitiful creatures prisoner? Where some of them don't have food, water, or even clothing to keep them warm?"

"I understand how bad it must appear to an outsider, but as such you don't have the facts." Nick's tone was firm but patient as he explained. "Block R stands for 'Rescue and Rehabilitation.' All of the inhabitants there are getting the best care we're able to provide, given the considerable lack of knowledge and resources available to us. Complicating matters is how very dangerous many of these species are to humans, their confusion and fear, and our inability to communicate with them."

Jaxon added his take. "Not only that, our docs are stretched too thin just doing their normal jobs to give them the personal care they deserve."

Kira was not placated. "So why haven't you hired someone to fill that role? There's no excuse for the neglect I saw. You can't stick intelligent beings in cells and leave them frightened, unable to comprehend what's happening to them! It's wrong on so many levels I don't even know where to start! And then to terminate them when they become unmanageable—"

"Hey, wait a second," Nick interrupted with a scowl. "We've never 'terminated' any of the residents of Block R. Where did you get that idea?"

"From Aric. He said—"

"Well, there's our first problem—Aric opened his mouth." Jaxon rolled his eyes.

"He *said* that when the creatures can't be rehabilitated, they're killed," she continued, insistent. "Is that true or not?"

Jaxon felt a surge of annoyance. Trust Aric to spout shit out of context to get a reaction from the sensitive newbie.

Nick clarified. "We eliminate rogue creatures only when there's no other choice. But that's typically done on the spot wherever we're sent, and only when lives have been or are threatened. The only ones we bring back here regularly are those who haven't taken lives, but can't be released until we can send them home or they learn to cope in our world. The one exception is when we need to incarcerate a dangerous rogue because we need information, but he wouldn't be kept with the others."

"So . . . Block R isn't like death row?"

"No. Are some of our guests lethal? Yes. But we feel the ones there now can be reached, with time. Which brings me to your question before—I haven't hired anyone specifically to work with them because none of the candidates whose names have been sent to me by my commander have been quite right for the job. It's not like we can put an ad in the paper."

Kira went quiet for a few moments, then asked, "Would it be possible for me to combine my duties in the lab with taking care of them? I could work on gaining their trust."

Nick smiled, looking extremely pleased. "I have a feeling you'll be good for them. Spend today getting oriented around the compound and you can start tomorrow. Just be sure to take one of the team with you, for safety reasons, until you make some headway. Take Zander or Aric—"

"I'll go with her," Jaxon said gruffly. Like *hell* was Aric going to spend more time alone with her than necessary.

Kira nodded at him before addressing Nick again. "What about the pretty guy with the wings? Why is he locked up? He seemed so sad. He looked malnourished and cold, too."

The plea in her voice got to Jaxon. There was so much she didn't understand, and the woman had a big, soft heart that had already gotten her into trouble twice.

Nick sighed. "We call him Blue for obvious reasons, because we can't get him to tell us a name. He's never spoken, but we know he's highly intelligent. We captured him in Ireland after getting an emergency call a few weeks ago that something resembling an angel was running amok in a village, causing quite a stir. By the time we arrived, he'd gone into hiding, but we found him, thinking that bringing him in would be relatively easy compared to some of the weird stuff we've dealt with."

"He certainly appears harmless enough."

"Doesn't he? Well, that 'pretty angel' rendered half the team unconscious with a single wave of his hand. Fortunately, the other half used their Psy powers to subdue him before he could do more damage."

She frowned. "But he only knocked your men out, causing no permanent harm. Right?"

"Yes, and once we got him here, we thought he was calm enough for us to let him go. We wanted him to realize he had a safe haven here. Instead, he tried to bolt and put up quite a fight. Wasn't as easy the second time to subdue him. He's fought us ever since, and we had no choice but to lock him up for his own safety."

"What about food? Clothing and bedding?"

"He won't eat. He's become increasingly despondent and a few days ago things finally reached a breaking point."

"What do you mean?"

Jaxon said quietly, "He used the chain on his collar to try and hang himself."

"Oh my God!" she cried. "Poor thing. That's why there's nothing in his cell—so he can't use anything else to try it again."

"I'm afraid so," Nick confirmed. "His wrists are bound for that reason, but the silver mesh gloves prevent him from tossing spells at us. Or whatever he does."

Kira slumped back in her chair, clearly upset. "There must be a way to reach him."

"You're welcome to try. Just be careful."

"What type of being is he?"

Jaxon answered. "Best we can figure, given his physical characteristics, powers, and the fact that he was found in Ireland? Possibly Fae."

"Fae . . . as in a faery?" Her eyes widened.

"Yep. Specifically Seelie, because of his physical beauty and his unwillingness to do us any real harm, which are typical traits of his kind. How he ended up on our plane of existence is anyone's guess. Unless you can get him to talk."

"Jeez," she muttered. "No pressure or anything."

Nick chuckled. "A lot to take in, huh? The important thing is not to rush him, or any of them. I think you'll do fine."

"What about the black wolf? I think he's going to be my toughest challenge."

The boss's humor died. "You're right about that. Raven is completely feral, but we haven't given up on him. We can't."

"Why not? I'm all for rehabbing, but if there's no hope it seems cruel to let him pace that cell day after day, going mad."

Jaxon cleared his throat, which had suddenly gone tight. "We can't give up because Raven is one of us. Five and a half years ago, he was the finest SEAL we'd ever known. After we were attacked by rogue weres in Afghanistan, he turned wolf. Unlike the rest of us survivors, he never came back."

Kira's head reeled with the overload of information Nick and Jaxon were dropping in her lap. Never had she imagined having such a bizarre conversation with anyone.

Fae. A Seelie running scared through Ireland.

A maddened wolf with his human counterpart stuck inside.

Weirder and weirder.

Which led to the obvious question. "What about the others? The snake and the furry gremlin thing?"

Jaxon folded his arms, causing his biceps to bunch enticingly. "The furry guy is just what he appears—a little pain in the ass. He bites. Ask me how I know," he deadpanned, causing Nick to laugh. "The snake isn't your typical garden variety, as you no doubt noted by his size. But it's not just the fact that he's the size of a small horse. He's a basilisk. And before you ask, forget almost everything you've read in the legends about them."

"I haven't heard much. Just that they're extremely

venomous and supposedly kill with a glance. Fairy-tale stuff."

"The venomous part is correct, but they can't, or don't, kill with their gaze or everyone in the compound would be dead. The most interesting thing is that he can take human form."

Of course he can. "So he's a shifter. Does he talk?"

"Unfortunately, yes." Jax curled his lip. "Belial is . . . Well, you'll see for yourself."

"What?" She glanced between the men. "Is he hideous or something?"

"No, quite the opposite. His power is seduction and he knows how to wield it. He's a sly son of a bitch, and that makes him more dangerous than anything. I can't get a vision of his past. Even Nick can't get a good reading on whether he'd hurt anyone in the future, though he swears he wouldn't."

"Despite biting and nearly killing Ryon," Nick added, his voice hard. "The only reason he wasn't terminated is he insists he never would've struck if he wasn't terrified when we tried to take him in."

"With all due respect . . . most of us mere mortals will never know if we can truly trust the most sincere-sounding person not to hurt us. We have to abide our neighbors because we have no choice. We can't go around locking people up just because we're not *sure*. Is it really fair to hold this person to a different standard just because he's a basilisk and he rubs you the wrong way?"

Both men had the decency to look guilty at that statement. Still, Nick wasn't totally sold. "Most people can't swallow you whole while you're sleeping."

She sighed. Seemed she had a lot of work to do with her new charges before they could even begin to be integrated into life at the compound. But she was looking forward to the challenge more than she had anything in ages. Sure beat working for Bowman, the jackass.

"Okay, I'll make a prediction," she began, watching their reactions. "Within one month, I'll have them ready to socialize with kings. Well, maybe not kings, but a bunch of flea-bitten wolves and the occasional human."

Jaxon gave her a smoldering look that made her nerves tingle, but didn't rise to the teasing "flea-bitten" remark. "I say it can't be done within a month. Six months, if you're persistent."

"Wanna bet?"

"You're on. If it takes you longer than one month from today, you have to do the entire team's nasty, sweaty laundry for six weeks." He grinned at the idea.

Smelly underwear and bloodstained shirts? "Eww. Three weeks."

"Four. That's fair—same as your month with our so-called guests."

She thought about it. "You're on. I believe they'll come around. And if they prove me right, you have to . . ." *Take me to dinner.* Right, like she'd blurt that out in front of his boss.

Forget that. With Jax, I'd rather be *dinner. And dessert. Yum.*

And where the heck had those naughty thoughts come from, anyway? Couldn't be those full lips or the angle of his cheekbones. Those smoky blue-gray eyes regarding her in amusement. Or that sexy tribal tattoo creeping from under the sleeve of his T-shirt to run down his muscular arm.

"Kira? If you win?"

She shook herself, struggling not to blush. "Um, you have to promise to do your best to see that they get home, or wherever they wish to go, within reason."

Jaxon glanced to Nick for confirmation. When his

boss nodded, he agreed. "Okay. If it's within our power, they'll leave if they wish. But just so you know, it might not be possible for them all. I don't have a portal to the Fae realm hidden under my bed."

"It's a deal."

Nick stood, signaling a conclusion to the meeting. "Kira, welcome aboard. Give me a regular end-of-week report on Block R so we can discuss their progress. I'll have Mac see you about starting in the lab, too."

"Thank you, Nick. I won't let you down."

His gaze softened, and for a second, he appeared melancholy. "I know." He turned to Jaxon as he walked them to the door. "Tell the guys I'll see everyone in half an hour, in the smaller meeting room."

"Will do."

As she and Jaxon walked out together, she was hyper-aware of the big man at her side. He must put off some serious pheromones because all she wanted to do was rub against him like a cat in heat. She'd been attracted to men, but never like this. It was almost as if she had no control over the need to be close to him, and that scared her a little.

"I'll show you around outside, if you want," he offered. "If you've never been to Shoshone, you're in for a real treat."

Just being with Jax was a treat, but she kept that to herself. "I'd love that."

"Come on."

He offered his arm and after a second's hesitation, she slipped her fingers around his biceps. The gesture was sweet and so old-fashioned, and so at odds with the raging beast that had torn out two men's throats, she didn't know what to say. It did funny things to her heart, and brought her defenses down several notches, which made her uneasy, too.

She found it hard to comprehend that this man and his friends were shifters. Where was the line between man and beast? Or was there no definition, one simply meshing with the other to create an altogether different being? Could a woman fall in love with such a man?

Could she make love with a shifter? And then came the inevitable disturbing thought—*who would I be making love to? The man, the wolf, or both?*

She shuddered, and Jax misunderstood the reason. Thank God.

His voice was concerned as he looked down at her. "Are you cold? It's usually warm during the day in the summer, but it can get chilly up here at night."

"No, I'm fine, but thanks." He led her out a side door and she stood gazing in awe at the view. Towering aspen and pine skirted the edges of the compound, and beyond that a wide lake sparkled perhaps a half mile away. In the distance, the Rockies rose majestically toward the sky, defying mankind and the changes wrought by millions of years.

She'd only seen one thing more impressive.

"Stunning, huh?"

She met his gaze squarely. "Very." Damn, she hadn't meant for that to come out so low and husky, betraying her inner turmoil. The awareness of him and how good he smelled, how warm and right he felt beside her. Solid. Why did he have to be so danged sexy?

His pupils enlarged, and his voice was deep as he pointed to a part in the trees. "Want to take a walk? There's a great footpath and a stream that way. The view is awesome."

So tempting. "You have a meeting in thirty minutes. I don't want to make you late."

He shrugged. "I'm a big boy. Besides, we won't go far."

"Lead the way," she said, already cursing herself for her weakness. What was it about this guy that clouded her judgment?

Gently, he peeled her hand off his arm. Disappointed, she started to put some space between them, but he took her hand instead, completely swallowing it in his. The spark from the contact zinged up her arm and spread all over her body. Tightened her nipples and made her ache to get closer.

Lips hitching up, he tugged her hand and they started off. As they entered the mouth of the trail, she forced her attention to a different kind of scenery.

"It really is beautiful here. I like to walk in the mornings if I get up in time, and I can't imagine any place more scenic to get my exercise."

"The trails are great for that purpose, but never venture out alone," he said, his tone deadly serious. "The grizzlies have been really aggressive again this summer. There are also black bears, moose, and any number of dangers. If you went off alone and got hurt, we could find you by following your scent, but it might be too late."

"I knew that, but it's easy to forget that dangerous things can be found in pretty packages."

He gave her an odd look. "Don't I know it."

Jax didn't explain and she didn't ask, though she was curious. She wondered what made the man tick, what pain lurked in his past. She sensed whatever rode him was more than losing his former life as a Navy SEAL, being turned into a shifter, though that was bad enough. Without being told, she knew it would take a lot more than a fledgling friendship and a few strolls in the woods to crack his armor.

Had any woman ever managed that feat before? Had there been anyone serious?

There wasn't now, she decided, or he wouldn't be

holding her hand. There wouldn't be this spark that threatened to ignite when they touched. Jax didn't seem the sort of man to stray once he'd set his romantic course. If he ever did.

Did he date? Did he do hearts and flowers? No. This man would take and possess. He'd envelop his lover and have her drowning in such a way that she'd never want to come up for air. He'd *be* her air, demand everything of her, and she'd willingly give.

What nonsense! Daydreaming would never make the ultimate man of her fantasies emerge from the mist and carry her away to be delightfully ravaged until the end of their days.

Men like that didn't exist, except in movies and books.

"This is one of my favorite spots," he told her, pointing ahead to where the forest grew sparser. A small stream burbled, the sun catching the water tumbling over rocks. The area around it was green and lush, just right for lazing the day away.

Too bad they couldn't. "Do you come here much?"

"Not as often as I'd like, but I get out here now and then, mostly when I go for a midnight run."

She'd give anything to see his wolf in this enchanted place, in the moonlight. What would it be like to run with him, to be like him? Instead, she observed, "You told me not to come out alone, but you take the risk."

"I have an advantage, don't forget. The only creature that's likely to bother me in wolf form is a human, and out here there's little chance of that happening."

"Still." She huffed.

He turned to face her, stepping real close. "You worried about me?" Reaching out, he stroked the curve of her jaw with his fingers. She was too distracted to answer as he lowered his head. Took her mouth.

Fire. Sweet, unmerciful flames, licking at her as sure

as his tongue slipping inside. Tasting, stroking. She pressed into the hard line of his body, savoring his full lips claiming hers. His earthy male scent drove her crazy, and she wanted more. Against her stomach, his erection came to life, plumped, grew long and stiff, burrowing in as though seeking what it wanted most.

Both hands framed her face and he explored, swirling his tongue, muscles bunching against her straining body. This man made kissing an erotic, seductive art form. No one else had ever compared to how damned good he felt. Right here, taking what he wanted.

Pulling back some, she opened her eyes. She wanted to see his face, and she wasn't disappointed. He was as lost as she was to the moment, eyes closed, black lashes fanning on his cheeks like lace. Groaning, he opened his eyes and broke the kiss. The glaze of arousal lifted bit by bit, and his expression grew fierce.

"I can smell him on you," he rasped. His lips pulled back some, showing his sharp canines. The same teeth that had killed those men.

"Wh-what?" she stammered.

"Aric. I smell him on you."

This morning. Aric's kiss. He was jealous! "Oh. Well, he's a pretty good kisser." Anger darkened his face and she figured teasing him on that issue wasn't smart. "But he didn't do a thing for me. Zip."

He subsided some. "Oh? What about *my* kiss?"

She pretended to think about it. "Hmm. It was marginally better." At his crestfallen look, she couldn't keep up the charade. Grinning, she twined her arms around his strong neck. "I'm kidding. You sexy thing, that was the most wonderful toe-curling kiss I've ever had. Rocked my world."

"Really?"

"Really."

He yanked her against him, hand splayed at her waist. Narrowing his eyes, he rumbled a warning. "Don't let me smell him, or any man, on you again. I won't be responsible for how my wolf reacts. I wouldn't hurt you, but him? All bets are off."

Swallowing hard, she could only nod, not certain how she felt about the mandate. Looking smug, he planted another steamy kiss on her mouth, stepped back and took her hand.

"Now, unfortunately, I have a meeting to get to."

He walked her back to the compound, never letting go of her hand. She didn't understand his reaction to Aric putting the moves on her, and had a feeling he didn't, either.

"I don't know what Nick will have us doing this afternoon, but I'll see you later," he promised, once they were inside.

"Sure. Later," she managed. He swung around and she watched his fine ass sway back and forth in his jeans until he turned the corner.

Good God. Maybe a man from her fantasies could become a reality after all.

Five

Jaxon could barely concentrate as Nick moved to the front of the meeting room. His erection throbbed in time to the headache pounding at his temples. What in God's name was wrong with him? Half an hour alone in Kira's presence and he was ready to jump the woman and have his way.

Her scent was driving him insane. It was like he had a zillion ants crawling under his skin, the urge to mate her—fuck her until they were both limp and exhausted—almost a physical pain.

He'd been nuts to kiss her, much less make demands they weren't ready for. Who was he kidding? He'd never be ready to settle down with any woman. Not after—no. *She* was a nightmare he would not revisit. The only purpose Beryl served now was as a fitting reminder of why he was alone. Why he would stay that way?

He'd take back what he said to Kira about staying away from other men. Tell her it was a mistake, which was the truth. It was as though someone else's mouth had been saying the words, but he hadn't been able to stop them.

But this itching under his skin was abominable. He had to find sexual relief ASAP. And not from his own hand. He needed to bury his cock in a hot, willing sheath and fuck until he couldn't breathe any longer. It wouldn't be Kira, no matter that the idea made his wolf whine in distress.

Any woman would have to do. Today, tomorrow night at the latest, he'd call on Jacee. She had never turned him away, and probably never would. He didn't need Kira, just a sleek body, and he'd remind himself of that soon.

"Jax, are you with me?"

Jerking his head up, he found everyone's attention on him. Great. Meeting Nick's gaze, he schooled his face into a cool mask. The man saw far too much. "I'm sorry. I missed what you said."

After shooting Jaxon a look of irritation, the older man started over. "We've got two cases Grant dropped on my desk early this morning. The first is a string of murders that have happened around Cody. Or more accurately, the bodies were dumped outside town, but the victims were killed elsewhere. The second is a guy who's been hanging around the cemetery not far from where the bodies were found and is doing a bang-up job of making the locals nervous. Whether or not he's responsible for the killings or knows anything about them, we don't know, but we're going to find out."

Zander spoke up. "Why'd we catch this? Sounds like a job for the sheriff's office."

Ryon smacked his friend on the back of the head. "Why do ya think, idiot? These aren't just any bodies and this dude is no ordinary drifter. Otherwise, Grant wouldn't have become involved."

A few snickers ensued before Nick continued. "Correct. There have been four bodies discovered in shallow graves on the northeast border of the Shoshone, all within a few yards of one another. After the sheriff's office and forensics went over the area, the county coroner was called out. He immediately ascertained what the cops suspected—all four bodies were in varying stages of decomposition, the most recent one dead only a few days."

"They found a dumping ground," Jaxon guessed.

"Right. All were men, approximate age range early twenties to early thirties. No IDs, and no men have been reported missing from Cody or the surrounding areas. In layman's terms, the men were tortured to death. It appears they were kept in captivity—ligature marks on the wrists and ankles—and were malnourished. Scalpel marks and missing tissue from several areas of the body suggest they endured some kind of medical procedure."

"Jesus," Ryon whispered. At first Jaxon thought his friend was reacting to what Nick said. But his eyes were closed and his face had paled, his skin gray and clammy. "I don't know what you want. I don't *understand*."

"Crap, somebody bring him back," Aric blurted. It always unnerved the normally brash wolf when Ryon's spirits came to call.

The sole Channeler and Telepath on the team, Ryon was often sought out by the dead beseeching him for help he didn't know how to give. Like now.

Jaxon would take his ability as a RetroCog any day. He had no control over events that had already occurred, but at least he wasn't barraged by dead people, and that suited him just fine.

Leaning close, he gripped his friend's shoulder and shook gently. "Hey, buddy. Let them go, come on back." The blond's eyes fluttered open. "Ryon?"

"God, I hate when they blindside me," he rasped. "Why can't they get that there's not a damned thing I can do to help them?"

"How many this time?" Nick asked, frowning.

"Two. They were yelling at me, but as usual, the words were garbled. One kept pointing at you, like he was all worked up by what you were telling us."

"One of the four victims?"

"Maybe. I don't know. You got photos?"

"Not yet. Grant is sending them by e-mail shortly."

"Okay." Ryon rubbed his temples.

"You all right?"

"I'm fine. Not gonna toss my cookies or anything. Sorry about that, guys."

Hammer thumped him on the back. "Give yourself a break, man. It's all good." From the quiet one of the bunch, it was practically a speech.

Nick got the meeting on track again, keeping a wary eye on Ryon. "So the coroner determines cause of death. Imagine his surprise to discover the men weren't human."

Aric whistled through his teeth. "Let the fun begin."

"No shit." This from Zan.

"Shifters?" Jaxon wondered aloud. His mind drifted to the suspicions Kira had shared with him and Nick, and the gene/DNA report she'd read. Nick's eyes met his, and Jaxon knew his boss was thinking the same thing, though how they could be related was a mystery.

"Bingo. To say the coroner got excited is an understatement. Thank Christ Sheriff Deveraux is in our loop and got to the man before he had the chance to blab the news to everyone he knew. Deveraux called Grant, and now we're 'assisting' the sheriff's office in the investigation. Off the record, of course."

"Who's got the bodies?" Zan asked.

"Melina and her team will have them as of this morning, when they pick them up from the coroner. We'll be able to learn a lot more about the victims after they conduct some tests, much more than a few crime scene pics will tell us."

Aric leaned back in his chair and propped his feet on the table. "This is all real fascinating, but I don't see what we can do here. I mean, point me at a demon or whatever and I'll smoke it. Fuck, we're soldiers, not detectives."

"Well, it looks like you'll have to be both," Nick snapped. "Unless you've got another Paranormal Black Ops team on speed dial to take this mess off our hands. No? Didn't think so."

Aric shut his trap, but shook his head, his displeasure clear.

Nick parked his ass on the corner of the table. "Our advantage is our Psy skills. We'll use all of our resources to get a lead on what happened to these poor guys, and why. Which brings us to the drifter in the cemetery. Witnesses report he's young, early to midtwenties, with collar-length black hair. Deveraux personally ran him off night before last. Said he's very Goth, wears a heavy silver pentagram, three studs in each ear, black eyeliner, and a black leather duster. Translation—he ain't from Wyoming."

That got a good laugh from everyone.

"All kidding aside, in light of the discovery of the bodies and their proximity to the cemetery, he's a person of interest. Deveraux got his name—Kalen Black. Go figure. If the bodies had been found at the time, he would've held the guy for questioning. Tonight we'll stake out the cemetery, see if he shows. If he doesn't, we'll ask around and try to pin down where he might've gone. We'll leave at sunset. Questions?"

No one had any, and Jaxon made himself scarce before anyone could ask him where he was going. Hell, this was supposed to be their weekend off, and that had sure been shot to shit, hadn't it? He was entitled to some of the R & R they'd all been forced to abort last night, and he didn't feel one bit guilty about taking his due or not inviting his friends to ride into Cody. They were big boys.

And where he was going, he didn't need any tag-alongs.

Instead of taking one of the team's black Mercedes SUVs, he jumped onto his baby—a sleek silver and dark blue Honda Shadow ACE 750, a big, bad boy with plenty of power for the road. Aric and Zan were Harley men, but in Jaxon's opinion the brand was overrated. Appalled, the other two declared that was just "un-American." It was a friendly debate they kept going while tinkering in the garage and flexing their muscles, so to speak.

Slipping on his shades, Jaxon took the winding road away from the compound, relishing the wind in his face, raking cool fingers through his hair. Wearing a helmet would've been the smart thing, regardless of the fact that adults in Wyoming weren't required to, but he was feeling a little reckless. Even a shifter couldn't heal from his brains being splattered all over the pavement, but for a while he simply wanted to feel free. Not trapped by rules and regs.

Not to mention by his own nature.

The miles slipped away and he roared into Cody more relaxed. But no less aroused. The purr of the machine between his legs hadn't helped, but he was going to get that remedied very soon.

Forcing himself not to think about how he'd gotten into this state, or who was responsible, he turned onto the familiar street in the older neighborhood and turned up a weed-choked driveway as he'd done several times before. An ugly thought crept in and he tamped it down with an effort.

He was *not* using Jacee. Hell, she got every bit as much satisfaction from their scorching interludes as he did. All she had to do was say no and order him not to come around anymore, and he wouldn't. No big deal. But she never once had.

So he parked behind her Focus, shut off the engine, and strode to the door. Fist raised, he hesitated, and then knocked, ignoring the greasy feeling in his gut. It was probably his breakfast refusing to settle. Eggs messed with his stomach sometimes.

When Jacee opened up wearing a big smile and stepped aside to let him in, he pushed everything but her from his mind. As she locked the door, he took in her skintight jeans and the snug white top with spaghetti straps that rode just above her midriff and showed off her flat, toned belly. She wore no bra today, and the white cotton hugged full breasts, dark nipples clearly outlined underneath. They puckered under his hungry gaze, anticipating what was to come.

"Wonder what brings you to my humble abode, hmm?" Stalking him like a cat, the brunette stepped up and pressed her lush body against his, twining her arms around his neck. Her full breasts were squashed against his chest and her crotch rode his erection, grinding into him suggestively.

"What do you think, gorgeous?" he replied teasingly. "You got a problem with that?"

"Do I ever?" Her voice was like whiskey, smooth and dangerous. "Damn, it's been too long."

His body responded and he captured her mouth, thrusting his tongue inside. She was a tall woman, so he didn't have to bend his head to enjoy the kiss. She was all curves, built like an Amazon, arms strong from tending bar and tossing out drunken patrons at work. She was tough, rough, sexual, and liked her men the same.

So unlike pretty little Kira.

The thought was so unwelcome, he broke the kiss in reflex and stared into Jacee's brown eyes. They were smoky with lust as she grinned and palmed the rod in his jeans, stroking it.

"Why don't we get right to the good stuff?"

He chuckled. "What, no stimulating conversation? Maybe I want to talk about my week."

She snorted. "Since when? If you want to talk, I'm obviously doing something wrong. Come with me and I'll cure that for you, hot stuff."

Taking his hand, she pulled him through the tiny living room into her bedroom, which wasn't much bigger. But it was large enough for the king-sized bed they'd put through the paces in the past.

Stopping beside the bed, she grabbed the edges of the minuscule top and slowly pulled it over her head, revealing her bare breasts. As she tossed it aside, curtains of dark hair tumbled past her shoulders and framed them the way she knew he liked. They bobbed, begging for his mouth, and he obliged, cupping them both and lifting their weight in his palms. He suckled each nipple, scraped gently with his teeth.

Would Kira's nipples taste as sweet? *Better*, his mind insisted. *Much better*.

Annoyed with himself, he continued laving the taut peaks until Jacee moaned, dropped to her knees. Hard as an iron spike, he watched as she worked on his jeans, unzipped them. She parted the denim, shoved it down his hips, out of the way. His cock sprang free, flushed and leaking, pointed at her lips. Her tongue swept away the drop of moisture on the bulbous head and he groaned, thrusting his hips toward bliss.

Burying his fingers in her hair, he guided her as she swallowed his cock down her throat. "Fuck, yeah. Suck me."

She did, sliding it deep, out again, and then repeating. Slow and easy, making him feel so good. He sought the spark they'd enjoyed before, the one that would ignite a tiny flame into an inferno and make it more than good. Spectacular. He reached, but couldn't find it.

Frowning, he closed his eyes and wondered what it would be like if the hair sliding between his fingers was blond and shoulder-length. If her mouth were smaller, so much so that she might have trouble taking all of him, both sucking and fucking. If her eyes weren't brown, but sky blue. If her name was different.

With the image he wanted firmly in mind, he found the spark and moaned. *Yes, just like that. Suck my cock, pretty little angel. And then I'm going to fuck you. Slow and easy. Hard. Rough. Any way you like.*

The scent of her arousal invaded his nose, cinnamon and spice. But instead of enhancing his drive, inciting his lust to a new high, it broke through the fog of desire and began to clear his head.

Because the scent was all wrong. Dark. It wasn't citrus and vanilla. It wasn't crisp and sunny, blue skies and fresh air.

It wasn't that of his Bondmate.

The knowledge washed over his body like icy water. And just like that, in about two seconds flat, his erection went completely limp, like a balloon popped with a straight pin.

Jacee pulled off of him and crouched there holding his flaccid cock as if she'd never seen it before. And she hadn't—not in this pathetic state. "What the hell?"

Wasn't that the million-dollar question?

Embarrassed, he eased back from her, ruefully tucking himself into his jeans once more and zipping them up. "I'm sorry, honey. It's not you," he lied. It *was* her, he just didn't know who to thank for it—the man who wanted Kira, or his stupid shifter biology. But Jacee didn't have a clue about his true nature, and it wasn't like he'd ever tell her. "Nothing personal. It's been a tough week."

She was not happy. "Join the club." Standing, she retrieved her top and yanked it back on, smoothed it in place. "Want some coffee? Something stronger?"

He gave her points for trying to salvage an awkward situation. And he knew in that moment he'd never be back. He sensed she knew it, too. "No, thanks. Some other time?"

"Sure."

They made nice as she walked him to the front door, for which he was profoundly grateful. Women scorned could be a nasty business.

"Take care, Jax." There was a sad finality to her words.

"You, too, honey." Giving her a quick peck on the cheek, he did his best ghost impression, and vanished.

As he drove away, the ants under his skin returned. Without considering why, he turned his bike in the direction of home-sweet-compound and drove as fast as he dared.

Once he got back, he'd be fine. Normal as could be.

For a man who was really a lusty beast inside.

Kira told herself she wasn't disappointed when Jax practically ran from the building as Nick's meeting dispersed.

Where he was going was none of her concern despite his earlier caveman impression—*Unga-unga, you smell like rival male!*—but his defection without a backward glance left her at loose ends. Sort of lonely.

She didn't know anyone here very well, even Jax, but she'd thought she and Jax made a connection by the stream. She'd hung around until their meeting was done, hoping he'd take her down to Block R like he'd said he would to get better acquainted with the "residents," and now it seemed she'd have to find someone else to accompany her since she was under orders not to go alone.

While his mandate not to let him smell another man on her had been kind of exciting at the time, it now infused her with irritation. How much did he really care if he just waltzed off like she didn't exist? The temptation to seek out Aric to be her protector in Block R rode her shoulder like a mischievous devil, but she wasn't stupid. She'd seen the results of her failed kiss with Jax's friend, and wasn't about to have a repeat of the ugly scene.

Nick would no doubt be too busy doing whatever Alpha leaders did. That left Dr. Mac, or one of the other team members. She'd be more at ease with another woman, but Mac was human. Would she be able to protect her if one of the detainees became violent? She thought not.

Resigned, she went in search of a willing assistant. At the end of the corridor near the dining room, she spotted Zander leaning against the wall, talking with the big, bald man she'd seen earlier. Curious, she studied the bald guy as she approached. He wasn't classically handsome, but was impressive in a macho, muscled, Vin Diesel kind of way. His resemblance to the actor was remarkable, and he smiled tentatively as he looked away from Zander and saw her approaching.

Her stomach fluttered a bit as she returned the smile, and she decided for sure, homely men were not allowed to apply to work with Alpha Pack. The whole place was a testosterone feast that was about as healthy as downing half of an entire strawberry cheesecake in one sitting.

"Hey, guys," she said in greeting, and turned to Zander's friend. "We haven't officially met. I'm Kira Locke. Call me Kira."

He held out his hand, which she took. "Kira, I'm Hammer. Nice to meet you."

"Same here. Did Nick tell either one of you what my new duties are?"

Zander rubbed his chin. "Come to think of it, no. What's up?"

"He offered me a job. I'm starting tomorrow in the lab as an assistant."

"Wow, that was fast," Zan said, studying her. "Then again, the boss isn't known for dragging his heels when he feels something is right. Congrats."

Hammer echoed the approval, and she wondered how they'd take the next bit of news. "I'm also going to work with the guests in Block R to get them ready for life in our world. Well, life outside their cells will have to do for now, but you know what I mean."

"You're kidding." He shook his dark head, looking at her in sympathy. "Good luck with that."

"I need more than luck, I need an assistant. I'm under strict orders from our boss not to go in there alone, and my self-appointed helper seems to have flown the coop."

"Jax?"

"The one and only. So which one of you is going to volunteer to beard the lion's den with me?"

Hammer laughed and backed away. "Not me. The last time I went in there snake boy almost ate me. That bastard's evil."

Zan arched a brow. "I think he takes exception to being called snake boy to his face."

"Now ya tell me."

She looked to Zan. "Come on, I need somebody to step up to the plate here. What do you say?"

"I don't think so . . ."

"I thought you were wolves, not chickens," she muttered. "Fine. I'll just go find Aric. He'll be willing to—"

"No!" Zan blurted. He cleared his throat. "That won't be necessary. One dogfight in a week is enough, and next time one or both of them will end up in the infirmary."

That made her feel sort of bad for coercing him into seeing things her way, but not enough to relent. The memory of the winged guy sitting on his bed, lost and alone, tugged at her. "I don't want that any more than you, but I can't do this by myself and those poor souls deserve a fair shake. Can you imagine what it must be like to stare at four walls day after day, not even being from our realm or comprehending our rules? To be without any of your kind to communicate with, devoid of hope?"

"I can more than imagine," Zan said, eyes softening. "Since it happened to us."

She groaned aloud at her thoughtless words. "Oh, no. I didn't mean—"

"Don't worry about it. I may regret this, but I'll help."

Hammer sighed. "Shit, me, too."

"Thanks," she said, shoving aside her embarrassment. Of course these men had been through hell when they'd been turned. How stupid could she be? "Show me the way. I was turned around before, so I'm not sure how to get back there."

As they started off, Zan commented, "Persuasive little thing, isn't she? Jax is so screwed and he doesn't even know it."

"Hmph," followed by a small smile was all his friend contributed.

Zan led her in the direction of the place she suspected was the lobby of the infirmary she'd stumbled onto earlier where nobody had been working the desk. Before they reached it, however, he made a couple of turns and strode down a long corridor she recognized. It had a set of double doors at the end marked "Restricted Area."

She waved a hand at it as they approached and pushed through. "I didn't see the sign before, but I was able to enter with no problem. How come there's not a pass card or code required?"

"We don't get any visitors," Zan replied. "Besides, this isn't the high security area for the staff. That would be Block T, in the basement."

A chill crept down her spine. "What does T stand for?"

"Termination."

Halting just before the row of cells began, she gaped at Jax's friend. "What? Nick told me none of the residents of Block R have ever been terminated!"

"That's true."

"Then what's the deal with having a death row on site? I'd like a straight answer to my questions, damn it!"

"He wasn't lying to you, Kira. He simply isn't in the habit of giving away more information than is absolutely necessary." Seeing this wasn't going to placate her, the dark-haired man continued. "Beings that are not only deadly but evil beyond hope are sent straight to Block T. Do not pass go, etcetera. Not every paranormal creature is redeemable, sweetheart, just as not every human is."

Kira swallowed hard, struggling with this. She didn't consider herself a bleeding-heart liberal by any means, but life was precious. Yes, she stood by the law and the guilty deserved to be punished accordingly, but if there was any hope that a soul might be saved, it seemed a waste to extinguish it.

"Are there any residents there now?" she managed in an even tone.

His eyes hardened. "Yes, there's one. And don't even *think* of going down there, hoping to play savior to that scum, do you hear me? He doesn't want or need Mary Poppins to sweep in with a spoonful of sugar and fix him, and the only reason he isn't worm food is because he has vital information we need. End of story. Got it?"

"Yes." She wondered what type of creature he was, but it didn't matter. No point in arguing. If he was as bad as all that, she'd stay away. Despite her awful curiosity. Dropping the subject, she gestured toward the cell she was most anxious to visit. "Shall we?"

Hammer spoke up, sounding amused. "What, we're not checking out snake boy first?"

"From the way his disposition has been described, I think he can hold his own for a while."

"That's putting it mildly."

The basilisk was going to be a pill, it seemed. But looks could be deceiving and she had to wonder how hard any of them had tried after their help had been initially rebuked. Even humans would snarl or lash out when afraid. Why would these guys be any different?

Zan entered a code on the keypad beside the door, but blocked her view with his body, so she couldn't see the number sequence. She'd have to earn their trust to gain the codes, and she didn't blame them. He gave a shove and the heavy door swung inward with a groan. He and Hammer went in first, Kira close on their heels.

She wasn't sure what to expect, but the sight that greeted them hit her even harder than when she'd seen him before. The slim figure huddled on his bed, wedged in the corner where the walls met, sitting up, knees bent, large azure wings draped protectively around his body, crossed in front. Only the top of his head and his toes were visible, and she couldn't tell whether he was asleep or not.

Stepping around her two companions, she tried a soft greeting. "Hello? Are you awake?"

No response.

She edged closer, brought up short by Zan's hand on her arm, pulling her back in warning. She shook him off, but stayed put and tried again. "Hey there, are you hungry? Have you had any breakfast?"

Immediately, she felt like a fool. Would a member of the Fae know the term "breakfast"? Stupid.

"We're not going to hurt you, I promise. Would you please speak with us . . . Your Highness?" The last, she'd added on impulse. Why, she wasn't sure. Just that it seemed right, as though she was picking up a vibe from the gorgeous man. Whatever the case, it turned out to be the right thing to say.

Slowly, he raised his head, his wings lowering just enough to allow him to study her and still shield his nakedness. She expected his eyes to be blue, but they were gold. Brilliant, luminous, clear gold, like the eyes of an eagle she'd once seen behind bars at a zoo. But unlike the bird, there was nothing proud or fierce about his gaze, though she sensed his bearing might've been different, once.

Defeated. Whatever he'd been before, that was the best word to describe him now—not to mention tired, and more than a little wary of what the newcomer wanted of him. There might have been a brief spark of curiosity as well, but she couldn't be certain.

Cocking his head, he surprised them all by ordering her softly, "Come closer."

As she started to obey, Zander laid a hand on her arm, and again she shook him off. Perhaps she was naive not to be more afraid, but she felt she could trust Blue. Or whatever his name was. Getting him to trust *her* or anyone else might be a challenge. When she'd moved nearly to the edge of his bare mattress, he held up his gloved, bound hands, indicating for her to stop.

Immediately, both men stepped in front of her and growled a dual warning at the winged man. Belatedly she recalled that this being had supposedly immobilized half their team with a single gesture. But he'd been fighting for his life then, or so he'd undoubtedly believed. Something told her that even if his hands were free, he wouldn't do the same again without a very good cause.

She hoped she wasn't wrong.

"Honestly, how am I supposed to make any progress with you overgrown bullies getting in my way?" Crossly, she stepped around them and caught their incredulous expressions.

"Bullies! That firefly over there just about turned us into pillars of salt," Zan protested.

"Hush and let me concentrate." Giving her attention back to Blue, she had another pleasant jolt. He was sitting up straighter, regarding her with rapt attention, lips curved the smallest fraction.

"Who are you?"

The smooth, melodic quality of his voice rushed over her like cool water. "I'm Kira Locke. Like you, I'm new here. Really new—today's my first day."

"You are my jailor?"

"What? No! I'm going to be a lab assistant and sort of a caretaker."

He looked puzzled. "Lab assistant?"

"It's someone who helps a doctor around the lab with—well, never mind that at the moment. Too much information. The important thing is, I'm going to take care of you and the other creatures here, make you feel at home."

Instantly she regretted her poor choice of words as his face fell and sadness once again replaced the curiosity. "I have no home. I am outcast."

"From where?" she prodded gently.

"The Seelie High Court. I was a prince. Now I am nothing," he whispered.

She shook her head. "I disagree there, but we'll work on it. Is that why you were running loose on the streets in Ireland when the team found you? Had you just been cast out?"

"Yes. I was in Ireland once, as a child, but when I was tossed through the gate, I was disoriented and frightened. People were screaming and I ran. I meant no harm." Remorse colored his voice, and she knew he spoke the truth.

"Why didn't you just tell that to the Alpha Pack guys when they came for you? Could've saved yourself a bunch of trouble."

"As I said, I was frightened. I thought they were sent by my sire to kill me."

"What's your name?"

"Sariel."

She smiled. "What a beautiful name. It suits you."

Ducking his head, he flushed. "Thank you."

"Who's your father? Do you think he'll follow you here?"

This evoked a bitter laugh. "My sire is Malik. He'll stop at nothing to see me dead. He is Unseelie, and is the reason I'm no longer welcome in my world."

Not promising. "You're royalty, right? Can't your people protect you?"

"From Malik? You know nothing of Unseelie, then. They are little better than demons, and Malik is the worst. When the Seelie High Court learned that I'm a Halfling, they were upset enough. But when they found out Malik is my sire, public outcry forced them to banish me rather than risk facing his wrath. You see, he's on a quest to destroy me and will kill anyone who gets in his way."

"Why? I don't understand." How awful for Sariel.

"Does it matter? He is a rotten stench, a pestilence in any land he chooses to corrupt." Sariel paused, as though searching for the right term.

"Malik is the evil that time forgot. And now he is risen."

Six

"That's kind of melodramatic, isn't it?"

Sariel leveled Zan with a cool look. "Malik likes to paralyze his prey with his venom and then strip the flesh from their bones, eating them alive—and that is when he is in a jovial mood."

"Jesus," Hammer muttered. "You sure you don't have any other relatives we can contact who'll take you in? A distant cousin or something?"

Hurt flashed in his golden eyes, and was quickly gone. "My family is the reason I am here. But if you'll kindly step aside and allow me to pass, I'll no longer be your problem."

Zan disagreed. "You will when we get dispatched to wherever you've caused a stir after being spotted by humans again. Bad plan."

"I cannot imagine that all areas of your world are overrun by your kind." His wings rustled and he negligently waved a hand. "Point me to one of those places and I'll spend the last centuries of my life there."

Kira wanted to ask how old he was, but the pain behind his declaration concerned her more. "Alone, and with no one to help if Malik locates you? I don't think so."

"*When* he finds me," Sariel said with total surety. "And none of you will wish to be within leagues of me on that day. No, it's best I go."

"And I believe it's in your best interests to stay." She glanced at the guys, who didn't look pleased. "What, you're going to tell me you guys are a bunch of wimps who can't take on one nasty Unseelie?"

"Nasty *flesh-eating* Unseelie." Zan sighed, apparently deciding she wasn't going to budge. "Fine. It's not like we've ever backed down from a fight, anyway."

"Great, it's settled! And no arguments from you, Highness," she said firmly. "I can't think of anywhere better for you to be than here, where most of the folks aren't human and can relate to your situation. Well, I can relate, but I'm human—there's nothing special about me."

He studied her, bemused. "I'm simply Sariel now, not royalty. And you're wrong about your worth. If you possessed wings, you would be Seraphim—highest of the Angel Hierarchy, a being of pure light and love."

Clearly, the wolves could use a lesson in charm from this guy.

"Well, aren't you sweet? Maybe your manners will rub off on certain others around here." She turned to Hammer. "Would you get Sariel some clothes? He can't go parading around naked." *Darn it.*

"Sure." He eyed their newest resident. "Tall and slender? I'll see what I can find."

After he left, she addressed Sariel again. "If we let you out, do I have your word you won't try to harm yourself again?" She should've thought of this before sending Hammer on his way.

The faery had the grace to appear ashamed. "Yes. I wouldn't have succeeded anyway, not by attempting

strangulation. The Fae are not so easily killed, and I dis-
honored my name even further by attempting such fool-
ishness. I was feeling very hopeless and I still don't see
how things can end well for me. But I give you my word
I won't attempt to harm myself again."

Eyeing him, she felt he was telling the truth. "I believe
you, but not the part about dishonoring yourself. Everyone feels alone at times, like they have nowhere to turn
and no options. But you have us now, so put your trou-
bles aside for a while and let us take care of you. Okay?"

He hesitated, then smiled. "All right. I shall try."

*My goodness, what a lovely male specimen, no matter
his species.*

Too bad that ill-tempered, possessive wolves were
more her type. One tattooed, goateed, übermacho wolf
in particular.

"Zander, is there another empty room he can occupy,
perhaps one close to mine? I'll take full responsibility
for his liberation."

"I don't know, Kira," he began, frowning.

"Nick gave me the chance to prove I could make a
difference. How can I do that without a little cooperation? Work with me. Sariel won't harm anyone here, and
he wouldn't have fought you all if he hadn't felt threatened. Right?"

"This is true," he said gravely. "I would never harm
another unless in self-defense."

She gave Zan her best pleading look, and after a few
seconds, he relented—though he wasn't thrilled.

"It's not only your ass on the line if you're wrong; it's
all of ours. But I'll go with it, for now." He gazed past her
to Sariel. "You cause trouble, and you're on your own.
Nothing personal."

The faery pressed his lips into a thin line and inclined
his head. "I understand."

Hammer returned, thrusting a pair of army green and brown camouflage pants and a green T-shirt, along with socks and boots, at Sariel. "Couldn't find that fancy getup you were wearing. Best I could do on short notice."

Sariel eyed the garments dubiously. Kira doubted a Fae prince had ever had an occasion to dress up like a clump of turf, but he was too nice to say so.

He took them, managing a polite, "Thank you." Which earned some points of approval all around, however un-intentional. "But I can't put them on unless these are removed." He lifted his bound hands.

Here was the test. If she was wrong about Sariel, they were screwed. Zan looked to Hammer, who nodded. They were aboard. Zan removed a set of keys from his pocket and flipped through them. Finding the one he wanted, he unlocked the silver cuffs and the attached mesh gloves. The Fae male flexed his hands, and then expressed his thanks.

"Once again, you have my gratitude. Allow me a moment?"

She breathed a sigh of relief, and they slipped into the hallway, leaving the door cracked a bit so he could come on out when ready. Kira heard clothes and feathers rustling, some muttering, and finally he joined them. He was dressed except for the shirt, which he held aloft. She was struck again by how thin he was, and made a mental note to get him to eat.

"I can't get it in place over my wings," he explained. "Perhaps one of you might be of assistance?"

"Shoulda thought of that," Hammer said. Reaching into his pocket, he fished out a small knife and flipped it open. "Hold it up so I can see the back."

He did, and Kira grabbed the edge of the shirt, pulling the material taut. Hammer went to work and made two long vertical slits at the shoulder blades.

"Try it now."

Sariel pulled on the shirt, and then Kira helped by gently guiding each wing through the slit. They were a bit tight going through and the fabric tore some, but once in place he stretched one, then the other, seeming satisfied. Kira stared, unable to get over their magnificent span and iridescence.

"Much better." He swept his long, blue locks over one shoulder and regarded them with a regal tilt of his head. "To my quarters?"

On the way, they caused a little excitement. Dr. Mac and another woman wearing a white coat were walking with a couple of people wearing scrubs—one young man and a third woman—who might've been nurses or lab techs. The group stopped and stared, openmouthed, at the entourage. The woman with Mac, the one in the lab coat, stepped into their path, her expression morphing from incredulity to anger.

"Excuse me, but what's going on here?" Her eyes swept over Kira and then apparently dismissed her as unimportant in the matter. She turned her attention to Zander and Hammer as the others with her exchanged whispers. "Where do you think you're going with Blue? I didn't authorize any order for my patient to be moved."

The woman's chin lifted, dark eyes snapping with anger. Her tone left no doubt about who ruled this little corner of the compound. Behind her, Mackenzie gave Kira a nod, her expression encouraging.

Kira returned the gesture and turned her attention back to Mac's friend. She immediately recognized this woman's type from her own work experience. The names and address had changed but the song remained the same. This steely woman with the short cap of black hair would be the alpha bitch, the one who could choose to make her life here a living hell, or not. Whether or not she was also a fair-minded person and well liked among her colleagues, Kira would soon find out.

Zan handled her smoothly. "Hey, Doc, good to see you. Now that our new pal is up and around, we have some introductions to make." He waved the Fae male forward, who came to stand at his side. "Sariel, this is Dr. Melina Mallory. Melina, this is Sariel, prince of the Seelie High Court."

"Displaced, as it happens." Sariel swept a bow, and then regarded her steadily. "Doctor, we've met before, but it's good to make your acquaintance under less stressful circumstances. Call me by my given name; it is much simpler."

The doctor in question stared at the faery in amazement, mouth agape. Quickly, she regained her shaken composure. "Sariel. It's good to see you up and about, and willing to talk. Who do we have to thank for this positive turn of events?" Though she sounded sincere, she also appeared a little wary.

Sariel waved a hand at Kira. "My new friend persuaded me to give your hospitality a chance to make a difference for me. I don't know how long I can impose myself upon you all, but for the time being I will live here and abide by your leader's rules."

Dr. Mallory nodded thoughtfully. "I don't think you'll be sorry."

A wave of emotion rolled off Sariel, catching Kira by surprise. Had she really felt a deep, profound regret and sadness emanating from the Fae prince, or was she simply projecting her own feelings? It had happened the first time she'd seen him weeping, his emotions pouring over her like a waterfall.

It had happened when she met Jaxon, too.

Before she could puzzle over this more, Dr. Mallory addressed her. "You must be the new assistant Nick and

Dr. Grant told me about this morning. You're quite the busy bee already."

While not unfriendly, her tone held a note of censure as she slid a brief side glance toward Sariel. In doing so, she silently made it plain that while she wouldn't take issue with Kira's initiative in front of the others, she'd appreciate being kept in the loop in the future.

"I'm Kira Locke. I apologize if I've stepped on any toes," she said, injecting as much sincerity into it as possible. "I simply couldn't stand to see Sariel so unhappy and I wanted to help."

"Yes, well, that's understandable. Nobody wants that for anyone living here. We'll discuss the other residents of Block R later, all right? I'll give you some insight on them before you continue your work." So the doctor was tough, but wasn't the type to berate her subordinates in public.

Good to know. "That sounds fine. I'll come down to see you this afternoon, if that's okay by you."

The older woman looked satisfied. "Buzz me first to make sure I'm not in the middle of something in the lab or with a patient, but that should work."

"I'll do that."

"Nice to meet you, Kira. Sariel, I want to examine you after you've had a chance to settle into your room. How about after lunch. Three hours?"

"As you wish." The faery leveled the doc with the full force of his brilliant smile, causing her to blink at him a couple of times before looking to Zan and Hammer.

Lust. It was suddenly radiating from the outwardly stoic doc, as well as a distinct wave of . . . fear? Vulnerability? Didn't anyone else notice? Nobody seemed to. Kira stifled a giggle and thought she must be losing her mind—though if she hadn't already, she was probably safe.

"Later," Dr. Mallory said. Then she left, her staff following. Mac waved at Kira and hurried after them.

"Why do I feel like I just passed inspection?"

"Because you did," Zan said with a chuckle. Placing a hand on her shoulder, he gave her a friendly, one-armed hug. "After getting the equivalent of a green light from Melina, the rest will be gravy."

"If you say so." Kira paused, recalling something in retrospect. "I sensed a lot of anger in Dr. Mallory. And oddly enough, a feeling of vulnerability, as though she's not as in control as she'd like others to believe." She glanced at the men, who were gazing at her intently. "What?"

Hammer crossed his arms over his massive chest. "Does that happen a lot?"

"Does what happen?" she asked, mystified.

"Getting 'feelings' from people."

"No, I don't think so." She frowned, remembering. "At least not before I met Jaxon last night. Weird, huh? It's probably this place and the sudden submersion into all this woo-woo weirdness frying my brain. No offense."

Hammer looked at his friend and raised his brows, and the two seemed to share the same thought before Zan turned to her.

"Maybe you should mention this to Melina when you meet with her."

"Why? Other than suffering from delusions because I talk to faery princes and think I see men shifting into wolves, I'm perfectly healthy," she deadpanned.

Both men gave a quiet laugh, and then Zan answered. "I know you are because I'm a Healer and I'd know if you weren't. Still, it won't hurt to tell her and see what she has to say. Since the Institute of Parapsychology was established, Melina has made it her life's goal to learn what makes every supernatural creature tick. Tell her, and then she can log your information in case it's important."

Kira thought he was going overboard, but didn't see the harm. "Sure. Why not?"

"Have you ever had any leanings toward paranormal ability? Ghosts in your house, seeing things others don't, anything at all?"

"Not in the slightest." She frowned, recalling the voice she thought she'd heard when fleeing NewLife with the tissue samples, then dismissed it. Surely that had been her imagination. "But I'm a big fan of *Ghost Hunters*!" They gave her a blank look. "You know, on the Syfy Channel?"

"Um, we don't watch much TV. And when we do, it's probably not going to be anything dealing with the paranormal."

"Kind of like folks who work in an ice cream parlor not eating the stuff because they're sick of it," Hammer put in.

"Exactly."

"Oh. Well, you'll have to make an exception in this case. Great show. I'm completely addicted; even follow Jason and Grant on Twitter." She grinned at their perplexed expressions. "Never mind. Baby steps."

"What are Syfy and TV?" Sariel asked in confusion. Everyone had forgotten him as he tried to follow their conversation.

"Jeez, what do they do for fun in the Seelie High Court?" she teased.

The Fae prince made a face. "Fun? Very little. My existence there was all about pomp and proper behavior. I believe humans call it 'kissing ass.'"

The three of them laughed and Kira patted his arm. "Goes to prove some things don't change no matter where you are."

"I can believe that."

They walked Sariel to a room just a couple of doors from Kira's. She and the others did their best to reassure the Seelie that he was safe and welcome.

"I'm staying there," she said, pointing. "Dr. Grant is there, and Jaxon is across the hall. The others are close by as well. Don't hesitate to knock if you need anything."

"Or use the phone," Zan put in. "There's a list of extensions beside it."

The faery stared at them helplessly. "The what?"

Zan smiled. "It's a communication device that looks like a box. Come in. We'll show you." He led the way and Sariel trailed him, taking in his surroundings.

Zan gave a short tutorial on how to use the phone, while Sariel studied the thing as if it were a strange insect and declared that in his world there was no need for such a contraption. They simply used Mindspeak or flashed to another location to talk in person. Then he looked sad and she figured it had reminded him that he'd lost his home and people.

Afterward, the trio spent some time showing the wide-eyed Fae some more earthly devices, like the oven, microwave, and refrigerator. Their new friend began to look more and more dejected.

"I cannot cook," he murmured. "I don't know how."

"No worries." Hammer clapped his shoulder. "The kitchen and appliances are here only in case you want to eat in private. We have a cafeteria and the cook is real fine. You won't go hungry."

"And that reminds me," she began. "I heard you haven't been eating."

A slight flush colored the prince's pale cheeks. "I wasn't hungry. But I will not continue to shun your hospitality."

She figured that meant he *had* been hungry and was too damned proud to admit it.

"Lunch is in a couple of hours," Zan told him. "Why don't you rest and I'll make sure someone comes to get you right before we eat?"

Sariel nodded. "I would like that."

"Will you be okay here?" She couldn't help but worry. When she'd seen him earlier, he'd been the picture of abject misery, and now he was almost too calm. She hoped that didn't mean he planned to do something drastic the minute their backs were turned.

"This will be most comfortable. Thank you."

Zan started for the door. "We'll get out of here, then. If you get tired of being alone, just come on out and go for a walk. You're bound to see someone who can point you toward wherever you want to go."

He swallowed hard, and looked to each of them, including them all in his next words. "I appreciate your kindness and I'm indebted. Somehow I will repay you."

"Let's not worry about that, huh?" Zan winked. "We'll let you get some shut-eye."

As they left, Kira glanced back over her shoulder to see Sariel standing in the middle of the small living area looking very alone. She didn't really want to leave him but he needed time to adjust. He wouldn't want someone hovering over him constantly after he'd given his word he wouldn't harm himself. It would be a breach of trust in his eyes.

In the hallway, she voiced her concern as they walked. "What if he tries to leave?"

"We can't stop him," Zan answered. "And we can't keep him caged. After you got him to open up, anyone could see that wasn't right. But if he tries to walk out, he won't get off the grounds without us knowing. We can try to persuade him again to stay."

"If he translocates, though, he's gone," Hammer said. "Nothing we can do about that."

Zan attempted to reassure her. "Try not to worry. He said he'd stay and he seems like a man of his word."

She hoped so. The thought of such a gentle soul facing exile by himself was not acceptable.

Kira thanked the guys for their help and they told her to call on them again if she needed to. She said she would and headed in the direction of the recreation room, forcing herself to look on the bright side. Sariel was liberated from that awful cell, and though bewildered, he would adjust. He'd be fine.

What should she do with herself until lunch? Dr. Mallory had made it crystal clear she wanted to speak with Kira before she took on any more of her duties. And really, she wasn't officially an employee until Nick said so. She wasn't worried about the background check as it was a simple formality. Not even an unpaid parking ticket marred her record.

Until last night, her life had been critically boring to the point it needed CPR.

In the rec room she froze. Jax was sitting on the sofa, arms crossed over his chest, shit-kickers parked on the coffee table. He was watching a talk show on TV, but from his glazed expression, she had her doubts that he even knew what the topic was.

God, he was so wickedly sexy, her heart beat faster simply being near him. Short black hair sort of stuck out in that messy, spiky style that wasn't as easy as it looked to pull off. Did he use gel? She'd love to offer to do the job for him, run her fingers through the black silk and mess it up real good.

While he kissed and licked his merry way down her body, making places tingle that hadn't in ages and desperately needed to—

"You going to come in or stand there all day?"

She hated when people threw out challenges like that.

It was tempting to turn around and leave, but then she'd look like an ass. "Coming in, I guess. I've done my good deed for the morning and I don't dare do any more without Dr. Mallory's blessing."

His eyes met hers as she moved to the sofa and plopped down. "Why? What's going on?"

She shrugged. "Sariel is out. Zander and Hammer helped me."

He frowned. "Who's Sariel?"

"Oh, that's right." She snapped her fingers and glared at him. "You don't know because you weren't here to help me in Block R like you said you would!"

"Wait. You went there alone?"

"I just said your friends helped me. And Sariel is the name of the winged guy. He's a Fae prince who was outcast from the Seelie Court. The lousy asswipes tossed him through the gate, and only because his daddy is some Unseelie guy with nasty eating habits."

"You found out all of this while I was gone?" He eyed her in disbelief.

"Yep. All I did was talk to him, and I guess he was ready to get out of there." She was pretty proud of herself for that one.

"He's *out*?" Jax sat straight up in alarm. "Where is he?"

"Relax. He's fine. He's staying in the living quarters two doors down from me and across the hall from you. We got him settled in after he promised not to try and harm himself again. Said he couldn't really do much damage, anyway, because the Fae aren't easy to kill."

"And you all believed him? Kira, he's despondent," he said in concern. "If he wants to die, he'll find a way."

That led to a horrible thought. "You don't think he'd give himself up to his father, do you?"

"Hell, how should I know? He's never said a word until you came."

She worried her bottom lip with her teeth. "He promised to give life here a try. I believe him and so do the others."

"Well, if he goes back on his word, there's nothing we can do."

"That's what Zan said."

"You and Zan are getting awfully chummy, aren't you?" Leaning close, he sniffed her neck and shoulder. "He touched you." A growl started low in his throat and only stopped because she smacked him in the arm. He blinked in surprise, the noise ceasing.

"Don't you start that crap with me. He gave me a brotherly hug—that's all—and it's not any of your biz, anyway!" Leaning over, she sniffed his neck in return . . . and her blood started on a slow boil. "Seems I smell a woman on you, and it's not me."

Oh, that deer-in-the-headlights expression. Priceless. "What are you talking about? You're not a shifter, and I highly doubt you can discern scents like we can."

Seething with righteous anger, she stood, fists balled at her sides. "You arrogant jackass, I don't need a wolf's nose to know cheap drugstore perfume when it hits me like a ton of bricks. I don't have on any, and if I did I wouldn't choose something that makes me gag."

"Shit." He rose to face her and held out his hands. "It's not what you think."

"Oh? You were attacked by a drive-by perfume spritzer at the mall?"

"No. It's not—I didn't . . ."

"You know what? It's none of my business what you did or didn't do. I don't care." Okay, that was a teensy lie. She did care, but she wasn't about to let some womanizing jerk know it. "What *is* my business is who I decide to kiss or touch. You don't have any right to demand that other men stay away from me and then come back smelling like a skank."

"You mean skunk?"

"Read my lips—*skank*." She gave him a hard shove in the center of his chest, and he took a step back. "And if I want to screw my happy way through the whole Alpha Pack team, there's not a frigging thing you can do about it!"

"All right!" Ryon enthused from the doorway. "I've got the welcome banner right here for ya!"

Kira realized she'd pushed a Jax a bit too far about a half second before he grabbed her wrists and bared his canines. Yanked her flush against his hard body.

And crushed his mouth to hers.

Seven

He was pushing her, too much too soon. She'd had too much to deal with and he wasn't giving her time to process everything that was happening.

But goddamn, she was driving him bat-shit crazy. Jax devoured her mouth like a starving man at his last meal, hand around her waist, crushing her small frame to his much larger one. No way could she miss the erection nestled into her belly, seeking relief.

That's all it was, right? A physical need that would be satisfied when he buried his cock inside her, and afterward, when they were both drenched in sweat, whatever hold she had on him would be broken and they could go their separate ways.

Breaking the kiss, he took her hand and pulled her in his wake, shoving past a smirking Ryon. He'd break the dipstick's face later. Right now, he needed to get her alone.

"Hey!" she squeaked. "Where are we going?"

He glanced down. Took in her flushed cheeks, eyes alight with desire, as she jogged to keep up with his long strides. He slowed a bit but kept on toward his destination. "Anywhere my interfering brothers aren't. At the moment, the closest place is my quarters."

"But—but . . ."

She didn't finish the protest and that was fine by him. If she couldn't dredge up a reason why this was a bad idea, he wasn't going to give her one. When they reached his room, he keyed in his personal code and ushered her inside. Blessedly alone with her at last, he surrendered to the animal that wanted nothing more than to mate with his female.

Pushing her against the inside of the door, he set about overwhelming her senses while divesting her of the baggy clothing that hid way too much. He nuzzled her neck, kissing and flicking the vulnerable skin with his tongue, puzzled as to why he felt the nearly overwhelming need to bite her. And why denying that need seemed to make the burning itch even worse. Perhaps he would give in, but not today. He wouldn't risk it without talking to Melina about the possible ramifications.

His hands found the edge of her shirt, and his palms slid over her flat tummy. Moved upward to her small breasts, so different from his usual busty type. Hers were barely a handful and yet they were perfect. His thumbs grazed the nipples, pleased when they pouted and hardened. A little whimper escaped her throat and she arched into him, begging without words.

"You like that, angel?" he murmured.

"It's been so long." Her voice was breathless, husky with arousal.

"Do you want me to stop?" He plucked the peaks, pinching just enough to give a tiny jolt, make her want more.

"This isn't a good idea."

Scraping the tip of one fang along the spot where her neck and shoulder met, he nibbled, careful not to scratch her pretty skin. "That's not an answer. Do you want me to stop?" he enunciated, putting more force into the question.

"No."

"Tell me what you want," he coaxed. Moving one palm downward, he had no problem sliding his hand inside the front of the too-big jeans. Slowly, he brushed his fingers through neat curls, giving her time to protest. Instead, she widened her stance with a moan, inviting him to touch, thrilling him. But he had to hear it. "Tell me, baby."

"Touch me," she whispered, burying her face in his chest. "Give me everything."

Yes. "I can do that. Trust me?" She had no reason to, not to this degree, and her acquiescence was a gift.

"O-okay."

Her borrowed T-shirt went first. He pulled it over her head and tossed it in the general direction of his sofa. Then he reached around and unclasped the bra, slipping it off her shoulders. She let it drop but then raised her arms, trying to cross them in front of herself protectively. He was having none of that, and pushed her arms down, baring her to his hungry gaze.

"Uh-uh. No hiding from me," he scolded gently, cupping the creamy globes. "You're perfect."

Her cheeks turned rosy. "I wish they were bigger."

An unwanted image of Jacee's breasts, full and pendulous, came to the fore. A few days ago, he'd been happy lusting after them—and the rest of her as well—whenever the mood struck. Studying Kira now, he couldn't imagine what he'd ever found attractive about women like Jacee or Alexa. They were nowhere near Kira's class of lady in his mind—smart, spunky, and adorable.

"Does this make you feel good?" Bending low, he captured a nipple with his teeth, grazing the peak.

"Oh, yes. It does." Her hands buried themselves in his hair.

"And this?" He sucked the pebble, laved it.

"Yes! Jax ..."

"Feel how you affect me." Taking one of her hands, he guided it to the bulge between his legs. Cupped her fingers around his tight balls through the denim and moved it upward, rubbing along the rod that reached damn near to his belly button. Her touch was like fire even through his clothing. When he got naked, she'd probably roast him alive. "Does that prove I find you incredibly desirable?"

She smiled, lifted her chin to gaze at him. "Well, it does make a pretty strong case."

God, he couldn't wait anymore. "Hang on. Wrap your legs around me."

With little effort, he hoisted her up and she did as he asked. Wrapping his arms around her, he cupped her bottom and strode for his bedroom, enjoying how she fit in his arms. He liked carrying her and the action did weird things not only to his libido, but to this protective side that continued to plague him. The one that shouted *Mine!* in his brain and confused the hell out of him.

Beside his king-sized bed, he let her slip to the floor and wasted no time shoving the offending jeans down and off her slim hips. She toed off her shoes, held on to him as she got rid of her socks, and stood before him in nothing but a pair of peach-toned panties. He drank in the sight of her.

She was a pretty, petite package with slender legs that seemed to go on forever despite her short stature. Delicate toes sported a dark hue of red polish. Her shoulder-length blond hair was mussed some from taking off her shirt and if he had his way, it would soon be tousled beyond repair.

"No fair," she protested, blue eyes wide. "I want to see some skin."

Another wave of citrus and vanilla teased his nose, this time darkened with the unmistakable aroma of pure want. Something about her called to him in a way no other female ever had and he was too weak to resist.

He made short work of his clothes, ripping off his shirt and kicking aside his shoes, socks, and jeans. His turgid cock pointed straight at her, begging to be stroked. She stepped closer and reached out to smooth a hand over his right shoulder, admiring the tribal tattoos. He let her explore, loving her curious touch. Gradually, she inched around, examining how the scrollwork spilled down his back.

"This is beautiful. Do all of your friends have one?" With one finger, she outlined the design on his right shoulder blade. The silhouette that symbolized his inner beast, ears flat, jaws open, canines ready to shred his enemy.

"Yes. We had them done as sort of a memorial." He thought of how to explain. "When we were attacked by rogue wolf shifters in Afghanistan, most of our squad was killed. We thought the tattoos made a fitting tribute to them, to what we'd become, and how we'd never let our enemies get the best of us again. A ward against evil, I guess."

"Did it work?"

"No," he said softly. Now was not the time to get into the ambush that had wiped out half of the Alpha Pack team and left him crippled. The massacre he was partly responsible for because he'd let the wrong woman past his defenses.

Beryl. Treacherous whore.

The team refused to believe Jax was just as much at fault as Terry. But Jax knew better. Not only had he trusted Beryl, which had led to disaster, but he had a chance to use his gift as a Timebender when he realized who'd betrayed them, and squandered it.

My fault. I own that failure, no one else.

Ruthlessly, he shoved down the horrible guilt and focused on Kira. Her scent, her warmth pressed to his side. He'd never let another woman hold his heart, but his body was another matter. And his burned for the angelic blonde with the innocent blue eyes.

But maybe she wasn't as "innocent" as she appeared.

To her credit, she didn't ask any more questions about the tattoo and from what evil it had failed to protect them. Nor did she ask about the scars marring the flesh on his right leg, though her eyes briefly drifted over them. She continued her journey, mapping his body with those soft hands as though memorizing every hill and valley. Her warm palms skimmed his pecs, teased his nipples. They poked out for her and he shivered involuntarily, gooseflesh breaking out on his chest and arms.

Laughing quietly, delighted, she ventured lower, fixing her gaze on his straining erection. From the hum of approval as she trailed one finger over its length, she was indeed no blushing innocent in the bedroom. Why did thinking of her with another male make him want to rip something apart? Clamping his mind down on that train of thought, he concentrated on soaking up her attentions.

When she wrapped her fingers around his cock and gave a couple of strokes, he nearly came like a fifteen-year-old getting his first diddle under the bleachers. "God, Kira," he rasped. "On the bed, before I lose control."

She smirked, appearing very pleased with herself. "What if I want you to?"

"I will, when I'm buried inside you."

The unmistakable scent of lust rolled off her, inciting his wolf to near-mindless excitement. His beast was clawing his gut, howling at him to claim her, and he held the urge at bay with a superhuman effort as he flung back the covers.

She climbed onto the bed and he pounced, flipping her onto her back. Her merry squeal, that inner light radiating from her, did something funny to his insides, but he chose to ignore the feeling. Because if he didn't, he might be forced to acknowledge that she was too good to be here, rolling around with him. And his conscience wasn't welcome at this party.

He suckled and laved her breasts as she ran her hands over his shoulders and squirmed. Then he headed south, kissing his way down her flat belly, dipped his tongue into her navel and made her giggle. And then lower until he crouched between her thighs, hooked his fingers in her panties, and began to work them down.

She lifted for him a bit and he pulled the peach silk down her legs and off, tossing it away. All humor fled her expression and she spread wide for him, granting him a tantalizing view that made his mouth water.

"Oh, yeah," he murmured.

Crouching low, he nuzzled her mound. Gave her pretty slit a long, slow lick. Damn, she tasted good, sort of sweet, just like her scent. Her flavor was like ambrosia exploding on his tongue and he laved her greedily, his selfish desire to lap up as much of her essence as possible almost equal to his desire to please her.

She squirmed, burying her fingers in his hair and clutching his scalp. He licked every inch and then parted the tender folds, stabbed his tongue into her entrance, fucking the slick channel as her hips began to move, grinding her into his face. God, he loved it!

"Oh! Oh, Jax, yes!"

"Taste so fine, angel." Lick. "So fuckin' sweet, like candy."

Jesus, she was so damned responsive, opening like a flower after the rain. He never knew a woman could be both sweet and sexy, vulnerable and yet a firecracker when treated right.

Latching on to her clit, he suckled until she trembled, started to unravel, and then moved to crouch on his knees between her legs, poised and ready. "You want this?" He wouldn't take any woman for granted. She'd have to let him know what she wanted, with no chance for misunderstanding.

"I do, but . . ." She hesitated, uncertainty clouding her gaze.

"I can't get any sexually transmitted diseases, nor pass any to you," he said. "And I couldn't make you pregnant unless we were mated. We're still learning about our kind, but the doctors have confirmed that much. I would never risk a lover by not being sure."

Kira nodded, looking relieved. "All right, then. Yes, please."

"Please what? Say it."

She flushed but didn't look away. Her voice was thick with desire. "I want you inside me. Now."

"My pleasure."

Giving her a wicked grin, he rubbed his fingers along her folds, spreading the moisture. "You're nice and wet. So hot and ready for me." His cock throbbed.

She arched her hips. "Yes."

Ignoring the twist of pain in his bad leg, he remained on his knees, and brought the head of his cock to her slit. Parted the slick flesh and began to guide himself into her heat. Cupping his hands under her bottom, he lifted her, shifted forward and drove his rod deep with a throaty growl of sheer bliss.

"Fuck, you're so tight, angel."

Her moan, the way she submitted to him, completely opening to his possessing of her body, electrified his blood. Where their bodies were joined, the connection sizzled, sent fire rushing along every nerve ending. His world narrowed to the delicious clasp of her silken sheath hugging his cock, the little blonde spread for the taking. For *him*.

Mine.

"Nobody's but mine," he told her, his tone brooking no argument. He didn't know where the words came from, and the odd protective instinct confused him more and more. He didn't know anything except how right she felt under him as he drove into her snug channel. Thrust, long and slow, all the way to the hilt, his balls hugging her ass. Out again.

"Ohh, Jax." She clung to his shoulders, hooked her legs around his waist. "Oh, God, fuck me harder!"

He pumped with more force, careful not to hurt her. She met his passion with equal fervor, not seeming to mind it a bit rough. In fact, the sprite was stronger than she looked, evidenced by her hands digging into his muscles, giving as good as she got. When blunt little teeth sank into his shoulder, it was all he could do not to return the favor with his sharp canines.

But he wouldn't stop with a gentle bite. No, he'd sink his fangs deep, and her blood would taste so fine ...

His control shattered and he stiffened with a shout, emptying himself into her so hard he damn near turned inside out. His spasms were soon joined by Kira's as she clutched at him with a cry, milking him until they both lay spent and panting.

After a minute, he moved off her, not wanting to crush her under his weight. As he did, he realized that while the maddening itch had subsided, it definitely wasn't gone. With dread, he took stock, suspecting that the reprieve might be temporary. If it didn't go away, he'd have to see Melina for a checkup whether he liked it or not.

He didn't want to hear what he feared, deep down, she was going to say.

Rolling off the bed, he headed for the bathroom, aware of her gaze following his progress. He cleaned up quickly, cursing himself as lust cooled and reality set in. What a goddamned idiot he was for complicating things between himself and their new charge. What had he been thinking?

Simple—he wasn't. He'd let his fifth leg do the thinking, and look where that got him.

Padding into the bedroom, he wondered what the hell to say. He sucked at small talk, and in truth, conversing had never been at the top of his agenda when a beautiful woman graced his bed.

Kira lay on her back, the sheet pulled modestly over her nakedness. She studied him with as much caution as he felt, as though uncertain what to say. But she gave it a stab. "You were fantastic. I feel like a limp noodle."

He couldn't help but puff up a bit. "Thanks. You were pretty incredible yourself."

They stared at each other, an awkward silence stretching between them.

Sitting up, Kira sighed and shoved a strand of blond hair from her face. The sheet slipped to reveal one rosy nipple. "Look, this was fun, but don't think I'm going to go all clingy on you. I realize we were two consenting adults blowing off some steam, and I'm fine with that."

Jax stared at her, thrown for a loop. "What?"

"I mean, the last thing I intend to do is put a strain on your relationships around here, and in spite of what I said earlier about screwing my way through the team, I don't plan on being the resident slut." She slid out of bed and began to hunt for her clothes. "So this was great, but we'll just leave it at that. Right?"

"Uh, sure." He should be relieved she was letting him off the hook so easily. Why wasn't he?

Locating her panties, she slid them on and reached for her bra. "And now that you've scratched your itch, I'm assuming the possessive 'don't let me smell another man' thing shouldn't be a problem for your wolf."

He blinked at her. "Are you asking me or telling me?"

Grabbing her borrowed jeans, she lifted her shoulders in a shrug. "Asking, I suppose."

Watching her dress, he stumbled over the question. Was he fine and dandy with the idea of her suddenly reeking of another man's stench? With the knowledge that she'd been touched, pleasured, by someone else?

His wolf bristled, rumbling ominously inside him.

"I don't know what came over me before," he said, striving to sound casual. "It's none of my business who you spend time with."

His skin prickled, the burning itch worsening, the reprieve apparently coming to an end. His own words felt like acid on his tongue, and he stood like a statue, willing down his wolf's rage. And it wasn't only the beast that was unhappy, he realized—his very human side was pissed as hell at her calm dismissal of their fling and even worse, his own stupidity in agreeing with her.

"I'm glad we have that cleared up," she said. But a flash of something that might've been hurt clouded her eyes, and then was hidden as she sat on the edge of the bed and bent to tie her sneakers.

At a loss, Jax pulled on his clothes as well, hiding his conflicting emotions. He knew she was right, that his possessiveness was nothing more than a by-product of his beast flexing its muscles, but for some reason it didn't make him feel better.

"How did you hurt your leg? If you don't mind my asking."

He did mind, very much. But she was looking at him with such honest concern, not pity, that he found himself answering. "Six months ago, my team was ambushed and five of us were slaughtered. The mangled leg was my souvenir from that night. Guess I got lucky." The bitter sarcasm in his voice wasn't lost on either of them.

"I'm so sorry," she said softly. Her eyes locked with his. "But I thought you said shifters were almost impossible to kill."

"Almost being the operative word. But we were lured to an abandoned building, and lowered our guard when we saw it was unoccupied. The next thing we knew, bullets were flying. Silver ones." Remembered horror had him swallowing hard.

Screams of agony, his friends falling. Writhing on the cold concrete floor.

Creatures unlike any they'd ever seen, conjured as though from the worst of their nightmares, swooping from the rafters. Screeching in salacious joy as they ripped through flesh and bone, tearing him apart.

Blood everywhere, flowing like a river.

"Jax?"

Shaking himself from the terrible memory, he noticed she'd stood and was patting his arm. "I'm fine. It just sneaks up on me sometimes."

"Six months isn't long to heal, either physically or emotionally. I apologize for bringing up a painful subject."

"Not your fault," he assured her. "Anyway, we couldn't shift into our wolves because of the silver bullets. Silver shuts down our systems, and it's agonizing no matter what form we take. While we were incapacitated, these creatures attacked. Black leathery bastards, with gaping maws of jagged teeth. All we could do was lie there while they sliced and diced us."

She shuddered. "Demons?"

"No. None of us had ever seen anything like them. Four of us survived—me, Zander, Aric, and Ryon. Zan escaped the worst of the attack and healed the three of us as best he could. Nearly killed himself trying to save the others. I woke up back at the infirmary and learned the rest were dead, including our leader, Terry Noble."

"Then Nick and Hammer came in as the new guys," she finished.

"Yeah. They've fit right in, and Nick is a good boss. Different from us, though," he said, anxious to steer the topic from the massacre.

"How so?"

"He's a born shifter, not made. He's also a rare white wolf and a PreCog. All of that has made him a favorite subject of study with the docs here at the Institute."

"I'll bet." Her expression lit with interest. "Understanding his physiology and his lineage should go a long way toward helping the doctors learn about the life cycle of your kind. Like whether being a shifter shortens or lengthens your life span, what happens when you take a mate and try to have a child—all sorts of stuff."

Mating. Another subject he didn't want to discuss, though he *had* opened up the subject before they made love, in trying to ease her concerns. But he'd have to talk about it in more depth when he saw the doc, and he should get going soon if he wanted to speak with her today. In a few hours, they'd leave to stake out the cemetery and wait for Goth Guy to show.

He nodded. "They're studying everything they can

about what makes us tick, and I figure you'll assist with the research and testing. When you're not making nice with your new buddies from Block R."

"I guess I'll learn more after I see Dr. Mallory." She cocked her head, curious. "By the way, what's the 'evil' creature currently making its home in Block T?"

His eyes narrowed. "Who told you about that?"

"Zander. He also told me not to go down there for any reason."

Way to go, Z-Man. Now Mary Sunshine is sure to try, you dipstick. "He's right—don't even think of finding Block T. None of the creatures who're put there can be rehabbed, and our guest at the moment is no exception."

"What is he?" she repeated.

Damn it. The woman was tenacious when she wanted an answer. "During the massacre, one of the things that attacked us was injured. His buddies left him for dead and he ended up here as our prisoner in hopes of getting information from him about who set up the attack. He either can't communicate, or refuses. We're not sure which."

"You know, I got Sariel to talk when no one else could. Maybe I could—"

"No fucking way!" he practically shouted. "Keep your nosy self far from that piece of shit or I'll turn you over my knee and spank your ass until you can't sit for a week."

Stepping away from him, she stiffened in anger. "A simple no would have sufficed. I'm quite capable of following the rules."

"Says the woman who stole from her employer not twenty-four hours ago," he shot back.

"I explained why I took those samples, and it's a good thing I did since something really weird is going on there that's even weirder than what goes on *here*. Now, if you'll excuse me, my *nosy self* has pressing business with my new supervisor."

Sailing past him, she exited the bedroom.

"Hey, wait! Kira, I'm sorry!"

A few seconds later, the door to his apartment slammed and he was left alone.

"Well, fuck!"

Even Mary Sunshine had her limits, it appeared. This wasn't how he'd envisioned their interlude ending. But it was probably for the best. He'd never wanted to tie himself to any one lover, even more so since his last disastrous relationship. Nothing good could come from leading on someone as genuine as Kira.

Wandering into the living room, he tried to decide what to do next. Kira was on her way to meet with Melina, so Jax's own visit with the doc would have to wait. Maybe he'd see if Zan wanted to do some sparring in the gym.

Nothing like a little friendly bloodshed to keep his mind off a cute blonde.

Already, he knew the odds of the distraction being completely successful.

Damn it.

"Nosy!" she seethed, stalking away from Jax's place as fast as her feet would carry her. "Insufferable jerk. Where does he get off yelling at me?"

She was inquisitive. So what? And if that undesirable trait helped uncover something illegal or immoral, then it wasn't all bad. No, her biggest problem at the moment seemed to be Jax believing he had the right to tell her what to do.

Being shouted at tended to shut her down, always had. Her dad had been one to shout whenever he conveyed his displeasure over anything, no matter how small. She and her mother had to put up with it when Kira was growing up, and her mother still endured his bullying. But Kira didn't have to take it from Jax, or any man.

God, if only she could forget the play of his muscles under her palms. The way he moved inside her, took control. Owned her body as no lover ever had.

"Kira? May I walk with you?"

Halting in her tracks, she turned to see Sariel close his door and stride toward her. She was struck anew by his ethereal beauty, so different from Jax's rough-around-the-edges male potency, but no less effective. If it wasn't for Jax—no. She wasn't going there, not with the Seelie and not with Jax, ever again. She'd been a fool to fall for his seduction knowing full well that she was a substitute for his failed liaison with someone else.

"Sure. I'm going to see Dr. Mallory. Which reminds me, I was supposed to buzz her first."

Catching up with her, he smiled. "Would you like to use my communication box?"

"Your phone," she corrected, laughing.

"Yes, that thing."

"Might as well." She was going to suggest that she use her own phone since her door was closer, but Jax chose that moment to leave his apartment and spotted them. "Your room, then."

Okay, that was probably mean of her, saying that loud enough for Jax to hear. But he needed to get the point. She wasn't going to follow orders where her personal business was concerned.

Even if he was hot enough in bed to set the sheets on fire.

She was glad his Psy ability wasn't setting fires because the look he gave her and Sariel as he stalked past would've fried them both in their shoes. Lifting her chin, she trailed the faery into his room and walked to the phone, scanning the list of extensions. Finding the correct one, she punched in the numbers and waited for the doc to pick up.

"Dr. Mallory."

"Hi, um, this is Kira Locke. I know it's early, but I was wondering if you had time to see me before lunch." She glanced at her new friend hovering nearby. "Sariel, too."

There was a pause, and the sound of papers shuffling. "I was just finishing a couple of tests, but I should be free in ten minutes or so. I'll see you first, then him. Does that work?"

"Yes, that's great. Thank you."

"You're welcome. See you in a few minutes."

Kira hung up and replaced the receiver in the dock. "She'll see us in ten minutes. Me first, then you." She looked at Sariel and felt a tremor of anxiety roll from him, despite his placid expression. "Don't worry. She seemed warmer than when we met earlier."

His brow furrowed. "Warmer? Was she cold?"

She stared at the prince for a couple of seconds before realizing that he'd taken her words literally. Not wanting to hurt his feelings, she stifled a giggle. "No. What I meant is, she didn't seem as unfriendly."

His confusion cleared, if not his fear. "Oh. Well, I suppose that's good."

"Sariel, I don't believe either of us needs to worry about being in danger here. These people are only trying to protect the world from evil."

"It's not the people here who concern me," he said, golden eyes darkening. "And none will be able to protect me from Malik once he learns where I'm hidden. He will destroy me, and if I'm fortunate, he'll allow me to die."

His words, so matter of fact, sent a chill through her. She longed to offer him comfort, but knew he wouldn't appreciate empty promises she had no business making.

"The Alpha Pack team will do their best, I have no doubt. We have to believe that's enough."

His smile was accompanied by a wave of sadness that made her want to cry. "Perhaps it will be."

But he didn't believe that. Sariel fully expected to die at the hands of his own father.

Their walk to Dr. Mallory's office next to the infirmary was a quiet one, punctuated only by their footsteps and the occasional rustle of his wings. Giving him a curious sidelong glance, she noted his regal bearing never wavered despite the onslaught of emotions battering at him. Unlike earlier, when she'd seen him quietly falling apart in his cell. That couldn't be good.

How could his people have so callously thrown him away? She'd like to give those uptight snobs—cowards, more like—a piece of her mind.

They found Dr. Mallory's office without incident, thanks to a nurse who was heading the same way. The doc's space was located in the infirmary she'd found before, past the reception area and down a short hallway. The door was open and Kira peeked in to see the woman entering some sort of info into her computer. At Kira's knock, she looked up and then stood.

"Come in," she invited. Her tone was pleasant enough, though reserved. "Sariel can wait in the reception area."

Kira glanced at the prince, who merely shrugged and turned to do as the doc said. Weird, but now his emotions weren't coming through at all. Like they'd been locked behind an invisible wall.

Now wasn't the time to try to puzzle it out, though. Closing the door behind her, she took a seat and waited for Dr. Mallory to begin the meeting. The other woman got right to the point.

"I had a word with Nick," she began, sitting back and toying with a ballpoint in one hand.

I'll just bet you did.

Her dark eyes pinned Kira in place as she continued. "Let's get one thing clear. No question, Nick is the boss and has total say over the compound and the beings under our care. He can even decide whether outsiders can receive sanctuary here."

Ooh, and I'll bet that just chaps your ass, huh? But she kept her lip buttoned.

"But *I* am the chief of staff at the Institute of Parapsychology and I have final say over who joins my team, not Nick."

The doc paused, apparently awaiting some sort of response. Kira lifted her chin and met the woman's gaze squarely, refusing to be intimidated. "He never said otherwise. He merely asked if I would be interested in helping in the lab and with the residents of Block R, and said if so I'd have to pass a background check and you'd have to agree to take me on."

Well, she didn't recall Nick mentioning Dr. Mallory by name, but figured she'd leave that out. This last bit of info seemed to appease the stiff woman, her posture relaxing some and the hardness of her eyes softening a tad.

"That's what he told me as well."

Hadn't she believed him? Hmm, friction between the good doc and Nick. What was that about?

She cocked her head. "He also sent down some remarkably interesting samples that you *liberated* from your former employer."

"Did he tell you why I took them?"

"Yes. I'm willing to give you the benefit of the doubt because Nick insists you'll play a vital role here—and I have to admit he would know. From what I've seen so far, with your astounding progress with Blue, I'm inclined to give you a chance."

"Sariel," she corrected automatically. The woman didn't take offense.

"Right. But back to the samples—I believed them to be human, at first, but some interesting markers presented themselves. I then called in two assistants and we're working to verify what it is, exactly, that you've brought to us."

"Why can't Jax and Nick, you know, do their woo-woo thing on them and find out?"

The doctor gave her a piercing stare that spoke volumes about what a stupid question that had been. "And if they handle the tissue, and fail to get a reading?"

Kira flushed. "The sample is likely harmed."

"Not only that, but do you have any idea of the adverse effects using their Psy gifts has on their bodies? In some cases, it can leave them drained for days. And if they're called out to deal with a rogue? It could be deadly."

"But with all due respect, science can't tell us everything," she said, careful to keep her tone respectful. "It can't always tell the story, or the process of investigating is so slow, critical time is lost."

"Well, that's what still makes us all human, no matter our gifts," the doctor responded softly. "We all have to make our judgment call, and learn to live with it."

Kira wondered what decisions Dr. Mallory was trying to live with.

"What about me? Will you take a chance, or do I need to beg Nick for a job scrubbing toilets?"

For the first time, the other woman's mouth quirked with humor. A small crack in the shell. "I'm sure that won't be necessary. Report to me tomorrow morning after breakfast. You can observe while we continue testing on your samples and see what we find. Your afternoons will be free to work with your new charges in Block R." She stood, concluding the meeting.

"Thank you." She offered the doc her hand, and got a brisk shake.

"Send in Bl—I mean Sariel, if you don't mind. I'd like to talk with him a bit, and then give him a checkup."

"Sure."

As she went to get Sariel, she pondered her conversation with the doc. Strange, her emotions had been every bit as guarded as the Seelie's were a few minutes ago. Impenetrable.

And I must be crazy, thinking I can read emotions all of a sudden!

She made a note to ask Dr. Mallory about it tomorrow—among other things. Sariel stood, quickly masking the trepidation that flashed across his face as she approached.

"Relax," she told her new friend. "She just wants to talk to you and then make sure you're healthy. Okay?"

"If you insist," he managed. "I'll trust you."

"Do you want me to wait until you're done?"

There was no mistaking the profound relief as he answered. "If you don't mind."

"No problem."

He tried a smile and then walked past her, head high, as though to his doom. But she wasn't worried. Dr. Mallory might not be all shits and giggles, but she seemed fair.

Maybe the doc just needed to get laid.

Thinking of Jax and where that mentality had gotten her, she made a face.

Then again, maybe not.

Eight

"Watch out! Brace with your *left* leg, not your right!"

Jaxon grappled for leverage, fighting both a losing battle with Zan and his own goddamned bum leg. He wanted to yell at Aric that he was *trying* and to kindly fuck off, but he couldn't bellow at his friend and breathe through the pain at the same time.

Sweat trickled down his face and sides and his mangled leg trembled as Zan used his position to his advantage, bowing Jax backward to force their combined weight onto the limb. Zan had him in a bear hug, his embrace every bit as powerful and unbreakable as a grizzly's. All he had to do was be patient and wear Jax down, drive him to exhaustion.

It was pathetic how quickly he'd done it.

Then suddenly, Zan let up, loosened his hold. Distracted by the relief of being able to straighten, thinking their bout was over, Jax was taken completely by surprise when Zan delivered a swift kick to his injured leg.

"Aaah, fuuuuck!" he yelled, agony sweeping through his muscles like a blowtorch. The leg buckled and he went down hard, the thick gym mat cushioning his fall. To his shame, he could do nothing but writhe on the mat, breathing hard and pounding his fist, riding out the waves of sickness rising in his throat.

"Hey, low blow!" Aric shouted. Jax was barely aware of the redhead leaping from his spot on the bleachers and jogging over to shove Zan. "What the hell, asshole?"

Zan ignored him and raised his thumb and forefinger as though shooting a gun aimed between Jaxon's eyes. "And boom, you're dead."

Aric shoved Zan again and got right in his face. "I'm talkin' to you, needledick. What gives with that bullshit? You're supposed to be his best bud, and you put him on the ground like a fuckin' dog!"

Jaxon wasn't sure what amazed him more—Zan doing just what Aric said, or Aric leaping to Jaxon's defense. Wasn't it just this morning that he'd taken a chunk out of the red wolf for getting too cozy with Kira? And here the man was, ready to do the same to Zan for delivering the cheap shot.

The two men glared at each other as Zan replied. "What do you think a demon would do in battle? Or someone with a gun? Apologize and offer to kiss his boo-boos? Get a grip, man. We can't help him improve his skills by coddling him."

Aric's lip curled. "But you're not the enemy, you prick. He can't get better with you whacking away at the damage."

"I disagree."

"Why don't ya take a shot at someone who can whoop your ass?"

Jesus. Sitting up with a grimace, Jax reached out and tapped Aric's calf. "At ease, soldier. He's right. Help me up, would you?"

The pair stared each other down a few seconds longer. Aric relented first and reached to lend him a hand. Zan grabbed the other and together they hauled him to his feet. Another bolt of pain rocketed through the complaining limb, but he managed to steady himself by briefly holding on to Zan's shoulder.

At their questioning looks, he nodded. "I'm good. Gonna go grab a shower and see Melina before lunch."

"Christ, Jax, did I hurt you that bad?" Zan asked, eyes wide. "God, I'm sorry!"

"No," he said with a short, humorless laugh. "Something else entirely."

"What's going on?" This from Aric, who was frowning in concern. "You sick?"

"Don't think so." He paused. "Not sure. I've got this burning itch—"

"Eewww." Zan gave him a teasing grin. "Thought we couldn't get those kinds of diseases anymore."

"Ha-ha, very funny. It's not that sort of itch; it's all over, just under my skin. No rash or anything, but it's driving me insane." *Especially when* she's *around, and then I have the unbearable urge to bite her.* But he refrained from telling them that part.

Zan pushed a hand through his black hair. "Huh. Well, if anyone can figure it out, Melina can. Let us know you're okay after you talk to her."

"You bet. Walk me out?"

He didn't really need any help, but he wasn't about to leave them there alone to possibly get into another argument. Aric's combustible temper was going to be his downfall someday.

In the hallway, at the junction leading to his quarters, however, he had no option but to leave them to their own devices as they headed toward the rec room. At least they both seemed calm now. They could handle their difference of opinion like adults. He hoped.

In his bedroom, he stripped and showered without rushing, letting the hot water cascade over his aching muscles. Bracing his hands against the tile, he hung his head and fought back the feelings of worthlessness threatening to take over. He was no good to his team in this condition, but Nick had stood firm against him quitting Alpha Pack. God knows why.

The boss had his reasons and Jaxon was sure he didn't want to be privy to them.

A small, insistent voice in his brain reminded him that he'd handled the bastards attacking Kira just fine. In wolf form, he wasn't weak. Wasn't *less*. But how could she, or any woman, love the beast as well as the man?

That brought his head up, eyes wide. Love?

No. Uh-uh. Not now or ever.

Lust? Bring it on.

And Kira was too good to be used that way. Her soft little heart would get broken in nothing flat, hanging with the likes of him. She deserved better.

The goddamned itching returned at that very moment, seizing him with a vengeance. Arms, legs, and torso, he inspected every inch, and nothing. Groaning, he scratched like a madman, only to learn that made it a million times worse, and inflamed the burning sensation. Yet his skin was totally unblemished.

"Son of a bitch!"

Smacking the nozzle to shut off the water, he flung open the glass door and stepped onto the rug. Then he grabbed the towel hanging on the nearby bar and dried off, and hurried to the bedroom to put on fresh jeans and a T-shirt that declared THE HEAT I'M PACKING IS JUSTIFIED without really paying attention to what he'd picked.

Then he studied himself in the mirror, wondering if he should change the shirt.

He grinned. Nah.

His good humor was short-lived as he limped toward Melina's office. He probably should've called first, but he was in too damned big a hurry to stop. Didn't make a difference whether she was busy or not, he had to see her and get something to stop the itching before he lost what was left of his mind.

Hobbling into the reception area, he saw Kira sitting in a chair flipping through a magazine, but paused only long enough to bark at the young female receptionist, "Is Dr. Mallory back there?"

"Yes, but— Wait! She's with a patient!"

Tough shit. He was *dying*. Rushing to her office, he found the door standing open, the space empty. She must be in one of the exam rooms, then. Going from room to room, he had the presence of mind to knock before pushing open the doors. In the fourth one, he found the doc standing next to the Fae prince, who was sitting on an exam table. The white paper underneath him crinkled as he peered around the doc at Jaxon.

His movement alerted Melina, who was holding a cotton ball tightly to the bend at his elbow. Glancing over her shoulder at Jaxon, she shot him a look of annoyance and then turned back to her patient.

"I'm going to put a Band-Aid over this. Leave it on a while, until the bleeding stops."

"All right." The prince gave her a smile. "That wasn't as bad as I'd feared."

"Usually isn't." Jaxon watched in amazement as she beamed at the man in return.

There was still a warm, fuzzy woman under those cactus spines after all. Who knew? He waited patiently as she patted Sariel on the arm in a comforting gesture and then collected a vial of sapphire blue liquid from the nearby counter.

"Is that his blood?" he asked, raising his brows.

"Yes," she snapped. "Not that it's any of your business. Is this a social call or are you having a problem?"

"A problem."

"Wait in exam room two while I finish." She pointed the way in curt dismissal.

She was pissed, but he was too damned miserable to care. He walked two doors down and paced the empty room, listening to their conversation as she concluded business with her patient. He didn't mean to eavesdrop, but even with the carpeting, the acoustics afforded him every word.

"Okay, I'm going to run a few more tests that I haven't yet done on you, mostly for research, to study and record how the system of a Fae male works. How it compares with the humans and shifters."

"All right."

"However, some of them are going to tell me what I already know. Such as the fact that you've lost too much weight. You've got to start eating, even if you don't want to, in order to get back your energy and regain your health."

"I'll try," he said in a grave voice. "But as I said, I don't eat meat and anything else I've sampled has made me sick. Which doesn't make sense because your vegetables are not that different, from what I've seen."

"We'll work on that. Now, what about you trying to take your own life? Do I need to worry about you attempting it again?"

"No! On my honor, I will not." He sounded sincere, and ashamed. "I was feeling like I had lost everything. But I can see perhaps that was not true."

"It's not true at all. You have friends here, if you want them, and I think you'll do well. But come to me immediately if those depressed feelings return."

"I will."

"Good. As soon as I'm done with Jax, I'll speak with the kitchen and have them prepare some other dishes for you to try. If that doesn't work, we'll keep digging until we get to the bottom of this, I promise."

"Thank you, Doctor."

"Melina, please," she said softly.

Oh-ho! Jaxon stopped in midstride and grinned, wondering whether the guy had any clue what a gift had just been dropped in his lap. If not, he'd soon find out if things got up close and personal between them.

"Sariel." He paused, then added, "But *you* can continue to call me Blue if you'd like."

"I will, then."

This was getting more and more interesting. Too bad the doc was walking him out, ending the fascinating drama. As they reached Jaxon's room, she stopped there and said she'd see him again soon. Sariel thanked her again and left.

She came inside and shut the door. "What's so important that you barged into my examination with another patient? And it had better be good, because you don't look like you're dying," she said, eyeing him.

"No, but I feel like I am," he muttered, tugging at his soul patch. "Christ, Melina, I'm itching all fucking over. And look at me." He spread his arms wide, and then tugged up the hem of his T-shirt so she could see his stomach. "No rash, nothing."

"Have you been in contact with any strange or unidentifiable plants, maybe while running in the forest?"

"No, and I'm pretty sure I would've noticed."

The doc frowned, her irritation vanishing. "Take off your shirt."

"You won't find anything." But he complied, and she circled him, nodding in agreement.

"You're right. Clear as a bell." Grabbing her stethoscope, she gestured to the table. "Let's begin with all the standard stuff, like the heart, lungs, and throat. Have you run a temperature?"

"Nope. I don't feel hot, and shifters can't get diseases anyway." He scooted onto the paper-covered surface.

"That we've been able to learn," she pointed out. "That rule might only apply to the sexually transmitted ones." After listening to his heart and lungs, she removed the instrument from her neck and set it on the counter. Next came the tongue depressor. "Clear so far. Open up."

She placed the nasty wooden thing inside far enough to reach his frigging colon and pushed down. "Hmm. There's some redness and swelling. Is your throat sore?" The depressor came out and she tossed it into the trash can.

Swallowing, he took stock. "A little. I hadn't really noticed until you asked. It's not bad, though."

"Scale of one to ten?"

"Uh, a two."

"Which means it's really a three or four, knowing how you guys never admit to crap, even when you're gushing blood." Knowing the doc was right, he didn't argue as she opened a drawer and removed a vial and a syringe sealed in sterile wrapping. "I'm going to have one of my assistants run the usual tests—blood cell count, hormone levels, thyroid, you name it. We'll put a rush on it. Should be ready by tomorrow."

"Melina . . . I need to ask you some questions. As a patient," he clarified. They all worked in such close quarters, living together for years, he counted her among his friends. It could have been personal, but this time it wasn't.

"We'll talk in my office after this. I have questions for you, too."

He studied her angular face as she deftly swabbed the skin at the crook of his elbow with alcohol and then opened the package containing the syringe. Black fringe framed her forehead and cheekbones in short spikes, longer than his own haircut but still severe to him. Her hair had once been long and glorious, a black silk curtain that she kept pulled back while working, loose when off duty. Once, she'd smiled more, too, the rough edges smoothed by contentment.

She'd been married then, to their former leader, Terry Noble. After he was killed in the massacre six months ago, she'd cut her beautiful locks. And her smiles—the ones that actually lit her eyes—were now as rare as Nick's white wolf. Or a Fae prince.

But she'd smiled at Nick not long ago, when he wasn't looking.

And she'd done the same today, with Sariel.

"Why are you staring at me like that?"

He started. She was done and had stuck the cotton ball with the Band-Aid on his arm without him even noticing. "No reason. Just thinking that I miss your hair being long."

What he really missed was the friend she'd been to them all before Terry died. But he could hardly tell her so without alienating her further. Especially when Jax was the cause.

She eyed him, a funny expression on her face. "Where did that come from?"

"Don't know. Just being a stupid guy, I guess."

"That I can believe."

"Jeez, anesthetize a guy before you stab him, would ya?"

"You started it." Her lips quirked, and it saddened him to realize that was as close as she came to teasing anymore.

"So I did."

"My office. Wait for me there. I'm going to drop these off at the lab."

"Sure."

He pulled his shirt on and did as he was told. Once he was seated, it took her only a minute to join him. Taking her place behind her desk, she folded her arms on the top and began.

"My questions first, then yours." She gazed at him thoughtfully. "Exactly when did the itching begin?"

"Last night. After we rescued Kira."

Her gaze sharpened, along with her tone. "Have you touched her?"

And then some. "Yeah. Last night I touched her cheek and got a faint impression. Then I took her wrist and got a clearer vision of her stealing something, and running from men who wanted to kill her."

"It started after that."

"Yes, probably before I was even aware of it."

"Are there times when the symptoms seem worse than others?"

There wasn't going to be any way around telling her the truth. Not when it related to his own questions. Damn it. "Definitely," he said with a sigh. "It got a helluva lot worse after we went on a walk this morning and I kissed her. And then . . ."

"Don't leave anything out, Jax. It could be important," she urged.

He cleared his throat. "And since we made love, it's gotten to be damned near unbearable."

She blinked at him and then blew out a breath. "You sure didn't waste any time."

He fought down a surge of embarrassment. "That's another thing—I *had* to be with her. To—to *mate* with her, I guess is the right word, and it couldn't happen fast enough. I wanted to sink my teeth into her neck, Melina, to taste her blood! I didn't, though, and the need to take her again and follow through this time is driving me insane! What the fuck is wrong with me?"

"Jax," she said gently. "What you've described is exactly what Terry went through before he took me as his mate. Once he bit me during sex, the symptoms disappeared."

"Oh, God." He closed his eyes, slumping in his chair. This was what he'd been afraid of, the very thing he dreaded.

"There's something else."

He shuddered to imagine. "What?" Opening his eyes, he took in her grim expression.

"Once he mated with me, he was never able to become aroused by another female. It was physical, as though the mating rendered him incapable."

"But . . . Christ, you mean it's irreversible? And we have no say in who we're mated with? That fate or genes or whatever the hell decides for us? That's totally screwed up!"

She studied him for a long moment before answering. "I think that's the negative way to view it. I prefer to believe that shifters will experience these symptoms when they meet the one who's perfectly suited to them. The one who completes them in every way."

"Like you and Terry?" he blurted.

"Well, almost perfectly. He bit me, but I never turned into a shifter. He felt a bond with me that he claimed was like a slim golden thread, but I never felt it with him. I'm not sure we were true Bondmates, but we were happy."

A stab of remorse went through his gut like a bayonet. *Happy until I fell for a whore who led us all into a trap and got your husband murdered. And then I had the ability to bend time, change what happened, and failed to use it.*

That last fact was his greatest shame. His horror to bear.

But Melina had never blamed anyone. Not even Jax.

"Do you think Kira is my Bondmate?" he managed.

"Only one way to know for sure."

"Bite her."

"Yes. However, if you do and she's not your mate, you still run the risk of turning her into a shifter. You'd have to make certain it's what she wants either way."

He swiped a hand down his face in aggravation. "What a nightmare. And if I don't?"

"You might recall that Terry got really sick before he finally gave in and took the plunge, so to speak. His powers were almost drained and he was so ill he almost waited too late to bite me."

"Are you saying he nearly died?"

"No, but as a doctor who saw his rapid decline, I fully believe he would have if he'd waited a few more days. And you should know that once he mated with me, his abilities vanished for weeks. They did come back eventually, but we didn't know if they would."

Jax hadn't known that. He doubted the others did, either. The news was unwelcome and quite frightening. He didn't want fate, genetics, or anything else picking his mate. Fuck, he didn't want a mate at all!

"I need time to process this," he said. "You've answered my questions."

"And you answered mine." She stood at the same time he did and rounded her desk, laying a hand on his shoulder. "Take some ibuprofen for your sore throat. Would you like a sample of Benadryl capsules for the itching? I don't know that it will help much, if any, but it's worth a try."

"I'd take anything to get rid of it," he muttered, scratching his stomach.

"I know," she said in sympathy. "It'll all work out. You'll see."

"I'm not sure about that, but I appreciate the pep talk, short and sweet as it was."

A trace of humor lightened the starkness of her features. "Anytime."

After she fetched a bottle of the medicine, he told her good-bye and headed out, scanning the reception area for Kira. Of course she'd been waiting for her new buddy earlier—the one who looked like a frigging otherworldly runway model—and was now long gone.

And that made him seriously want to kick some faery ass.

Kira was sitting at one of the big oak tables in the dining room, eating lunch and talking with Mackenzie and Sariel when Jax stalked in, looking hotter than sin and loaded for bear. His steely gaze immediately focused on the Fae prince sitting next to her and narrowed, and he made a beeline straight for them, situating himself in a chair next to Mac and across from Kira.

"Mind if I join you guys?" His tone said he didn't care whether they did or not. Spying the sandwiches and chips served family style in the middle of the table, he grabbed a paper plate from the stack and began filling it.

"Only if you can put up with a nosy busybody like me," she lobbed back.

"Hey, I tried to apologize for that." He stuffed a bite of sandwich in his mouth as her companions looked on with great interest.

"Maybe not hard enough."

Setting the sandwich on his plate, he looked at her earnestly, ignoring their audience. "Listen, I *am* sorry. I was only concerned about you putting yourself in a dangerous situation again. If you say you won't, then I believe you."

He sounded sincere, and his gaze held hers, steady and serious. And it had never been in her nature to hold on to irritation for long. "Then I accept your apology. For the record, I'll try not to trespass or do anything else to put myself in harm's way."

"That's all I can ask."

As they ate, she mused over why he'd gotten so angry in his room. Why he seemed to care about her welfare more than a virtual stranger should. Because while there was a definite connection of some sort between them, and she liked his friends more and more with every minute, that's what they were—strangers.

Nobody's but mine.

His words returned with the force of a punch, and she choked on a sip of her soda. Waving away their concern, she grabbed a napkin and pressed it over her mouth as she coughed, eyes watering. Sariel patted her on the back, and nobody at the table missed the deep-throated growl of warning that rumbled in Jax's chest when he did.

The two males locked eyes and Sariel's hand froze. Kira's heart did a sharp jerk at the very real threat on Jax's face. One lip curled up to reveal a lengthening fang and his entire body was suddenly tense as a bowstring, ready to leap across the table and tear out the other male's throat. Anger smoldered, reached out like smoke to curl around them all, especially the Seelie.

She'd seen Jax cut through two human thugs like they were chew toys, but could he win a fight against a faery? Sariel's strong, firm voice broke the silence, and all eyes in the room riveted on the scene. Unknowingly, he answered her fearful question.

"Stand down, wolf. I have no designs upon your female, and trust me when I say that you have no wish to do battle with a nine-thousand-year-old Seelie."

Holy shit! At another table, a couple of the guys murmured to each other in surprise. Zander and Aric stood, ready to intervene if necessary.

Wait a minute—*your female*?

"Take your hand off her," Jax advised, each syllable enunciated with barely contained rage.

"I will, after you are calm." The prince's expression was now every bit as forbidding as the other man's. He might be pretty, but he was definitely no pushover.

"I'll rip off your fucking arm and beat you with it." Jax started to rise.

"Before you can, I'll turn you into a slug."

"Nice," said Aric with a chuckle.

Jax paused. "That's cheating."

The prince shrugged. "Whatever works. As you are the one threatening me, I reserve the right to end the conflict, preferably without bloodshed."

The Fae male was so self-assured, no one in the dining room appeared to doubt he could do exactly what he claimed. Kira's attention was fixed on her onetime lover, all the spit drying in her throat. Jax stilled, his expression cold as ice, the planes and angles of his face taking on sharper definition. Before her eyes, beast and man waged war over which would rule, neither of them wanting to avoid bloodshed at all, yet knowing they must back down.

How could this deadly predator be the same man who'd taken her to the heights of pleasure just hours ago? His struggle for control was scary as hell, but not nearly as frightening as what he said next, his throaty voice low and gravelly.

"Can you bend the very fabric of time, Prince?"

"Jax, don't." Zan quickly closed the distance between him and his friend and tugged his arm.

The prince frowned. "Such a thing is impossible, even for the Fae."

"Not for me." Ignoring Zan, he gave a humorless laugh. "I'm a Timebender, and my teeth would rip into your fine neck before you even realized I was no longer in the same place as before."

Sariel read the truth in the wolf's statement and his face paled, if that was even possible. "By the gods," he murmured, shaking his head. "Now, *that's* cheating, in its finest form."

"Whatever works."

For some reason, having his boastful words tossed back at him made Sariel laugh. A genuine hearty sound that shattered the dangerous tension in the room and had Jax's friends exhaling heartfelt sighs of relief. Including Kira, though she wasn't yet sure she counted as a friend.

"I like you, wolf." Pointedly, he removed his hand from Kira's back. "Perhaps one day you'll unleash that particular talent upon my sire."

The other man relaxed, his canines receding along with his anger. "Now, that's a war I'll look forward to winning."

For her part, she failed to find any part of the exchange the least bit humorous. Why did males of any species feel the frequent need to whip out their dicks and compare sizes?

She wasn't sure how she felt about being fought over like a steak bone, either. Perhaps it wouldn't have been so embarrassing minus the roomful of gawking people.

"Well, that was fun," she said stiffly, glaring at Jax. "Next time why don't you hike your leg on me like I'm a frigging tree?"

Pushing away from the table, she made herself scarce, dumping the remains of her lunch on the way out.

Behind her, Zan said, presumably to Jax, "Way to go, dumbass."

She couldn't agree more.

Nine

Morose, Jaxon stared out the window of the SUV and cursed himself for the zillionth time for how badly he'd handled the confrontation with Sariel. It was his own stupid fault. Now his team thought he was losing his damned mind, and worse, he'd pissed off Kira.

From the driver's seat, Ryon nudged him. "Dude, quit scratching."

"I'm trying," he hissed. "Melina gave me some medicine, but the crap's not helping."

"You got fleas?" Aric, the smartass.

"Boy's got a bad case of *somethin'*," Zan said from the back, a smirk in his tone. "Could it be an itch for a tasty little blonde?"

Aric snickered. "A tasty little blonde who was eating up our boy with those big baby blues, just about as much as his were doing to her."

His wolf snarled inside. "Shut up. You fucktards have no idea what you're talking about."

"Sure we don't. That's why her scent all over you is about to gag us," Aric said.

They all busted up laughing, even Hammer, sufficiently blowing off his heated denial. They knew him too well, which made living with his best buds in such close quarters a big pain in the ass sometimes. But paybacks were hell. He'd return the favor someday as each one of these jerks found their—

No. Kira was *not* his mate. Just because Terry had gone through the exact same symptoms before mating Melina . . . symptoms that were eased only by giving in to his primal urges.

Oh, Christ, I am so screwed.

Hammer changed the subject. "Who's got the photos of the four victims? Want to take another look."

Jaxon passed them back and the team took another look at the crime scene pics Nick had been sent courtesy of Sheriff Deveraux. The simple act of touching the paper the photos were printed on gave him chills. Nick had reluctantly asked Jax to do a reading on the bodies, which were now with Melina and her team, and Jax was damned glad to be able to put off the task until tomorrow.

"Nothin' special about these guys," Hammer observed. "Unless you notice how they all appeared to be really fit at one time. Broad shoulders, muscles, no extra fat. I think this guy might've been military." He tapped a pic.

Aric leaned in. "Let me see. Oh, yeah, the tat on his biceps. Didn't clue that."

"What do you think it means?"

"Dunno. Could be something, though."

Ryon turned onto the narrow, rural road that led to the cemetery. After a few miles, he pulled the SUV off the road into the trees, where it would be well hidden since the sun had set an hour ago. They'd travel the last mile or so in wolf form, the better to see and smell in the forest and graveyard at night.

And it would make walking much easier on his leg, which throbbed more than usual from the hard kick Zan had delivered while they were sparring. He should've had Melina look at it, but he'd have to do that later.

"How long do we wait for Black to show?" Aric asked as they got out of the vehicle.

Jaxon faced his buddies. "Give him until two, three in the morning?"

Ryon spoke up. "Whatever biz he has in a cemetery, I'd guess if he hasn't shown by three, he's not coming. The night begins to wane by then; the force of the witching hour fades." As their expert on the dead, he would know.

Nobody disagreed. They undressed in silence, tossed their clothes in the SUV, and shifted. Jax relished the stretch and pop of bone and muscle, and the moderate relief that being in wolf form brought to his injured limb. It would make fighting easier, too, though he hoped it didn't come to that.

Jaxon's enhanced vision adjusted to the darkness, his wolf enjoying a clear picture of the dense forest bathed in moonlight. The colors washed around them in tones of pale white, royal blue, and black, glowing in a way that the naked human eye could never see without the aid of technology. He sniffed the air, caught the scent of rabbit, and something bigger. Deer. Hiding in the shadows, trembling, aware that death was near.

But they needn't fear him tonight. He didn't have time to run and hunt, and his mission called him back to attention.

He kept his senses alert as they picked their way through the forest with stealth, barely making a sound. They made good time, arriving at the clearing in minutes. Once there, they hovered on the edge, keeping to the undergrowth where they'd remain hidden yet able to observe. They had a good scope of the area and were crouched on the back side of the property, a safe distance from the main entrance and any cars that might arrive—though at this hour there shouldn't be any except for the one their man might be driving. Never hurt to be safe.

They watched. After a while, they lay on their bellies, still alert but growing more bored by the hour. As the hour passed one in the morning, Jaxon was struggling with the need to doze when Ryon's urgent voice telegraphed into their heads, bringing them fully awake.

Showtime, boys. Our prey is here. A pause. *Jesus, get a load of this guy.*

No way. Jaxon blinked, just to make sure he wasn't seeing things. Yep, Nick was right—not from Wyoming at all.

Their quarry was on foot, carrying a backpack. He stepped from the shadows directly into a pool of moonlight and slowly began to walk in their direction with a loose stride Jax knew all too well—that of a fellow predator. As his clothing and features took on more definition, he couldn't help but be a little awed by the sight before them.

The male was tall and lean, just over six feet. He wore a black leather duster that had seen better days, cracks and tears marring the surface. Underneath he wore all black, jeans and a snug T-shirt hugging a sculpted chest and long thighs, and heavy shit-kickers on his feet.

Jaxon's gaze traveled to the ebony rock star hair falling in messy layers around his face and barely to his shoulders. Even from here, he could see the black nail polish and guyliner. Jax had heard some women dug that shit on a dude, but he'd pass, thanks. The only contrast on the man was his pale skin and the impressive silver pentagram pendant hanging on a chain around his neck and resting on his chest.

And the eyes that shone like emeralds in that face . . . He'd expected someone older. Thirtysomething. God, he was young, barely more than a kid who *might* be old enough to order a beer. And there was something else.

Kalen Black radiated power from every inch of his body. Ancient spine-curling power that created an aura around him, not so much visible as present in the air like the pressure, electricity, and the earthy scent from a coming storm.

Ryon posed the question in all of their minds—*What the fuck is he?*

The love child of Criss Angel and Adam Lambert? Jaxon tossed back.

His friend gave a soft snort that might've been a laugh. *With a little Nikki Sixx thrown in, sure.*

He couldn't hear the others' thoughts, only Ryon's since he was the Telepath, but he imagined they were pretty much in agreement. He couldn't tear his eyes off the kid, who was now searching the headstones. Carefully, Black picked his way up one row, down another. Oddly enough, he'd stop every so often, crouch, and trace the deceased person's name that was carved into the granite. Sometimes the date of death, too, but never the date of birth. Weird.

What the hell was he looking for? It was almost as if he was considering each for some purpose, and was discarding them one by one. Yeah, that's exactly what he was doing, but they'd have to wait to find out why.

This process continued for almost a half hour, the pack keeping as close as possible from their cover. Finally, Black's fingers paused over the name of one Henry Ward, recently departed from the world. He closed his eyes for a few moments, and then let go of the stone to kneel beside the fresh grave. They watched in rapt fascination as he removed some items from the backpack and arranged them in a circle over the mound. Then he opened a vial, sprinkled a white powdery substance over the circle, and put the small container back into his pack. He began a low chant, hands spread palms-down above the mound.

At first, Jaxon thought *whatever floats the freak's boat*. But in his profession he should've known better than to be so quick to dismiss the kid, especially given the power he wore like a mantle. After about fifteen seconds the earth began to tremble, vibrating the ground under their paws and shaking the very leaves on the trees. Jax and his brothers exchanged uneasy glances.

Tell me he's not doing what I think he is.

But none of them could reassure Ryon that his suspicions weren't on the money. Especially when the soil on top of the grave began to rise like a cake baking in an oven, splitting in the middle, the items that had formed the circle rolling down the sides. Through the split a hand appeared, gray and withered, gnarled from age and death. Then the skinny arm, followed by the head and shoulders of an old man with only a few silvery wisps of hair clinging stubbornly to his scalp.

My God, Jaxon projected to Ryon. *The kid's a Necromancer!*

Oh, yes, but he's much more than that.

Jaxon was afraid his friend was right, but they didn't have time to speculate further. The ground seemed to give birth to the old man in a gruesome manner as he clawed from his former prison and sat on the edge of the seam in the earth, staring blankly at his liberator.

Still kneeling, the young man waved a hand at the corpse in a slow palm-out motion, and spoke, his voice ringing with authority. "Henry Ward, I command you to speak with me, to answer all of my questions truthfully so that I may return you to your eternal rest. State your full name for me so I know we're ready to begin."

Jax and his brothers were riveted to the scene.

The corpse blinked at him, the eyes little more than gooey pewter marbles in his skull. "Who . . ." The old man's voice cracked and he coughed, apparently from using vocal cords that were never again supposed to be in working order. "Who are you? Why have you disturbed me?"

The Necromancer sighed in exasperation and rolled his eyes heavenward. "Why do they always answer questions with questions?" He looked at the old man, redirecting him. "I'm Kalen Black. State your name, please."

"Humph! Henry Allen Ward." Henry glanced around, his confusion apparent. "Where am I? My daughter is expecting me for dinner and I'm going to be late."

"No, Henry," the young man said gently. "She's not expecting you. Someone hit you over the head three weeks ago as you were walking home. Do you remember?"

Jaxon wondered where this was going. Had the kid killed the old man for his wallet or something, and now he needed to find out who might've seen the crime? But that didn't seem right.

"I . . . Wait. Yes, I do." The old man paused. "I bought milk and bread, and walked home. I had just enough time to get home and get ready for dinner. My Tina makes a great stroganoff." He gave a gummy smile that was decidedly macabre in his hollow face.

The kid didn't react to the sight. "I'm sure she does. But I have to ask you about what you saw right before you were hit on the head. You lived in a semirural area outside Cody, correct? Close enough to walk home but not many other houses on your road?"

"Yes."

"And as you walked home that afternoon, your path took you past a side road where you saw something and went to investigate."

"I did."

Black leaned forward, intent. "What did you see, Henry? This is very important."

The old man thought. "A truck— No, a van. Dark blue. Pulled into the trees. Thought it was odd cuz I never seen it before, so I walked that way. Maybe somebody had car trouble."

"But they didn't?"

"Nope. Two men were comin' from the woods when I got to the van." He frowned. "One had blood on his hands and I thought maybe they'd been hunting, but they didn't have guns. The other man had a shovel. I asked what they were doin', he swung it at my head, and that's the last I knew."

So the kid hadn't done in the old man. Who had and why, and why was the Necromancer investigating the killing?

"Henry, can you describe the men?"

"Oh, middle-aged white fellas. In good shape, I guess. The one with the bloody hands was average-looking with dark brown hair. The one with the shovel had sandy hair."

Not much help.

"Can you recall anything about how they were dressed?"

"Nah. Except one had on a blue polo shirt with something stitched above the pocket in white thread."

"What was it? Think, Henry."

"Uh, letters."

"Like initials?"

"Yes. With a logo," he recalled. "Three letters and under those, two hands holding a heart."

"What were the letters?"

"Don't know. Can't remember."

The young man blew out a breath. "Can you remember anything else, Henry? Anything at all?"

"No." Henry looked at him, expression blank. "Can I go now? Tina's expecting me for dinner."

Jesus, it creeped Jaxon out how the dead man kept repeating stuff, and he felt sorry for the poor victim's confusion, as though he couldn't grasp his situation. Apparently it affected the Necromancer the same way, because he was looking at Henry in sympathy, his caring for the man's plight etched on his face.

"Yes, Henry, you can go. And thank you."

Black waved a hand, murmured a few words in a different language, and a translucent green smoke drifted toward Henry, swirled around him. The old man stiffened, and then mechanically lowered himself through the seam in the grave, bit by bit until he'd disappeared from sight. The kid repeated the procedure over the grave and more green mist shrouded the ground. Once again, tremors shook the earth and the dirt began to push inward, filling the seam, and in moments, the scar was repaired and nobody would be able to tell such an amazing thing had ever taken place.

Holy shit, I've never seen anything like that in my entire life.

Considering some of the shit Ryon had seen, that was saying a lot.

"Rest well, old man." Pushing to his feet, Black brushed the dirt off the knees of his jeans and then suddenly turned without reaching for his backpack, his posture deceptively relaxed with his hands at his sides, and gazed directly at the spot where Jaxon and the other wolves were hidden in the darkness.

Or so they believed.

"Did you enjoy the show? Afraid I'll find out who you are and why you murdered poor Henry? Or maybe you were just passing through the graveyard in the middle of the night, out on a romantic stroll." The words were tossed as a challenge, laced with a touch of sarcasm. One thing was for sure—the kid wasn't one bit afraid of who he might face.

Come on, let's see what he thinks about taking on a pack of wolves.

As a unit, they emerged from the trees and padded forward, fanning out some in an attempt to surround him. Careful not to make any abrupt moves, they made their way toward him as he studied them in return, fists clenching and unclenching as though revving up his magic to hurl at them if necessary. His expression was hard, those green eyes glittering like cold jewels, none of the warmth or caring that he'd shown with Henry in evidence.

When they were within about twenty yards, Jaxon, Zan, and Hammer in front of him, Aric and Ryon to each side, the Necromancer held up a hand. "Far enough," he ordered. "Now I think it would be wise of you all to change, shifters, and tell me what the fuck you want."

Jaxon gaped in astonishment as a ripple of shock went through them all. The kid had to have known they weren't exactly human when they came out of the trees after he acknowledged them, but to call them exactly what they were—shifters—without batting an eye?

They might be in deeper trouble than they'd thought.

Jaxon half-expected the man to at least make a crack about their state of undress, especially given his youth, but when they shifted and stood, he didn't smile. Didn't so much as blink. He simply let his gaze travel over each of them as though memorizing details that might be useful later.

Jaxon got the heart-to-heart rolling. "Kalen Black? Why did you raise Henry Ward and question him about his murder?"

"What's it to you?" he challenged, pinning Jaxon with a cool stare.

"Not a damned thing. But it'll matter to Sheriff Deveraux, since he's the one who asked us to see why you've been hanging around." Indirectly, but he didn't need to get into the particulars.

"That asshole?" The kid gave a humorless laugh. "He couldn't find his dick with both hands and a tube of K-Y."

Now *that* sounded more like a young dude.

"Be that as it may, we need an acceptable answer or you're going to come with us for a more private chat." He glanced at his brothers. "Might not be a bad idea anyways."

"Second the motion," said Aric. The others agreed.

"Forget it. Deveraux doesn't have any grounds to arrest me if he called in the canine squad, and what I'm doing here is nobody's business. I left everything the way I found it."

"What about the murders of four men who've been dumped around Cody in the past few months? Know anything about those?"

The kid's jaw ticced and his eyes narrowed, the first sign of his control slipping. "Don't know what you're talking about."

He's lying, Ryon projected. *Get ready to take him, on three. One.*

"Or perhaps those two men who killed Henry are buddies of yours and you were making sure their tracks were covered?"

Two.

"You're full of it, man." Those fists, clenching. Unclenching.

He was going to bolt.

"According to Henry, one of those men had blood on

his hands, the other a shovel. If I was a betting man, I'd say that the perpetrators had just finished disposing of the newest victim of the string of murders we're looking at. That makes you a person of interest in the crimes, and that means you're coming with us."

"Fuck this."

Three!

Everybody flew into action at once. Shouting a word, the kid flung his arm at Jaxon, palm up and fingers spread, firing a blue ball of pulsing energy that would've hit him in the chest if he hadn't shifted at the same time. Instead, the orb merely singed some fur as it whizzed past, doing God knows what damage to the graves behind him as it exploded.

Black raised an arm, but before he could fling another nasty surprise, Jax leaped, hitting him square in the chest and taking him to the ground. He didn't want to hurt the guy, but that might not be an option. Black was strong as an ox for someone so lean, almost too thin under the bulk of his coat, and was fighting like a wildcat.

And that analogy turned out to be correct. The writhing body underneath them rippled, and in an instant they found themselves wrestling two hundred pounds of pissed-off . . .

Black panther.

"God*damn*!" Ryon shouted. "Hold on to his ass!"

Whether he was getting weak or was too worked up, Black couldn't maintain the shift and morphed back to human form. Still, though Jax had him pinned and Aric jumped on board, the red wolf closing his jaws around the young man's wrist to help immobilize him, it took four of them to hold him down. Hammer and Ryon stayed in human form, Hammer sitting on the kid's legs, Ryon pinning his other arm.

"Go back and get the SUV, and bring the iron restraints!" Hammer shouted at Zan, halting him in mid-stride before he could add to the pile.

Zan shifted and took off as fast as his four legs could carry him. Wouldn't be quick enough, though, if Black got his dominant hand free to let loose more of his impressive mojo.

Shifting back to human form, Jaxon grabbed a handful of the young man's raven hair and muttered, "Sorry, kid."

Then he slammed the back of Black's head into the ground, wincing at the soft *ughnnn* that burst from his lips before his eyes rolled back into his head and he went limp.

Hammer's brows lifted and he grinned at Jax. "That's cheating."

"Whatever works." But he didn't smile back.

Jaxon felt like a piece of goat dung for knocking out the kid. Yeah, it was dirty pool, but Black would've fried them all if he'd had the chance. Wouldn't he?

Turning in the passenger's seat, he glanced over his shoulder to where the young man was slumped between Hammer and Aric, dark lashes resting against white cheeks. His chest rose and fell steadily, so Jax wasn't worried that he'd killed the kid. He'd come around soon, and then they'd all have more questions for him.

Such as why he was practically starving, and didn't seem to weigh nearly as much as he should have when they'd picked him up to take him to the SUV. His T-shirt had ridden up as they carried him, and despite the guy's cut musculature, his ribs were prominent and his stomach concave. His face was a little too thin. He needed three squares a day and then some for about the next month to regain his health, which might be why they were able to easily get the drop on him. Jaxon shuddered to think how powerful he was when at full strength, if the supercharged display was any indication.

"A freaking Necromancer," Zan muttered from the back. "Who'da thought?"

"Ryon said he's more than that," Jaxon reminded them. "So what is he? Besides that and a panther shifter."

Ryon turned onto the main road, glanced into the rearview mirror, and blew out a breath. "He's a Sorcerer. And I think that's the basis for all his abilities, including his animal."

Stunned silence met his announcement. If their friend was right, Kalen Black might just be the most powerful being they'd ever run across. Including Nick and Sariel.

Finally, Zan spoke up. "Did you see how he shifted without even getting undressed? His clothes just vanished, then reappeared when he shifted back."

"Too cool," Hammer said. "Wish we could do that."

"Sorcerers gather power from the elements and can use it to command . . . hell, just about anything." Jaxon sighed. "Won't be so cool if he's really gone rogue and tries to use dark magic against us. Everything went down too fast and there was too much adrenaline pumping for me to get a reading on him."

After that sobering reminder, there wasn't much to say on the way back, each of them lost in their own thoughts. About ten minutes before they arrived, Black moaned and awakened gradually, eyes fluttering open. He tried to move his arms only to find his wrists were shackled behind his back, and Jaxon hoped the irons were strong enough to do their job.

Apparently they were, because the kid sat quietly, expression betraying nothing. Not fear or even anger. He just bided his time, patient, as though this was merely a side trip on the cracked and rocky road of his life.

What kinds of hardships had this young man endured?

The compound was quiet when they arrived, but then it was nearly two thirty in the morning. The only person who was awake to greet them was Nick, standing at the back entrance as though he'd expected them, which he probably had.

Jaxon took their detainee by an arm and led him inside, unprepared for the rush of darkness that swamped him from the young man—not the darkness of malice but of sorrow and desperation. Of long nights suffering from cold and hunger, the agony of abandonment, bleak despair.

But I have nowhere to go! I can't help what I am!

Huddled in a filthy alley, alone and scared. Stomach growling, in pain.

Hungry, kid? I know how you can make a few quick bucks.

Shame. Wanting out, but too afraid to make the cuts. Has to end. Make it stop.

But if I give up, they've won. Gotta keep going.

All of these images and emotions were much more than he wanted to see, and Jax felt like a voyeur, intruding on the young man's horror when he had no right. But he hadn't done it on purpose. Normally readings like this were a painstaking process that took several minutes to find the memories, catch the threads and follow them. But the Sorcerer was like a conduit for an endless flow of energy and Jaxon had no defenses against the man's roiling emotions that poured through the connection like blood.

At least he'd gleaned one important thing—Kalen Black was no enemy of theirs. With the right cultivation, he'd make a powerful ally, perhaps even a new team member to bolster their numbers again. He hoped the others, especially their boss, got the same feeling. Their group stopped in front of him, waiting for instructions.

Nick got right down to business, addressing the younger man directly. "Mr. Black, we're going into the meeting room where we're going to have an honest discussion about why you're here. You're going to tell us what we need to know, and then we'll decide what course of action to take. Is that clear?"

"Yes, sir." His gaze didn't waver, and revealed no deception.

Nick nodded in approval and they trooped down the hall and into the same room in which they'd had their briefing about the four dead men and the suspicious cemetery visitor, who was now in their custody. Black was directed to sit in a chair at the large table as the focal point of a rough circle, hands still bound behind his back. His backpack was placed on the floor next to him. He volunteered nothing, no doubt having learned the value on the streets of keeping one's mouth shut unless necessary.

Everyone sat except Nick, who remained standing with his arms crossed over his chest. He studied the kid for a long moment, no doubt seeing many of the things Jaxon had felt minutes ago. "You're a Sorcerer." A statement, not a question.

"Among other things." A slight crack in the kid's armor revealed the self-loathing behind those words.

Jaxon knew what "other things" he meant, and they had nothing to do with his magical talents.

"Shifter. Necromancer."

"Yeah. So what?"

"How long have you known?"

The question seemed to throw him a little, and he paused, thinking. "Always, I guess. Though I didn't have labels for my abilities when I was a kid. I just knew I was weird and my mom and stepdad hated me."

"Feared you is likely more accurate," Nick corrected.

"Maybe. What difference does it make? I've been on my own since they kicked my ass out at fourteen and I haven't looked back. Not once in nine years."

Fourteen. God, for what this young man had suffered, mommy dearest and the stepbastard ought to be tortured and hung.

"You're right. It doesn't make a difference except their actions made you what you are—a survivor traveling a road that will lead to either your salvation or destruction, depending on the choices you make. Starting tonight."

The Sorcerer stared at him a few seconds and then gave a short laugh. "Right. Isn't that true of everyone, Seer?"

A hush fell over the room and all attention swung to Nick. The undisguised challenge of his talents from this newcomer wasn't surprising, given the young man's isolation and his inexperience in dealing with others, but their boss wasn't inclined to go easy. The kid didn't need that right now, nor would he appreciate it.

"I'm not speaking in generalities and I think you know that, just as you know most men could never handle learning their fates. What you decide here tonight will set you on a very specific course, one that will lead to the toughest challenges and greatest enemy you'll ever face."

For a second the guy seemed unnerved, glancing around at all of them. Rallying, he shook his head. "What do you want from me?"

"Cooperation, for starters. Tell us what brought you to Cody, Wyoming."

He shrugged. "Nothing specific. Just sort of go where the wind blows me, performing street magic for tips to get by."

"Like that David Blaine dude," Ryon put in.

"Yeah, like him. Only I can't speak for him, but my stuff is the real deal. I could've done Vegas, but I don't like the thought of selling out to the big fish, having them watching over me, putting me on a schedule and telling me what to do with my magic. That would suck out loud."

The corner of Nick's mouth kicked up at his choice of words. "Plus somebody might find out it's not an act."

"Can't have that, either. So it's just me and the road." He cocked his head. "I don't know why I came here, but now that I'm giving it more thought, it's almost like something called to me. I mean, it's a good place away from the city to let my panther run, but there was something else. Once I got here, I sensed death. My panther smelled it."

"We're in the forest," Nick pointed out. "Animals die, sometimes campers and hikers who aren't careful."

"Yeah, but I'm not talking about natural death or accident. What I sensed after I arrived was more like … something that makes your skin crawl, makes you want to run and hide, shaking in terror and hoping it'll pass by without noticing you. Know what I mean?"

"Yes, I do. And that's why you started snooping around the cemetery?"

"Partly." He heaved a deep breath, looking afraid for the first time. "Before I started hanging at the cemetery, that awful feeling and the scent led me to one of the bodies of those four guys. At least I'm pretty sure it was one of them."

Nick laid a palm flat on the table. "What? Explain."

"I'm the one who anonymously called the sheriff's office about that victim, but I don't know how they found the others. I did my duty but I didn't want to be in the spotlight, so I made the call and stayed out of the picture."

"But you didn't, not completely. You were noticed hanging around."

"I knew that was a risk, but I couldn't leave town. Not when I had such an unsettled feeling in my gut, like I'd crossed paths with something truly evil that most wouldn't have the capacity to understand or figure out. Shit, I'm not sure I do, either, but I might have a better chance than the average guy."

"So you decided to play amateur detective." Nick allowed a hint of doubt to seep into his tone. "How convenient."

Jaxon knew Nick was playing the kid, that from what he'd said so far he didn't really believe the Sorcerer was responsible for any of the deaths, but was testing his worth. His determination. He'd been on the receiving end of Nick's scrutiny in the beginning often enough to know.

"I didn't kill those men," Black asserted, his expression fierce. "I've never hurt anyone, and I'm not stupid enough to stay in the area if I did."

Nick let him hang for a moment, then said, "I know. Tell me why you raised Henry Ward."

"If you *saw* what I did, don't you know why? You're the Seer."

"Humor me."

"Fine. It wasn't rocket science to connect the local buzz of an old man found bludgeoned to death with the body of a man found in the woods nearby. Like the cops, I thought there was a good chance Ward might've seen something, and I have a tool in my kit they don't."

"You can raise the dead and talk with them."

"Yep."

Quickly, he filled in Nick on what Ward had told him. The logo on the one man's shirt proved to be a good lead, and their boss nodded in approval.

"That sounds like the logo used by NewLife Technology," he said, and Jaxon stiffened in surprise.

"That's Kira's former employer." Damn, she hadn't been far from his mind all evening, and simply mentioning her name brought back all his physical discomfort with a vengeance.

Nick looked to Jax. "Who she alleges is possibly conducting some sort of DNA experimentation on human tissue, morphing it into a different strand altogether. Something animal."

"And the photos and autopsy reports show slivers of flesh removed from the men while they were still alive." Jaxon heaved a breath. "This is emerging into a terrible picture."

Nick agreed. "The question is, if NewLife is behind this, what the hell are they trying to accomplish? And at the cost of human lives, no less."

The Sorcerer spoke up. "This is fascinating, but am I free to go?"

Their boss pinned the kid with his blue gaze, and then gestured for Ryon to unbind him. "You can leave anytime you want. As a rule, I don't interfere with free will, especially if the individual intends no harm."

"Why do I hear a 'but' in there?" Black asked quietly, rubbing his wrists.

"Because your destiny is here," Nick said in a low voice, expression grave. "You may go, but if you do, know that your life will follow a path it was never meant to take, and you'll never find what you're searching for. I can't tell you more than that. The decision must be yours."

It was more warning than Jaxon had ever heard Nick give anyone.

"Trust him, Black," he advised the Sorcerer.

The kid studied each of them, those emerald eyes

shining with something like hope that didn't come easily. "Call me Kalen. It's been years since I've had a pillow and a mattress. That'll make sleeping on the decision a lot easier."

"You do that. Sleep on it; take all the time you need. Tomorrow, or I should say later today, Jax and a couple of the other team members will show you around, explain what we do and how things work. We'll get you checked out in the clinic, too. Get some food in you."

"Thanks. I appreciate this." Kalen didn't say the words lightly. He was a man who had nothing and no one.

Until today, even if he didn't realize it yet.

"Prove yourself a good soldier and that will be thanks enough." Grinning, Nick reached out and flicked the pendant on Kalen's chest. Gestured to the earrings both Kalen and Jax wore. "Might have to lose some of the bling, though. That goes for everyone."

The kid didn't look bothered. "I'm willing to negotiate. Some."

Jax wasn't really concerned, either. Nick had lost the argument over the decorative hardware before—or rather, gracefully conceded that they didn't interfere with the job—though the boss didn't like them.

Aric laughed and handed Kalen his backpack. "Come on, I'll show you to a room."

The red wolf led their newest recruit out, the others trailing them, talking and attempting to put the younger man more at ease. Jaxon hung back, concerned to see the smile melt from his boss's face as the others left.

"Is the kid going to be okay?" he asked.

"Definitely not if he leaves, but even if he stays . . . I don't know. His storm is still a good ways off, but it's coming."

"And when it arrives?" He was almost afraid to learn the answer, with good reason.

"Kalen will either find it in his soul to do the right thing, make the hard choice. Or he'll destroy us all."

Jaxon raked a hand through his short hair. "Who's his greatest enemy, Nicky?"

"Himself," his boss said grimly.

Ten

"**W**ho's that?"

Kira nudged Mac and both women watched with great interest as a young man entered the dining room, pausing uncertainly to study his surroundings.

"He must be the new prospective team member Nick was telling us about," Mac whispered. "Kalen Black, Sorcerer."

Dr. Mallory was chomping at the bit for them all to get started on their study of the four dead men. This morning after breakfast, Nick had filled them in on everything the sheriff and Alpha Pack had discovered. Including the short-lived battle in the cemetery with this guy. Not only was he a Sorcerer, but a Necromancer and a black panther.

"He sure *looks* like a Sorcerer."

"I'll say."

Kira couldn't help but notice that Mac's voice had grown a little husky, and how her pupils dilated as she studied the man. She couldn't blame her friend. The guy was seriously hot, messy black hair falling around a face that belonged on a model and a tall, lean, sexy body

dressed in black jeans and a T-shirt. The only adorn-
ments were the silver pendant around his neck and the
studs in his ears.

Glittering kohl-lined green eyes surveyed the area
warily, and then he strode inside, choosing a place at the
end of a nearby table. He sat by himself, back to the wall,
where he had a view of the whole room and who might
enter it. Kira wondered if he'd positioned himself this
way on purpose and thought it likely, given his body language.

His gaze found them and he nodded in acknowledg-
ment before turning his attention to the steaming dishes
the kitchen staff had placed on the tables for lunch. Politely, he took a plate and eating utensils from the stack.
Then he served himself a hearty portion of shepherd's
pie and took two rolls. Gripping his fork, he stared at the
meal like he'd never seen food in his life and then slowly
began to eat. One bite, then another. Faster and faster
until he'd wolfed down the entire serving and consumed
both rolls in less than five minutes.

He filled the plate again and started over.

Kira and Mac exchanged glances and she knew they
were thinking the same thing—Kalen was literally starving. They made small talk and tried not to stare as he
dished a third helping, but it was almost impossible. Finally Mac couldn't stand it anymore and rose, walking
over to greet him.

"Hello," she said, her tone friendly, offering her hand.
"I'm Dr. Mackenzie Grant. I work at the Institute of
Parapsychology, which is housed here on the com-
pound."

He stared at the hand, swallowed a mouthful of food,
and then shook with her. "Kalen Black, Sorcerer at large.
I work everywhere, and nowhere," he said with a wry
grin.

Her eyes lit with good humor. "I heard a little about that. Are you going to join Alpha Pack?"

Kalen didn't take those striking green eyes off Mac as she brushed her dark curls over one shoulder in an unconscious feminine gesture. "I haven't decided. The guys are going to show me around later. We're getting a late start today since we didn't go to bed until almost three this morning."

So that explained why Jaxon and the guys hadn't shown at breakfast, or anywhere today for that matter. Nick had been the only one present.

"Well, I for one hope you choose to stay. You won't find a better team to work with than our guys, and there's never a dull moment around here," she said with enthusiasm.

"I can see that," he drawled, sitting back lazily in his seat to stare at her.

Mac flushed, but brushed past the blatant male appreciation in his gaze. "I think you'll fit right in. In the meantime, come down to the clinic when you get a chance. You'll need a physical and I'd love to give you one." Instantly, she realized how that sounded and sputtered a bit, especially when he laughed. His genuine, broad smile made him exponentially sexier. "I mean, someone will check you out. Make sure you're healthy."

"Thank you, Mackenzie. I'll do that."

"My friends call me Mac," she said, then waved a hand in Kira's direction. "That's Kira Locke. She's new, too."

"Hi," Kira said, waving.

"Hello."

Mac went on, capturing his attention again. "Anyway, as a doctor I wanted to say that you might want to slow down on the food, especially if the team intends to spar with you later. You'll end up getting sick."

His humor faded and he laid his fork on the table, lowering his eyes in obvious embarrassment. When he looked up again, he nodded. "Good advice. Thanks." Wiping his mouth on a napkin, he stood. "I'll see you ladies later, right?"

They chimed an agreement and watched the Sorcerer's delectable backside disappear through the door.

"I'm such an idiot," Mac groaned, slapping her forehead. "Why'd I have to go and say something so stupid?"

Kira patted her friend's arm as she returned to their table. "Hey, you were only expressing a valid concern, and you were right. Eating like that when you're not used to so much food will make a person ill. He'll get over it."

"I hope so."

"Ready to get started in the lab?" The distraction worked, though it really was time for them to go.

"Ready as I'll ever be." She grimaced as Kira rose. The two of them left and started for the clinic. "They aren't a pretty sight, and I don't mean just because they're dead."

She tried not to think about it too much as they headed for the lab. But the condition of the bodies was hard to ignore when they walked into the large sterile room wearing their gowns, masks, and latex gloves.

Each of the men lay on a metal table, spread far enough apart so everyone could work around them without running into one another. Kira wasn't surprised to find Nick already there, waiting with Dr. Mallory. He was the boss and he'd want to know what they found. But she was a bit taken aback to find Jax present, leaning negligently against a wall, his steely blue eyes all but devouring her the second she entered. She couldn't look away.

Like Nick, he wasn't wearing protective clothing. Low-rise jeans hugged his hips and his biceps bulged even more from his arms being crossed over his yummy chest. His lips quirked, the dark humor in his expression doing nice things to his handsome face. Things that made lunch churn in her stomach and made her long to drag him off, throw him down, and have her wicked way with his sexy body for the rest of the afternoon.

He winked and she shook her head, breaking eye contact. Wasn't she supposed to be mad at him? She didn't feel upset at the moment—just really hot between her thighs. Damn it.

Dr. Mallory claimed everyone's attention. "Let's get things rolling, shall we? First of all, let's make sure we all know why we're here. The autopsies have already been performed, and the coroner was quite thorough. Did everyone have a chance to study the copies this morning?"

Answers were affirmative all around, including those from two techs Kira had met earlier but didn't yet know very well.

"Good. Our purpose here is not to redo what was already done, but rather to think outside the box. To study the victims, taking into account all that we know so far, and to try to create a portrait of not only what happened to these four men, but what might be going on in the big picture."

The woman was a pro, even if she was sort of aloof.

The doc glanced at a tablet on which she'd written her notes. "All four victims have ligature marks clearly visible at their wrists and ankles. They were underweight at the times of their deaths, but not mortally so. Each victim has scarring from very precise wounds made with a sharp instrument, such as a scalpel. From this scarring, at various stages of healing at the time of death, we can surmise that tissue was removed from them—while alive—at regular intervals. Their bodies were pumped full of an array of drugs as well."

Kira began to regret eating lunch before this. Scientists weren't always able to turn off their sensitive button.

"They were held captive," Nick said. "And they endured some form of experimentation."

"That would be my guess," she agreed. "The question is, for what purpose? I believe that the tissue samples Kira liberated from her former employer, not to mention the connection these four men have with one of their alleged killers who was wearing the company's logo, might provide some answers. Ones we're not going to like."

"The men who dumped the bodies aren't necessarily the murderers," Jax pointed out. "They might be the lackeys doing the disposal."

Nick nodded. "True."

"Whatever the case, my initial findings indicate that the changes in the DNA and gene strands undergone by both Kira's tissue samples and ones taken from these men are almost identical. The implications of these changes are quite alarming."

Jax shifted, his expression uneasy. "Nick and I spoke with Kira about the tissue data she found on Dr. Gene Bowman's computer. Are these the types of changes you're referring to?"

"I'm afraid so. In layman's terms, my professional opinion is that someone is taking humans—willing or not—and attempting to force their bodies to take on animal characteristics."

"They're creating shifters," Nick said, seething with anger.

"Or something like that, yes." She waved a hand at the bodies. "And *this*, in my opinion, is indication that they haven't yet perfected the process."

The idea was stunning. "And then they just dump

them like trash," Kira whispered. "That's sick." Jaxon
looked like he wanted to cross the room and hold her,
but didn't. Instead, he carried her thoughts a step farther.

"It's totally fucked up. If they can figure out how to
mass-produce shifters, bypassing natural methods like
mating or biting and clawing, which don't always work,
just think how that would affect the world as we know
it."

"And if they're imbuing them with any other special
talents, like your Psy abilities, or if the targeted humans
already possess those abilities . . ." Dr. Mallory let the
statement hang, the meaning ominous.

Nick stared at her. "The entire human race could be
in real danger within a matter of years. They'd be the low
rung on the hierarchy of intelligent beings. My God."

Jax pushed away from the wall. "We can't let that happen, but to stop them we have to know for sure if the
doctors at NewLife are the ones responsible, and how
high up the food chain this project goes—whether or not
Orson Chappell is aware of it, and if so, who's involved
along with him."

"Chappell must be heading this and I'll bet he has
partners outside the company," Nick said. "Something of
this magnitude needs big backing, bigger than he can
pull off by himself."

"First we have to find out where they're holding the
captives, assuming the participants are unwilling. Or become unwilling once they realize what torture they face."
Jax paused. "I'm thinking they must have more than one
facility. Kira's samples came from the NewLife building
in Vegas, but these four bodies were dumped a long way
from there."

"I'll get on finding out where their facilities are located," Nick said. "If there's one here, that might ex-

plain why these men were discarded nearby. But even if the Vegas building is the closest, it's only a day's drive by car or two hours by plane. Not a difficult trip if our lackeys were sent to dispose of the bodies in a forested area."

"That would make more sense," Kira speculated. "I doubt they'd dispose of the bodies in their own backyard."

Jax looked at her. "I'd say Las Vegas is the place to start. Plus, Henry Ward told Kalen the men were in a blue van. I think they either drove out here with the bodies, or brought them in a private plane and *then* rented the van, and returned to Vegas afterward."

Nick agreed. "All right. I'll check, and if NewLife has no building here, we'll assemble and head to Vegas." He paused thoughtfully. "Where are they getting the shifters for the experiments? I wonder. They have to use shifters to make the changes in the humans work. And why haven't any of *their* bodies been found?"

"We heal faster," Jax reminded him. "We can take a lot of abuse before we succumb."

Well, that wasn't a comforting thought. Kira felt sorry for the victims on both sides.

Nick sighed, and glanced at one of the bodies. "I hate to ask you this, but can you see about getting a reading?"

"Sure. Let's do it."

He sounded so casual, but Kira had seen firsthand how much this took out of him. And today, though sexy as always, he appeared tired, like he hadn't been sleeping well. He was scratching every now and then, too, really digging at his arms and stomach. She frowned, unable to spot a rash.

He moved to the oldest of the corpses, touching only the wrist without the benefit of latex gloves, which could hamper his ability. He concentrated for several minutes, but shook his head and moved on. "Nothing. He's been gone too long, with the elements working at him."

Kira hid her revulsion as he went on to the second victim. He had the same bad luck with that one and the third. It wasn't until the latest victim that the tide turned.

Closing his eyes, he took the abraded wrist and breathed slowly and deeply, settling himself. After a few moments, his head tilted back and his body tensed. As the minutes passed, the color drained from his face and he began to shake. That was frightening enough, but the agonized scream he suddenly let out nearly made her heart explode.

"Nick!" Frantic, she looked to the boss, who'd taken a step toward his friend.

But before he could intervene, Jax moaned, "Oh, God, no. Please don't . . ."

Then his knees buckled and he hit the floor, sprawled on his back.

"Oh, my God! Jax!" Everyone converged on him, but Kira reached him first. Dropping to his side she patted his cheeks, shook him. "Jax!"

He didn't respond, but his breathing was steady, she noted in relief. Mac pushed in next to her and took his pulse. Next, she opened an eyelid and shined her penlight, testing the reaction.

"Has this ever happened to him before?" Kira asked the group anxiously.

"No," Nick said, voice rough. "It's never easy on him, but he's never passed out."

Dr. Mallory's voice cut through the rising panic. "We need to get him into an exam room. Nick, get his shoulders and I'll take his feet."

Between the two of them they managed to pick him up and maneuver his big body out, down the hall, and onto one of the clinic's exam tables. Kira tried to ease into the room, but Dr. Mallory wasn't having it.

"Everyone out so we can see to our patient. Either Mac or I will come as soon as we have news."

From nowhere, a powerful emotion hit Kira hard. *How dare that woman keep him from me?* The fierce rage swelled in her chest, strangling her lungs. A low sound emerged from her throat that very much emulated the noise Jax had made at the idea of others touching her. That reaction from him had pissed her off, and now she was doing the same thing.

Dr. Mallory froze, her efficient mask slipping long enough to gape at Kira in astonishment. Then she turned back to Kira's lover. "Nick, get her out of here."

"Come on," he said, taking her arm. "Let's get out of Melina's way. Jax will be fine."

As he led her to the waiting area, the red-hot anger began to subside, only to be replaced by a terrible anxiety. Jax was in there, only God knows what was happening to him. She couldn't touch him. Speak to him. Make certain he was okay. She needed to do those things or she'd go crazy.

"Nick, what's wrong with me?"

He sat her in a chair, took a seat next to her, and remained silent for a long moment. When he met her eyes, the expression in his dark blue ones made her heart lurch. "You're a scientist, Kira. Look at his reactions and yours with that analytical brain, and you tell me."

Unwillingly, she did. Protectiveness, bordering on violence, on both sides. The unexplainable animal attraction from the first instant he morphed into a man before her eyes. The constant desire to be near him.

"No," she said in denial. Her hands started to shake. "It can't be. That kind of thing only happens in the movies."

"Sweetheart, it's true. Jax is your Bondmate."

She stared at him, trepidation curling in her stomach. "What does that mean, exactly? Spell it out, please."

"Melina can give a better explanation than me."

"I'm asking you," she insisted.

After a long pause, he continued with some reluctance. "You're his perfect match. The one who completes him, both the man and the wolf. Whether a made shifter like Jax, or a born shifter like me, we all have a Bondmate out there somewhere."

"Is this bonding thing triggered by feelings a shifter is developing for the other person?" she asked hopefully. The analytical part of her brain could accept that—but not the answer she actually got.

"No. Whether feelings develop before or after the shifter recognizes his or her Bondmate is irrelevant. The two are fated to be together, period."

"I won't accept that! No way." Her vehemence surprised them both.

"Jax is a good man. There's obviously chemistry between you two. What's so bad about being his mate?"

Bombarded by conflicting emotions, she struggled to explain. "Nothing, if he loved me! Yes, we've had fireworks, but that doesn't mean anything. We still don't know each other very well, and he sees other women—"

"He won't anymore. Not now."

"What? How come?" She refused to acknowledge the bubble of happiness that news caused.

"Once wolf shifters find our mates, we're physically incapable of being with anyone else in the carnal sense. No worries there." He said that as though she should be thrilled.

And she was, except for one tiny detail. "You don't understand. I want my man to be with me because I'm *me*, not because his glands are dictating to his libido! I want him to fall in love with me and vice versa, not be stuck together because science says so."

"Kira, what makes you think you two won't fall head over heels? Personally, I believe you're well on the way already, and you just need to give yourselves a chance."

"But how will I know?"

"The same way anyone does. In here," he said, pointing at her heart.

She considered this. "Have you ever been in love?"

Pain flashed in his eyes, there and gone. He smiled, but it seemed a little sad. "Hey, we're not talking about me, remember? Just give it time. Trust me."

She didn't answer, but the whole idea still bothered her a great deal. It was the thought that basic feral nature could force two people together, and before either of them were ready. That did not sit well at all.

Forty minutes later, Mac and Dr. Mallory appeared. Kira didn't like the almost tangible aura of gloom surrounding them, the anxiety.

"What's wrong? Isn't he okay?"

Mac glanced at her colleague, who nodded, indicating she could go ahead. "The reading really knocked him for a loop, but as far as recovering from that goes, he should be fine."

"That's good, but what do you mean 'as far as that goes'? There's more?"

"Unfortunately, yes. He's experiencing some symptoms that are causing him discomfort."

"I noticed him scratching," Kira said with a frown.

"He's itching and it's getting worse, starting to burn. He also has a sore throat and a fever, which he didn't have yesterday. He's getting sicker and if the proper steps aren't taken, his life will be in danger."

Kira blinked, chest squeezing. "What do you mean? What kinds of steps?"

"One important one, really." Mac paused. "Did Nick tell you?"

"I told her," the boss confirmed.

"Wait a second. Is this about me being his mate? You're telling me that not only do we have this attraction we can't help, but his cure depends on me?"

"That's what we're saying," Mac told her gently. "His *life* depends on you."

She gasped. "He's going to *die* if I don't mate with him? Oh, my God!" She rounded on Nick. "You said I could give it time! And now I find out I have no choice? I'm supposed to just hand my entire life over to a man who's half canine, and not really a man at all?"

As soon as the words left her mouth, she knew she'd crossed the line. Especially when a hoarse voice spoke from behind her.

"I'd never ask you to make such a horrible sacrifice. Don't worry. You won't be saddled with a filthy dog like me."

With that, Jax limped past the group. His cheeks were still pale and he was holding his stomach as he walked slowly across the waiting room and out the door.

Kira's face flamed, her heart aching with shame. And something else, a yearning for the man who'd left, looking more dejected than she'd ever seen anyone. She wanted to call him back, but the words had lodged in her throat like a melon.

She'd put her own feelings before the well-being of a good man. He could die, and she'd only thought of herself.

The scathing look she received from Dr. Mallory

spoke volumes. "Why don't you take the rest of the afternoon off? Go see Jax and make things right."

"I will," she said softly.

Ducking her head, she rushed from the room. She had to apologize.

And somehow make him understand these feelings she didn't even comprehend herself.

Jaxon's stomach churned, and his head pounded. His throat, his whole body, felt like he was slowly being roasted in an oven, but those symptoms weren't the worst.

No, the worst was Kira's words still ringing in his brain. Cutting him off at the knees, bringing him lower than he'd ever been. Even after Afghanistan, with more than half his soldiers slaughtered. Or following the ambush on Alpha Pack, when Beryl had betrayed him.

I'm supposed to just hand my entire life over to a man who's half canine, and not really a man at all?

Not a man at all.

What else had he expected? But God, it hurt. So badly he wanted to curl up in the fetal position and die. A warrior and a shifter with special abilities, cut down by a woman's tongue as surely as if he'd been run through with a sword or shot between the eyes. The latter would be kinder than this.

Breathing through the pain—both kinds—he let himself into his apartment and headed for his room. Without bothering to remove his boots, he flopped onto his bed and lay on his side, covering his eyes. That's when he realized the burning in his throat wasn't all from the fever. Sweet Jesus, he hadn't cried in years and he wasn't about to give in now.

He'd dealt with a lot of shit and he'd deal with being rejected by his mate.

He would.

But that didn't stop the hot moisture from seeping between his lashes. Angrily, he rubbed his eyes, willing the ache to ease. Was this the reaction of the dirty dog, or the man? How sad that he didn't know.

Oh yeah, you're not a man, remember?

He heard a rapping at the door to his place. He lay there willing it to stop, but his visitor wasn't going away.

"Son of a bitch."

Hauling himself up, he started for the door. Halfway there, Kira's familiar scent wafted to him, freezing him in his tracks. If she'd come to apologize, he wasn't ready to listen to excuses.

Growling in frustration, he limped across the distance and yanked the door open, schooling his expression to appear calm. "What do you want?"

His curt greeting took her aback and she fidgeted nervously. "Can I come in? I really don't want to do this where someone might hear."

"Funny, you didn't have a problem with that in the clinic."

"Jax, please?" Her small face was pinched, blue eyes shadowed with worry.

He sighed. "I guess. Come in."

Leaving her to follow, he shuffled into the living room and sat on one end of the sofa. She took the other end, perching close to him but not touching. Since this was her dime, he let her struggle.

"Look, you don't know how sorry I am for what you heard," she began with difficulty. "But I didn't mean it the way it sounded."

He snorted an ugly laugh. "That I'm not a man? Really? I'd love to know how else to take that except you believe I'm an animal, or subhuman."

"No!" Leaning toward him, she clutched his knee. "That's not what I meant! I just find it sort of scary to learn that I don't have a say when it comes to you being my mate. That I have to be bound to someone for life because of biology, and not love."

He studied her, decided she was being honest. "I get that. But how do you know this attraction between us is not becoming love already?"

"How do I know it is, for absolute sure?" she countered. "I've never been serious about anyone before, not serious enough to marry or even live together. And then I suddenly learn that there's a whole world I never knew existed, and that the creatures of my childhood fables aren't so fictional after all. There was no time to adjust, to catch my breath. And then, bam! Sudden, life-altering changes and a man—and yes, you *are* a man, and I'm a jerk—a man is claiming me for his own. And, oh yeah, he and his friends are like critters out of a J. R. R. Tolkien novel, and I'm walking around half-expecting to run into Gollum looking for his precious!"

Her eyes were wide, cheeks flushed from the passion of her speech, blond hair framing her face. Damned if she wasn't the cutest thing he'd ever seen.

And fuck it all, he was going to forgive her.

Reaching out, he brushed back a pale strand. "Yeah," he said softly. "I guess that would pretty much mess with your day."

Arousal flared on her face, pupils dilating. Breath hitching, she scooted closer, capturing his hand. "Pretty much. Forgive me?"

"Sweet baby, I forgave you at 'I'm a jerk.'"

Her lips tilted into a smile. "Don't get used to it."

"I'd like to get used to you, period."

"How flattering."

"I'm working on my delivery. What can I say?"

"Say you'll kiss me," she whispered.

He smiled, all his pain forgotten with her one simple request. "Baby, I'll do much more than that."

Pulling his woman close, he crushed his mouth to hers.

Eleven

Kira reveled in his mouth on hers, his tongue slipping inside to taste. Being held in his strong arms was heaven and she loved his size, how she felt surrounded. Safe.

His hardness poked against her stomach, causing her to squirm. He moaned and a little spurt of satisfaction went through her that she was the cause of his arousal. His need.

Big hands skimmed her sides, worked underneath her shirt. Found the cups of her bra and palmed them as he thrust upward, grinding his erection, seeking relief. The action caused an answering heat between her legs that spread low in her womb. She needed to be filled by him. Owned. Ravaged.

"Too many clothes," she hissed, tugging at his shirt.

Briefly, his eyes seemed to glow. "We can remedy that."

She yanked the garment over his head and then scooted back some, attacking his belt. With a low chuckle, he raised his hips to help her along and she freed his thick cock, lifted out his heavy balls. She'd never thought of a man's package as particularly beautiful, but Jax was everything a man should be. And much more.

Suddenly she couldn't think of anything she wanted more than to taste the precum seeping from the slit of his cock. To wrap her lips around the head and drive him crazy with lust. In the past, giving a guy a blow job was something she could take or leave—mostly leave since the act was usually all about *his* pleasure, not hers—but this time was different. With Jax, the pleasure would go both ways.

Sliding to the floor, she pushed his knees apart and crouched between his denim-clad thighs, smoothing her palms on top of them. She loved the feel of his muscles bunching under her fingertips and wanted to see more.

"Off with the jeans," she ordered, smirking at his surprise. A slow grin curved his sexy mouth as he complied, sliding the offending material down his hips.

"Whatever the lady wants."

"Smart man."

As she eased the jeans and boxer briefs down his legs and pulled them off his feet, she glanced up to see a shadow darken his expression. His gaze flicked to his injured leg and away, so quickly she might've missed it if she hadn't been paying attention.

Gently, she kissed the scarred flesh that twisted around his right thigh. "Your scars don't make you any less handsome to me. They don't matter."

"You think I'm concerned about my looks? No, I deserve exactly what I got and more for trusting the wrong person and leading my team into a trap."

His voice was filled with such self-loathing her heart went out to him. "I don't believe that and neither should you. Someone took advantage of your trust and broke it, and that person is responsible for what happened. Not you," she stressed.

"But I—"

"Hush." Bending over his lap, she grasped the base of his cock and gave the slit a lick, catching the drops. Salty-sweet flavor burst on her tongue and he sucked in a breath. Oh, tasting him was going to become addictive, real fast.

"Kira," he moaned. His head fell back to rest against the sofa and he spread his legs wider, raising his hips the slightest bit, a silent encouragement to continue with the welcome attention.

She didn't need much convincing. As she took the spongy head between her lips and began to suckle, it was readily apparent that giving in to him was to be its own reward. His tanned skin was hot, his long, thick cock flushed dark, balls heavy with need. He was sprawled before her like a feast, one hand buried in her hair, the other clutching the arm of the sofa as though he might blast off any second and had to somehow anchor himself.

She watched his face as she took him deeper, sucked his rod and laved the silky underside, pumping the base. His eyes were closed in ecstasy, chest rising and falling more rapidly, making the swirling tattoos on his shoulder move and seem almost alive.

"God, I can't take much more," he told her roughly.

His control was admirable, but he was no match for her bobbing up and down. Taking him to the back of her throat, and out again. She slid along his length until he pushed her back carefully with a low chuckle.

"Damn, woman, I'm about to lose it. My turn," he insisted, his dark tone making her shiver in anticipation. He slid to the floor next to her and patted the sofa cushion. "Brace yourself, honey."

Moving forward, she laid her front half down on the comfortable seat, hyperaware of him positioning himself behind her. Even though he was exposed and vulnerable moments ago, she wasn't certain she liked feeling that way herself. She was too skinny, shaped too much like a boy without womanly curves and the lush bosom that appealed to so many men. She didn't know what a hottie like Jax saw in her body, but he seemed to appreciate it just fine.

Can't fake a gigantic hard-on.

"Spread for me, baby."

She inched her knees apart more, and the position had her offered with her ass in the air, ready and willing to be his.

"That's it. Jesus, you're so pretty." Two fingers dipped into her slit, already hot and wet. Rubbed and smeared her juices, played with her clit. "You like that, baby?"

"Y-yes. Please . . ."

"More?"

"Please, don't stop!"

"Don't worry. I won't leave you hanging."

Suddenly his lips were bestowing soft kisses to the small of her back. It was slightly ticklish and she stifled a giggle, and then he moved on. He caressed her rear and then nuzzled her sex, taking a tentative swipe with his tongue. Arching her back, she opened for him as much as possible, telling him without words to take what he wanted. Give them what they both needed.

As he laved her folds, tongue dipping inside, she started to feel too big for her own skin. Like she was swelling, a balloon becoming more and more full, heat pushing at her from inside out. The feeling began in her sex and washed to her limbs, filtered into her blood, bringing it to a gradual boil. Searing her.

"Oh . . . Oh, Jax."

"You taste so sweet," he whispered. "I'm going to fuck you so hard."

The image his words inspired, his mouth working her

into a fever, shattered whatever resistance was left. Her bones melted and she submitted completely, his to do with whatever he wished. She was his. Nothing else mattered.

She needed him as close as possible. Inside her. *Please! Fuck me!*

Had she shouted out loud? She wasn't certain. Only knew that he was holding her hips now, bringing the head of his cock to her slit. Nudging her entrance. Her skin was scorching and she needed him.

"Gonna take what's mine," he growled.

Moaning, nearly out of her mind, she pushed backward, and that was all the assent he required. His cock slid inside, stretching and filling her. So good, so right. He was huge but it didn't hurt, simply made her feel complete as he slid all the way home. His balls nestled against her, springy hair from his groin and thighs sensitizing her to every nuance of him. Of them together, connected as they should be.

Then he began to thrust, spearing deep into her core. Tantalizingly slow at first, letting her feel every inch of him. Then picking up speed, putting some power behind the pumping, his fingers digging into her flesh.

Not just fingers, but claws. Stinging just a bit, but only adding to the wicked pleasure.

Somewhere in the back of her mind, she was surprised she didn't object to his feral nature coming out during sex, and wasn't afraid. Instead, his barely leashed wolf only turned her on even more, and she was shocked to realize she embraced them both as they fucked her into oblivion—Jax and his beast.

Beyond that, she couldn't think. Her body was caught in a raging inferno only he could sate. Flesh slapped against flesh as he impaled her repeatedly, driving even harder when she made helpless whimpers. Almost there.

"B-bite me," she begged. The words slipped out of their own volition, a reflection of the need she couldn't acknowledge before. Almost as though she had no choice.

"God, baby. You don't know how much I want that."

Her orgasm exploded and she cried out, convulsing around his cock. He stiffened and followed her over the brink with a shout, pumping her full of cum. Emptying into her with such force, he was plastered to her back for several moments after.

Panting, she floated back to earth, the post-orgasmic haze leaving her boneless. And very unsure where they now stood.

"Why didn't you bite me?" she asked quietly.

Kissing her shoulder, he pulled out and then turned her around, gathering her into his lap. "Because that would have mated us, and you weren't ready."

"How do you know? It felt like I was ready. It was all I needed at the time, so badly I couldn't think straight."

His eyes were a little sad when he replied. "Exactly. You feel so strongly about not giving in just because it's nature, yet you were helpless to the pull of mating while we fucked. Think about it, baby. If I'd done what you asked in the heat of the moment, you would've hated me for taking advantage."

"No, I wouldn't have."

"You would," he insisted. "Has your opinion changed about mating before love, then?"

She stared at him with a sinking feeling in her gut. "No."

"Then you would've hated the sight of me, and I might never have earned another chance to win your trust."

Oh, God. He's right. Face heating, she looked away and wished she could disappear.

"And there's something else you should know." He paused, obviously reluctant to continue as he took her chin, made her look at him. "If I bite you—hell, if any shifter does—there's a very good chance you could become one of us. You need to decide if you can live with that before we mate. Because if we do, I *have* to bite you."

Her mouth fell open. Of course there was a chance. Why hadn't she thought of that possibility? She might become like him. A wolf.

"Jax, I—I—" Overwhelmed, she fumbled for a response that wouldn't hurt him more than she had already. "I need time to think."

"Hey, it's okay. I understand, even if my wolf is howling like a banshee and threatening to claw his way right out of my skin, leaving me nothing but an empty husk."

His attempt to joke made her feel worse. "I'm so sorry. I know you're in pain and it's all because of me."

"No, angel," he said softly. "It's nobody's fault. Let's just take this as it comes and we'll be fine."

"You won't be fine." She touched his face. "You're burning up, and it's not just from having hot sex. I'm scared to death about what Dr. Mallory told me could happen to you. *Is* happening."

He shook his head in dismissal. "Melina is overly cautious. That's her job. Us shifters are tough and it'll take more than a few raging hormones to bring me down. We've got plenty of time to decide what we want, and I don't want you worrying about this anymore."

"I can't promise that."

"Do your best, because I'm okay." He kissed her nose.

"Promise you'll tell me if it gets too bad?"

"Sure."

He didn't exactly say the words and she frowned,

knowing he'd keep his misery to himself as long as possible. That he'd put her feelings before his own needs, no matter how much it hurt him, caused something warm and wonderful to expand in her chest.

"I'm glad you forgave me for what I said in the clinic," she told him.

He winked. "Me, too. Got me laid, didn't it?"

She dug her fingers into his ribs. "Smart-ass."

Falling backward, he laughed, pulling her with him, and the tickle fight was on. She managed to get a few more digs in his ribs before he latched on to an ankle and tortured the sensitive bottom of one foot.

"Uncle!" she squealed. "You win!"

"I'm the boss. Say it!"

"Ahh! You're the boss," she gasped, trying in vain to wrench away her foot.

Mercifully, he released the appendage and helped her up. "The boss demands you shower with him."

"Humph. I suppose you'll want me to wash your back, too."

"Of course. But I'll do yours, too." His voice promised more extracurricular fun than a simple shower.

The hunky wolf delivered, too, soaping certain crevices perhaps a tad more than necessary, making her laugh and shudder in delight by turns. She wasn't laughing, however, when he guided her to brace herself on the tiles, his hardness rubbing the crack of her butt, declaring that they weren't finished playing.

"Gotta have you again," he murmured. "What you do to me ..."

He made love to her there with the water cascading over them, nice and easy, with such gentle heat her eyes burned with unshed tears. Never had there been a connection like this with any other man. Never anything that felt so right. As though everything she'd been searching for had coalesced here, with this man, in this place filled with strange inhabitants.

He took them to the peak and they exploded together, him buried deep inside her, whispering endearments in her ear. She was so at peace, yet when he withdrew again without giving in to the need to claim her as his own, guilt pricked at her conscience.

Despite his insistence that he was fine, she couldn't help but imagine what terrible price his patience might demand.

And whether she'd ever be able to reconcile the man as one with the beast without the fire of his touch blowing apart all reason.

"Jax?"

"Hmm?"

Kira trailed a finger over the broad expanse of his chest, hoping he didn't close off when she pried. But she had to know more about the man at her side. "Tell me about Afghanistan. When you were changed."

He went so still for a few moments, she wasn't even sure he was breathing. When he finally began to speak, his voice was so low, bleeding with remembered pain, that she held him tighter.

"What's to tell? We ventured into the mountains on a routine patrol, and encountered creatures out of our worst nightmares. Then some of us awoke to realize the lucky ones were dead, and the rest had to live with the fact that we'd become freaks at best, enemies of the human race at worst."

She hugged him tight. "Obviously neither was true. You guys were put in the unique position of protecting the world from creatures most people don't even know exist. Have you ever stopped to think about all the lives that would've been affected if you *hadn't* been changed? How many would be lost by now?"

After a moment, he admitted, "It's crossed my mind. But it's hard to get that through my head when the personal cost has been so damned high. Call me selfish, but that's how it is."

"That's not selfish, just human." She cursed herself for her blunder. "You know what I mean."

He kissed the top of her head. "Yeah, I do."

"You're not a freak."

"And yet you don't know if you can embrace both sides of me."

Rising up, she propped herself on his chest and looked him right in the eye. "Get it through your head, that's not true the way you mean it. I'll admit I was a little unnerved by the shifting at first. But the only problem I have is with the biology of the mating thing not giving us a choice. It's like we're not in charge of our destinies."

"Everyone has a choice." He arched a dark brow. "You're here, for instance, and nobody forced you to get down and dirty with me. Twice. Three times if you want to get technical."

"You've got me there." She couldn't help but smile at his self-satisfied expression. "You're a hard man to resist."

"Just hard, period." He leered at her.

"You have a *point*," she teased, wiggling against the hardness in question.

The chirp of his iPhone interrupted them. With a put-upon sigh, he grabbed it off the nightstand and peered at the display. "Text message from Nick. We're meeting in one hour, and he wants you there."

"Me?" She frowned. "Must have to do with my old employer."

"My guess is he's ready to plan the recon on the New-Life building. We can obtain the floor plans, but you might have other information we can use."

"I don't know. I've told you everything."

"We'll see. In the meantime we need another shower."

"Without the messing around, or we'll be late."

His grin made her pulse leap. "Punctuality is over-rated."

They were almost ten minutes late. Holding her hand, Jax pulled her into the room where the rest of the team was already assembled and talking among themselves, waiting for Nick to start. All eyes swung their way and a couple of the guys snickered. Nick gave them a knowing stare, appearing curious. And if she wasn't mistaken . . . was that a wave of sympathy, maybe laced with a touch of sadness, she felt from the boss as he studied them? What was that about?

Embarrassment colored Kira's cheeks at the others guys' razzing, but she kept her head high as she and Jax found seats. She was grateful when Nick began the meeting without any remarks about their tardiness. He hadn't struck her as that kind of man, but the lack of censure was still a relief.

"First off, I invited Kalen to join us so he can get a feel for how we work," Nick said. "Does anyone have an objection?"

"Not as long as he keeps his wand pointed in the other direction," Aric cracked. The others laughed, except for Nick and Jax.

Kalen accepted the challenge. "I wouldn't point my wand at you if you were the last ugly, one-eyed, three-legged shifter on earth." One corner of his mouth quirked up. "Not that I use one, 'cause those are so last century. Just sayin'."

"You're all right, man." Aric slapped him on the back,

and a couple of the others did the same, as though he'd passed some sort of male test.

Kira slid a glance to the young Sorcerer, who was unusual to say the least, even among present company. She'd never seen someone who seemed so alone in a roomful of people, though he appeared okay with the group's good-natured ribbing. If he planned to stick around, he'd have to get used to that.

"Since there are no protests, let's move on," Nick said, gaining their attention once more. "I checked on the NewLife facilities, and the closest one is in fact the Las Vegas location. As most of you are aware, our newest staff member, Kira, used to work at that building and fled from there with some tissue samples and a suspicion that her bosses are involved in altering human DNA and gene strands. Based on study of the four bodies provided courtesy of the sheriff's department and coroner, Melina and her lab assistants have concluded that these same changes were being forced on these men at the time of their deaths."

"And your team heard the corpse, Henry Ward, tell me about one of the bastards who killed him wearing a polo with the NewLife logo on it," Kalen put in.

"This guy is powerful shit," Jax whispered in her ear, referring to the Sorcerer.

She glanced at her lover. "No kidding."

Nick acknowledged Kalen's statement with a nod. "And that's why we're sending a team into the Vegas building in forty-eight hours. You're going to do a search, see what you can find. Which brings us to why I asked Kira to come." He turned to her. "Tell us what you can about the level of security there."

Put on the spot, she fumbled for a few seconds. "Well, I'd say security is what you'd expect for a company of that size and reputation. It's not Fort Knox, but an outsider would have a difficult time breaching their perimeter."

Ryon smirked. "They didn't count on *us*."

Kira doubted most of the population would be a match for Alpha Pack.

Nick ignored the comment. "Give us the rundown of what they've got—how many guards and so forth."

"There's a security guard on each level of the building at all hours, and they work in three shifts—day, evening, and deep nights. There are cameras on every floor . . . except in the basement," she recalled, sitting up straight. Why had she never realized that before?

"I'm guessing the basement is where you found the tissue samples," Jax said.

"Yes, in the restricted lab area down there. And when I was escaping that night, it's also where I could have sworn I heard a male voice begging for help." She shivered at the memory. "It was brief, but terrible. I thought I was just frightened, imagining things."

"But you don't think so now?" Nick asked.

"No. With everything that's come to light, I believe it's highly possible I heard someone in need of assistance. Or at least got an impression of pain and desperation."

"An impression?"

She nodded. "I get feelings from people, pick up their emotions. It's gotten much stronger since I've been here. Actually, it wasn't until I got here that I really was sure of it. I'd say that sounds crazy, but among this group . . ."

Nick's tough veneer cracked some, his eyes warming. "You're an Empath. It's an occupational hazard."

Silence fell and she became aware of the others staring at her. She'd thought it possible, but to hear Nick announce it in a room full of guys with unrivaled special abilities made her more than a bit self-conscious. What good was one puny Empath in comparison?

"That may be, but it's hardly a useful talent," she demurred. "Anyway, I have a friend inside who I'm pretty sure will help us. His name is A. J. Stone and he's a security guard."

Nick welcomed the news with caution. "What makes you think he'll be willing to place himself at risk? He could lose his job over this, or worse, if anyone suspects him."

"I wasn't the only one who thought something weird was going on at NewLife. A.J. believed it, too, and we talked about it in private more than once. That night, though, I didn't tell him what I was doing. He'd called in sick, which was just as well. I didn't want to get him in trouble."

A pang of guilt went through her. A.J. was probably worried and thought something bad had happened to her. If it hadn't been for Jax, something terrible would have.

"Can you—all of us—trust him?" Nick asked.

She didn't even hesitate. "Absolutely. He has a good soul. It shines from him like a beacon."

Jax winked at her. "And you thought your talent wasn't useful."

"I'm not convinced it's anything but plain old intuition," she said, flushing. "But I believe in A.J. If you want, I can give him a call and explain what's up, and then let Nick talk to him so they can discuss the details of getting you all in and out."

"That sounds fine." Their boss let out a deep breath. "I just know that whatever we do, we have to take action fast. There's something a lot more important than lab samples waiting for us in that hellhole, and time is running out."

The guys were grim now, none of them participating in the usual joking around. To see them so serious, knowing Nick's visions were nothing to take lightly, formed a ball of ice in her stomach.

"Are we taking the jet?" Jax asked.

Nick shook his head. "Not enough room, and we'll need plenty of space on our way home. We'll take two Hueys and a doc to ride in each. Once we get to Vegas, we'll land at our usual hangar and take a van and the SUV. Any questions?"

Jax had one. "What about Kira and Kalen?"

"They'll ride along, but they won't participate. Maybe next time for Kalen."

The Sorcerer nodded his agreement.

"I think Kira should stay here," her lover protested with a scowl.

"We need her there, just in case. Anything else?" Subject closed. Nobody spoke. "Then we'll go wheels up in forty-eight. Get your rest; you're all going to need the energy."

As the meeting broke up, Kira playfully punched Jax in the arm. "Come on, don't get pissy. Nick wouldn't have let me come if it wasn't safe."

"He can't interfere in free will—you know that," he said in a low, unhappy voice. "If something bad was going to go down, he couldn't change the fact. Besides, I just don't want you anywhere near that building."

"I'll be fine. I promise to stay out of the way, like he ordered."

"You'd better or I'll put you over my knee." He made the threat sound like fun, and followed it with a half smile.

"Haven't I told you not to threaten me with a good time if you don't intend to follow through?"

"Hey, it's not a threat—it's a sure thing."

"We'll see about that, big guy."

"Oh, yes. We will."

His grin sent a sizzle to her nipples, fingers, and toes. And everywhere in between.

She couldn't wait.

Twelve

J axon went in search of his wayward woman, though he had little doubt where to find her.

When they weren't testing the durability of his mattress and bed frame, she could be found in Block R working with Chup-Chup, as she'd named the mischievous little gremlin critter for the sound it made, socializing it and teaching it all kinds of stuff. First and foremost, to go outside to do his business and not to bite the hand that fed him. He had to admit, she'd already begun to make good progress.

With the aid of a sturdy pair of gloves to protect her from nips and scratches.

"You're in an awful big hurry. Guess I don't have to ask why."

He looked up to see Nick in his path, stopped and gave his boss a sheepish grin. "Guess not."

"How're things going with you two?"

"Fine. As long as we avoid the subject of mating," he said with a grimace. "I was always the one who was downright against creating a forever kind of bond with any woman—even Beryl—and now that I've found my

Bondmate she won't even discuss it with me. She shies from the subject when I bring it up. Ironic, huh?"

"Give her time. She'll come around."

"Nicky, in spite of what I told Kira, I don't *have* much time," he confessed, then wished he'd kept his mouth shut.

"You hurting bad?"

He nearly lied. It was on the tip of his tongue to say he was A-okay, no problems. But holding the man's gaze, he couldn't do it. Besides, he knew he looked terrible and couldn't fool his boss. "Yeah. Pretty fucking bad. You don't know how much this sucks."

"I have some idea." Nick sighed. "Listen, you're not going to want to hear this, but—"

"Then don't say it. I'm not staying here tonight, especially when Kira's going to be with you guys. In danger."

"You're in no shape to travel, much less fight if the need arises. I want you to stay here."

"Is that an order?"

"Would you follow it?"

"Not if Kira's going. Surely you can understand where I'm coming from."

"You know I do." The older man pushed a hand through his dark hair. "And you know damned well I'm forbidden to keep mates apart. Even if they haven't made the union official."

Actually, he hadn't known because it wasn't as if there were tons of mated pairs around, but the rule made sense. And as a born shifter, Nick would know more than the rest of them in some areas. "I'll pull my weight, watch my back and theirs. No worries."

"Why don't I feel better?" he grumbled. "Be at the hangar in three hours."

"With bells on."

Nick left him to his own devices and Jax continued in

the direction he'd been headed. Now he had an excuse to find Kira, not that he needed one. It was enough to long to see her sweet face, hear her laugh at something that stupid gremlin did, or chatter away with Sariel, Mac, or any number of the friends she seemed to have so easily made here. The sight of her settling in, happy, made his heart clench with joy and also fear that she'd never belong to him.

God, he was such a sap.

Block R was quiet as he entered the corridor. Raven was mercifully asleep, curled up with his bushy black tail over his nose, the only time the poor bastard ever knew any peace. Belial, on the other hand, had chosen to be in human form today, and was dressed in simple jeans and a T-shirt, pacing his cell like the caged beast he was. Jax felt bad for the basilisk, but they couldn't yet trust a lethal snake shifter loose in the compound.

Even Kira's honest charm was no match for the sneaky wiles of that one.

When he reached Chup-Chup's cell, it was empty, the door standing open. Alarmed, he glanced in each cell again and then headed out of Block R. Where could they be? If that little shit had bitten her again, he'd tear its head off and eat it for a midnight snack.

Growing more concerned with every step, he diverted his course to the clinic. Mac was leaning over the front desk talking to the receptionist when he stomped in.

"Where's Kira and that little demon? I'm going to rip his teeth out if—"

"Hold on, Cujo." Mac straightened, eyes sparkling with humor. "Last I saw them, she was taking Chup outside for some fresh air. They were getting along fine, so get your boxers out of a knot."

"Fresh air? What if he runs off? Attacks a hiker or something? Jesus H., that woman is going to be the death of me!" With an effort, he willed himself to calm down. "Where'd they go, exactly?"

"I'm not telling if you're going to approach them like this," she informed him. "You'll scare poor Chup to death and put Kira back at square one."

Damn it. She was right.

"I'll be the perfect gentleman. Promise." He smiled for effect, earning him the evil eye from the good-natured doc.

After a few seconds of debate, she relented. "They're out on the lawn, on the side by the rec area."

"Thanks, Mac."

"Don't mention it," she called to his departing back.

All the way across the building, he couldn't help but worry. As he crossed the rec room, Aric glanced up from the war game he and Zan were playing on the Wii.

"Better get out there before the furball steals your girl," he said, going back to the game.

Not bothering to answer, he ducked down the hallway on the other side of the room, made a turn, and pushed out the side door leading to the area where their pool, tennis court, and covered barbecue/outdoor kitchen area was located. There, just beyond the covered patio, lying flat on her back on a quilt in the sunshine, was his woman.

And sprawled on her stomach, tiny, furry legs hanging on each side of her like a cat sunning on a branch, was Chup-Chup. Unnoticed by either of them, he stopped and stared. Her little friend was making a sort of whir-ring, hiccupy noise nobody could mistake as anything but sheer bliss. His round body, which almost resembled a baby koala bear's, rose and fell with each breath as he dozed.

The pair was so fucking cute, he couldn't really form the words to describe what the sight did to him. All he knew was it tightened his chest with an emotion he wasn't ready to name. To see this creature, formerly scared and snapping at everyone, lying there so trusting and content, was a measure of her goodness. The bright light that no one was able to resist.

Including himself.

Turning her head, she spotted him standing on the porch and waved him over. "You can come closer. Just don't make any sudden moves."

That seemed to be true of the woman as well as Chup. Wisely, he didn't say so. "Okay. Walking slowly." He made his way over to where they lay and crouched. The creature hadn't moved. "Now what?"

"Nothing. He'll notice you soon enough and we'll see what happens."

"That's reassuring." He eyed Chup warily.

"Don't tell me the big bad werewolf is afraid of this little guy," she teased.

"Shifter, not werewolf. A werewolf is that half-man thing from a B horror movie. And that 'little guy' can chew my face off. Have you seen those teeth?"

"Pardon me, *shifter*. And he won't bite unless you startle him." She looked entirely too amused by his trepidation.

"Then I'll have to be sure not to startle him again, won't I? Remember, he got me once before." He frowned at her hands, which bore red scratches and a few bite marks. "You aren't wearing your gloves."

"I don't need them anymore."

"I'm not so sure."

"Trust me."

Oddly, he did. After Beryl, he thought he'd never willingly trust anything out of a woman's mouth again, but Kira was not Beryl. The two women couldn't be more different. "I do trust you."

That made her smile, and his groin tightened. Damn, he couldn't get enough of her.

"When do we leave?" she asked, interrupting his lustful thoughts.

"Three hours. We're supposed to meet the team at the hangar." That awful, strange emotion rose up again to nearly strangle him. He wanted to order her to stay here, but knew how well that would go over. "I wish you weren't going tonight, baby. Please reconsider."

"And miss the chance to give my old boss the finger?" When he didn't laugh, she sobered. "Seriously, if there's the slightest possibility that I might be able to help, I have to go. But I promise to try and stay out of the action."

"I don't like it, but I guess I have no choice," he said, taking her hand. The odd feeling in his chest persisted. Was this love? He'd never been in love before, only thought he had been. Whatever he was feeling, he now understood that what he'd known was a pale imitation of the real deal.

For some reason, he wanted to tell her all of it. The whole sordid truth about his relationship with Beryl and what it had cost him. What it had cost the entire team.

Just then, a low growl of warning stalled his confession. Chup was awake, eyeing their linked hands and leaning out to sniff him in suspicion. Recalling his last tango with the imp a few days before Kira came to the compound, he kept still and let the creature check him out.

Sitting up carefully, Kira took the gremlin and set him on the grass between them. "Chup-Chup, Jax is a friend. He won't hurt you." Gently, she stroked the fur between his batlike ears. "See? Friend."

Chup wasn't convinced. On his hind legs, he toddled closer to Jax, nose working, still not getting too close. The growling stopped, but neither did he make the content chupping noise Jax wanted to hear.

Letting go of Kira's hand, Jax held his out to the creature, hoping he didn't lose a chunk of flesh for his trouble. "Good boy," he crooned. "Aren't you cute? Remember me? I'm not so scary, honest. I only eat bad little gremlins who bite, and only when I'm really hungry. Friends?"

Chup looked back at Kira as though seeking reassurance, so she made encouraging noises, urging him forward without pushing too much. Emboldened, the small critter turned his attention back to Jax and closed the remaining distance, sniffing all over his hand. The stubby whiskers tickled but he didn't dare jerk away.

Then, to his amazement, Chup began to rub his head against Jax's fingers like a cat wanting a good scratch. He complied, lavishing attention on both ears, the broad face, under the chin. And there it was—the noise of happy contentment. Chup crawled right up into his lap and closed his big brown eyes in obvious ecstasy as Jax continued to scratch.

"Well! Looks like you've got a new friend," Kira declared with a grin. "He won't let you out of his sight now."

"That might make it hard to leave for the op. Think I can use 'I have to babysit the gremlin' as an excuse not to go?" he joked.

"Hmm, somehow I doubt Nick will accept that." Reaching out, she stroked Chup's fur. "I'll have to ask Mac if she'll watch him while we're gone. I hate the thought of putting him back in that cell."

"Me, too. It could undermine the trust you've worked to gain, especially since he hates being locked in there." He paused. "What about Belial? Have you made any headway with him?"

"I'm not sure," she said thoughtfully. "He's really hard

to read, so full of bullshit I don't know if even *he* is capable of separating the truth from the lies. It just seems to be his nature to deflect questions and kindness with blatant attempts at seduction, but things aren't always what they appear."

"True. So what's your gut feeling as an Empath—can he be trusted? Will he be able to fit in here?"

She bit her lip, uncertainty clouding her blue eyes. "Eventually, yes, I believe he'll get there. I sense a basic goodness in him that's well hidden underneath the layers of self-hatred and anger, and I don't buy his 'Look at me—I'm such a manwhore' act for a second."

He nodded. "Okay. I trust your judgment. But whether it's an act or not, I don't pretend not to hate the hell out of knowing he puts the moves on you every time you get close. It makes me want to rip his heart out. Just so you know."

"I'll keep that in mind." Eyes twinkling again, she leaned over and kissed him on the lips. "You're so sexy when you're jealous."

"I'm not jealous! Well, I am, but you'll have to admit I'm handling it. I'm here, for example, rather than busting down the snake's cell door and chopping off his smarmy head."

She wrinkled her nose. "Good thing, or you'd never even make it to first base with me, buddy. I don't do homicidal lovers."

"Duly noted." He couldn't resist the opening. "What kinds of lovers have you had in the past?"

"None who were violent! I did date one guy who was really pushy. Wanted me to do as he said, monitored how much time I spent with friends as opposed to him, had to comment on everything I bought for myself. Always found something wrong with what I cooked for dinner. Stuff like that."

Jax snorted. "I'll bet he didn't last long."

"Just about a New York minute. Honestly, I haven't had too many boyfriends, or even second dates for that matter." She had no idea how happy that made him as she studied him curiously. "What about you? I can't imagine you've had too many dry spells in the female department."

"You'd be surprised," he murmured. "I don't let people in easily, and the one time I did before you ended in disaster."

There. Now he was committed. If she hated him afterward, so be it.

"What happened?"

"The ambush I told you about, the one six months ago?" She nodded and somehow he found the courage to reveal the truth. "It was my fault. I'd fallen head over heels for Beryl, or thought I had. Looking back I can see that I was blinded by lust, pretty much thinking only with my cock."

Kira let the comment pass, expression serious, and guessed, "She betrayed you."

"In the worst way possible." God, he didn't want to talk about this. "We'd been seeing each other a few weeks when she revealed that she knew what I was. She had some special abilities of her own, which is how she claimed to have figured me out. I didn't question it. I was just relieved not to have to lie about myself."

"Had she known about you all along, before you met?"

"Yes. I didn't know she was a plant, and that her job was specifically to ensnare me, gain my trust."

"What was her ability? Who was she working for?"

"She was a witch practicing the dark arts. As to her contact, we've never been able to find out who was behind the ambush. All we know is Beryl's goal was to integrate herself here, gaining our trust and learning our secrets, like the fact that silver can kill us. She and her contact planted false information about a family being held by vampires, so we scheduled a rescue op. I trusted her. That night, the ugly bastard down in Block T and his murderous comrades were waiting for us. Taking us out was like shooting fish in a barrel," he said hoarsely.

"How did she know about the existence of Alpha Pack in the first place?"

"That's a question we've all asked. If one of us had been a traitor, then Beryl wouldn't have needed to pass along information and set us up. So that theory is out."

"But one of you might have let it slip by accident," she speculated.

"Yeah, that's possible."

"I'm so sorry." Laying a hand over his, she stared intently into his eyes. "Is there any chance at all she wasn't involved? Do you know for sure she's the one who sold you guys out?"

"Oh, there's no question. She was there, in the aftermath, laughing as five of us lay dead—Terry, Micah, Jonas, Ari, and Nix. I can't describe the horror of knowing what I'd done to my team." The agony was almost unbearable. "The building was on fire and I used the last of my strength to throw her into the flames. I can still hear her screaming."

His lover swallowed hard. "She's dead?"

"Yeah."

"I'd say good, except it might have been useful to keep her alive and force her to give up who was calling the shots."

"Another idiot move," he admitted. "I should've used my gift as a Timebender to go back and warn my team of the ambush. A few minutes were all we needed. But I was in shock, running on nothing but rage, and I reacted, using up what little strength I had left. Now we may never know."

Unless they try again.

Shoving away the overwhelming guilt, he looked down at his lap, where Chup had curled up and fallen asleep. Sucking his thumb. There was proof that sometimes all a seemingly vicious creature needed was a little TLC. Too bad that wasn't always the solution.

"So you can really bend time, go back and live something over again?"

"Yes."

"Wow." She thought about that. "Can you go back to when you were ten and beat up the school bully who kept tormenting you? Stuff like that?"

He laughed at the idea. "Wouldn't that be nice? But no, I can't jump around. I'm not a human time machine. I can bend it enough to gain back the previous few minutes, and that's all."

"Huh. Well, that's still pretty cool. Sort of like that movie where the prince guy uses his knife filled with magic sand to go back in time. Only you don't need anything but yourself."

"Right." But the one instance where it would've done the most good, when he could've saved his team, he'd screwed up his chance. "I can't use the gift, though, except in the direst of circumstances."

"Why not?"

"For the same reason Nick rarely tells anyone what he sees happening in the future. Because every little thing a person does to interfere with that future affects those around us, and those we haven't even met, in ways we can't possibly know until it's too late."

"That makes sense," she said. "It just seems like a waste."

"It's not a waste that one time you really need it."
Except if you fuck up and don't use it.

"True."

They fell silent for a few minutes, enjoying each other's company. Or at least he enjoyed hers as much as he could, knowing he didn't deserve to be happy.

"Why don't we hand off Chup to Sariel to babysit while we're gone, instead of Mac?" Kira suggested. "I just realized Mac might be with us tonight."

"Good idea. Taking care of the little guy will give Sariel something positive to do."

"It's settled, then. Now the question is what to do with him while we're all eating dinner."

"The cook would throw a fit if she saw a gremlin in the dining room." The idea made him grin mischievously. "We'll just have to promise to teach him not to beg at the table."

"If she spots him, you're on your own," she said with a wink. "I had nothing to do with your plan."

"Traitor."

"Survivalist."

With a quiet laugh, he gathered the furball and stood, then offered her a hand up. "Come on, let's go see who we can rile."

"As long as it's not Chup, we're good."

"Agreed."

As they walked inside hand in hand, Jax felt lighter than he had in months. He still believed the massacre was partly his fault, but it had been nice to trust her with the truth as he saw it.

Now he just had to fool her and his team long enough to make it through tonight. They absolutely could not find out that he was in so much pain that he could barely keep moving. The reason was simple.

He wanted Kira more than he wanted his next breath.

But he'd die before forcing her into a decision she wasn't ready to make.

Jaxon gripped the leather armrest as the van neared their destination. His throat burned and his skin was hot. Tight and dry. His muscles cramped, as though they were being slowly twisted and torn apart. But that wasn't the worst.

No, the worst was sitting near Kira, her sweet scent driving him mad, and not being able to touch her. Because if he did, he'd finally lose control. Throw her to the floor of the van and give everyone a lesson in mating they'd rather not witness. His cock was hard enough to hit a home run and he was too damned miserable to be embarrassed about it, though he vaguely hoped his cammos were loose enough to hide the problem.

Hammer guided the van onto a dark side street a block over from the NewLife building, and Nick, sitting next to him in the front, gestured to a good spot to park both vehicles. Also riding in the van with them were Kalen and Mac, who'd been eyeing each other the entire first leg of the road trip. The SUV carrying Ryon, Aric, Zan, and Melina pulled up behind them.

Hopefully they wouldn't need the docs, but better to be prepared.

"Um, guys," Kira began, glancing between him and Nick. "This isn't going to be a popular opinion, but I need to go in with you."

"No fucking way," Jax snapped. "You're not getting within a hundred yards of that place. Are you forgetting how you barely escaped a few days ago?"

"I remember very well," she replied evenly. "But I'll have the team with me, not to mention A.J., and—"

"Your friend is putting himself at plenty of risk without adding you to the mix."

"But he doesn't know the labs like I do," she argued. "I think we need more samples, as well as photos of every document we can lay our hands on, and I'm the only one of us who knows exactly where to find them."

Hammer shut off the ignition and Jax seethed while they waited in silence for Nick's decision. Finally he nodded.

"Kira has a good point. We're going to need the items she mentioned, and I don't foresee any immediate danger in allowing her to help lead us through the building."

"I still don't like it."

In the end, she and Nick were right, so he could snarl all he wanted and it wouldn't make a difference. He chose to save his energy. He had a suspicion he'd need it.

The docs remained with the vehicles, but everyone else climbed out and got a few quick reminders from their leader.

"Remember, the goal here is to search, locate any possible evidence that NewLife is involved in experimentation on humans and shifters, and then get the hell out. A. J. Stone will be coming with us when we're done here. He has no other option—if he stays, he's a dead man."

A ripple of surprise went through the group, but Nick's men trusted his judgment. They were, however, visibly curious. But the questions would have to wait.

"Ready?" Everyone was. "Let's get this done and get home."

The street was dimly lit, and the adjoining alley almost completely dark, which helped hide their progress as they approached the edge of NewLife's property. The problem getting in and out would be crossing the vast parking lot, which was mostly empty this time of night. They'd be completely exposed both entering and leaving.

Targets for the ramped-up security Orson Chappell

had no doubt ordered in the wake of Kira's theft and escape.

Nick ordered Kalen and Hammer to remain at the mouth of the alley and keep watch over the back of the building. Cover them if necessary. The rest of them would enter through the big bay area of the garage, where A.J. would be waiting.

If nothing had happened to him.

As they left the alley and made their way to the high chain-link fence topped with razor wire that surrounded the parking lot, Jax had to force himself to concentrate on the op. Not on the curve of Kira's delectable little rear hugged by her camouflage pants. The way she moved, lithe and graceful. How cute she looked with a black knit cap pulled down on her head to hide her shiny blond hair. Like some sort of tiny ninja assassin among a bunch of Neanderthals.

Breathe, Jaxon, old boy. Patience, and she'll be yours.
Maybe.

Wielding a pair of bolt cutters, Zan opened a hole in the fence wide enough to allow them to squeeze through. Leaving the pair of cutters on the ground near the fence, he came through last and pulled the snipped ends of the wires together so the gap wouldn't be so noticeable. They'd need this route when they left.

They crossed the parking lot without being spotted and entered the bay through the side door A.J. had told Kira to use. Nick went inside first, then motioned for the others to follow. The garage was a cavernous space, dimly lit by a couple of wall fixtures. One was situated next to a service elevator they'd take into the basement.

"Where is he?" Ryon whispered, glancing around, body tense. "I don't like this."

Kira's reply was barely audible. "He'll be here. He won't let us down."

Jax hoped like hell she was right. If they'd trusted the wrong person—or if the guy had been found out—they were all dead.

When a slim figure emerged from the shadows, it became apparent that neither was the case. The security guard stopped before their group, hand resting on the butt of his gun in a deceptively casual pose. He was taller than Jax, maybe six-four, sandy brown hair framing one of those good-looking, all-American faces people liked right off the bat. Pale blue eyes regarded them warily, but brightened when he saw Kira.

"Hey, girl, it's good to see you," he said, moving forward to envelop her in a big hug.

The low, ominous growl escaped Jax's throat before he could stop it. His canines lengthened and fingernails became claws as sharp as daggers.

The man released Kira and stepped back, gazing at Jax without a trace of fear. "Is there a problem?"

"Not as long as you keep your hands off her." He returned the newcomer's stare without flinching.

"Kira?" he asked, the question obvious.

She shot Jax a look before answering. "Please pardon Jax. His animal side gets a bit testy when other guys so much as breathe in my direction."

"Yeah, well. No harm done." He dismissed the incident.

Good thing, because Jax offered no explanation or apology. There wasn't time for the first, and his wolf said screw the second. Kira was his. Period.

Introductions were brief, Nick getting right to the point. They were in and out, and A.J. was coming with them. The man's lack of resistance made Jax think the guard and their boss had discussed this beforehand, and he suspected A.J. had been briefed on what the Alpha Project was all about.

In fact, there was something about the way he held himself, the ease of his movements, that told Jax this man was more than a run-of-the-mill security guard. A.J. kept an eye on the position of each man, and was also very aware of his surroundings, keeping his ears open. Oh, his scent was human, but Jax would bet his life savings the man had a military background, or was a former cop.

And if so, how had he wound up working here? It would be a definite career step down.

There wasn't time to speculate further, because A.J. took the lead, pointing to a corner. "See that camera? When it points toward the bay doors, we haul ass to the elevator. Get ready . . . Go!"

Kira right behind him, they jogged for the elevator. A.J. punched the down button and the doors slid open, and they hurried inside. Before the camera completed its circuit, they were on their way to the basement.

"How many other guards are on duty tonight?" Nick asked.

"Two, as far as the regular uniformed ones like me. But Kira's disappearance coupled with some items we heard were missing from the lab have the big guys really nervous. There are some suits hanging around, and they're armed."

The guard's choice of words caught Jax's attention. "You *heard* about some items reported missing? There wasn't an official notice or memo to the company's employees about the theft?"

A.J.'s smile didn't reach his eyes. "Of course not. Wouldn't that be like a serial killer publicly complaining that someone had swiped his victim from under his nose?"

No one found fault with that logic.

"That's one more nail in Chappell's coffin," Nick said

as they exited the elevator. "Assuming he's the apex of the power structure."

"But you don't think so," Jax observed.

"No, I don't. That's too easy, and if I've learned anything in my existence it's that no move in the game of world domination is *ever* simple."

Too true. His boss's quiet words made him shudder, and wonder where all of these threads would lead. Even a powerful PreCog like Nick couldn't know everything. But if the white wolf could keep them one step ahead of death and destruction, it would be more than any of their former leaders—human or not—had been able to accomplish.

The group trekked down a long brightly lit corridor, everyone strung tight, waiting for discovery. The sound of a raised alarm. But the building was eerily silent as they went, footsteps shuffling on the concrete and echoing off the stark walls. Close to the end, Kira gestured to a closed door, no different in appearance from the others lining the passage.

"This is the lab where I got the samples," she told them, keeping her voice low. "I didn't get a chance to do a very thorough search, but the corresponding paperwork to whatever tests they're conducting should be here unless they've moved it."

"Let's give it a try," Nick said. "Even though they brought in extra muscle, I doubt they banked on the cavalry showing up so soon."

Inside, they found pretty much what Jax expected. There weren't any grisly body parts hanging from the ceiling or spread on the counter for dissection, à la *Texas Chain Saw Massacre*. The space was clean and orderly, so sterile one could eat off the counter. Not that anyone would.

Kira removed a Ziploc bag from one of the large

pockets of her camos. "I'm going to grab a few more samples from the cabinets. The records will be on the computer, through there," she said, pointing toward an office. "They might also have hard copies in the filing cabinet we can copy, but if one of you can hack in, it'll be much easier to download all the info onto a thumb drive."

Zan held up the small device in question and headed for the office. "I'll give it a shot. How will I know what I'm looking for?"

Nick answered. "Just download everything and we'll sort through it later."

"Gotcha." Ryon and Nick followed him, while Aric and A.J. stood near the door, listening for any sign of unwelcome company.

Jax accompanied Kira across the room and watched as she fished an old key from her pocket. She tried to use it to unlock the cabinet, but it wouldn't fit.

"Damn it. This is the key I stole from Dr. Bowman and used to get in before. They must've changed the lock." She tossed it aside in frustration.

"Here, let me help."

Reaching up, he grabbed the handle and pulled with steady force. He was tempted to smile at her dubious expression, but his macho display was using the precious reserves of energy he still had left. The wood began to creak, groan . . . and then snapped with a sharp crack. He tossed the cabinet door onto the counter and gestured to the many containers inside.

"There you go. Have at it."

"Wow. Thanks."

"Anytime."

Quickly, she set about sorting through the samples, discarding some and taking others. Soon her baggie was filled with more of the type of tissue she'd brought them before. "That should be enough," she said, sealing the plastic. "Let's go see if Zan is having any luck."

In the small lab office, Zan was hunkered at the computer, frowning at the screen along with Ryon and Nick. The thumb drive was in place, downloads apparently progressing.

"What's so interesting?" Jax asked. Kira moved to his side, pressing close.

"I can't make much of this testing stuff—nothing at all, really—but I've noticed that each document has a number at the top. I think they're using case file numbers instead of names to ID their test subjects."

"That would be standard," Kira said. "NewLife has to protect the identities of organ donors and their recipients."

"Yeah, but even so, their corresponding names would be recorded somewhere, right?"

"They should be," she told him. "Also, see how there's a date at the top of each section of the document? That shows the date each test was done on the subject, with a description of what was done and how the subject reacted to whatever they did."

Nick spoke up. "So what we've found is the doctors' files on what's being done to each person and when, whether they're human or shifter."

Kira nodded. "Looks like it. I'd feel better if Zan hurries and gets it all, like you said, so we can get the hell out of here and study this stuff later."

"She's right," Jax said, a sense of urgency riding him harder than before. "And we've still got more poking around to do before we can go."

Nick let out a breath. "There's a stench permeating the very walls of this place. Blood, sweat, hunger, terror, death. We need to hurry, or more lives will be lost."

Zan completed the transfer of data in a matter of

minutes and pocketed the thumb drive. Jax prayed the proof they needed was on the device, because they'd never be able to get inside a NewLife property again without launching a full-blown attack.

When they were ready to move again, Nick glanced between Kira and A.J. "Where to now?"

"I found something interesting after Kira took off the other night," A.J. said in a low voice. "This isn't the only area restricted to regular staff."

"You located another one? How? Where?" Kira asked anxiously.

"I was thinking about it—if they're down here doing their mad scientist gig, then where are the lab rats?"

Kira's eyes widened. "You found them?"

"Maybe. But we won't know unless we can get past the big-assed solid steel vault-style door that's standing smack in our way."

"I've got an idea of how to take care of that," Aric said with a grim smile. "You play tour guide and I'll be the demolition man."

Thirteen

Being back here was harder than Kira had anticipated. She'd barely escaped before, and now a sense of impending doom was closing bony fingers around her throat, urging her to get the hell out. Fast.

That wasn't the worst of it, though. Jax was doing his best tough-guy routine, but she could tell he was hurting. His limp was more pronounced than ever, his face pale. He wasn't scratching anymore, but she wasn't entirely certain that was a positive sign. What if his body was giving up the ghost? Shutting down?

What if the choice to mate wasn't hers anymore? If she'd waited too long, would he die?

Oh, God. It was more imperative than ever that they finish up and make tracks. Whatever was hidden in this building couldn't be worth Jax's life and the lives of his friends. Could it?

But she knew none of them could leave without knowing for sure whether there were people hidden here. Being sliced, experimented on, tortured beyond what any being should be forced to endure. And for what purpose? It was madness.

A.J. stuck his head out to check the corridor, then motioned for them to follow. She wasn't surprised when he led them in the opposite direction from the service elevator that would ascend to the parking garage and to escape. Every step made her more and more uneasy. No, downright scared.

She tried reminding herself that she was with a team of badass shifters, ones with special Psy abilities to boot. But on the heels of that thought came another; if Dr. Mallory and the other researchers at the Institute were correct, then whoever was experimenting on humans and shifters clearly knew how to capture and hurt them. Endlessly. Until their bodies gave out.

Stop it!

By the time they reached the far end of the corridor, she was sweating, pushing back mind-numbing fear. It was an effort, but she couldn't afford to let them down. If this went south she refused to be the square cog that upset the machine.

A.J. gestured to a door marked HIGH VOLTAGE—KEEP OUT! and produced a key. "Got hold of the master key ring a couple of days ago, and found the one that opened this lock. When I saw that the warning sign is either wrong or more likely a fake, and there's not anything electrical in here, I went looking. After I discovered the hidden passage, I made a copy of the key and put the ring back."

"Hidden passage?" Aric snorted. "Jeez, I'm starting to channel a little Indiana Jones."

"As long as there are no flying poison spikes or boulders rigged to crush our asses, I'm good." This from Zan, who was only half-joking. The other half was ready for anything.

Once inside the room, A.J. closed the door quietly and waved a hand at the space, which was filled with empty boxes, crates, and palettes. "As you can see, nothing much here but junk. When I first came in and looked around, I almost left right away. But then I was struck by how orderly this *junk* is. Almost too neat."

"Strategically placed," Nick observed. "There's not much dirt or dust."

"Right. So I looked around a little more. And I found this." Picking his way between stacks, he left them to follow.

Single file, they did, careful not to upset any of the boxes or crates. On the far wall, in the corner, was another door. Her friend used the same key to unlock this one, and pushed it open. Well-oiled, it didn't make a sound. As she moved closer to get a good look, she blinked at the sight of a staircase on the other side, descending into nothingness, it seemed.

"The vault, and whatever is inside, is at the bottom," A.J. told them. "No regular key, just a security panel with card-key access—and sorry. I couldn't lay hands on one. There's also a number pad that I'm guessing is an override if the card doesn't work, but I was afraid to try and hack it. Might set off an alarm. Plus, I wasn't prepared to face by myself whatever I might find. I was damned glad when Kira called me and said you all were coming."

"You did the right thing," Nick assured him. "Let's move."

As they went into the bowels of the earth, Jax reached out and squeezed her hand, gave her a reassuring smile that made her heart trip. Damn, could it be love between them?

At the bottom, the group closed the remaining distance to the steel vault, which did indeed appear to be impenetrable. Aric walked right up, laid a palm on the smooth surface, and nodded.

"Piece of cake. Stand back, guys."

They gave him space and he closed his eyes, keeping his hand flat against the center of the door, leaning his body into the touch. At first nothing happened, and then after one long minute, the metal around his hand began to glow. Fascinated, she remained silent, guessing that he intended to blow up the entire barrier or perhaps make the vault slide open.

Wrong on both counts. As the metal glowed red and began to melt away from his palm, spreading outward, she stifled a gasp. She had no idea a Firestarter could use heat energy to manipulate metal—or at least this one could.

When at last he staggered backward, panting, sweat trickling down his temples, auburn hair sticking to his face, a man-sized hole had been torched in the middle. Jax caught his friend, steadied him.

"Gotcha. You okay?"

"Yeah," he said quietly, none of his usual snarky bravado in evidence. "Thanks."

"You need to stay here, catch your breath?"

"Nah, man, I'm gold. Let's do this."

"Holy shit," A.J. breathed, gingerly touching a finger to the edge of the melted steel. "Who the fuck are you people?"

"Told you explanations wouldn't do us justice," Nick said, clapping him on the shoulder. "You just have to watch and learn."

"Apparently so."

Their boss gestured to the newly made entrance. "I'll go in first. Wait for me to make sure it's clear."

Nick ducked slightly and stepped through the hole, vanishing. Tension rose as the seconds ticked by, his team antsy, not liking their boss and friend in uncharted territory without them at his back. Kira didn't blame them. As her eyes adjusted and senses heightened, she saw a dim glow in the room beyond, and smelled something really . . . putrid.

Nick appeared, his expression stony. "We have three dead and a couple of captives in bad shape. Got to free them and get out of here. Right fucking now."

As the others started after him, Jax took her arm in a gentle grip. "I don't want you in there."

"Any more than I want to go, but I'm not staying here by myself. So forget it."

Reluctantly he let her go. "All right, just stick close."

She snorted. "Like that'll be a problem."

She was practically glued to his back as they climbed through the hole and surveyed the gloomy prison.

"Oh my God," she whispered. "Jax . . ."

"Jesus Christ." He tried to block her view with his body. "Baby, don't look."

Too late. Stepping around him, she stared in horror, her brain struggling to comprehend such depraved cruelty. The stench took her breath away, a close second only to the awful sight before them.

One corner of a large chamber was taken up by what could have been nothing else but a place to torture the captives. A vinyl dentist chair was coated in dark stains and surrounded by tables of instruments—pliers, rope, saws, knives, drain cleaner, funnels, and other tools. More than she could name.

The rest of the room was filled with cages. Literally stacked with them, no more than three feet square, not nearly large enough for a full-grown human or shifter to stand, sit, or lie down in comfortably. And in those cages, the victims.

Emaciated, skin pulled taut over bones. Naked, curled into fetal positions, wasting away in their own filth, eyes devoid of hope. Eyes sunken and staring, some empty of life.

Kira's gorge rose and she spun, found the nearest corner, and dropped to her knees. She promptly lost her dinner and was vaguely aware of a large hand rubbing circles on her back. Jax, comforting her. Always there, strong and silent.

"You okay?"

"Yeah," she said weakly. Using the edge of her shirt, she wiped her mouth and stood, too queasy to be embarrassed. "Or I will be, when we get the survivors home."

Something flashed in his eyes, and he nodded. "Let's see what we can do to speed things along."

There wasn't much to do but hover anxiously as Nick and Aric extracted one captive, Zan and Ryon the other. Both were males.

"They're shifters," Ryon said, studying the unconscious male in his arms. "Not sure what kind, but I don't scent a wolf."

"Me neither." Zan sniffed, and then froze. Slowly, he walked to a cage next to the one he and Ryon had pulled their victim from. Leaning close to the bars, he scented the area and shook his head. "It can't be."

Jax stalked over. "What?"

"Micah," Zan whispered. "I smell him. In that empty cage. My God, is it possible?"

The others exchanged stunned glances.

"Z-Man, Micah's dead," Jax said quietly.

"Are we sure? How do we know?" His friend's voice took on a note of desperation.

"I saw them myself. They were dead, Zan."

"How do we *know*?" he practically shouted. "Grant sent in a clean-up crew to take care of the bodies. We were injured, out of commission, and we never *saw* them afterward, dead and on a slab! And now I'm telling you, I caught Micah's scent in there."

"Which would mean our high-up government

friends—the assholes who're supposed to be on our side—lied to us," Aric put in, voice cold. "Ain't like that's never happened before."

The words fell between them like stones, and Kira watched helplessly as they realized what they'd uncovered tonight was a mere thread that would unravel a much bigger scheme than they'd dreamed in their worst nightmares.

Jax's jaw worked in impotent rage. "Then what really happened that night? How did Micah end up here, and where the *fuck* is he now?"

"And if he's alive, or was . . ." Ryon trailed off, looking shell-shocked.

Nick finished. "Then where are the others? I don't have all the answers, but we're going to get them." A groan from one of the freed shifters brought them back to reality. "Unfortunately we won't get them tonight. We have to go."

As they made their way out and up the staircase once more, an unpleasant niggle teased Kira's mind. But fear, the urge to escape from this hellhole intact overrode the niggle before it could form into a thought. She'd have to examine it later.

They made it back to the HIGH VOLTAGE room above without incident. Luck had been with them so far, but it ran out just as they entered the bright corridor and approached the lab they'd looted earlier. Another security guard and three armed men in suits burst from the lab, apparently having discovered the intrusion. They froze, momentarily thrown by A.J.'s presence in the lead.

"Stone? What the fuck are you doing?" the other guard barked.

"What does it look like? Giving my friends a tour of the building," he sneered in return.

"They got the prisoners!" one of the suits, a fat man

with a ring of hair encircling his balding pate, shouted. "Kill 'em!"

The security guard who'd spoken looked thoroughly confused, and clearly had no clue what the hell was going on. The suits did, though, and brought their guns up.

Jax shoved Kira behind him and down to the floor as shots rang out, deafening in the confined space. Aric and Ryon dropped into a crouch, shielding their charges with their bodies. Dropping to one knee, A.J. returned fire, putting a bullet in the center of one goon's forehead while Jax, Zan, and Nick shifted in midrun, going for the other two.

Bullets struck bodies, ricocheted off the walls. Sprawled on her stomach, arms over her head, Kira didn't have the best view but she saw enough. Three wolves ran right out of their pants, boots, and socks, straight for the two men who were still firing, eyes going wide at the unbelievable sight.

The black and silver wolves took down the fat man with relative ease. The black wolf—Zan—went for his throat, and his high-pitched scream was abruptly cut off, ending in a sickening gurgle. Next to them, the big white wolf had the other suit down, the body twitching underneath his bulk.

Crouching, the silver wolf raised his head and fixed his steely gaze on the security guard, who'd slid down the wall and was staring at the carnage. Fur retracted, limbs reshaped, but Jax didn't shift back all the way. Instead, he remained at half-shift, muscular body huge, long muzzle pulled back into a snarl, revealing deadly canines. A terrifying and awesome sight, especially to the blubbering guard.

"You," Jax said, his voice rough as gravel. Deliberately, he pointed one four-inch claw at the horrified young man. "Do I need to take care of you next?"

The guard was so stricken with terror, he hadn't even drawn his weapon. A dark stain spread across his crotch. "N-no! I d-don't know wh-what the fuck's g-goin' on and I d-don't care! Just don't eat me, please!"

Jax tilted his head, as though considering the request. "Then here's what you're going to do. Wait fifteen minutes after we're gone and then tell your boss you found these guys just like this. You didn't see a damned thing. Then if I were you, I'd put in my resignation and move far, far away. Got that?"

"Y-yeah! Shit, I got it!" The guard nodded emphatically, but didn't move.

Jax looked to Kira. "He telling the truth?"

For a second she was surprised, and then a little spurt of pride went through her. He was treating her like a team member, asking for her help as an Empath. Trusting her judgment, and in front of the others.

She opened her senses to the guard and was battered by waves of fear, confusion. Hope. He only wanted to make it out alive.

"Yes, he is. There's no deception in him."

"Then he lives." Jax stood and retrieved his pants, completing his shift to human form. "We're out of here."

Then he lives. Simple as that. Based on her perception of the jumble of feelings rolling off him, the guard would walk away. The power of that idea was frightening.

Jax offered her a hand up and she took it, averting her eyes while Nick and Aric yanked on their camos, shoved their feet into the discarded boots. In seconds they were ready to continue, the whole horrible episode having taken less than five minutes.

With a quick peek, she saw everyone was decent. Zan was wiping a seeping bullet wound in his side with the edge of his T-shirt, grimacing in pain.

"You all right?" Nick asked sharply.

"Think so. It's a through-and-through. I'm already healing," he replied. He was a little out of breath, but standing on his own.

Nick looked around. "Anyone else? I know I heard at least one other hit."

"Took one high in the chest," Jax muttered. His face was pale, sweat rolling down his temples.

"What?" Kira gasped. "Let me see."

He shook his head. "No time. Mac can take a look in the van."

"Are you healing?" Nick's voice was tight with concern.

"Not sure."

Which wasn't an answer. Eyeing his chest, she spotted the small hole in the dark fabric on the left side, barely noticeable. On closer inspection, she could see wetness spreading on his shirt, and it didn't seem to be slowing any. A chill shook her. When he'd rescued her from the two men that first time, he'd been hit and had healed almost instantly. And again, when he and Aric had fought, their scratches and bites had vanished quickly.

He wasn't healing now. With every step they took to the elevator, and then across the parking garage, making their escape, he slowed. When they reached the hole in the fence, his limp was worse than ever, he was breathing hard, and his friends were exchanging worried looks. His shirt was almost completely soaked with blood, and the front of his cammos was fast becoming saturated. He stumbled and Zan was there, slinging Jax's right arm over his shoulders, half-carrying him.

Halfway to the van, his knees buckled, and his eyes rolled back in his head.

"Shit!" Zan caught him as he collapsed, lifting him into a fireman's hold.

"You got him?" Kalen asked as they reached the mouth of the alley where he and Hammer were waiting.

"Yep. Damn, he's heavy though."

They were moving fast and Kira had to jog to keep up. Fear gripped her by the throat and wouldn't let go. He hadn't felt well to start with, but he'd insisted on coming anyway. And now he'd been shot and couldn't heal.

Because of me?

If that was true, if she caused the death of the man she loved, she'd never forgive herself.

The man I love. Oh, my God, I love him. He's my mate. Mine.

And he can't die.

Back at the vehicles, the two doctors met them, faces grim but determined. The scene took on a surreal quality as the sick pair of shifters were loaded into the SUV with Dr. Mallory, Ryon, and Aric. Kalen helped Zander get Jax into the van, and once inside, Zan refused to let go of his best friend. Kira crouched in the back, close enough to hold her mate's clammy hand, but giving Mac room to work. Tears sprang to her eyes, rolled down her cheeks.

"Jax?"

No response. He lay horribly still as Mac cut his shirt up the middle and parted the flaps, exposing the wound. Blood was streaming from the hole located high on the left side of his chest, inches above the nipple, close to the collarbone.

"I'm pretty sure the bullet missed his lung," the doc said. The relief in the vehicle was tangible. Quickly she checked his back, and put a damper on the good news. "But it's still in his chest and he's losing too much blood."

"Let me do my thing." Placing a hand over the wound, Zan pressed down firmly. A blue-tinted glow lit his hand, and Kalen sucked in a breath, eyes wide.

"You're a Healer?"

"Yes, but it's not working." Zan, holding his friend's head in his lap, removed his bloodied palm and swallowed hard. "Why the hell isn't he healing, Mac?"

"I've got a theory, but it's privileged information."

"What? That's bullshit! Is he dying or something?" Zan barked at the doctor, dread stamped on his handsome features.

"Or something," she agreed, her gaze flicking briefly to Kira.

Who felt like a steaming pile of shit.

"He'll recover, though. Right?" Zan asked.

After a pause, Mac nodded. "I believe so."

"You *believe* so? What the—"

"Easy, man." Kalen touched Zan's shoulder. "Let the doc get to work so she can help your friend. Okay?"

For a few seconds, Zan visibly struggled with himself, perhaps to keep from snarling at the newcomer. In the end, however, he just sagged against the side of the van. "You're right."

Mac kept working, placing a pressure bandage on the wound. Next she hooked up an IV, and Kalen held the bag of fluid aloft for her. "Thank you."

"No sweat," he said softly.

Kira wiped the tears with her shirt, but they wouldn't stop coming. She'd never felt so helpless. And the guilt ate her guts like a worm pushing through rotten soil. She clung to Jax's hand, brushing the rough skin with her thumb, contemplating whether his team would blame her for this.

But they couldn't possibly hate her more than she hated herself.

His sternum had been cracked open with a rusty screwdriver and a mallet, liquid fire poured into the cavity.

He opened his mouth to yell, or thought he did, but

couldn't make a sound. Nothing worked the way it should. He knew where he was, though. In the speeding van, head in someone's lap, every bump in the road jarring his pain-racked body. A small, feminine hand held one of his tightly. Kira.

"Jax?"

He knew it was her, but he couldn't scent her anymore. Couldn't speak or move at all, not even to squeeze her fingers, let her know he was alive.

For how much longer?

Goddamn, he didn't want to go out like this. He struggled to breathe, thinking it shouldn't be this hard. When he'd been hit, he was certain the bullet had missed his lung. It had, right? He'd been shot before, and the wound should've healed with no problem.

Instead he lay as if dead, along for the ride, unable to communicate in the slightest. He was aware of Kira and a couple of other voices speaking to him in soothing tones, telling him that he'd be all right. He tried to take heart, to push back the encroaching fear, but wasn't entirely successful. Something was very wrong, besides the gunshot wound. The talking around him grew even more worried as the vehicle stopped and doors opened.

People were shouting. His body was jostled and he couldn't cry out.

Something hard slid underneath him. A backboard.

Then he was out of the van, being carried fast. Loaded into another transport. He remembered the helicopters and realized they must be at the hangar. Two hours to home.

And the truth flooded in—he wasn't going to make it.

It shouldn't be possible, but it was becoming a reality. His body was shutting down, like the lights in a house winking out one by one. He hung on as long as he could. Counted in his head, and when he lost count, tried to concentrate on the loud drone of the engines. Imagined the compound getting closer with every mile, whisking him to safety.

"Breathe, Jax! Come on, buddy!" Zan shouted next to his ear.

"Jax? Please, stay with us." Kira. He heard her tears. "Don't leave me."

He tried to obey. Really fucking tried.

Made it all the way to landing before their frantic calls began to fade. His last awareness was of being lifted, flying. Wishing he could see the stars, shift into his wolf, and run.

Make love to Kira.

And then it all vanished into mist.

"He's not breathing? Mac!"

Kira bailed out of the helicopter after the doctor. Zan and Kalen were already out, holding each end of the backboard, hurrying up the walk toward an entrance marked EMERGENCY. The other woman didn't answer or spare her a glance, just ran, shouting orders at the nurses and other medical personnel who met them at the double doors.

Heart pounding in fear, Kira rushed after them. She would've followed them all the way into the ER had strong arms not wrapped around her waist, hauling her back.

"You can't go in there, honey," Nick said, voice full of regret.

"Let me go!"

"Can't do that. He's in good hands, though, I promise."

"He needs me! Nick, please."

"I'm sorry." Gently, he guided her to a chair. "Come on, I'll wait with you."

"We all will," Aric declared, dropping into a seat. Obviously he and the others had handed off the two survivors they'd liberated from the NewLife building, but she hadn't been paying attention.

After a moment, she calmed herself enough to ask, "Are the two shifters okay?"

"They'll make it, physically. The rest, we'll see, but I think they'll pull through."

She nodded. "That's good."

The respite was brief and took her mind off Jax for only about three seconds. The team crowded into the waiting area, none of them willing to leave without word. Zan and Kalen walked back in from the OR, faces weary. A barrage of questions from the guys was met with little info, none of it encouraging.

"He wasn't breathing," Zan choked, dropping into a chair, head in his hands. "That's all I know."

"Jesus," Hammer mumbled in shock.

Aric responded by putting a hole in the wall with his fist and letting go a stream of profanity. The others just moped. Someone went for coffee.

Time passed. Kira wasn't sure how long it had been when Sariel strode into the room, heading straight for her. Jumping up, she launched herself into his arms. He caught her against his chest and enfolded her in his wings, and the dam broke. She sobbed in terror, babbling that she couldn't lose him.

"You won't, dearest." He placed a kiss on the top of her head. "I swear to you."

"H-how do you know?"

"I just do. Now dry those tears, or else your wolf is going to be treated to the lovely vision of a puffy, blotchy mate when he wakes up."

Pulling back, she managed a small laugh. "Gee, thanks."

"You're welcome. What are displaced princes for?"

It was a lame attempt at a joke, and she loved him for it. Wrung out, she let him tug her over to a chair. At Zan's urging, he fetched a box of tissues from the front desk—he was puzzled about their purpose at first—handed them over, and settled in beside her for what might prove to be a long wait.

It was worse than long. Interminable was a better word. Half the team was dozing when both Mac and Melina pushed through the double doors into the waiting area, but everyone immediately snapped to attention.

Dr. Mallory got to the point. "The two shifters are stable but still unconscious. Jax is also stable at the moment, and the bullet has been removed. But his condition is critical." She gave Kira a pointed look. "I'll need you to come with us."

"Of course." She rose on rubbery legs and followed the doctors. Whether either of them was ready or not, she had a suspicion that the moment of reckoning was at hand.

A sexy silvery-eyed wolf was about to become hers.

Fourteen

"Jax, open your eyes."

Don't want to. He preferred to keep sleeping, safe in his cozy cocoon. Besides, hers was the wrong voice. Not the one he loved.

Wait, loved? Ah, shit.

"Sweetheart, can you hear me? Come on, handsome. Let's see those peepers."

Kira. For her, he tried. His lids were like wet concrete, but he managed to crack them open a tiny bit. Her small form was leaning over him, blurry. But there. Holding his hand, stroking his brow. So good.

"I . . . can't smell you," he rasped.

Her touch stilled. "What?"

"He means his sense of smell is gone," Melina said. "He can't scent you."

"Oh. What do we do? How do we fix it?" She was so upset, his baby.

He couldn't comfort her. Couldn't move a damned muscle.

"This is undocumented territory, but I'd like to try something. Are you willing to let me make a small inci-

sion in your wrist? I can give you a local anesthetic."
Obviously she was talking to Kira.

Wait a minute. Melina wanted to cut his angel? Why?
Jax tried to growl but only a pathetic whine came out.
His eyes closed again.

"Yes! Anything that will make him well."

No! his mind shouted. But his lips wouldn't budge.

Noises ensued, the clank of metal on a tray. Melina
spoke to his mate, but he couldn't make out the words.
He was tired and he hadn't even been awake that long.
His energy was nonexistent.

Suddenly a slick finger parted his lips, began to rub his
tongue. He sputtered, tried to turn his head away from
the latex-covered digit, but the doc held him fast, smearing something wet on his tongue. His gums and canines,
too. What the hell?

Automatically he swallowed, and caught the sweet,
earthy taste on his tongue. His initial impression was
that it was nice, if kind of weird, and then . . . the effect
hit his system like rain in the desert. Warmth flowed to
cells and muscles, liquid sunshine. And he knew.

Melina had given him Kira's blood. Lifesaving, nour-
ishing blood from his mate. Doing the job that no medicine could hope to perform in pulling him back from the
brink. Slowly, he cracked his lids open again, glad to find
his vision mostly clear.

"Hey," he croaked, giving Kira a lopsided smile.

"Oh, my God!" Scooting her chair close, she hugged
him tight, laying her head on his chest, on his right side,
opposite the bullet wound. "I was so worried. Everyone
was. *Is*."

Carefully, he brought his arm around her, holding her
snug against him. "I'm okay, baby. Don't cry."

"Sariel says I'm blotchy." She sniffed.

"Yeah? What does he know? You're always beautiful." He kissed her head, and would've growled if he had the energy. "I can smell him on you."

At least he could scent again. A bonus.

"He was comforting me because I thought you were going to die." Another sniff. "Get over it."

He snorted a laugh, but it hurt and he sucked in a breath, waiting for the pain to subside. Apparently his healing powers weren't at full speed yet.

"Doc?"

Melina moved into his line of vision, angled face filled with concern. "Yes?"

"Is this, you know, temporary?"

"The boost you're feeling now?"

"Yeah."

She sighed, showing more emotion than he'd witnessed in months. "I'm afraid so. Kira's blood has strengthened you because it contains the properties you require to be a healthy wolf shifter male. But you aren't mated. In short, this is a stopgap measure to get you strong enough to finish the process."

He frowned. "But if I take her blood when I bite her, what's the difference? Why can't I take it through the cut in her wrist or something?"

"Good question. I think the answer lies in your saliva, in the chemical change that occurs when mates bond during sex. I could be wrong." She shrugged. "Only two ways to find out."

"Two?"

"First, we'll let you take blood from Kira's wrist—provided she agrees." Kira nodded, so Melina continued. "Then we give you a few hours, see if the bond forms between you and you're completely well. If it hasn't worked, you'll feel progressively worse in a relatively short time."

"And then?"

"We give you more blood, and release you to do as wolves do in the wild." She actually smirked at this.

Jax looked to Kira, who was blinking rapidly, cheeks turning pink. "Not unless that's what Kira wants."

Melina was silent for a moment. "Are you saying you'd rather die than force Kira into mating you?"

As much as it broke his heart, he had to let her go if that's what she wanted. "That's exactly what I'm saying."

Big blue eyes fixed to his. "Jax," she breathed. "You don't mean that."

"Every word."

"I'm not going to let it happen," she whispered.

"Then stop me."

"Oh, I intend to."

"I'll give you two some privacy," Melina said with a grin. "I'll be back."

Neither of them noticed when the doc left. They just stared into each other's eyes, and Jax wondered where to go next. What to say.

All that came out was, "Thank you." Which was completely inadequate. He wasn't a man prone to long, mushy soliloquies, hearts and flowers. He'd rather *show* a woman what she meant to him, and he sure couldn't do that laid up in the infirmary. Damn it.

An impish smile curved her lips. "You're welcome. Though I had sort of a selfish motive for saving your bacon."

"Really?" His hand sought hers, clasped their fingers together on top of his stomach.

"Sure. A take-charge wolf man with woo-woo powers and a smokin' hot bod? And I might get to be a wolf, too. Where else am I going to find all that?"

He laughed, and immediately regretted it. Sharp pain blasted through his shoulder and he gasped, riding it out. As the sick waves subsided, he noted that her teasing mood had disappeared and tears swam in her pretty eyes. "Hey, none of that. I'm going to be fine."

"What if you're not? I can't help but feel this is my fault," she said, voice breaking. "If I had—"

"No. This is most definitely not your fault, or mine. Nature isn't fair, that's all." Studying her expression, he thought it only fair he give her one more out.

"Kira, I want you to know I meant what I said. You're under no obligation to mate with me. If you don't want to do it, I'll let you go. You can't leave here until it's safe, but I can. I could ask Nick to assign me in the field for a while, and this mating fever, or whatever it's called, might pass."

And the mere thought broke his heart. Made him want to tear the room apart, shred the furniture. When had she burrowed so far under his skin?

To his amazement, her expression turned fierce. A little bit pissed. His angel got right in his face. "Listen to me, Jaxon Law. There's something really good here, between you and me, and I'm sticking around to take it all the way. So stuff the self-sacrificing crap and get out of this bed so we can get our animal goin' on."

Okay, his inner wolf liked the attitude. A whole helluva lot. The rest of him did, too, and made his desires known with throbbing intensity, injuries be damned.

Reaching out, he traced a finger over her lips. "Yes, ma'am. You always so bossy?"

"No, but I'm learning."

With that, she took his mouth, licked inside. Her flavor excited him as no woman's ever had, and he wanted to pull her on top of him. Have his way right here. She must've felt the same, because she broke the kiss to nibble along his jaw.

"You could bite me right now," she murmured.

"Baby, even if it would work, there's no way I'm going

to create the most important bond either of us will ever experience sitting in my oh so sexy hospital bed." He arched a brow. "Give me a little romantic credit."

She brightened. "I'm glad to hear you say that."

"Why? Was that some sort of test and I passed?"

"No! Well, maybe a little," she teased. "I don't want to do it here, either."

"Why do you want it at all?" His quiet question pierced the playful mood, but he had to know. His own change of heart concerning taking a mate wasn't such a mystery. Kira, he wasn't so sure about. "Why me? Have you made peace with the fact that I have an animal half who's every bit a part of me as the man?"

Her gaze slid from his and moved to his lap. "I keep telling you that wasn't the problem."

"Then what—oh, right. You didn't want nature to force your choice." Taking her chin, he tilted it up so she'd meet his eyes. "I don't want that, either. But for my part, I don't have to worry anymore."

"What are you saying?" She bit her lip.

"That I'm falling for you," he said, smiling a little. "Because of *you*, not some souped-up version of my genetic code. This might sound stupid, but I knew you were all I wanted the second I saw Chup sleeping on your stomach."

"That doesn't sound stupid at all." Leaning in, she kissed the corner of his mouth. "In fact, that's the greatest thing anyone's ever said to me."

"What about you?" He attempted to keep the sudden strain out of his tone. "Do you still feel trapped?"

"No," she said, taking his hand. "I'm scared and a little overwhelmed, but not trapped. I think that's because I'm not fully adjusted to this lifestyle yet. To the enormity of all of this—otherworldly beings, evil forces and soldiers who battle them. Plus there's a big possibility I'll be a shifter like you guys. But my feelings for you have become stronger than my fear of what I can't control. Does that make sense?"

"Perfectly."

She has feelings for me. Yes! It's a place to begin. A terrific place. Still . . .

"So you're really okay with the idea of becoming a shifter?"

After a pause, she nodded. "I'm nervous, but at the same time I can't help but wonder what it will be like. You know, the process itself. Not to mention being stronger and faster, being able to defend myself with claws and really sharp teeth. It's kind of cool, now that I'm getting used to the possibility. I think I'll be disappointed if it doesn't happen."

"It might not," he said gently. "Melina didn't change after she and Terry mated."

"I know. If it doesn't, I'll deal with it." Lapsing into momentary silence, she played with his hair. "It's weird for me to think about being shifter, but at least I get a warning. I can only imagine what a shock it was for you guys."

"Damned right it was. Thought we were losing our minds at first."

She studied him, obviously chewing on something. "You told me that you, Zan, Aric, and Ryon were Navy SEALs. And you were all turned after you were ambushed on patrol. Right?"

"Yes, plus Raven, who's in Block R. Why?"

"So is that when your Psy abilities manifested? You were all able to do cool stuff after you became shifters?"

He frowned. "No, we had our abilities already. They just became much more powerful."

"Did any of the other men—the ones who were killed—did they have powers, too?"

"I don't know," he said slowly. "It's never occurred to me to ask."

"Did any of you know one another before you joined the Navy?"

"No, we met in BUD/S training and were placed on our team together. What are you getting at?"

"I'm not sure. It just seems strange that out of all the people in the military, a group of guys with Psy abilities ended up on the same team unbeknownst to one another, and all of you survived when so many others didn't. Doesn't that seem weird to you?"

Suddenly, Aric's earlier declaration returned.

Which would mean our high-up government friends—the assholes who're supposed to be on our side—lied to us. Ain't like that's never happened before.

A chill gripped his heart. What could it all mean? Were they played from the beginning, set up, used? The strong turned into paranormal soldiers, the weak discarded like broken toys?

That would be abominable. And it could be true.

"When you put it like that, it does," he said. "I don't know what to make of what's going on with NewLife and these experiments, disappearing Alpha Pack team members, dead bodies, what the government does or doesn't have a hand in, none of it. What I do know is I want out of this bed."

Mischief sparked in her blue eyes and she leaned over, nibbling his neck. "My poor wolf pup," she teased. "Feeling a bit anxious? Cooped up?" Her hand slid under the covers.

"Kira." His intended warning became a plea as her fingers sought their prize, rooting under his gown to find his lengthening shaft. "God."

"Let me help you get rid of some of that tension."

Her hand began stroke him, sending shivers of delight through his burgeoning erection, up his spine. "I'll make a mess," he gasped. "The doc will know what we've been up to."

"There won't be a mess," she promised him with a wink. "Sit back and enjoy, and I'll take care of everything."

When she flipped back the covers and exposed him, bent over his throbbing flesh, his dazed brain grasped her meaning. All half-formed thoughts of protest died on his lips and he groaned, arching his hips.

Her mouth surrounded him, took him in, hot and sweet. The sensation fired his blood, not to mention the sight of her blond head bobbing over his lap, his cock disappearing between her lips. Just the idea that she planned to swallow his essence nearly made him lose it way too soon.

"God, Kira!"

She hummed in apparent pleasure, small fingers squeezing, manipulating his balls as she sucked. The dual stimulation was challenging enough in holding off his orgasm, but when the hand slid down his perineum, ventured into his cleft to massage the forbidden pucker there . . . Jax almost came totally undone.

"Baby, I can't last," he rasped. "Please . . ."

Please stop? Or please eat him alive? He wasn't sure. His world had been reduced to a whorl of intense, mindless pleasure. Nothing existed but what she was doing to him, how unbelievably incredible it felt to surrender to her.

Mine!

Unable to hold back any longer, he erupted with a shout. On and on his cock pulsed as she drank him down, not missing a drop. After what seemed forever, his spasms finally stopped and she pulled off him, wiping the corner of her mouth.

"Oh, my God," he breathed, the words a reverent praise of her talents.

She gave him a self-satisfied grin. "Did that help?"

"Did it ever! I think my bones melted."

"Good, that was the plan." Kissing his cheek, she arranged his gown over his lap once more and fixed the covers. "Can you rest some now? You look tired."

"Not sure. Maybe I could take a nap," he mumbled, suddenly drowsy.

"Go ahead." She took his hand. "I'll be right here."

Worn out from the naughty interlude, Jax fell into an exhausted, sated sleep. When he woke again, hands were shaking him, urgent voices calling from far away. He tried to ignore them but they were persistent, and he finally managed to crack open his eyes, blinking against the sunlight that shone around the edges of the blinds.

"You're awake! Thank God." Kira smiled down at him, eyes shadowed.

"Did I sleep all night?"

"Yep." Melina beamed a penlight into his eyes. "It's a quarter past eight."

"Jesus," he muttered, jerking his head from the light. "That's my brain you're skewering."

"At least you still have one. Do you remember me bringing in a cot for your lady to sleep on? Us giving you more blood?" She slipped the wretched device into her coat.

He thought. "No. Must've been out of it."

"You were, but I thought you might've had some awareness. The fact that you didn't is telling, Jax."

"My body is failing." God.

"Faster than I expected. This is it—do or die. You're going to drink from your mate's wrist, gain some strength, and then I'm releasing you. Go where you like, but if you don't come back mated, there's no coming back," she said bluntly.

Kira winced, and he wanted to snap at Melina to use some sensitivity, but it wouldn't do any good. The doc didn't believe in candy-coating the facts.

"Remember what I said about what could happen to your abilities after mating. Now, I'll leave you two alone. As soon as you feel strong enough to get up, do it." Then she was gone.

Kira watched her go. "That woman is so hard to like. But for some reason, I do."

"Because she's a good person, just shit on by life. Now, give me your hand."

She did, and he nuzzled the delicate flesh inside her wrist. Flicked out a tongue and tasted. His senses might be shot, but her sweet vanilla and citrus came through, making him dizzy. He needed her so much.

Resisting the urge to bite, he grazed the skin with one canine, making the small cut so fast she barely felt it. Little drops beaded in the slice and he captured them, soothed the area with his tongue. As before, the flavor was so strong and heady, he couldn't wait to learn how it would feel to be truly joined.

Strength seeped into his bones, that soothing warmth returning. Along with a more insistent heat in his groin. He wasn't going to get any stronger without the mating. Now was the time.

"My clothes?"

"Here." She handed him a pile of freshly laundered jeans, a green shirt, socks, and shoes. "Zan brought them. Everyone's worried about you."

"They won't have reason to be, soon."

She blushed. "They're all going to know."

"And be jealous as hell." Sitting up, he swung his legs over the side of the bed. "If any of those dipsticks give you a hard time, remember that's just their way of showing you how much they like you. If they ignored you, then you'd have to worry."

"I suppose so."

He dressed quickly, glad that he felt pretty good. One a scale of one to ten? About a seven at the moment. He'd work with it.

"What do you say we go for a walk?" he asked with a grin.

"To your favorite spot by the stream?"

"Unless you'd rather drive into Cody. I can book us into a nice room, order some bubbly and—"

"I think the stream is the perfect spot. And you're the only high I need," she said, almost shyly.

"And I think that's the greatest thing anyone's ever said to *me*." Chest swelling, he stood and held out a hand. "Shall we?"

"Let's go."

Putting her hand in his, she allowed him to walk her outside, into the new day. She trusted him to take care of her, now and always.

He'd do anything not to break that trust.

Anything.

Staring out the window, Nick watched them go, with a heart heavy.

So little time left, and they didn't know. How short life is. How unfair.

Turning away from the glass, he clenched his fists. "This isn't a gift, it's a curse. Take it back," he whispered.

But no one listened, or answered. No one ever had.

Not once, from the day he was born.

As they walked, fingers linked, Kira's nerves started to get the best of her. Because the truth was, Jax was every fantasy come to life.

As he tugged her along, walking slightly ahead, she ogled his ass hugged just right in the well-loved jeans. His broad back flexing under his T-shirt, his trim waist. The scrolled tattoo winding lazily from under the right sleeve to trail down his arm. She couldn't wait to see the rest of it again, lick it. Taste his skin.

"What are you thinking about so hard?" Turning his head, he looked back at her, lips curving into a sensual smile.

For a second, her brain fritzed, totally short-circuited by his sheer beauty. Not the pretty kind, but dangerous. All raw, sexual male. She'd never been one to prefer any sort of facial hair, but his goatee was the perfect complement to his masculine face and bad-boy, motorcycle-riding image.

"Earth to Kira."

She shook herself out of the drools. "Sorry. Too much on my mind, I guess."

"I'll fix that by blowing all those pesky thoughts to dust." He grinned at her, his meaning clear.

"I'm sure you will." His words reminded her of something. "What did Dr. Mallory mean when she told you to remember what can happen to your abilities when we mate? Can something go wrong?" The idea of anything happening to him scared her.

"Not wrong, exactly." He paused. "She told me the bonding could negate my powers for a while."

"Oh, no! Will you get them back?"

"Most likely."

"You seem pretty nonchalant about it."

"I'm not. But when it's a choice between losing my abilities or my life . . ."

Not much of a choice at all. She hoped he didn't regret their mating, but couldn't bring herself to say so. In spite of nature forcing life-altering changes upon them, she and Jax had formed their own connection. One based on mutual trust, friendship, and attraction. Nothing could take that from them.

Except death.

She shivered.

"You cold, baby?"

"No, I'm fine." She smiled and the worry in his eyes eased.

When they reached his favorite spot by the stream, he turned and gathered her into his arms. Pulling her flush against his hard body, he cupped her face. "Relax, angel. I'm not going to devour you. At least not until you're begging for it."

She was there already. His hands on her face, the heat of his erection burrowing into her tummy, his strength surrounding her ... Oh, yes. She wanted more of that, with the two of them naked, tangled, and sweaty.

His kiss was slow and thorough. Sweeping and exploring. Like a master, he eased her gently under his spell, and she wondered whether he might be part Sorcerer. She rubbed against him, needing to be closer, to crawl inside him.

Breaking the kiss, she knelt on the spongy ground and unzipped his jeans. "First I want to devour *you*," she said, voice husky. "Will you beg for it?"

His eyes darkened with predatory hunger. "Make me."

"I like that sort of challenge."

Hooking her fingers in the waistband, she pulled down his jeans, slid them off. He kicked off his running shoes, stepped out of the pants, and spread his legs, standing with his feet braced slightly apart, and then pulled off his shirt. All of the glorious skin she'd been eager to touch and taste was right there, a living sculpture of male beauty.

Reaching out, she cradled his heavy balls, squeezing, manipulating carefully. He moaned and widened his stance, encouraging her to do what she wished. What she wanted was to drive him out of his mind with a tongue bath, and so she grasped the base of his cock, lifting his stiff erection. Bending forward, she licked the silky sac, determined not to leave an inch unloved. He squirmed, buried a hand in her hair and thrust his hips, clearly enjoying the attention.

Getting into her ministrations, she kissed and suckled each orb as though savoring a juicy peach. Delicious, too, smooth and creamy, just like—

"Kira," he rasped.

"Mmm. Ready to beg yet?"

Whatever reply he might've made was silenced when she swallowed him to the root. A cock this magnificent deserved her undivided attention and she gave it, sucking him with firm pulls, laving the underside, worrying the sensitive flesh with lips and a slight grazing of her teeth.

Her wolf lasted longer than she expected, and she smirked to herself as he disengaged with a low growl of warning. "Get those clothes off, because if I do it there won't be anything left but scraps."

"You wouldn't want me to traipse back in the buff?"

His eyes narrowed. "I don't share."

"Good to know, because neither do I."

Kneeling, he helped divest her of the pink cotton shirt she'd worn this morning, followed by the lacy white bra. Both were tossed aside and he literally crawled up her body, pushing her to lie on the grass. Straddling her, he tweaked a nipple and it immediately perked to attention, seeking more of the same. But he moved on, attacking her jeans with the same impatience she'd demonstrated, stripping them and her underwear down her legs. The shoes and socks went next, and the whole pile joined the rest of their clothing.

"Christ, you're so pretty," he breathed in reverence.

She resisted the impulse to cover herself. Barely, and because she knew he didn't like it when she did. "I'm happy you think so."

"It's a fact." Bending, he sniffed her neck, inhaling her scent. "So good. Sweet. You're not afraid of the Big Bad Wolf eating you up?"

"Should I be?" Oh, God, he felt so good above her, his hard cock rubbing her belly.

"Oh, *yeah*. Be very afraid," he deadpanned.

Then he gave her nipples his full attention, treating them with the same care she'd lavished on his balls. He suckled, scraped, and licked, making every nerve ending sizzle in joy. She clutched his short black hair as he began to kiss his way south, humming to himself in pleasure. Callused fingers parted her folds and it was his turn to drive her wild, his tongue lapping at her clit, her channel, sending tendrils of delight spiraling through her abdomen and to her limbs.

Somehow he knew when she couldn't take anymore, but instead of backing off, he upped the ante. "Am I driving you crazy, baby? Who's going to beg now?"

A smart remark hovered on her lips—and was instantly forgotten when his mouth went back to work on her slit. And when a slick finger teased her back entrance.

Her eyes widened and she gasped. "What are you doing?"

"Relax, angel," he purred. "Give yourself to me. Just feel."

She started to refuse. She really did. But the wonder of his tongue combined with the finger rubbing sensually around the sensitive ring of muscles *there* reduced her to a puddle of mush. He was never too invasive, simply teased and stroked in time to feasting on her, to the point that she was nothing but his.

"Jax, please!"

"Please what, my angel?"

"Fuck me," she begged. "I need you, inside me."

"What my lady wants, she gets." He sounded rather pleased with himself.

Deftly, he urged her to flip over and grabbed her hips, pulling her up on her knees with her ass poking in the air. Offered to him. The man and the beast.

She knew what would come with the fucking and she welcomed it. Wanted it hard and feral, no holding back, and she made sure he understood. "Take me, like a wolf takes his mate. Show me how it can be."

"I'll show you how it *is*," he asserted. "You're *mine*."

The blunt head of his cock pushed into her, sliding deep. He filled her to the hilt, his strong body covering hers, and still she needed more. Her blood called to him, every cell in her body yearning for the completion only he could give them. To be his Bondmate, the one at his side for life, loving him. Fighting their battles, celebrating their triumphs. She wanted it all, with him.

"God, yes," he hissed. Gripping her hips, he began to thrust, slamming into her core with almost brutal force, skirting the edge of pain.

Breathless, she moaned, pushing back onto him. Tempting him to increase the intensity, to own her. Spearing her again and again, he drove them higher, to the brink. His nails lengthened, became claws needling her flesh. He seemed to grow bigger all over as he pounded into her channel, his muscles taut and unyielding.

About to go over, she reached back, trying to touch his face. "Jax, I can't . . . Please!"

Sitting back, he brought her into his lap, the position burying his cock deep. Instinctively, she tilted her head to the side, offering her neck in submission to her mate. A finger brushed aside her hair and he licked the vulnerable skin where her neck and shoulder met.

"You're mine."

"Yes, I'm yours! Don't make me wait any longer . . ."

He struck, sinking his canines into her flesh like razors slicing through paper. She cried out, the pain unlike any she'd ever known, and then . . . ecstasy.

Pure, white-hot pleasure that boiled and rose for about five seconds and then exploded in the most powerful orgasm she'd ever experienced. Screaming, she writhed on his lap, spasming around his cock. Her release triggered his and he poured into her, warmth bathing her womb. She opened her eyes and was shocked to see the forest through a golden glow, almost like a veil surrounding them. A glow that sank right through their skin as they remained connected, winding into a tangible golden thread that ran between them.

From her heart to his.

Jax stiffened with a hoarse shout, emptying the last of his seed and then slumped, still holding on, his face in the crook of her shoulder where he'd bitten.

How long they remained there, joined, she didn't know. Finally he raised his head and peppered her neck, her cheek, with kisses. "Are you all right, baby?"

"I think I blew a fuse," she teased.

"I know I did." He sighed, and then said, "My wolf is gone, and so are my other gifts."

"What? How can you tell?" Something like panic pushed at her breast.

"I just can."

Easing off his lap, she sat facing him. "Well, try to shift."

"Okay." Scooting back some, he remained kneeling, and concentrated. After a couple of minutes, he shook his head. "Nothing."

She reached out, took his hand. "Oh, Jax, I'm sorry. But Dr. Mallory said they'd probably return," she reminded him.

He laughed. "I know. I was thinking how ironic it is that five years ago, when I was turned into a shifter, I thought I'd been cursed. I would've done anything to reverse it. And now I feel quite naked."

"You are naked, in case you forgot."

Fortunately, he responded to the tease. "Oh, my God! You're right. What're we gonna do about that?" Playfully, he got on his hands and knees and stalked her.

"I haven't the foggiest." Giggling, she began to inch backward. "Hey, you're bullet wound is healed! I guess that means something good came from bonding, huh?"

"It means I'm in good enough shape to stalk my mate."

He leaped, and she jumped up with a squeal, trying to run. She couldn't get away, though. Even without his abilities, he was still faster and stronger than she was. He easily caught her, spinning them around, and took them both to the ground.

He turned, taking the brunt of the fall, giving her a cushion for the landing. And she had to admit, she didn't mind landing on him at all.

"I'm your captive—now what will you do with me?"

He smiled, his canines oddly normal. "I'm sure I'll think of something."

Fifteen

"**D**id you mean it when you called the compound *home*?"

"Hmm?"

Kira didn't even look away from the TV as she munched on her popcorn, and Jax couldn't help the swell of love that blossomed in his chest, leaving little room for anything or anyone else. The little imp had gotten most of the team hooked on watching that ghost-hunting reality show. Even Sariel was sitting cross-legged on the floor with his wings draped around himself, eyes wide, fixated as though he'd never seen anything so fascinating.

"I said, is this home to you? That's what you called it the other night, when we were returning from the rescue."

"Did I?" She looked at him thoughtfully. "Of course I meant it. Why?"

He shrugged. "I was thinking you might want to move out and get our own house someday. I'm not required to live here. It's just easier."

Her eyes softened. "Honey, I don't care where we live. Home is wherever you are."

"Aww." He tweaked her nose.

"Oh, gag me," Aric snarked, but without much heat.

"Shut up, dickless. You're just jealous."

"Hey, I can get my knob polished anytime I want—without the ball and chain hanging on my ankle."

"Okay, boys, don't get started," Kira scolded with a frown. "I'm trying to watch this."

Jax and his friend made a face at each other over her head, and then he went back to his favorite pastime of studying his new mate. Was it his imagination, or did she have this really healthy glow surrounding her? He liked her pale blond hair pulled back into a ponytail, her cute nose, her little feet. He especially liked the mark of his canines at the curve of her neck, the two small punctures having made a faint, permanent scar in the four days since they'd bonded.

"Quit staring at me," she muttered, crunching more popcorn.

"Why? I love looking at you."

"You're giving me a complex."

"A good one, I hope."

"Is there such a thing as a *good* complex?" Exasperated, she plopped the bowl down on her lap and opened her mouth, most likely to give him hell, when Nick's voice broke in over the building's intercom.

"Alpha Pack, Kalen, Kira, and A.J., to the meeting room, stat."

"Goddamn," Aric grumbled. "The show's only half over. What's so freakin' important it can't wait until tomorrow? Can *I* move out and get my own place?"

"I'll help ya," Ryon quipped.

Jax didn't blame his friend for being pissed. Most folks didn't live at work twenty-four-seven and had no idea how annoying it was to be on call day and night. With an assortment of curses and rumbles, everyone rose except the Fae prince, Chup asleep in his lap, who waved them off without looking up from the TV.

Setting aside her bowl and giving the program a look of regret, she fell into step beside Jax for the short walk to the meeting room. When they trooped in, Nick was already waiting, as were Melina and Mac. That and the late hour could only mean some news was breaking, classified as "need to know ASAP." The team's lazy demeanor rolled off like oil on wax paper, and they took their seats, completely alert and professional. Not one complaint passed anyone's lips; they'd already voiced them all.

"I appreciate you all being so prompt and giving up part of your evening," Nick began. "You know I wouldn't interrupt unless it was extremely important. Dr. Mallory and Dr. Grant report that it appears our two rescued shifters will survive. One of them finally awakened a short while ago and is talking. What we've learned from him is the reason I've called you here." He paused before continuing. Jax and some of the others exchanged glances, but no one spoke.

"The shifter who's awake is a jaguar named Beck. He told us the other guy is an eagle named Archer who'd been held captive longer than him or any of the others, as far as he knows. He also said there were other captives who were moved a day or so before we arrived, but he's not sure exactly when because there was no way for them to measure time."

Zan spoke up. "How many and who were they?"

"According to Beck, three were moved. Two humans and another shifter." He took a deep breath. "I don't want you guys to get your hopes up, but . . . the shifter's name was Micah."

"Christ," Jax breathed.

"What the fuck?"

"Why were we told he was dead?"

"And where the hell is he now?"

"If he's alive, what about Terry, Jonas, Phoenix, and Ari?"

Nick weathered the explosion, fielding their barrage of questions as best as he could under the circumstances. "I know, and believe me, I'm with you all the way. If this is *our* Micah, then we've got a big fucking problem because we've been lied to, and maybe worse. But we have to take this one step at a time. Let me turn the floor over to Dr. Mallory for a few minutes so she can explain how what we've learned from Beck supports the findings from our lab and coincides with the information we liberated from NewLife."

Giving Nick a short nod, she moved forward. Jax thought she looked rather pale, and figured the idea of Terry perhaps being alive had shaken her. Badly. She wouldn't wish him dead, but theirs hadn't been a match made in heaven by any means.

"As I told Nick, the two new shifters will make a full recovery. The speed with which this has occurred is nothing short of remarkable, and our tests on Beck and Archer have given us some startling information." Scooping a sheaf of papers from the table, presumably her notes, she relayed their findings.

"Both shifters' bodies contain abnormally high levels of epinephrine, which has super-stimulated their adrenaline. As a side note, this overdosage may account in part for heart failure in at least two of the four bodies we received from the coroner that were found locally. Anyway, in our two survivors, their systems absorbed and accepted the drug, as well as a cocktail of a designer drug that has, by all indications, altered their DNA to contain more animal than human genes."

"And this means?" Nick prompted.

"In layman's terms, some of the doctors and researchers at NewLife are attempting to create a breed of highly advanced super-shifters. They're taking existing shifters and fit humans, enhancing their greatest and deadliest genetic strengths, and striving to perfect the process of making an intelligent man-beast that has Psy gifts and is virtually indestructible."

Ryon's eyes were wide. "Like that creature from the old movie *Predator* with Arnold Schwarzenegger? They couldn't kill that fucker."

"The premise is similar," Melina allowed, "except NewLife is working with humans and shifters, not extraterrestrials, and using DNA and genes rather than technology per se. But creating a ruthless, unbeatable soldier is the bottom line."

"That's what the dead guys were trying to tell me," Ryon said, looking tired. "They're agreeing with you right now, all excited. They've been driving me crazy."

Jax felt sorry for him, and hoped he got some peace from the ghosts.

"This all makes sense, except for why Beck and Archer were in such bad shape when we found them," Kira put in. "If they're strong enough to recover so fast, then why would the bastards starve and torture them?"

Nick answered that one. "How do you produce the best warriors? By breaking them down and building them back up again and again, until nothing can stand in their way. The weak perish; the strongest are made stronger."

"That's . . . evil."

"Yes," their boss agreed. "It's horrible for the victims, unethical, and dangerous for humanity. Worse, according to Beck these aren't volunteers in an aboveboard, sanctioned program. They're being stalked and kidnapped from all walks of life and forced into being test subjects. Beck said that he and Archer were two of the few who'd survived all of the doctors' engineering so far, and had been scheduled for 'mind reprogramming.'"

"Brainwashing," Melina clarified.

Jax sat forward. "We were talking about who's at the top of the pyramid. Does Beck know who they are?"

Nick sighed. "I wish. He says Orson Chappell's name has been whispered, and from what he's managed to overhear there are at least two figures above him. And every last doctor, researcher, or other employee who's in on the program is terrified of them."

A heavy silence followed. This whole deal was more terrible, more far-reaching, than any of them had envisioned.

"What now?" Zan asked.

"We put NewLife under surveillance," Nick said. "They might lie low at the Vegas location for a while, but eventually they'll have to make a move. I want to place two of you in Vegas, and two more to watch their building in Dallas, Texas. Just document everything and everyone you see coming in and out, nothing more. We need to learn where they're holding other shifters and humans so we can plan our next hit."

"I'll take Vegas," Aric volunteered.

Ryon piped up. "I go with him."

"Zan and I will take Dallas," Jax said. He was surprised when Nick vetoed the idea.

"No fieldwork for you until your abilities return."

"With due respect, I was a human soldier before I was turned, and a damned good one."

"We can't take any chances on this one. I'm sending Kalen with Zan, since he did so well in his first run."

Aric snorted. "Hard not to do good when you don't

have to *do* anything but stand outside and hold up the wall." That earned him a venomous look from the Sorcerer, which he ignored.

Nick shot a disapproving glare at Aric. "You know my expectations. If you're part of this team, ditch the attitude and act like it. You're mentoring a new recruit, so suck it up and teach him."

So Kalen was in. That was news, but Jax thought he'd fit in well. Whether their boss would offer a spot on the team to A.J. remained to be seen. He was human, after all.

Put in his place, Aric flushed and nodded. "Yes, sir. Sorry, witch."

"*Sorcerer*. Witches are female," Kalen said stiffly, expression pissed.

"Hey, couldn't tell through all the makeup. My bad."

Nick closed his eyes briefly as though he was getting a headache, and then returned his attention to group. "Tomorrow morning is soon enough to head out. Both teams, come by my office before you leave and get the city maps showing the NewLife buildings and the structures around them so you can plan where to set up surveillance. Check in with me daily whether you see anything or not. Questions? Good. Scram."

As the others guys filed out, Jax approached Nick. "Is there anything specific you want me to do while I'm hanging around here?"

"Yeah." His boss gave him a smile that seemed sad for a moment. "Get to know your mate and recover your strength. Life's too short to spend it working all the time."

Jax stared at him for a moment. It was so odd, the way he said that. But the weird feeling passed and he shrugged. "I can do that. And hopefully by the time we're ready to move, I'll be at full speed."

"I'm sure you will."

Turning, he walked to the door where Kira waited, and took her hand. "Back to the living room?"

A seductive smile curved her mouth. "Suddenly I'm not interested in television anymore."

"I love your devious little mind. And you look so sweet on the outside, too."

"It's part of the disguise."

"Let's go somewhere private so I can strip it off."

Laughing like teenagers, they stumbled to his quarters and practically fell inside, leaving a trail of clothes to his bedroom. He made love to her until they were exhausted and sated, and fell asleep wrapped in each other.

He awoke in the night, heart pounding, terrified by something. Not a nightmare, but what?

Shadows. The awful sensation of falling.

But the bedroom was quiet, only the gentle sounds of Kira's breathing next to him. Her warmth snuggled in, where she belonged.

It was nothing. Spooning, he pulled her close.

They were together, and he wouldn't let anyone tear them apart.

Holding Chup in her lap, Kira giggled, thinking if she could sell tickets to this show, she'd be rich.

Watching shifters, a handful of humans, and a faery play football—correction, make that *attempting* to play football—was the funniest damned thing she'd ever seen. The shifters weren't half-bad, though, and it was a good thing the NFL didn't know about them. Humans would never again stand a chance in the world of sports.

Mac blocked A.J., who tried to tackle Nick, the quarterback for her side. Nick drew back his arm and fired the ball at Sariel in the end zone. His pass was way too high, but the Fae prince spread his azure wings and leaped, catching the ball and floating to the ground in an impressive move.

"Flag!" Aric yelled, pointing an accusing finger at the receiver. "That's cheating, asshole!"

Sariel arched a brow and spiked the ball. "Whatever works."

Kira busted up laughing and got a glare from the red-head, but she couldn't help it. The whole thing was hysterical: Sariel strutting around like he'd won the Super Bowl and Aric pissed as hell, his competitive nature coming to the fore. She should've felt bad and would have if the red wolf wasn't such a pain in the butt. He had to learn to take it if he was gonna dish it out.

Jax playfully ruffled Aric's hair. "It's just a game, man. Lighten up."

"You lighten up." His friend swatted his hand away and stalked off to rejoin the game.

They watched him go, and Jax shook his head. "That guy's a trip. Always has been, even in the military."

"I can't imagine him being disciplined enough to last in the SEALs," she commented. "He's got a great sense of humor that comes through, but most of the time he's so snarky and sarcastic."

"Well, on that score he's changed a lot," Jax said quietly. "But then, we all have."

"I can only imagine." Her stomach lurched, but she put it down to being reminded of what had happened to Jax and his team.

Clearing his throat, he changed the subject, she suspected, before sadness could dampen the mood. "Don't know what we're going to do with all these displaced shifters, not to mention Sariel. Before long, we'll be running a home for wayward outcasts of the supernatural world."

They both looked to the Fae prince, who was still

cheating at football, him and Nick against the doctors and Aric.

The idea had merit and she looked at Jax, wondering what he'd think when he learned she was way ahead of him. "So? Why not?"

"A home for paranormal outcasts? For real? You're kidding."

"No, and what's wrong with that? You guys go out and destroy the dangerous, evil creatures, but what about the good ones? You've already got the holding cells for those who need rehabbing, the clinic for sick ones, extra apartments, and now the personnel starting with me and Sariel."

"Why do I get the feeling you've already discussed this with Nick?"

"Because I have." He didn't appear particularly happy, and she bit her lip. Her stomach lurched again, and she started to feel hot.

"I think you're taking on a lot, especially considering we've only been mated two weeks." Crossing his arms over his chest, he tried to look stern. And failed. A smile quirked his sexy mouth. "But as long as we still have time for us, I'm all for this, if it's what you want to do."

"Whew! You had me worried for a minute," she said in relief. With a trembling hand, she wiped a bead of sweat from her brow. "I thought we were going to have our first argument."

Crouching, he peered into her face, brow furrowed in worry. "Baby, what's wrong? It's not that hot today—and you're shaking."

"I—I don't know. Breakfast didn't agree with me, and the nausea seems to be getting worse."

"You want to go lie down?"

"I think that would be—" A terrible cramp hit her gut, a fist twisting her insides. Crying out, she slumped sideways clutching her belly. Chup, dumped from her lap, squeaked in alarm and ran to Sariel.

"Kira! Baby, what's wrong?" The pain was so bad, she couldn't speak. "Melina!" he shouted, pulling Kira into his arms.

Agony shot through her jaws, her torso, arms and legs. Every inch of muscle and bone seemed to be turning inside out, imploding. Curling in her mate's arms, she screamed, clutching at his shirt.

"Oh, God, what's wrong? Melina, do something!"

The doctor's voice came as if from a long tunnel. "How long ago did you bite her?"

"Uh, two weeks. But— Oh, Jesus. She's changing."

"I believe so. Talk to her, Jax. Try to calm her down."

His rough hand smoothed the hair from her scorching face. "Angel, I'm so sorry," he rasped. "But it's going to be all right. This first time hurts like hell, but it gets better, I promise."

She nodded, wanting to believe him. But a scared part of her knew it didn't always work out. She thought of their feral teammate, Raven, still isolated in his lonely cell in Block R. The one she hadn't yet been able to reach.

And she could very well end up next to him.

Muscles, bones, and tendons began to stretch and pop. The pain was excruciating and she screamed on and on while Jax desperately tried to soothe her, to no avail. Now she knew firsthand why a wolf shifter could go crazy.

Don't let me end up like Raven. Please.

Her screams became canine yelps. The hand clutching Jax's shirt became a paw, the rest of her body following. Reshaping until she lay in Jax's lap, his fingers buried in her fur.

Fur.

"Here, baby. Let me untangle you from these clothes." He helped free her and she looked up into his smiling face. "Wow, aren't you beautiful? You're a silver wolf like me, but not nearly as big."

Everyone gathered around, beaming and agreeing with her mate, whose blue-gray eyes were shining with pride.

Beautiful? She was completely freaked. Scrambling, she climbed off his lap and stood trembling on four slender legs. Frantically, she tried looking down at herself, and behind at her bushy tail. She tried wagging it, and it worked.

Oh, shit!

This couldn't be happening. Not yet. She wasn't ready.

Panicking, she scrambled backward, her first instinct to run. But the awkwardness of suddenly having four legs to control instead of two, plus the shape of her new form, trying to get used to redistributing her weight, was too much of a challenge all at once. Her legs tangled and she went down in a heap and sat up with a whine of distress.

"Kira, you're all right," Jax soothed, crouching beside her. Gently, he stroked her ears. "Easy, baby. There's nothing to be afraid of."

That was fine for him to say. He was already used to this. Tentatively, she stood again and looked around at the gathered group. Fear rose once more to override his words, and she did what came naturally—she pressed against his side and glared at everyone else, giving a low, ominous growl.

"Let's leave them alone," Mac said to their friends. "Come on."

They followed her back into the building, and Kira breathed a sigh of relief. Somehow, she felt better now that everyone wasn't staring. She took comfort in her mate's presence, strong and solid, easing her fright with his touch. She looked to him as he continued to stroke her face, her ears.

"See? You're fine. Try taking a few steps for me?" Standing, he moved back a few feet. "Just this far. You can do it."

She studied the distance doubtfully, the scant space stretching like a mile. But she moved one paw forward, placed it on the ground. Then another and another, until she'd moved all four and taken her first real steps. A tiny bit of excitement began to bloom in her chest and she smiled at Jax. Or thought she was smiling, but wasn't sure.

"That's it," he praised, beaming. "Now the rest of the way."

She did, slowly at first. Then a bit faster, until she'd covered the ground between them in no time. Arching a brow, he issued a challenge.

"Pretty good, but see if you can catch me."

He took off at a jog, not anywhere near as fast as she suspected he could run, but enough to test her new abilities. The predator in her exulted in the prospect of a chase, and running down her prize, and she bolted after him.

And promptly tripped over her gangly legs and went rolling, getting grass in her nose. Sneezing, she jumped up and spied her quarry making his escape—laughing, the jerk!—and she took off again. This time with much more success.

With every stride, her new wolf gained confidence in her control. Still, no one was more surprised than Kira when she caught up to Jax, gathered herself and leaped, and took him to the ground. They landed in a heap, his breath rushing out in an *umph*. Rolling, pulling her upper half onto his chest, he started laughing in pure joy. It was impossible not to be affected, and she licked his cheek.

"Not afraid anymore, are you?"

Hesitating, she realized she wasn't. Still a bit over-whelmed, but not scared. Because her mate was here, and he'd take care of her. She shook her head and he smiled.

"Good. Now, watch this." Slowly, he stripped off his clothes and then . . . he shifted. A handsome wolf, larger than her, stepped forward and greeted her, licking her muzzle.

You're gorgeous, my pretty mate.

Stunned, she blinked at Jax. *You can hear me?*

Loud and clear! Cool, huh? I guess Ryon isn't the only one who can do this after all—mates can!

She thought about that. *Yeah, it's cool. Wonder if we can do this in human form.*

I think so. We'll try it. Are you still in pain?

Not anymore. How do I change back?

Later. Let's run first!

But . . . you don't have your abilities back.

I do now—or at least I can shift. I think it was tied to you somehow. I felt my wolf return when you changed.

What about the Timebending thing?

Don't know. I can't feel it, though. Unconcerned, he ran around her, nipping at her flank and dancing around.

Watch it, buddy. I'll bite back.

That might be sort of fun, he teased.

He took off and she raced after him, surprising herself with the happy bark that came out in place of a laugh. Too frigging weird!

She tried to keep up with him, but started to fall behind. Running on four legs for a prolonged period was going to take some adjustment, and his stride was quite a bit longer than hers. She managed pretty well, leaping over rotting logs and dodging trees, but winced when she occasionally hit a sharp pebble in the trail that hurt her paws. Those would need some toughening up.

At one point, he glanced behind to see her struggling and stopped, waiting for her to catch up. When she did, he greeted her with affectionate licks to her muzzle—canine kisses. Nice, but strange.

When they started off again, he slowed to stay beside her, keeping their pace at more of a leisurely trot. Now she had the opportunity to marvel at how her senses were overwhelmed by the sights, sounds, and smells, all made much more sharp and clear because of her new status as a shifter.

It was like she could see each leaf on the bushes and trees. Smells hit her nose, those of other animals who'd been this way, or were hiding nearby. Her wolf half catalogued them for future reference, and she knew she'd recognize each of them again when she encountered them.

They reached Jax's spot by the stream, which she thought of as theirs, and took a long drink. Afterward, she stared at her reflection. A wolf with blue eyes and creamy fur tipped in black and silver stared back at her, pretty enough to be on any nature postcard.

See? I told you. His voice in her head was so happy. Proud. *You're stunning.*

Thank you. You're awfully handsome yourself. Sidling close to him, she nuzzled his face. *This is amazing.*

And the best part is, I never have to be alone again.

You've had your friends, your pack.

It's not the same as a mate.

I suppose it wouldn't be. Neither of us will be alone.

It struck her how fortunate she was to have Jax to help her through the transition. He'd been alone, no one to ease his fears the way he'd done for her. It made her love him even more.

Suddenly, he shifted and was a man again. An extremely sexy man kneeling by the stream, stroking her soft fur in wonder. *Can you hear me now?*

Yes! Guess it works.

"Good," he said aloud. "Shift back for me, baby."

A ripple of fear went through her. *How?*

"Focus all your thoughts on your human form. Imagine your limbs reshaping, reversing the process."

Will it hurt as bad as before? Because I don't want to do that again.

"No, it shouldn't. And it gets easier every time. Trust me."

Okay. She concentrated hard, but nothing happened.

"You're too tense. Relax."

It took several more tries, and then without warning, it worked. The process began, her limbs, torso, and face morphing in reverse. She cried out, dismayed that it was nearly as painful as the first shift, her bones feeling as if they were being ground into dust. Pulling her into his lap, he held on, murmuring soft words of encouragement until she was herself again. Her breath sawed in and out of her lungs and the pain gradually dissipated. After a while she became aware that she was a very naked woman being held tightly by her equally buck naked and horny mate. His erection pressed against her rear.

"Thank you," she said hoarsely. Eyes wide, she felt her arms and legs.

"Everything is back to normal. You did great, angel." Worry clouded his expression again. "Are you sure you're all right?"

"Much better," she assured him, cupping his face. "I'm so glad you were with me when it happened."

"Me, too." Moving in, he kissed her soundly, urging her back onto the spongy loam.

She pulled him down with her, spreading her thighs,

beckoning him inside. "Here," she whispered. "Right where you made me yours."

Settling over her, careful to keep his weight from crushing her, Jax kissed her jaw, her neck, using a bit of fang and making goose bumps rise on her skin. Shifting his hips, he positioned the head of his cock at her entrance and pushed.

"So hot and wet for me," he murmured.

"Yes." Kneading his glorious ass, she pulled him inside, impatient to have him fill her completely. Inch by inch, he slid deep, groaning in pleasure. "Feels so good."

"Like that, baby?"

"Love you inside me."

"And I just love *you*."

She stilled. "You mean that?"

"It's not the sex talking. I love you, Kira," he said softly.

Even without the waves of emotion pouring over her, she read the truth in his eyes.

"I love you, too." Her throat closed, tears pricking her eyes. "Don't stop."

He didn't ask whether she meant loving her or making love *to* her. He just murmured "Never" in her ear and started moving. Shafted his cock in and out, slowly at first, driving her mad with the delicious sensation of being filled over and over, driving them closer to the peak. When his thrusts became faster, more forceful, she tried to hold off her orgasm, but it was getting impossible. Her nails sharpened to claws that dug into his back, fangs lengthened, and she found she liked this new side of herself.

"Bite me," he demanded. "Claim me like I claimed you."

The idea called to the most primal instinct in her body—to leave her mark on her mate.

Without hesitation, she struck, sinking her canines into the curve of his neck. His shout was one of pure rapture as his blood splashed her tongue, hot and rich. His release exploded inside her and she clung to him, her orgasm matching his. They rocked together for what seemed an eternity, and yet wasn't long enough.

After a few moments, she released his neck and peered at the puncture wounds, an absurd sense of pride swelling in her chest. *My mate.*

Yes. All yours.

Rolling to his back, he pulled her on top of him and they lazed for while. "This is perfect. I wish this moment would never end," he said in contentment.

She propped herself up, looking into his sated, sleepy face. "It doesn't have to. You could use that Timebending thing you can do and relive it over and over."

"True. But I can do that in my memories just fine." He kissed the end of her nose.

How sweet. She gave him a leisurely kiss and rested her chin on his chest. "If you could go back and relive any perfect moment in your life, which one would it be?"

His smile took her breath away. "You know I'm forbidden to use that 'gift' except in the direst of circumstances. And it doesn't work like that—remember, I can only bend it to gain back the last few minutes."

"I know, but *if* you could. Humor me."

He thought for a long moment. "None of them."

Disappointment stabbed her. "Why not?"

"Because the perfect moment can never be improved, and should be remembered, cherished, just the way it was. Like every moment I spend in your arms," he said. "We should just go forward and make more of them."

"Oh," she breathed. A tear slipped down her cheek. "You had to make me cry, didn't you?"

"Only happy tears, baby."

"I'm holding you to that."

"Same goes for you."

His arms tightened around her, and they didn't speak again for hours.

They said it all without words.

Sixteen

Their idyll lasted exactly one more week.

Three weeks after he'd mated with Kira, their guys in the field reported movement at both NewLife buildings in Las Vegas and Dallas. Aric and Ryon flew home from Vegas, while Zander and Kalen stayed put since most of the action seemed to be centered at the Dallas site. The minute Aric and Ryon got in, Nick called a meeting to discuss what they'd learned and what action to take next.

Everyone settled in, and he got to the point.

"Dr. Gene Bowman and Orson Chappell are moving their operation to the Dallas site. Aric and Ryon reported that they'd spent last week with a small crew, moving equipment out in the wee hours while most of the regular staff was gone. Two nights after the last load was moved, Zan and Kalen watched the same crew arrive in Dallas and spend the last few nights moving it all into the Dallas building."

"Any sign of captives?" Jax asked, body tense. He had a bad feeling about this op. Real bad.

"A couple of large square containers have gone in,

but they were covered. Could be cages, or they could be nothing. In light of the information we recovered from their computer, not to mention our rescued shifters, I'm betting on the former. And one more thing." Pausing, Nick looked right into Jax's eyes. "There was a woman with them."

Jax's blood froze. The room tilted slightly and he had to remind himself to breathe. Beside him, he was aware of Kira's sudden tension. He had to ask. "Was it Beryl?"

"Zan said she fit the description—tall, long dark red hair. But her skin wasn't burned."

Jax clenched his fists, barely aware of Aric's loud curse. "That can't be. I threw her into the fire and I saw her burn. Unless . . ."

"Unless her powers were greater than you thought," Nick finished. "She was a witch, right? Or is."

"Fuck." This couldn't be happening. That conniving, murderous bitch could *not* still be alive and working with Chappell on his sick scheme.

But she was, and had been all along. The truth was unavoidable, forming a knot of fresh guilt and shame in his gut. And now he knew he'd have to revise what he'd told Kira.

If he could bend time back far enough, he'd make certain Beryl was dead. And then maybe Micah and the others would be safe right now.

Clearing his throat, Aric leaned back in his chair, shoving a fall of auburn hair over his shoulder. "How're we goin' in? Quiet, or a fast strike?"

"Both carry bigger risk than before, because they'll be ready," Nick said. "What we need is a layout of the building to study first, and Kalen offered to take care of that."

The red wolf frowned. "How?"

"Magic. He'll demonstrate when we arrive." Nick glanced at the clock on the wall, which showed it was just past one in the afternoon. "We're going wheels up in four hours, same crew as before, except Kira won't be going in. She'll stay with Melina in the van."

His mate frowned, but didn't argue. Wouldn't do her any good, because Jax was in agreement with the boss on this one.

"Just so it's perfectly clear, our goal here is to shut down their operation, one facility at a time if need be. Destroy their research, and take out Chappell and his minions *if* they can't be captured alive. Be ready. A.J., you and Sariel hold down the fort."

"Yes, sir." Their newest man appeared a little disappointed.

Those were the breaks. The human was too green to join the party just yet. Kalen was an exception—he had quite the arsenal of tricks up his Goth sleeve.

The meeting broke up and those who were leaving in four hours went to pack and attend to other business. Jax took Kyra's hand and they headed toward their quarters. As they walked, he put the disturbing news about Beryl out of his mind for the moment and worked up the nerve to address the issue foremost in his mind.

"I have something to ask you," he began uncertainly.

"Shoot."

"It's about our living arrangement. You're always at my apartment and I figured, you know, that's a waste of space and . . ." He trailed off, feeling stupid. "I totally screwed that up."

She grinned up at him. "Are you asking me to move in with you?"

"Yes, I am. Will you?" Jesus, he'd never been so nervous. He felt like a boy asking a girl to the prom.

"Well, I'd need a better reason than it being convenient. I'm sorta picky that way," she said, poking him in the ribs.

Stopping outside the door to his quarters, he turned and pulled her into his arms. "Move in with me because I'm madly in love with my pretty mate and need you with me more than I need air to breathe."

She blinked. "Wow. I believe the only answer to that is yes!"

Picking her up, he hugged her to him and swung her around, laughing. Squealing, she hooked her legs around his waist and held on, then gave him a kiss that fried his brain.

"Dang, get a room." Ryon stepped out of his apartment, closed the door, and walked off.

"We intend to! She's moving in with me," Jax called to his retreating back. His friend waved and kept going.

Without letting go of his mate, he walked them inside and proceeded to show her just how happy he and his wolf were with her decision. They barely got packed and to the hangar on time. They loaded into the two Hueys, a little bit of déjà vu unsettling him for some reason. They'd come away from the first op successful, despite his life-threatening injury. He was back to full strength, his shifting abilities restored, if not his Psy gift, so there was no reason to think this op wouldn't be successful as well.

The ride in the flying tank was loud and boring, and he was glad when they landed. They climbed out to find themselves at a private hangar in a rural area outside Dallas that they'd never used before and didn't belong to them. Grant had pulled some strings and two plain, dark vans were waiting. Quickly, they loaded their gear and headed for the hotel close to downtown.

Kalen and Zan had booked two adjoining suites for the whole group so they could have plenty of room to move about without attracting too much attention. Forty-five minutes later the team was gathered around the dining table in one of the suites, where Kalen had placed a hunk of brick, right in the middle.

"So, are we ready to make a model?" Seemed he was talking more to himself than the group, since his green eyes were fixed on the brick. He took a couple of deep breaths, appearing to find his center or something, and smoothed a palm over the pendant on his chest.

Jax and Kira exchanged curious glances, and she shrugged. Sorcerers were interesting, for sure.

"With what, a hunk of stone?" Aric snorted, but the younger man ignored him.

In fact, Kalen seemed to forget about everyone as he focused all his attention on the object, holding his palms just above it as though warming his hands over a flame. "You're going to reveal to me your secrets, take the form of the whole. Show me," he murmured.

Softly, he began a chant in the strange language he'd used before, the words lyrical and hypnotic. Maybe Latin, but Jax wasn't sure. A blue light enveloped the brick under Kalen's palms, which was really cool. But it was nothing compared to his amazement when the brick began to break down. Grain by grain, swirling around the object like a miniature sandstorm, the brick growing smaller until there was only the sand.

Whirling, it appeared to grow in density. Multiplying and reshaping.

Four walls formed, stretched upward. From the walls, flooring ejected, creating four stories. Then dividers for the many rooms. Kalen chanted another spell and two of the walls disappeared, creating a cutaway section they could see through, like a dollhouse. He left off the roof.

Kalen stepped back, removing his hands, and the blue light vanished along with the wind. There on the table was a replica of the NewLife building, created by stone and magic. The Sorcerer wiped his brow, and then gestured to the model. "This should help."

"Fuckin' awesome," Hammer said, impressed.

Jax and the others agreed. Even Aric, who clapped Kalen on the back. "You're all right, kid. What can't you do?"

The younger man shrugged off his touch. "Plenty of stuff."

Sensing his discomfort, the redhead backed off. "Yeah, that's true of us all. Why don't we take a look at this thing so we can get going?"

With the spotlight off him, Kalen began to appear more at ease. As Nick got started, Jax caught Mac gazing at the Sorcerer with barely concealed sympathy—and perhaps something more. Oh, boy. If the doc wanted to bark up that tree, she might be in for a rough ride, if Jax's glimpse into Kalen's little slice of hell was any clue.

"This is going to prove invaluable," Nick said by way of praise of Kalen's work. He didn't belabor the point, though, to the Sorcerer's visible relief. "The building is located in an industrial area just a few miles from here. We'll park on a side street and go in as before. Luckily, this property has no fence, which will make the approach simpler. However, when we go in, we're going to split up. According to Kalen and Zan, there's a helicopter parked on the roof, so Aric and Ryon are going to scale to the top to cut off that escape route. Ryon, as our Telepath, will let us know when they're secure, and we'll bust inside. Quick strike."

A rumble of varying opinions followed the decision, but none voiced an outright objection. Everyone understood that no plan would be foolproof.

Nick went on. "Looking at the model, the first and second floors have the largest spaces, with the third and fourth floors divided into smaller areas. I'm guessing the bottom floor is reception and conference areas, based on the layout and their business of disease research, and dealing with the public. At least part of what they're doing is legit, and they must have the facilities to conduct studies. That's where the second floor comes in—I'm betting these are the lab and research areas."

"The third floor is basically two long hallways with rows of cubicles," Zan pointed out. "I'm betting these are the holding cells, which are convenient for the lab folks to access their subjects."

Nick nodded. "With the executive offices on the top floor. The setup keeps the captives away from the public, trapped between floors with no easy escape going up or down." He pointed to the model. "When Ryon gives the go-ahead, we'll bust in and take out the guard in the lobby with a tranquilizer. No killing unless necessary, and no elevators in case they cut the power. We'll take the stairs straight to the second floor, where Zan will download the hard drive and then destroy the database. Then on to the third and fourth floors, doing a sweep to make sure any prisoners are liberated and the building is clear, and then all of us back down to the first floor and we get the hell out."

"Seems simple enough," Jax said.

Aric leaned on the table. "Which is usually when we need to worry."

All too true. There was a weighty pause.

"We carrying?" Ryon asked.

"Personal choice, as always," Nick told him. "Some of you have abilities that more than make up for lack of a gun, so use your judgment."

Hammer, Nick, and Ryon were the only ones who opted for man-made firepower this time around. The rest, Jax included, preferred to rely on their own talents. To the skeptic, Jax would retort that they'd been carrying

M-16s in Afghanistan and it hadn't made a goddamned bit of difference to the pack of rogue shifters who slaughtered them. They might as well have been using flyswatters.

"We doing this tonight?" Aric asked their boss.

"No reason to wait. We'll head out at midnight; after Aric and Ryon secure the roof, we should be ready to take the building by one." Nick checked his watch. "It's almost nine. Everybody try to get some rest. You'll need it."

Mac and Melina took a bedroom, Kira another. Some of the team spread out on the sofas and the floor, and some sat at the tables, or paced. Jax and Nick were among those who couldn't sleep, and so they leaned against the counters in the small kitchenette talking in quiet tones. Something about Nick's demeanor struck him as off, but he couldn't put his finger on what.

"What's bothering you, Nicky?"

The man gave him a long, searching look, but shook his head. "Just thinking about tonight. Strategizing."

"It's more than that." An awful thought occurred him. "We're going to get our asses kicked, is that it?"

"Not exactly."

"Come on, don't give me that shit," Jax said irritably. "Tell me what's going to happen."

"You know I can't do that, Jax. I don't know everything, and even if I did—"

"I know. You can't interfere with free will. You can't change the future." Damn, this burned.

"It's not that I'm not allowed, it's that I *won't*. Every decision we make affects those around us in ways we can't possibly foresee," he insisted, his voice full of regret. "I learned that the hard way and it's a lesson I won't ever forget."

"We're going to fail tonight." A ball formed in his gut.

"Define failure."

"Meaning we're not going to accomplish every task we set out to do."

"Does anyone?"

"Damn it, Nick!"

"What do you want me to say?" He was getting angry, probably because he hated carrying his burden and was torn by the knowledge.

"Tell me if we're going to lose anyone," Jax hissed, grabbing the front of the man's shirt in his fist.

Nick's silence, the anguish on his normally hard features, told him all he needed to know. Slowly, Jax released his grip and sagged against the counter.

"Who? Is it me?"

His boss met his gaze, jaw clenching, obviously waging war with himself. Finally he pushed from the counter. "I'm sorry. Just watch your back tonight, okay?"

Cold numbed him to his toes. "You'll look after Kira if something happens to me. Promise."

"You know I'll take care of anyone in my fold. You have my word." For a few seconds, he debated saying more, then walked out of the kitchen.

Oh, God. It's me. I'm going to die.

What would Kira do after he was gone?

She'll grieve, but she'll be okay, in time. Nick and the others will take care of her. I know it.

Heart heavy, he went to the bedroom where his mate napped so peacefully. So pretty and innocent in sleep. His angel.

If they were alone, he'd make love to her until they had to leave. As it was, he contented himself with holding her in his arms, settling her head on his chest. Cuddling was loving, too, just as much as sex.

He kissed the top of her blond head. "I love you, baby. Always."

Mumbling, she snuggled closer. He counted himself a lucky man.

For a few more hours, he'd have everything he'd never known he wanted, until it was too late.

It would have to last an eternity.

Nick and Jax were acting weird.

As the team got ready to move just before midnight, Kira watched the two men speaking only when necessary, avoiding looking at each other directly. A couple of times, though, she caught the boss staring at her or Jax when he thought they weren't aware. Several times she tried to get one of them alone to learn the source of the tension, but with all the activity around them, it was impossible.

The most she and her sexy mate managed was a quick kiss as they left the suites behind and headed for the vans. In the parking garage, they divided into the same two groups riding together as before, and were off in a matter of minutes.

Jax clutched her hand for the short ride. No one spoke. The nicer, chic area north of Dallas soon gave way to the sparse, depressing run-down south side, with its haphazard mix of old apartment units, single frame homes, and businesses. Kira could see why Chappell and his goons would move at least part of their operation to this location—nobody in their right mind would want to hang out in this place. Even the police.

Hammer pulled onto a side street, parked right behind the first van, and said a quick prayer. "Lord, please watch over our tires and rims. Amen."

Jax and his friends snorted with laughter, and Kira smiled at the grim humor. Hammer never had too much to say, but when he did, it was either really funny, or really important. In this case, it was both.

She climbed out after Jax and he swept her into a prolonged hug, holding her against him as though he never wanted to let her go. A barrage of his emotions hit her at once—fear, regret, anger, and most of all, love. Pulling back, she searched his face, but his expression revealed nothing of the turmoil below the surface. She opened her mouth to ask him what was wrong, but he cut her off.

"Stay here and stay safe with Melina and Mac," he said. "I'll be back before you know I'm gone."

His kiss eliminated any further protest. She told herself she was worrying for no reason. His powers had returned and this wasn't his first rodeo. The whole team was there to watch one another's backs. Her mate would be fine.

He would.

"I'll be waiting," she said softly. "I love you."

"I love you more." His mouth quirked into a grin and then he turned to join his team.

As the hottest group of men she'd ever laid eyes on started out for their destination, the one who owned her heart gave her a wink over his shoulder.

Then he vanished into the night.

"Hey, he'll be okay," Mac said, putting an arm around her shoulder.

"Something's wrong." The words were wrenched from her soul. She'd never been so certain of anything.

"Trust him. You'll be snuggled together by dawn, after this is all over."

"Mac, I feel cold," she said quietly. "I just watched the love of my life walk away and I didn't do anything to stop him."

"But, honey, you couldn't have. Those guys are closer than brothers and where one goes, they all go. You might as well get used to it."

"I know. I'm sure I will, eventually." She gave Mac a brave smile, but wasn't feeling it. This op was big trouble. She could feel it in her bones.

Bad shit was going down, and she wouldn't relax until Jax was safely in her arms again.

"I don't like this. It's too quiet," Aric hissed.

Ryon rolled his eyes. "It's after one in the morning and there's, like, nobody here except us. You were expecting a marching band?"

"Smartass. I got a bad feeling is all I'm saying."

"Goes with the territory of breaking and entering. Ready?"

"Shit, yeah. Let's get this over with."

"Be careful," Nick told them.

Ryon gave them a thumbs-up and the pair disappeared around the corner, headed to the back of the building and the fire escape. From there, they'd scale to the roof.

Jax and his group kept to the shadows, pressed next to the building at a side entrance, waiting. Eight minutes later, Ryon's voice pushed into their collective consciousness.

Roof is secure. Let's kick ass!

Nick and Hammer positioned themselves on each side of the door, guns drawn. Jax delivered a punishing kick, busting in the door with one try, a feat he wouldn't have been able to accomplish if he was still human. Nick and Hammer led the team inside. They ran at a fast clip down the side corridor and into the lobby.

Where there was no security guard at the desk.

The group fanned out, circling, eyeing the large space. Nothing moved.

"The alarm isn't going off," Nick snapped.

Fear shot down Jax's spine. They'd lived this scene before. *Oh, God, it's a trap!*

"It's a setup!" he yelled. "Get out—"

Figures burst from the shadows all around them, became armed men bringing up their weapons. Flashes of gunfire erupted, the noise deafening in the open lobby. Nick and Hammer crouched, returning fire, taking out as many as they could, covering for the team.

Jax shifted, not taking precious time to strip off his shirt, glimpsed Zan doing the same, and then he scrambled out of his pants and shoes. Putting on a burst of speed, he leaped for the nearest gunman, taking him down. Before the bastard could shoot again, Jax ripped out his throat. A quick, easy kill. He whirled, seeking his next target, and saw his team had dispatched a number of their enemy, but several more remained.

His boss and Hammer had taken cover behind the guard's desk and were keeping the goons on the defensive, picking them off. Zan was struggling in wolf form with two men who had him pinned. Kalen stood off to the side of the melee, palms out, chanting. God knows what the kid was doing. Hopefully, turning all the fuckers into toads.

Jax ran for the two men who had Zan, but a blast of heat scored his flank. He spun and attacked the asshole who'd shot him, making short work of this one as he'd done the other. When he turned back, he spotted Zan unconscious, in human form, the two men dragging him to the closest exit.

In that moment, he understood that not all of them were meant to die. At least some of them were slated to be taken captive for use in Bowman and Chappell's hideous experiments. Just like the ambush six months ago.

Would Grant and the government have lied this time as well, told them Zan was dead?

Taking off across the distance, he launched himself at the man holding Zan's shoulders. Backpedaling, the guy dropped his burden, frantically reaching for the gun stuck in his pants. Jax was faster, clamping down on his wrist just as he drew the weapon and crushing flesh and bone in his jaws. Screaming, the gunman fell to the floor and, knowing he was incapacitated, Jax faced the other man, the one who'd had Zan's feet. Who now had his gun pointed right between Jax's eyes.

His heart stuttered and he waited for the shot that not even a shifter could heal.

The bastard grinned. "I'm gonna enjoy this."

But the shot never came. The grin became a grimace, his mouth twisting in pain, eyes going impossibly wide in their sockets. Jax watched, frozen by fascination and horror, as the guy just . . . shriveled. Like a grape drying out, turning into a raisin.

And then he collapsed, nothing but a bag of skin and bones. Just like all of his armed comrades, lying everywhere.

What the fuck?

At the edge of the lobby, Kalen lowered his palms and leaned against a support column, clearly drained. "People are mostly made of water," he informed his stunned team. "Remove that element and there isn't much left. As you can see."

Then he slid down the column and passed out.

Jax took a step toward Kalen, but Ryon's urgent voice pushed into his head.

Need some help up here— we're outnumbered! They're trying to take Aric!

Shit! Jax ran for the stairwell, shifted to human briefly

just to get the access door open, shifted back and kept going. His preternatural speed was much greater in wolf form and he covered the floors quickly.

He just prayed he was fast enough to avert disaster.

Beside the van, Kira paced, chewing her thumbnail.

"Honey, he'll be all right," Mac soothed. "Come into the van and sit down."

"I can't. Something's wrong. This whole evening it's like the world has been slightly off its axis, and now it's worse."

"Trust him. He's an experienced soldier and—"

Oh, God, it's a trap!

Kira froze, gasping. "Jax."

Mac grabbed her arm. "What is it?"

"He said it's a trap." The blood drained from her face, and she wrenched her arm from Mac's hold. "They're in trouble!"

"Kira, you can't go! Jax wants you to stay here where you'll be safe. You know that!" Her friend moved to block her way.

"I'm not cowering out here while my mate is in there and something terrible is happening, so don't try to stop me," she warned. The growl in her voice let Mac know she meant it. She'd put her on the ground if necessary.

Stepping around her friend, she sprinted down the street. The building seemed too far away. It took only a couple of minutes to reach the side door they'd broken down to gain entry, but it might've been forever. She covered the distance to the lobby quickly, and drew up short at the horrible sight.

Nick and Hammer were bleeding, but were crouched over Zan and Kalen, tending to them. All around them, what must've been the enemy were sprawled on the

floor. And they were shrunken and dried like prunes.
God.

"Where's Jax?" she choked out. "Tell me!"

"Roof," Hammer said. "But don't—"

She didn't wait to hear him order her not to go.
Wouldn't have done any good. Quickly, she found the
stairwell, giving a silent thanks to Kalen for the model
they'd studied. Once inside, she stripped and concentrated, calling to her wolf.

The change wasn't nearly as painful as the very first
time. She'd had plenty of practice during her runs with
Jax, and she was getting good at it. On all fours, she took
a second to adjust to her wolf senses—and scented her
mate. Smelled his fear, his determination.

Following in his wake, she bolted up the stairs.

Jax burst onto the roof and into chaos.

His friends were under attack, Ryon in his silver wolf
form, battling two men on his own. Two more were dragging Aric toward the waiting helicopter, hands bound
behind his back with silver cuffs. Which explained why
the red wolf hadn't been able to change, or even unleash
his fire on them. He couldn't use his telekinesis to move
objects while bound, either.

A glance in the helicopter confirmed his fears. Dr.
Bowman and Chappell were waiting in the craft, and
they weren't alone. Beryl, Jax's traitorous former lover,
sat in the open doorway, the face he'd once thought so
beautiful pulled into an ugly smirk.

He started to bolt for the men dragging Aric away, but
pain blasted through his crippled leg. With a yelp, he
twisted to see one of the men who'd been struggling with
Ryon had turned his attention to taking out Jax, popping
off a shot and hitting the injured limb.

Normally his bum leg wasn't as big of an issue in wolf

form, but as he leaped for the new threat, it buckled. He managed to take the shooter down, but the agony in his leg was distracting. Thank God they weren't using silver bullets. The bastard got in a couple of blows to his head that left his ears ringing.

Just then, a snarl caught his attention. Raising his head, he saw a smaller wolf barrel through the open doorway onto the roof and straight for him. Fear and pride warred within him. She was magnificent, but he was terrified she'd be hurt.

Kira! Go back!

No!

Jax had the man's shooting arm in his jaws and Kira went for his throat. The gunman's scream was abruptly cut off. She spun and teamed up with Ryon to quickly dispatch his assailant. Seeing that they had things under control, Jax went for the helicopter. But with his injured leg slowing him down, he wasn't going to make it in time before the craft lifted off with Aric inside.

Suddenly, a flash of gray and white streaked past him. Before he realized what she was about to do, his mate leaped into the open craft and went straight for the gunman holding Aric. Shouts ensued as she crushed the goon's throat in a vise. The man fell, letting go of Aric and in an instant, Kira shoved their friend with all her strength.

Aric landed on the roof with an *umph*, and rolled, wrists still bound. Scraped up but safe.

Jax ran, his limp slowing him down. But the copter was lifting. Kira tried to get to Bowman, who sat on the other side of Beryl. Desperate, Jax shifted to human form and yelled over the noise. "Kira, jump!"

Turning, she saw her opportunity to escape slipping away. Making the decision to let them go, fight another day, she shifted to human form and braced herself in the doorway.

"Jump!" he yelled again. The copter was pulling away, a gap forming between it and the roof.

Kira tensed to make the leap—just as Beryl grabbed her from behind, holding her back. The gap between the building and the copter widened even more. There was no way Kira could make the jump now. Then Beryl raised a booted foot and kicked her hard, between the shoulder blades. Jax could only watch in horror as his mate lost her grip.

"Kira!"

She was flung from the helicopter.

Eyes wide with terror, reaching for the lip on the edge of the building.

And missing.

Her scream pierced the night. Shattered his heart.

Then silence. He couldn't breathe. Could not fathom what had just happened.

His mate wasn't dead. She wasn't.

He took his wolf form and ran. As fast as his injured leg would allow, down the flights of stairs. Past his team who'd regrouped and was on the way up. All the way down, out of the building. Around to the side where she'd fallen.

She lay on the pavement, pale and still. His wolf approached, the animal half scenting and realizing what his human counterpart denied—death.

Shifting back, he gathered her into his arms, cradled her. Gently brushed the tangled blond hair from her bruised face. Her eyes were closed, dusky lashes on delicate cheeks, blood trickling from the corner of her mouth.

"Baby?" His voice shook. Trembled as he fought the knowledge. "Kira? Open your eyes, angel. Please, please . . ."

No heartbeat. No life. Her body was broken, their souls no longer connected.

The bond was severed. His mate was dead.

Clutching her to his chest, he threw back his head and screamed.

And screamed.

Seventeen

Jax, buddy, you have to let her go.
  Oh, God, somebody do something!
  Leave him alone, asshole! Can't you see he's grieving?
Their voices came to him from far away. Grieving?

Yes. He was grieving his mate. Murdered by his former lover and her evil partners. Nothing would ever be all right again.

All along, it was Kira who was meant to die. Not me.

Nick had known. There was nothing to do now except follow her into death and hope she'd be waiting for him. Except . . .

If you could go back and relive any perfect moment in your life, which one would it be?

He'd told her none. That they'd go on to live their lives and make more perfect moments. And now there was only one way to do that.

Use his gift. The one he'd failed to use that night six months ago, and as a result, had failed his team. He had the power to make this right. For him and Kira.

Lovingly, he kissed his mate's cooling brow and laid her carefully upon the ground. Time was literally of the essence.

Oh, God, please let my gift return.

He was hardly aware of his team surrounding him as he stood, held his arms out from his sides, palms up. Ignored their calls as he let the rage consume him, fuel his power, and they realized what he was doing.

It can't be gone. Because if it's gone, so is she. Forever.

Reaching out with his senses, he found nothing at first. Only blank silence where his gift used to be. *No, please!*

Nothing.

And then, just as he was about to give in to despair, a glimmer of something . . . There! The threads. The very fabric of time. Desperately, he snagged them one by one, gathered them, bent them to his will. Spun them, running the reel backward.

The scene before him fell away and he watched the film outside of himself, an observer waiting for exactly the right moment. He'd only get one chance, and if he failed, he'd not have the strength to do it again.

He was on the roof again, going for the helicopter as Kira helped Ryon dispatch his assailant. Now!

Jax let go of the threads and prepared himself for impact. With brutal force, he was slammed back inside his wolf's body, the shock taking his breath away. But he had only precious seconds to recover. The helicopter was about to lift off with Aric inside, and a lance of agony went through Jax at the decision he'd already made.

His mate's life, or Aric's.

There was no choice.

This time, instead of going for the helicopter, he spun and intercepted his mate as she tried to streak past him. He tackled her, pinning her smaller wolf's body with his much larger one. Even with his injury, she had no hope of dislodging him. She was no match for the strength of his desperation.

And of his love.

The helicopter lifted, engines throttling. He raised his head to see the men inside, holding a struggling Aric. Beryl's expression was catlike, satisfied. God only knows what they would do to his friend.

But it was the look of hurt and betrayal on Aric's face that Jax would never forget.

He'd saved his mate, but the cost had been great. Not just for him, but the entire team. Nick would probably fire him for what he'd done. But the memory of holding Kira's broken body shook him, and he knew he wouldn't change what he'd done.

Underneath him, she shifted, and he did, too. Big blue eyes gazed up at him, confused and worried. "Why did you stop me? I could've saved him," she whispered.

Tears escaped to stream down his face. He couldn't have stopped them if he tried. "I know you could have. You did."

"What?"

"You saved Aric, but Beryl pushed you from the helicopter," he choked. "You fell to your death."

Her eyes widened and her mouth fell open. "Are you kidding?"

"I wish I were. I'll never forget it as long as I live." Scooping her into his arms, he crushed her against his chest. He was barely aware of himself, Kira, and Ryon being joined on the roof by the rest of his team.

"I think I remember falling," his mate said after a few moments. "It's like a dream."

"A bad one."

He wasn't sure how long he'd held her when suddenly clothing appeared on him and Kira. Looking up, he saw Kalen standing nearby with a faint smile on his lips.

"You guys were blinding me," he said.

He gave a hollow laugh. "Thanks, Sorcerer."

"Don't mention it."

"I don't suppose you could flash that helicopter back here?"

Regret etched his face. "I'm sorry, man. I tried to perform a grounding spell, but it got away before I could get a good grip on it."

Jax stood and helped his mate up, limping a bit on his bad leg. He'd have to get the wound checked out. Later. "That's all right. It's my fault those sons of bitches got away with Aric. I take full responsibility."

He drew her into his side, unable to let go. Not now, maybe never. How was it possible for a man to be so elated, yet completely consumed with guilt? Whatever happened to Aric was on his head.

To have his mate alive and healthy, he would pay whatever price the future held.

"Is everyone else okay?" he asked Kalen.

The Sorcerer nodded. "A little beat up, but healing."

"That's good."

Nick walked over, his expression unreadable. "We'll talk at the compound." His gaze flicked to Kira. "I'm glad you're all right."

"Thanks to my mate."

"Yes." Their boss was silent for a moment. "Let's finish our sweep, make sure there are no captives here, and get out."

They finished their jobs, speaking very little. The others knew what he'd done, remembered more than Kira did. He could tell by the solemn stares directed his way. They'd never begrudge him his mate's life, but they were all sick about Aric.

No captives were found, nor was there any scent of Micah or any other shifters in the lab or holding areas. The computer hard drives contained no information they could use. The entire scene that Zan and Kalen had observed, with Bowman, Chappell, Beryl, and their henchmen moving crates and equipment into this building had been a ruse. A setup from start to finish to trap them.

Weary, the team began the long trek home, made interminable by the loss of one of their own. By the time they reached the compound, dawn had broken. They dragged themselves inside and headed for their separate quarters. Jax turned to his boss and awaited his instructions, stomach churning.

"You going to give me walking papers?"

Nick sighed. "I don't know. You two get some rest and I'll see you in my office this afternoon." He left them standing there, staring after him.

"Come on, handsome." Kira tugged on his hand. "Let's go."

He let her lead him to their apartment, pull him inside. As they undressed, he recalled his bullet wounds and inspected them in the bathroom mirror. Just a scratch across his right butt cheek, and the wound in his bad leg was already healed. It still hurt, but he could live with it.

He had his mate.

They brushed their teeth and then he turned on the shower. He let the water get hot and then pulled her inside with him. Just held her as the spray washed away some of the terror and sadness of the past few hours.

"I couldn't lose you," he said hoarsely, tightening his arms around her.

"You didn't, and you won't have to."

His cock filled to press against her belly. He'd almost lost her, and both the man and the wolf needed to reaffirm their connection. Reclaim their mate.

Nuzzling her, he kissed his way to her nipples, licked at the droplets streaming over them. He suckled them until she squirmed, tugging at his wet hair. He straightened and a small hand found his sac, fingers manipulating him. Driving him insane.

"I can't wait, baby. I need to be inside you."

"Then don't wait," she urged breathlessly. "Fuck me."

Holding her around the waist, he lifted her and pinned her back against the tile. "Hang on."

She clung to his shoulders, legs going around his middle, and he positioned the head of his throbbing length to her opening. Pushed slowly inside and impaled her, inch by inch.

"Oh, God! That's so good," she praised. "More."

He gave her all of him, supporting her with his hands cupped under her bottom. Began to thrust, loving the feel of her slick heat massaging his cock. Again and again he drove into her, knowing this wouldn't last long.

When she shuddered around him, crying out, he went over the edge. Pumped himself deep inside, giving her all of him. This was where he belonged.

"I love you, Kira."

"I love you, too. So much."

He drew back to see tears in her eyes, and wiped them away. "Don't cry, angel." Carefully, he pulled out and set her down.

"I can't help it. You saved me, and now Aric—"

"*Shhh*. I wouldn't change what I did even if I could. We'll find him. In the meantime we'll move forward and live all those perfect moments, just like we planned."

"And the not so perfect ones."

"Those, too." Drying them both off, he carried her straight to bed and held her close.

"Hey, I just realized I lost the bet," she said, voice drowsy.

"What bet?"

"I didn't get Raven or Belial rehabbed within the

month. Now I have to wash the whole team's dirty laundry."

She sounded so mournful, he chuckled. "I never told the others about that, you know. I think we can let it slide."

"Yeah?"

"Absolutely. Sleep, baby."

She drifted off, but slumber eluded him. Instead, he simply enjoyed her warm body tucked into his. Cherished the fact that she was here, whole and healthy. He wouldn't waste this second chance. He owed that to her.

And to Aric.

Nick was waiting when Jax walked into his office several hours later.

"Take a seat."

He did, certain the ax was about to fall. "I'll have my stuff cleared out and Kira and I will be gone by tonight."

His boss arched a brow. "Just like that?"

"Yes. It's what I deserve."

"Really? You think you deserve to run from the consequences of your actions? You think your team deserves to have you desert them just when they need you the most?"

Jax sat back, stunned. "Well, no. But I don't understand how you can go easy on me after I chose Kira over one of my own brothers."

"Is that what you think? That I'm going easy?" Nick smiled, but it didn't reach his eyes. "No, Jax. You'll stay here and do your part on this team. You'll help us win the war against Chappell and find out who's backing him. And you'll help us locate Aric, Micah, and anyone else they've gotten their dirty hands on, and bring them home. That's your mission. Is that understood?"

He swallowed hard. "Yes, sir. I won't let any of you down again."

"You didn't let us down with your choice to save your mate," Nick said softly. "Everyone understands, even me. *Especially* me. But actions have consequences, sometimes far-reaching ones."

"Have I completely screwed up the future, put us in even more danger?" He dreaded the answer. But it wasn't what he expected.

"No man should be cursed with knowing what the future will bring, or how the endless array of choices made every second affects the possible outcomes. Those choices are like balls striking one another on a pool table—you know?"

"I—I think so."

"Each choice affects another. A single deed or whispered word can topple an empire . . . Or save a loved one. All we can do is weigh the risks and rewards, and move on. That's all any man can do, and for all your abilities, you're still a man at heart. Nothing more."

His words humbled Jax. He hung his head for a moment, thinking. Then he looked at his boss, and friend. "I can't help but feel like we failed."

"No," he said firmly. "We learned what Chappell and his partners are up to, and we learned Beryl is alive and is one of them. We rescued two shifters and we're going to liberate more, including our own. We're on the trail of our enemies, and we're going to win."

"If we make the right moves."

"Of course."

Jax knew Nick wouldn't reveal more. He stood, offered his hand, which his boss shook. "I won't let you down," he repeated. "Or my team."

"I know. Now go find that mate of yours." He released his grip. "Tonight we rest. Tomorrow we'll regroup."

"And kick some ass."

Nick laughed. "That's the plan."

Jax walked out of his boss's office feeling optimistic. Chappell and whoever were pulling the strings might have won the battle, but they weren't going to win the war.

"Hold on, old friend," Jax said. "We're coming for you. Count on it."

With new purpose in his stride, he went to find his mate.

His heart and soul.

Aric awoke slowly, head pounding. His brain felt stuffed with cotton, and his entire body ached. Where the fuck was he?

He tried to move, only to find he was chained against something solid, maybe a wall, arms and legs spread wide.

And he was naked as the day he'd been born.

From the shadows, a tall slender figure emerged. A woman with long hair a darker shade of red than his own. She was dressed in black slacks and a skimpy top that left little to the imagination.

"Beryl, you bitch," he hissed.

Her laugh sparkled with amusement. "Is that any way to speak to your sister?"

His voice was cold. "I don't claim you. I never have."

"Is that why you never told your sexy friend Jax the truth? I wonder how your team will react to your betrayal," she mused aloud. The prospect apparently pleased her. A lot.

"I didn't betray them. I thought Jax was happy, and despite what a skank I know you are, I didn't want to interfere. I won't make that mistake again."

"No, you won't get the chance." Too late, he saw the

knife in her hand, glowing red from being placed in the fire.

"Scream, dear brother."

As she pressed the hot blade into his side, he promised himself he wouldn't. But half an hour later, he failed, screaming until his voice broke. Until consciousness began to fade.

Ryon? Someone, find me, he begged. *Even though I don't deserve it.*

Please find me.

Blessedly, the knife, Beryl, and the horror faded to nothing.

Read on for an exciting preview of

SAVAGE AWAKENING,

the next addictive Alpha Pack novel by J. D. Tyler

Rowan Chase jerked the wheel in a hard left, brought the car skidding to a stop in the filthy, garbage-strewn alley between two run-down buildings, killed the ignition and was out before her rookie partner, Daniel . Albright, even got his seat belt unbuckled.

One glance at the situation told her things had already gone FUBAR.

A crowd of about twenty Hispanic men of varying ages surrounded two who were rolling on the ground, the edgy group shouting obscenities, egging on the fight. Quickly, her brain assessed the struggling pair, taking in the information, rapid-fire. One stocky male, six feet, about two hundred twenty pounds. The smaller one younger, slender, five-seven, about one sixty. The younger man was Emilio Herrera. Both wore the East Side Lobos' colors. Family fight. Over what? Drugs, a girl, or some imagined slur? Who knew?

Sunlight glinted off a sliver of metal between the combatants, and blood blossomed on the smaller guy's shirt. *Knife. Shit.* Rowan unclipped her holster as she jogged toward them, adrenaline rushing through her veins.

"LAPD!" she shouted, her pistol clearing leather. "Break it the fuck up!"

"Get back! Give us some room!" Danny bellowed.

Danny was green but he was a good officer. She trusted him to control the agitated crowd while she dealt with the fight, and trust was imperative. A second unit was on the way, but that didn't mean it would arrive in time to prevent disaster.

The pair was oblivious at first, the young man completely focused on defending himself against his assailant. The stocky man was clearly the aggressor, his rage palpable. He was the one she needed to reach.

"I said break it up! Now!"

Switchblade in his meaty fist, straddling the younger man, the stocky one turned his head to glance at her, a snarl on his face. She sucked in a breath, recognizing him. Luis Garcia. She should've known. He was a dangerous bastard with a long rap sheet full of violence. Worse, he was unpredictable, his mind fried from a lifetime of drug abuse.

"Little *puta* stole my shit," he slurred, spittle flying.

"I didn't!" Emilio cried, holding up his hands. "I don't do the powder—you know that! *La familia* knows that!"

"You took it and I'm gonna gut you like a—"

"No, you're not," Rowan ordered, using her most authoritative voice. She held her pistol at her side, pointed at the asphalt. "Put the blade down and come talk to me. We'll sort it out."

"Shut up, *lesbiana*. You think you have bigger *cojones* than Luis, *sí*? Perhaps you do." He gave a nasty laugh.

Rowan let the insult roll off her. She'd been called worse. "Emilio is telling the truth, Garcia. I know him, and I swear to you he wouldn't take your blow." *Now, your car? He'd steal that in a heartbeat, but not your coke.* "I wouldn't lie to my own people. Put the knife down."

To her right, the Lobos' leader pushed through the crowd, apparently late on the scene. Salazar Romero was tall, muscular, and menacing, with long black hair and a soul patch, arms covered with tats. "Don't be stupid. Listen to *mamacita*, Luis. She's street. One of us—you feel me? Her word is good enough for me, so it's good enough for the Lobos."

Finally, a break in the ice. The bigger man visibly wavered, his grip on his quarry loosening. He tried to stare down Salazar, but looked away first, like the dog he was. But that didn't mean the danger was over. Rowan's stance remained tense as Garcia let the knife fall from his hand, let go of Emilio's shirt.

"Climb off him and stand," she directed. "Slowly."

Garcia let go a string of muttered curses, but did as he was told. On his feet, he stepped away from the bleeding man and turned toward her, shaking his head. Still cursing. Gesturing and swinging his arms as he became more agitated. She didn't like his body language. The man was going to lose it again.

"Kneel, hands behind your head."

His head snapped up. "You said we was gonna talk!"

"First, kneel, hands be—"

"Fuck you, bitch!"

Rowan knew what Garcia was going to do, even as he dropped his right arm, reached behind him to grab something at the small of his back. She reacted a split second faster, brought up her weapon and leveled it at his chest, shouting, "Drop it!"

But he brought the gun around, swung the muzzle toward her, his intent clear. She was hardly aware of her finger depressing trigger, and the deafening explosion was over before her brain registered the noise.

Garcia jerked backward, eyes widening in surprise. A bloom of scarlet began to spread across his chest as his knees buckled and he crumpled to the ground. Weapon still trained on his fallen form, she walked over and kicked the man's gun from reach of his outstretched hand. Wary, she crouched next to his head and placed two fingers on his neck.

"Dead?" Danny asked.

"Yeah." She heaved a shaky breath and stood, surveying the few people that were left.

Most of them had gotten the hell out of there when Garcia drew down and his act of stupidity proved fatal. Emilio was still sitting a few feet away, a hand pressed to his bloodied side, grimacing in pain. Salazar and a couple of his lieutenants were with him, praising the kid for facing down crazy Garcia, as though the kid had taken him out himself. The little car thief's street cred had just risen substantially, along with plenty of temptation for a rival gang to add him to their hit list.

And the cycle never ended.

Rowan holstered her weapon, feeling sick. *Oh, God. I killed one of my own. Right here on my home turf, among the people I'm supposed to keep safe. Could I have handled this differently? How?*

"Chase!"

Startled, she blinked at Danny, who was right in her face, hand on her shoulder. "What?"

"Whatever shit is going through your head right now, stop," he said in a low voice. "You gave him every chance to give up. Hell, you almost waited a hair too long to draw down and pull the trigger. It was a righteous shooting. No one is going to dispute that."

"The baby cop is right, *mamacita*," Salazar said in a loud voice. "Luis was broken, man. He acted on his own to jump Emilio, and the Lobos wash their hands of him. There will be no retribution."

Broken, meaning Salazar had recently demoted him. She supposed she should have felt relieved that Luis had already become a problem they wanted erased, or her east side upbringing might not have meant squat. Suddenly aware of several sets of eyes boring into her, studying her reaction, she clamped her mouth firmly shut and gave a curt nod.

Salazar waved a hand at his remaining followers. *"Vamanos!"*

No retribution. Staring at their retreating backs, she couldn't work up the gratitude. Eleven years on the force and she'd drawn her weapon fewer than a dozen times. Never fired it outside the shooting range before today.

And today, she'd killed a man. No matter his failings, Luis Garcia had had a wife and six kids who depended on him. Her breakfast threatened to make a reappearance, but she managed to keep it down.

"Chase?"

Rowan turned, blinking at Captain Connolly. She couldn't seem to shake the fog that had wrapped itself around her brain. "Sir."

"What happened here?" he asked, matter-of-fact. His weathered face was calm, his blue eyes patient.

Quickly, she gave their supervisor the rundown, in detail. Danny backed her up, and the captain nodded.

"All right. Looks like a clean shooting, but you know what happens next," he said kindly.

She did. Although she'd never had to fire her weapon, much less kill a suspect, other officers had done so over the years. They all knew the drill. She exhaled a deep breath. "I guess I'm on leave."

"I'm afraid so." Connolly squeezed her shoulder. "At

least until the investigation is over. It'll probably be just a formality in this case, but it still sucks. We've got things covered here. Head on back to the station, take care of your paperwork. Make sure all your i's are dotted and the t's crossed. Then surrender your weapon and go home. I'll call you."

"What about Albright?" She gestured to her partner.

"I'll temporarily reassign him pending the closing of the investigation."

"Yes, sir." Damn, she hated losing a good rookie to another officer. Even if IA closed her review quickly, she'd have to fight to get him back.

"Take it easy," Danny said, trying to be reassuring. "Everything will be fine."

"Sure. Take care, and I'll see you."

She walked away, aware of eyes at her back, measuring. Wondering whether she'd be the department's new head case, waiting to see if this would be what finally sent her careening over the edge. First, the loss of her younger brother, and now this.

Climbing into the patrol car, she forced herself to start the ignition and calmly drive away when all she wanted to do was sit there and fall apart. Later, she promised herself. She'd pick up a six-pack of beer on the way home and let go where no one could see.

For now, *compartmentalize* was the word of the day and the only way to get through it.

Three hours later, Rowan finished the last of her mountain of paperwork, surrendered her pistol, and headed out the door, thankfully unnoticed except for by a couple of buddies who'd heard the news and stopped her on the way to deliver brief pep talks. She felt decidedly naked without the comforting, familiar weight of a weapon at her side, and she just wanted to get the hell out of there before her comrades noticed and wanted to hear the lowdown firsthand.

She hurried to her truck and fired it up just as her cell phone vibrated on her hip. With a sigh, she left the vehicle in park, retrieved the device and checked the caller ID. This one, she had to take. "Hello."

"Hey, it's me."

In spite of herself, she smiled. "Hi, me. What's cookin'?" Her friend, FBI special agent Dean Campbell, never said either of their names on the phone. Paranoia was more than in his job description—it was embedded in his DNA.

"Plenty. I've got those Dodgers tickets you wanted," he said cheerfully. "Meet me for a burger, usual place?"

Her smile vanished and the blood drained from her face. Her mouth opened a couple of times before she could find her voice. "I'll be there in half an hour. I need to go home and change first."

"On my way. I'll get us a table."

After punching the OFF button, she tossed the phone onto the seat next to her and peeled out. *Oh, God.* Finally, after months of a fruitless, agonizing search for answers and a maze of dead ends, the call she'd been praying for had come. And for a few more minutes, she had to bleed just a little more inside, not knowing whether this was the end or the beginning.

Not knowing if Micah really was dead, as the government claimed, or if he was alive somewhere, waiting to be rescued.

And if her brother was alive, what the fuck was going on?

The questions and possible answers whirled in her brain all the way to her apartment, and they didn't let up as she hurriedly stripped out of her uniform and changed into jean shorts, a tank top, and tennis shoes. She couldn't stand another second of this torture, now that the end was in sight. The drive to Willy's had never seemed so long, yet she made it there in under fifteen. The bar and burger joint wasn't crowded this time of the afternoon, so she was able to get a pretty good spot on the side of the building.

After jogging around to the front, she pushed inside and spotted Dean sitting in a booth near the back. He waved and she went to meet him, returning his quick hug before sliding into her seat across from him.

Mustering a smile, she crossed her arms on the table. "You look good, my friend."

He always did. Dean was in his midthirties, with honey blond hair, big brown eyes, and a killer smile. The whole package stopped traffic. It was a shame she felt nothing more than mild attraction for the man, and vice versa, because it had been *way* too long since she'd had any sort of an intimate relationship.

"Back atcha." Sitting back, he eyed her in speculation. "I already heard through the grapevine about the shooting. How are you holding up?"

"Jeez, that was fast," she muttered. "I'm okay."

"You sure?"

"No."

He patted her hand, gaze softening. "That's normal. You'll be all right, trust me. Especially after I give you something else to occupy your mind." Reaching into his pocket, he withdrew a legal-sized white envelope and slid it across the table.

Swallowing hard, she eyed it. "My *tickets*?"

The agent glanced around, but there was no one nearby to listen. Still, he spoke in a low voice. "Read that, memorize it, and then destroy it."

Turning the envelope over, she glanced at her friend. "What's inside?"

"Directions to a place that doesn't officially exist." He paused. "A compound in Wyoming situated deep in the Shoshone National Forest. Top secret, black ops."

"Unless you know the right people to squeeze."

A corner of his mouth lifted. "Exactly."

Taking a deep breath, she asked the one question burning in her heart. "Is my brother alive?"

"I don't know," he said, tapping the envelope. "But those are the ones who will."

So close, but still no answer. Yet. She fought back the tears that would do neither herself nor Micah any good. "You risked everything to get this information for me. I don't know how to thank you."

"By not getting yourself killed." He wasn't joking.

"I'll put that on the list right after finishing with IA, taking personal leave, packing, and hitting the road."

"Call me when you leave town, and keep in touch."

"I will," she promised.

"You hungry? I'm buying."

To Rowan's surprise, her stomach snarled. Funny how a sliver of hope could revive a person's appetite. "I could eat, but it's on me. And if this lead takes me to the truth about what happened to Micah, there's a steak dinner in it for you when I return. It's the least I can do."

"Only if you bring Micah with you," he said softly.

Dammit, she would *not* cry.

"It's a deal."

Understandably, their meal was quite a bit more subdued than usual. Rowan was far too preoccupied to make a good companion, but that was the beauty of true friendship; neither of them had to say a word to be comfortable. They had each other's backs.

While they ate, her thoughts drifted to this mysterious compound and what kind of operation she would find.

Not to mention the reception she'd receive, especially when they learned of her mission.

But she wouldn't leave without learning, once and for all, what had happened to her brother. She and Micah had always shared a mental connection that most people would scoff at, and certainly wouldn't understand. They weren't twins, but she felt strongly that she'd *know* in her heart if and when he died. He was alive. Had to be.

No, this wasn't the end at all, but just the beginning. She'd find her brother if it was the last thing she ever did.

And then she'd make reservations for three at the finest restaurant in L.A.

With every mile that took her closer to her destination, Rowan's anxiety grew by leaps and bounds. The gorgeous backdrop of the Shoshone National Forest, resplendent in full summer greenery, hardly registered as she steered her truck up the winding road.

Gripping the wheel, she eyed the left-hand side of the road, looking for the obscure turn outlined in the directions she'd memorized and then burned two weeks ago. Three miles later, she found it. Or hoped she had.

Turning, she braked in front of a metal gate. It was simple, the kind any landowner might use, along with the black-and-white NO TRESPASSING sign nailed to a post next to the chain and padlock. Neither posed a deterrent to her bolt cutters or her determination.

Leaving the truck running, she grabbed the cutters and made short work of the chain, then unwrapped it, letting it hang from the gate. *In for a penny.* If she was in the right place, she'd soon have a lot more to worry about than a measly charge of trespassing on government property.

After swinging the gate open enough to drive the vehicle through, she returned to the truck and did just that. Then she got out and closed the gate again, wrapping the chain around it so that hopefully nothing would appear out of the ordinary to a casual passerby. So far, so good. She continued on her way.

A couple of miles deeper into the forest, the second barrier was an unpleasant surprise and a formidable obstacle. She could have screamed in frustration.

The chain-link fence was about ten feet tall and topped with razor wire. This gate was much more sophisticated, at least two feet taller than the fence on either side, and automated, with a pass code box on the driver's side. On top of the security box, a camera lens stared her in the face like an all-knowing eye.

"Shit."

She didn't have the code. And after several minutes of punching a green CALL button and waiting, it became evident that no one planned to answer her summons. The operatives inside were probably having a good laugh. Maybe they thought she'd get bored and go on her merry way.

They thought wrong.

Calmly, she reached for her purse. Extracted the Glock from within and, squinting, pointed the gun at the camera lens. "Knock, knock, assholes."

And fired, sending a shower of glass and metal raining all over the drive.

That ought to get their fucking attention. Best to meet them head-on. Stepping from the truck, she tucked the gun into the waistband of her jeans and walked over to inspect the gate. State-of-the-art stuff, a real fortress. What was this place and how was Micah involved? She wasn't leaving until they enlightened her.

A shuffle sounded to her left. And low growling.

Turning, she cursed softly, eyes widening. Guard dogs? Several of them, on *her* side of the fence, fanning out to surround her, heads down, ears flat, fangs bared. Moving almost silently through the sun-dappled forest.

But no, these weren't dogs. They were . . .

Wolves! Several of them, and one really large black *panther*?

She blinked rapidly as they approached. Then she backed slowly toward her truck, thinking she must have been seeing things. Wolves were now common in the Shoshone, thanks to wildlife rescue efforts. But she'd heard that wolves went out of their way to avoid mankind. Right? Just not *these* wolves.

And what about the big cat? Black panthers didn't even technically exist!

Tell that to this one.

"Stay," she called, holding out a shaking hand. "Nice doggies. I'm not going to hurt you."

A loud snarl came from behind her, and a glance nearly stopped her heart. One wolf had moved behind her, blocking her escape to the truck. She was completely surrounded. Her pulse beat a terrified tattoo in her throat.

Just then, the images of three of the wolves and the cat began to shimmer. Sort of like heat waves on hot pavement. Their bodies began to re-form, the fur retracting. Canine and feline limbs becoming arms and legs. *What the shit?* Staring, she told herself she was *not* seeing a group of sexy, naked men standing among the rest of the wolves with a range of emotions on their faces from amusement to grim resignation.

A dark-haired god of a man—wolf, whatever—strolled forward. "I'm Nick Westfall, commander of the Alpha Pack team. And you're in a shitload of trouble, Miss Chase."

How did he know her name? Rowan couldn't catch her breath to reply, even if she could've formed a response. Her vision blurred, and the tough woman raised in an East L.A. barrio did something she'd never done in her life. Not even when she'd been informed of Micah's "death."

She fainted dead away.

ETERNAL
ROMANCE

FIND YOUR HEART'S DESIRE...